RICH PRICK

TIJAN

Edited by: Jessica Royer Ocken

Beta readers: Crystal Solis, Amy English, Rochelle Paige, Eileen Robinson

Proofreaders: Paige Smith, Kim Holm, Chris O'Neil Parece, Amy English

Moral supporters: Debra Anastasia, Helena Hunting

For the readers!

A NOTE TO THE READER

Rich Prick is written as a standalone, but both Blaise and Aspen are first introduced in Crew Princess. Aspen has a very short cameo while Blaise is introduced as Cross' brother. If you've not read the Crew Series, you do not have to fear!

Blaise and Aspen's story *is* a standalone!

That said, of course I'd love if you went back to read the Crew Series.

Enjoy, enjoy, enjoy!!

1

ASPEN

Everyone knew who Blaise DeVroe was.

It didn't matter that he'd come to Fallen Crest Academy late in the year—and FCA was *not* a school you showed up late to.

I knew this because I showed up shortly after this year—my senior year—began, and no one, I repeat *no one*, knew who I was. Since my parents decided to have a mid-life crisis and tried to make up for some of their wrongs and bring me back to Fallen Crest, my last year of high school had sucked. FCA was filled with rich, stuck-up people. That meant you had to speak their language to be in their groups, and I didn't. Not because I didn't have money. My parents were movie producers and directors. We had money, and I previously went to one of the most exclusive private schools in North America, *and* a stint in a boarding school in Europe.

I could be fluent in stuck-up-ese if I wanted to.

But I chose not to. I've never been that girl.

I was the library girl.

I was the book nerd girl.

I was the wallflower.

On the whole, I tended to avoid people. I didn't people well. I had an affinity for blending into the background. It's a skill. I'd been perfecting it all my life.

But anyway, Blaise DeVroe was the opposite of that.

He may have moved to this school late in the year, but he walked in as if he already owned it. And to his credit, he kinda did.

The guy who ran the school before Blaise showed up was Zeke Allen. He's this wealthy jackass who's a bully, a muscular douchebag, and who slept with girls and then talked shit about them. He was king of the school by default, I guess—not because he was anything fantastic.

Then Blaise DeVroe walked in.

Guess who gave him a welcome-home hug? Zeke Allen did!

I was there, just coming out of the counselor's office, so I saw it all.

Blaise DeVroe strutted in with that cocky walk all the athletes had, and he was gorgeous. Like, seriously gorgeous. He had the high, arching cheekbones only the prettiest of the pretty-boy models had.

I knew this too because I'd done some reluctant gigs in the business.

But back to freaking stunning Blaise DeVroe. He had a chiseled, square jaw. He could have had his own waterfall off that jawline. Dark eyes. His hair was short, but long enough so he could rake his hands through it and let it be all adorably messy. And his body. Don't even get me started on his body—I was all crushing on it because it was *sick* and I mean that in the hot kind of sick way, not the real sick way. He was definitely not the real sick way at all.

He wasn't as big as Zeke, but he had these big, broad shoulders. Trim waist. And there were muscles everywhere. I swear I saw shape definition in his neck.

Blaise DeVroe: the *hottest* guy at Fallen Crest Academy.

One of the richest guys too.

I didn't hear the story of why he came here—not the real reason. Rumors circulated that his mom was going through a divorce, but there were also whispers about secret siblings. I wasn't on the up-and-up with anyone, so I never heard for sure if any of that was true. All I knew was Blaise DeVroe had walked into the hallowed and pretentious hallways of the private school in our town, and he was hailed like a long-lost son or something.

Or something, as it turned out.

Blaise and Zeke knew each other from childhood. Zeke considered him his long-lost best friend. So it was a coming home sort of situation.

Not that I could talk much about the history of FCA, because I was new myself, but I had been here almost a whole semester before Blaise. And full disclosure, I'd been here when I was much younger at the private elementary/middle school. That was before Mom and Pops decided they didn't like the influence my older brother's best friend was having on him, so they pulled both my brothers and me out of here.

But that's a whole different story.

The story for right now is that I'm being a total weirdo stalker and perving on Blaise DeVroe getting his dick sucked.

Like, right in front of me.

In hindsight, this was probably not the best idea I'd ever had. And I've had some doozy ideas. But this one takes the cake. I just couldn't help myself. As I've mentioned, I usually keep to myself, but something got into me this year. Every time I heard about a party, I couldn't make myself go, but I also couldn't *not* go.

So...I went.

But I stayed on the outskirts, so the people actually attending the party didn't realize I was there. There'd been a big bonfire that our town and the neighboring two towns had a while back. I was there, but I'd decided to make it a camping trip—just for me.

I was there, but not there. And that night had ended weird too, but nothing like this one.

This time the party was at Zeke Allen's lake cabin. Not that his cabin was a cabin. It was a mansion—a twenty-room *mega* log cabin, which no one even blinked at, because that's just normal for these people. Most everyone was staying at the cabin, not trekking back here into the woods like me. I'd set up my tent a bit away, doing my camping thing again (something I love, by the way), when I heard voices. They weren't down by the house, spilling out over the back patio, or even at the lake. Nope. These voices were up the hill, coming from farther into the woods.

I'd done my research. Zeke Allen's cabin was set a good ten miles away from the nearest neighbors. I should've been in the clear to sneak onto their land, do a little freestyle camping, and listen to the party sounds like the loser I was. But noooo. I was about to get company.

As I snuck out of my tent, and realized who it was, I almost crapped my pants.

It was Blaise DeVroe, holding hands with Mara Daniels.

As popular girls went, Mara Daniels was one of the nicer ones. She was on the dance team. Dark hair. Shorter, but athletic. The problem with Mara was that she was friends with the other popular girls. Some of them were nasty—hence the reason I wasn't friends with them. Not that they'd tried to get to know me. Not that I even registered on their radar. But then again, that's what I did.

I didn't engage. I didn't attend. I was on the edge. I was the invisible girl, and here I was, being the invisible girl once more, but man...

When I saw it was him, and then saw how his hand went from holding hers and guiding her to a tree to slipping around and grabbing her ass, something came over me. I couldn't retreat back to my tent. I couldn't even stay hidden behind a tree and just listen.

I know, I know. This was all sorts of wrong, but Blaise was Blaise.

He'd become the guy in my dreams, my weird schoolgirl fantasies. He was my high school crush. Everyone had one. If you didn't, you're even weirder than me, and that's saying something. So when I started salivating over Blaise DeVroe, I kinda just let myself go. I mean, nothing was ever going to happen. Guys like him didn't date girls like me. They didn't even notice girls like me.

I wasn't crazy. That'd make me all sorts of delusional.

I was a realist. I knew my place in life's hierarchy. I was at the bottom. I was not the very bottom—because of my family—but socially, I was barely one rung up the ladder.

Anyway, when Blaise started kissing Mara, when Mara knelt in front of him, when she opened his pants and took out his cock —I lost all train of thought.

I watched as she took his dick in her mouth, as her head began bobbing up and down over him.

And, oh my God.

My whole body was awash with sensations, and I was captivated. Captivated! Entranced. Mesmerized.

I could not look away.

Then I felt throbbing and a warm feeling between my legs, and it was game over. It was all I could do not to make a sound, because I wanted to. So bad. I wanted to moan. I wanted to touch myself, but I didn't. I kept myself reined in, but watch? Oh yeah. I watched.

I couldn't *not* watch.

I watched the whole thing.

I loved the whole thing.

And then at the end of it, I almost died.

～

BLAISE

I WAS GETTING my dick sucked while a weird chick watched us.

"Hmmm...Blaise." My girl moaned, readjusted, and took me in again. She reached up to stroke under, and damn, that felt good. My eyes almost rolled back, but I caught myself and held steady. My hands went to her head. Sometimes a little guidance went a long way, and as I applied gentle pressure, my girl was receptive. So I started to drive her mouth over me. All the while, I never stopped watching the other girl.

I couldn't place her.

I was pretty sure she hadn't been at Zeke's party, but who the fuck knew. He'd invited fifty people, way more than he needed to, but Zeke was a lovable bully idiot. He was mean. Some might say he had a slime effect on them, but he was my best friend. I couldn't judge. I had an attitude the size of fucking Alaska. Anyway, back to Zeke. He liked to go big, and that included his parties and his fuck-ups, and there were a lot of both.

That girl...

I liked her.

Fresh face. I could tell she was light on the makeup. Her face was one of those that would look jaded under a ton of crap, but without it, she looked the way she did right now: innocent and pure. Though the fact that she was watching my blowjob didn't fit either of those adjectives. She was tugging on her lip now, her hand lingering on her shorts.

Christ.

Her shorts.

My chick was wearing a bikini top and shredded jean shorts —and those shorts were hardly there. They were more decorative so she didn't get arrested for public indecency. All the girls at this party were like that. Bikinis, and anything else they wore was painted on their bodies. The old school way of thought might've labeled them sluts or whores, but since we were all liberal and progressive, we went with *sexually healthy appetites.*

I, currently, was enjoying my girl's appetite.

She opened her mouth wider, angled her head to the other side, and oooh yeah—I was in at a whole different depth now. Fuck it. I took hold of her hair and started moving. She moaned, but only widened her jaw and spread her knees a little more apart. She was bracing herself.

Fuuuuck yeah.

That meant I could go a little harder, which I did. I shoved her down a bit more, a better angle, and right there. I loved when they let me take over. But then I looked back up to watch Voyeur Girl. My friends and I did not hang out with girls like my voyeur. My dick got harder. I almost cursed, gritting my teeth. I had not expected that reaction, but I'd take it.

The girl watching wore a buttoned-up maroon shirt, the ends tied at her waist. She had a good rack. The shirt was bunched up to hide 'em, but I saw her girls. They would be a decent handful, almost perfect. And she wasn't wearing a bra. There was enough of a tease between the buttons that I could see just skin, just tits.

The rest of her... I had no words.

Khaki shorts that ended mid-thigh, and what a fucking thigh she had.

This girl could model.

Long. Lean. Legs meant to wrap around your waist—I thrust a little harder, and my girl groaned around me. I needed to ease up, but I was almost gone. Almost. Not quite.

Then Mara reached up and massaged my boys. That was enough.

I unloaded into her.

She swallowed like a champ and smiled up at me. She wiped her mouth with the back of her hand, and for a second, the weird chick was forgotten. I grinned at Mara. I always liked Mara's blowjobs, and because I wasn't an asshole, I tugged her up and moved her farther behind the trees so she was hidden from view.

Now was my turn to make her feel good.

Kissing her, I slid my hand inside her shorts and inside her, and when she was done and moaning, I looked over my shoulder. The other girl was still there, still glued to her tree, her eyes still right on us, but this time, she saw me.

Her eyes bulged out, and she inhaled sharply. She jerked back, and I grinned, lifting my hand to my mouth. I tasted Mara on my fingers as I watched her. Then I winked.

She uttered a muffled scream.

Chuckling, I grabbed Mara as she tensed in my arms.

Her head snapped around. "What was that?"

"Nothing." I kept her tight to my side as she fixed her pants. "Come on. Let's go back to the party."

As we left, I glanced back.

The girl was gone.

BLAISE

"Dude! Soccer superstar!"

I grimaced. I wasn't known here for soccer and a part of me was hoping to keep that on the down low, for now. Zeke welcomed us back into the house with a toga half draped over him, a drinking helmet on his head—both straws hanging down by the sides of his face—and nothing else. Wait, he had flip-flops on.

Mara giggled and disappeared into a side room as I kept going. She touched my back as she went. I knew Mara. This wasn't our first run around together. She'd stick with the girls for the rest of the night, but if I wanted her later, I just needed to give her the nod. She wasn't like other girls. Mara didn't make demands to be more than a hook-up. That's why we'd worked so far, but that chick...

Who was that chick?

I shook my head. "You forgot your pants."

Zeke grinned, swaying on his feet. He didn't say anything more about soccer and glancing around the room, no one seemed to be paying attention. The usual group surrounded him—Brian and Branston, brothers, who tended to wade into any stupid fucking fight Zeke liked to pick. I didn't really mind his friends, but they were *his* friends. Zeke was mine. That was about the best way to describe my 'friends' since coming to FCA.

Best friend.

He and I threw that phrase around, but it wasn't always accurate. Some days I loved my best friend. But I won't lie. Some days I couldn't stand the guy. And he also loved me more than I ever did him. He liked to use that word a lot too. He meant it in a fierce, bromance sort of way. His feelings for me had grown while I'd been gone, living in New York. I had buds out there, a few good ones—and right now, as Zeke's dick flapped in the wind and two girls giggled beside him—I missed my East Coast friends more than I wanted to admit. One or both of those girls had already knelt before Zeke this evening, and I was sure the three of them would end up together later tonight.

Still. Despite being mean, ugly, and slimy at times, Zeke was loyal.

I gestured back to where I'd come from. "You invite some chick to the party this weekend? Fresh face. Long legs. Blond hair." *Her eyes.* "Green eyes."

Zeke's eyes narrowed, but they were glazed over. And the effort left him swaying even more erratically. He belched. "Fresh face? What's that mean?"

One of the girls laughed. "That means hardly any makeup." She lifted her top lip in a sneer before looking at me and smoothing her face into a seductive smile. "No girls like that are worth our time." Her hands came over my arm, and she caressed my bicep. "But I'll make it worth *your* time."

I stared back at her, not impressed. Her name was Penny, and she was one of Mara's best friends. "I just came back with Mara." I looked her up and down, mirroring the disdainful look she'd shown a second ago. "What kind of fucking friend are you?"

Zeke belched again before pointing at me. Even his grin was sloppy. "*Fucking* friend. That's what she is. Get it, man?" He wiggled his eyebrows. "Because you can certainly *get it*. If you know what I mean?"

Yeah. Loyal. That's why I liked him.

I rolled my eyes. "Yeah, dude. Like your dick wasn't just in her today."

He frowned, because he honestly didn't understand why I'd have an issue with that.

I leaned in. "I don't share chicks."

Another reason I liked Mara. She kept herself for me and me alone.

But Zeke's grin was easy. He was always easy when it came to me. Anyone else said that shit to him, they'd be flattened in two seconds. I almost shook my head, staring at my "best friend." I was an asshole to him. He was a good friend to me. Why he was okay with me treating him like shit was beyond me, but he was.

There were moments when I had his back. Maybe those went a long way, but that didn't seem right. Brian and Branston were Zeke's true followers. They were loyal to a fault. If he jumped over a cliff, so would they. A lot of the other guys were the same. The girls too, now that I thought about it. Zeke had this whole school on lockdown.

Everyone did what he said, until I showed up.

I had a different opinion than his, but no matter how many times I voiced it, Zeke never got pissed with me.

I frowned at him, raking my hand through my hair. "Why you so fucking nice to me, man?"

He blinked, still swaying, and a shit-eating grin split his face. "Because you're my best friend."

I sighed. It wasn't the first time I'd asked, a moment of guilt eating at me. And it wasn't the first time Zeke had given that answer, as if it made perfect sense to him.

All it did was make me feel like shit, and confused. "Yeah, man." I nodded, grabbing a beer from one of the girls walking past us. She had a handful of them, and she looked up, smiling coyly, and winked. She wasn't one of Mara's best friends, but she was still *in* their group.

I held a hand up to Zeke, turned, and tipped up my beer.

I wanted to find a room, get wasted, and not think again until Sunday night when we had to go back home. That sounded like a better plan than anything else, except maybe getting Mara to ride my dick.

Or that weird chick.

3

ASPEN

Camping was terrifying.

Once Blaise DeVroe had caught me, no way could I stay out here and relax in my weird stalking manner. I'd been discovered. The fun was gone. He knew I was here. He didn't know I was camping on private property. He probably thought I was attending the party. It seemed half our grade was there, and I knew there were others from Los Angeles too, so I hoped he thought I was just someone he couldn't track down in the house.

But I couldn't shake the anxiety that he would come trouncing through the woods and find me in my tent. So after sitting up and shaking for five hours straight—jumping at any sound I heard in the woods—I gave up. I packed it in and trudged back to where I'd parked my car.

I'd pulled Maisie, my 1968 Dodge Charger, over on an abandoned road. The grass was long, but there'd been enough of a crossing for me to know it once had been a road to come onto these lands.

My parents hadn't wanted me to have a classic muscle car, but when I saw Maisie, she spoke to me. She told me that while she loved having the speed and muscle and girth that'd been built into her, she was truly a diamond princess at heart. I was supposed to free her inner diva, so when my parents asked what car I wanted, I told them Maisie and dug my heels in. It wasn't like I'd asked for a dog or a cat. It wasn't like I was complaining that both my brothers were nonexistent in my life. And that seemed to do the trick—mostly because the reason my older brother, Nate, wasn't around was because they'd tried to control his life. And *dude*, my brother could hold a grudge. I'm talking *years*. Actually, the grudge might've lingered until the point that he'd forgotten we existed.

I was being sarcastic, but with an edge of truth mixed in.

But it wasn't the older brother card that won the car argument for me. It was my *other* brother card, because, you know, Owen wasn't around because he was dead.

Yeah...

I hadn't wanted to play either card, because I wasn't that girl. But Maisie meant that much to me, and after my voice cracked, my parents gave in. They almost couldn't give in fast enough.

Maisie was in our driveway the next morning, and she'd been mine ever since.

In a way, Maisie was my best friend. She was the one I hung out with the most.

I had lunch with her. I had dates with her. I depended on her for things, like holding my bags and carrying my things from point A to point B. And she always showed up. She was always happy, the purr of her engine told me so. It was her hello to me, and I rewarded her every time with a smile, a hello back, and a pat. Sometimes I tickled the dashboard.

I knew she enjoyed it.

The radio always did a little skip after the tickling. That was her little wink back at me. So yeah, Maisie and me. We were the best of friends.

When I returned to where I'd left her, of course she was waiting. I stowed my camping equipment in her trunk and tossed my backpack in front. I slid behind the wheel and checked my phone.

Zero text messages.

Zero phone calls.

Zero voicemails.

Alrighty then.

I started Maisie, and we were on the road a second later.

Zeke Allen's cabin was an hour away from Fallen Crest. The drive back was relaxing. I enjoyed the scenery along the shoreline.

I got a peek of it as the road wound in and out.

When I got back to Fallen Crest, my stomach was cramping. I'd forgotten to eat today, and I wasn't altogether sure I'd eaten the granola bars I'd packed for yesterday either. Either way, I knew there'd be food for me at home. Though my parents employed a chef, I had a craving for a nice juicy, greasy cheeseburger, so I made a stop. One burger. One fry. One soda, and soon I was heading for the newest section of Fallen Crest.

I slowed, pulling up to the gate.

The attendant rolled his window down.

"Heya, Mr. Carl."

That's how he'd introduced himself to me, and though I didn't know if Carl was his first or last name, it's what I called him.

Mr. Carl was middle-aged. I never knew for certain how old he was, but in my mind he was fifty-three. Gray hair. Wrinkles all over his face. And a smile. He was always smiling. He had a little paunch, but he said it was because the "missus" enjoyed feeding him too many dumplings. Was it sad that I hadn't known what dumplings were? I'd had to google them, and then I asked our chef, Benny, to make them. He looked as if I'd committed a terrible crime, but he made me dumplings that night.

And chili. I liked his chili the most.

I now asked for it once a week. He made it with turkey meat, said it was healthier that way.

I didn't care. I enjoyed it.

Mr. Carl was smiling at me like he always did, but then he frowned a little. "You okay, Miss Aspen?"

"I'm good."

"Your parents aren't home. They're in the studio editing that new piece they're working on."

I nodded, not feeling a thing. "Thanks for letting me know."

He dipped his head, gave a wave, and the gate opened.

I drove through. These days we lived in the newly gated section of Fallen Crest. We were all the way at the end, set on a peninsula. There were woods and a river winding around the lot. We were the hardest to get to, and we had the most privacy.

Driving up, I pulled Maisie to the far garage door.

We had a five stall, and I used the last one.

Walking through the empty garage, I felt a mix of emotions.

I knew Sandy, our cleaning lady, was likely here. She was Monday through Friday, but I knew she popped in on weekends too. She took care of the entire house, and it was a large one, so there were always places to clean. She and Benny managed just about everything. There was an outside maintenance guy. He mostly tinkered with the lawn and landscaping. We really didn't need him that much. The back lawn didn't take too much work.

I think he mostly came because he liked to flirt with Benny.

It wasn't a lawn day today, so that meant it was just Sandy and Benny inside, and true to form, I found them having coffee when I walked in.

"Miss Aspen!" Sandy jumped up, but I waved her off.

"I'm good, Miss Sandy."

She wavered, frowning. "We thought you were on a camping trip this weekend."

See? It was something I liked doing, not just to eavesdrop on parties.

I shrugged. "I decided against it. Mr. Carl said my parents are in the studio today?"

Benny had gotten up, and now was coming back with a plate of cookies. He set them on the table, offering an encouraging smile my way, but he didn't push them.

I held up my fast food bag. "I got food, Benny."

He ducked his head with a shy smile. "That smells delicious as well."

We'd come a long way from his heart attack over making dumplings. Now I could bring fast food in here—and look at that. He'd just smiled and nodded. Progress.

I set the bag on the table and went out to get the rest of my stuff. When I came back inside, the cheeseburger was now on a plate, the fries in a small dish, and Benny had a dipping sauce in another smaller container.

Classy all the way. That was Benny's motto.

I smiled. "Thank you."

Another dip of his head. "Do you need anything else, Miss Aspen?"

I shook my head. I'd never really asked for anything.

He hesitated, glancing back before moving into the kitchen. I heard the faucet turn on and the clank of pots. Miss Sandy came in behind me from the garage. She'd helped bring in my bag and was already going through it, pulling out the clothes she thought needed to be laundered. That was everything, even though I'd only changed my shirt once. I didn't fight her.

"Your parents thought you'd be gone all weekend," she said, her head bent over my bag. "They're having a get-together this evening. A lot of business people are coming." Her head came up, her eyes concerned. "Do you want me to make arrangements for you?"

I knew what she was asking.

This house was huge. It was easy for me to stay an entire week in my room and not hear anyone else. That wasn't the issue. She was asking if I wanted any kids my age to be invited.

I gave her a look. "Miss Sandy." She should know better.

She smiled, a sad look flaring briefly before she covered it. She cupped the side of my face. "You spend too much time alone."

I shrugged, stepping away from her.

Her face tightened before she went back to digging through my bag.

"I'll be good. I'm going to rent some movies and just crawl in bed."

I didn't need a lot of attention. I didn't need a lot of anything, to be honest. And if I did need something, it was there. I just needed to pick up the phone or wander down a hallway, and I could make a request. Miss Sandy and Benny adored me. They doted on me.

I wasn't saying my parents didn't.

My parents loved me. I wasn't a neglected child. I never felt as if they'd shipped me off because they didn't want to deal with me. Even when Owen and I went to Hillcrest Academy, our parents checked on us regularly. They were around a lot of the time in the beginning too, but they traveled for their careers. Daily phone calls and sometimes hourly emails became the thing for us. I knew when I checked my computer, I'd have ten emails from my mom. So I never felt unloved. It wasn't that.

I just preferred doing my own thing.

After Owen, it was easier that way.

"You ask me for anything. You hear me, Miss Aspen?" Sandy's voice was hoarse.

I felt my throat close, and I bobbed my head. "I hear you, Miss Sandy."

She nodded, her eyes holding mine as I slipped down the hallway.

4

BLAISE

My phone woke me up on Monday morning.

Rolling over, I saw my screen. *Marie calling.*

I sat up, rubbing a hand over my face and hit the button. "Hey, Mom."

"Where are you?"

Fuck.

I hadn't gone home last night.

She was pissed, and glancing at the clock, I saw it was five in the morning. "I'm at Zeke's."

"You were at Zeke's all weekend."

"I was at Zeke's *cabin* all weekend. We came back late, and I crashed at his house."

She sighed loudly. Her voice went low. "I'm getting sick of this, Blaise."

Yeah. Well. There was a lot to get sick of, on both our ends.

I didn't say anything, though, because I got it.

I did my own thing. I never checked in with her.

It was different in New York. I'd been just as independent there, but she'd been busier. Luncheons. Banquets. Charities.

She'd had more friends there too. A daily text checking in with her had satisfied her there, not here.

When we moved to California, everything changed.

She went through a quick divorce. There's money, but now she wants to work too.

She changed. I hadn't. I wanted to go back to the way we used to be, when she let me do my own thing. Then again, why she was trying to keep a hold on me was beyond me.

"Mom. I have two weeks left of school—"

"Exactly. Two weeks. You're still under my roof for those two weeks, and then you have the summer."

Now I was the one frustrated. "I'm in New York this summer."

She snorted. "Yeah, right. I know how that's going to go. You'll say you're out there, connecting with your father—"

"He's not my dad, now is he?" I cut in, my hand tightening on my phone.

She faltered a second, and then kept on as if I hadn't said a word. "But you won't ever see Griffith. You'll spend all your time with Jaxon and Connor. And I love those boys as if they're my own, but I know the trouble you three get in when you're together."

"Mom."

Her voice rose. "I don't want to be a grandmother! Do not get anyone pregnant, Blaise."

I stopped, looking at the bed beside me and feeling a bit guilty. A tad bit. Mara lay on her pillow, watching me. I hadn't lied to my mom. We were at Zeke's house, but I'd talked Mara into staying too. And we hadn't gotten a full night's sleep since the last time I'd reached for her was an hour ago. Hence my exhaustion, and I knew I'd be even more wiped for school because my mom was not going to let me off the phone anytime soon.

I mouthed at Mara, "I'm sorry."

She nodded, but with a big yawn, she got up.

Silently, she began dressing.

This scene had played out a lot at my house; my mom just didn't know. Mara would dress, then slip out and head home. She had her own entrance at her house, so I wasn't sure if her parents knew she was gone and didn't care, or if she was just really good at sneaking out. I'd asked a few times in the beginning when she started sleeping over, but she always told me not to worry about it. So I'd stopped worrying about it.

This morning, I felt a bit shittier than I usually did.

I reached over, taking her wrist. I mouthed, "I'll drive you home."

She frowned, pulling her arm free, and shook her head.

"Blaise!" Mom practically shouted.

I scowled. "What?"

Mara slipped from the room.

I rose, padded over to the door, and opened it. She was already down the hall.

"Stephen invited Tasmin over for dinner tonight. I want you here."

Well. Shit.

Thoughts of Mara vanished, and I knew if I didn't let go of the phone, I was about to break it. It wasn't long ago that I'd learned my mom's new boyfriend was actually my biological father, and that he had two other kids.

The brother didn't want much to do with me. Fine by me.

Tasmin was not the same.

My sister was trying to force a relationship to the point that it was pissing me off.

My mom had tried this family dinner before, and I'd gone. I'd taken Zeke with me, mostly to act as a buffer because my brother's hate was palpable. And that'd been the last time they tried to put the two of us together.

Tasmin, or Taz as everyone called her, was a whole other matter.

She was at our house most nights now, and it was becoming exhausting.

It wasn't that I didn't like her. I just didn't want anything forced on me, not before I was ready. Let me relish in hating my non-bio dad for a while before I had to manage a whole kumbaya moment with the new family.

I'd been rifling through years of hatred toward Griffith when I thought he *was* my dad. When I found out I wasn't his kid, a lot made sense.

But he was still calling.

He claimed he wanted a relationship, but I didn't trust the asshole. That was part of the reason I was going to New York. I wanted to find out his real agenda—whether it was to mess with my mom or something else—because I knew he didn't give two fucks about me.

"Mom."

"Say you'll be there, and I'll let you go back to sleep."

I sighed. I knew my mom. She'd keep me on the line until I had to go to school. She'd done it before, knowing I couldn't bring myself to hang up on her. It just felt wrong, even though she treated me like she was my annoying older sister at times.

I'd take Zeke. Hell, at this rate, I'd take the entire group: Brian, Branston, Penny, all of them. Mara.

"Fine." I gave in, needing to sleep. "Just text me what time later. Love you, Mom. Bye." And I ended the call. That wasn't hanging up, in my mind. We'd discussed things. I'd agreed. The conversation was resolved. I was just getting off before she could remember to add limitations, like I had to come alone to dinner. If she texted, I could say I never got it, because I wasn't above being immature like that, not for dire situations like family dinners.

On the way to the bathroom for a quick piss, I texted Mara.

Me: You get home okay?

Scrolling, there were a few more texts. One was from Tasmin.

Taz: Hey! How are you?

I deleted it, tossing the phone aside. I was crawling back into bed when Mara's response came through.

Mara: I did. See you in a few hours.

I didn't reply, just collapsed into my pillow and hoped for more shut-eye.

5

ASPEN

Students at FCA had recently successfully petitioned not to wear uniforms anymore, so I was still getting used to that. We'd had to wear uniforms for elementary school, and then also at Hillcrest, so coming back and finding out I could wear normal clothes had been a kick. I'd loved it, until I realized the scholarship kids were being targeted because of it.

Not cool.

Not that we had a ton of scholarship kids, but there were a decent amount. Not every kid came from a wealthy family at Fallen Crest Academy. Just the majority of them.

Anyway, as I approached school, I instantly knew what I was witnessing ahead of me. One of the scholarship kids was being targeted by the mean girls: Penny Lancaster, Kit Carlson, Deja Lorenze, and Mara Daniels, though Mara usually kept off to the side. And the last one was Ria Richter.

I didn't know the girl's name, but she was crying and holding her backpack against her chest.

Penny laughed at her, crossing her arms. "I'm just saying, walk away. You weren't invited this weekend for a reason."

Annnnd that's why I chose to hide my eavesdropping.

I walked right past the girl, going around the others too, and veered through the crowd heading toward school.

I wasn't a warrior woman. I wasn't about confrontation at all. If it involved me, I'd stand my ground. Or I'd probably name-drop my parents. And if worse came to worst, I could spew out my brother's name, the alive one. I knew he was known about by certain power players in this school, i.e., Zeke Allen. But in general, I tried to avoid doing any of those things. Wallflower. Invisible girl. Those were my choices for a reason. I was not brave and courageous enough to take on the mean girls of Fallen Crest Academy. They were *ruthless*.

"Hey, Aspen."

I almost dropped my book as I jerked around in front of my locker.

Then I relaxed. It was my partner from biology.

"Oh, hey."

She gave me a smile. "How was your weekend?"

What was she doing?

I didn't do this.

I went to class. I talked to students for projects. I did what I had to do to get through my studies, but talking between classes? No. And we were two weeks away from graduating. What was she doing?

I eyed her, frowning. "Uh. It was fine. Why?"

She glanced toward the front of the school, shrugging. She held her books, ready for class. "So, do you, uh, do you have plans for graduation?"

I frowned even harder. "Like going to the ceremony?"

I'd always heard Nate complaining that he wished he'd skipped his graduations, so I wasn't telling anyone, but I was planning on adopting his philosophy. My parents had no clue when I'd be graduating. I was hoping to break the news to them when it was too late for them to rally and attend, or to throw a party for me. They were so involved with their latest project, I knew I had about a ninety-percent chance of pulling that off.

She flushed. "No, like afterwards. Are you going to any parties?"

Dear Lord, this girl really didn't know me.

I raised my eyebrows, opening my locker and stowing my backpack inside. "Um..." I pulled out my book, put my phone into my pocket, and made sure to grab the right pencil and pen. I toed my locker closed and faced her. "Parties aren't really my thing."

She blushed even harder. Her face was going from a definite pink to red. Her forehead looked a little sweaty too. "I know. I just... I'm having a party, and I wanted to invite you." She pulled out a piece of paper and offered it to me.

I almost jumped back.

An invitation.

My stomach churned.

There'd been parties at Hillcrest. But those were in the dorms, and it wasn't really the same thing. Dorm parties were easy. You walked through the stairs and hallways, then entered a room. You mingled. Sometimes people went to the community room, sometimes the quad. There was a lounge set up for people to hang out. Sometimes a car took everyone into town for more hanging out.

I wasn't a complete hermit. I'd done those events, but I knew those people.

This was my first invitation to an actual party at FCA.

I wasn't sure if I was disappointed that I hadn't gotten through the entire year without having to make the decision about attending one of these, or because it took until two weeks before graduation to *get* an invite to a party.

I was a mess of emotions, and it was uncomfortable.

I took the invitation and read it over.

Her address wasn't in one of the wealthy areas. "Are you a scholarship kid?" The question came out before I'd realized I was even asking, and I felt bad as soon as her face closed off.

"Uh..." She turned away. "Never mind. I mean—"

"No." I grabbed her arm. "Sorry. I'm just surprised. It doesn't matter to me." I pointed to myself. "Like I give a crap. I'm not popular. I don't have any friends. So, loser. Me." I laughed, and it came out forced because now she was looking at me with pity, and that wasn't my intention at all. "I mean..." Oh boy. I was messing this up.

Making up my mind, I shoved the invitation back at her and rushed off. "I don't do parties. Sorry."

Seriously.

What *was* my issue?

I cursed myself, but wait.

I almost forgot.

What had I been thinking?

I almost missed my favorite part of the day.

Right before swinging into class, I stopped and looked back.

Hearing the commotion in the hallway, I knew it was already happening.

I couldn't help myself. My stomach went all warm and fluttering, and I moved to lean against the nearest locker. Hugging my book and computer to my chest, I let myself indulge.

Blaise DeVroe had arrived.

BLAISE

"DUDE," Zeke greeted me, his hand in the air as I got out of my G Wagon.

I reached up, and we slapped hands.

"You snuck out this morning?"

"Yeah." I grabbed my bag, slung it over my shoulder, and shut the door. Locking it, we started for school. A few others trailed behind Zeke, falling in line behind us. Brian, Branston, and this time it was Jamie Conway and Oliver Ashlome next to them. The B brothers were useless to me—couldn't even respond when I asked how they were. Jamie and Oliver actually seemed to have their own minds.

This school, it was something else.

"Had to run home for a change of clothes," I added as we hit the sidewalk leading up to the doors.

Zeke gave me a cocky smirk. "Daniels sneak out with you?"

I shot him a look.

The guys snickered behind us.

I heard one say, "Dicksy Daniels."

I stopped.

The other laughed. "She likes those cocks, man. That's for sure."

"Shut it." I tossed a look back.

Brian drew up short at that. "Excuse me?"

I wasn't having this. Not today. I snapped and went right at him.

He was about to say more shit, give me more attitude, and his arms were on the way up.

I was there before they came even halfway. I fisted my hands in his shirt and shoved him against the wall. There were students around, but they beat it real quick.

I was in his face, grinding my teeth. "Yeah. I said shut the fuck up. Why are you making me say it again?"

Fuck. I wanted to fight. I wanted to fight so badly.

I didn't care who this asshole was. He could've had my non-bio dad's face, my half-brother's face. He could have my *real* dad's face. I didn't give two fucks. I just wanted to hurt because I was so sick of everything.

A crowd formed around us.

I didn't give a fuck about them either.

Crowds formed. It's what they did.

"Hey, man." Zeke tried to get between us. "Hey. Hey, *brother.* Come on."

Brian looked relieved to have him there.

Nope. It didn't matter. I was pissed, and I didn't care who was trying to come to his aid. I was ready to burn the school down.

A deeper growl ripped from me, and I pulled Brian from the wall, only to shove him back even harder. My hands ripped his shirt, and I was still in his face. Hands tried to pull me back, but it was pointless. No one could move me when I didn't want to be moved.

"You got something else to say to me?"

Brian's eyes were wide. I saw a flicker of anger before Zeke pushed himself between us once more. Then it was gone. Brian held his hands up, as if surrendering. "Nah, man. I'll shut it. I didn't know you were gone on her, that's all."

Gone on her? Jesus Christ.

I'd started to let go of him, until those words.

I clocked him in the face and stepped back as he moved over. The force of the hit was enough that he bent over, in serious pain, but I hadn't hit him hard enough to go down to the floor.

I leaned over and said, "One kick to your knee, another hit to your head, and you'd be down for the count. I don't owe you any fucking explanation, but I'm getting really tired of the shit you and your stupid-ass brother say about women. Grow the fuck up, dude."

Yeah, yeah. There could be an argument made about me— how mature was it to throw a punch? But I was tired of this bull-shit. I didn't want to go to Rape School, and those were the dynamics fucking Zeke was putting in place, whether he meant to or not.

"Hey." I felt an assertive pat on my arm, and Zeke hauled me backward. He wasn't using enough force to piss me off, but he did put himself firmly between us. He turned to face me. "Let's chill, okay? We don't need internal fighting."

I shoved him. "Get the fuck off me."

Everyone went quiet at that one.

Zeke was still considered king here. I got more leeway than others, but still...

However, as I mentioned, I was tired of this shit. I'd heard how he talked to girls, and knowing I had a sister out there changed things for me.

I went at him, not caring that everyone else had grown eerily still. "You've been setting the tone here." I pointed at Brian, then Branston. "They take your cues. They're followers. You're leading them. Lead better. Do better. You got a sister, dude. You want your sister to deal with someone like you?"

His eyes went flat.

Zeke was protective of his sister.

Then his nostrils flared and he dropped his tone, moving in closer to me. He made a show of putting his hands in his pockets, but his words were meant for me, and I knew they were a warning. "Walk, best friend. We can talk about this later."

I snorted. Zeke didn't talk. He'd either organize a beatdown on me or he'd let it go. Studying him, I was guessing the latter, but one never knew with this kid.

"Yeah. Right." I looked at Oliver and Jamie, but didn't say anything else. They hadn't stepped in to help Brian, and they hadn't moved in to back Zeke up. But that didn't mean they wouldn't have. I didn't know where their heads were.

I moved down the hallway, and a second later, I saw them following.

I didn't say a word. Neither did they. I wondered if Zeke told them to tail, but then Oliver nodded at me.

I took that to mean something. I just didn't know what. As I moved past a classroom, I caught sight of someone slipping inside. They had disappeared by the time I fully looked.

I kept going.

I wasn't looking forward to the wave of whatever I'd just set in motion.

6

ASPEN

"**Y**ou get off on watching? Is that your thing, or is it just my cock you like?"

I was heading to my car after school when I heard him.

My heart stopped, almost literally. If I looked down, it was likely the entire contents of my stomach would be at my feet.

He'd found me.

I looked up, and Blaise DeVroe stepped out from behind the truck parked next to Maisie. His hand was on her back end, and he waited there, in the shadows (thank God), his head tilted to the side.

He looked so good, so delicious. All hard edges and angles. That jawline. It could give me razor burn between my legs, and I'd climax just by breathing hard.

I saw the flare in his gaze and felt his edge. I had to rein in a bit of my inner weirdo.

I'd heard about what happened that morning. Hell, I'd witnessed it myself, but then I'd also heard all the whispering about it afterward. It spread through the school like wildfire. And

what they were saying hadn't been kind. Most bets were that
Blaise was going to be kicked out of school. Others said Zeke was
going to have him beat up. Still others thought Zeke could have
him arrested. How that even made sense, I had no clue.

But I also saw those guys interact through the rest of the day
as if nothing had happened. Zeke still smiled at Blaise, even if he
seemed more cautious. Some people said there was a rift forming
in school. But again, why did that even matter? We had a week
and four days left to be here. Then it was summer.

"You talk?" His head cocked forward. There was a slight bark
to his words.

I jumped, then gathered myself. "Oh. Um..."

Shoot. I bit down on my lip. What did I say here? Okay. I had
nothing, so I guess honesty was the best policy. Besides this guy
playing a major role in my schoolgirl fantasies, I couldn't deny
that I was a little scared of him right now. I'd always felt there was
something *more* in him, a wild edge, but no one ever said
anything. There'd been no rumors about it, until today.

Today, everyone had seen. Today, everyone was talking
about it.

"I, uh..." *Screw it.* I shrugged. "It was live porn. What did you
expect?"

His eyes lit up. His nostrils flared. And he stepped toward me.
"To turn around and leave." His eyes narrowed. "I looked for you
the rest of the weekend. No way were you there for the party, so
what's that mean? Were you spying on us?"

Ooooh boy. So not good. I didn't want him to get anywhere
close to that realization about me.

My stomach shriveled up. I swallowed over a knot. "Um..."

"Were you?"

Shoot. Shoot. Shoot.

I could not talk about that. No way. That was my big secret,
and it was embarrassing. If he found out, if he said something, I'd

be the laughingstock of Fallen Crest. I couldn't handle that—not at this school. At Hillcrest, they would've left me alone. People knew me there. They knew Owen.

"What the fuck is wrong with you?" His nostrils flared again, and he moved even closer. He was almost within touching distance now, his gaze locked on mine.

I had to distract him. That's the only way I could get out of this one.

"I like you," I blurted.

"What?" He blinked, seeming stunned.

I got him. Crisis averted.

And I doubled down. "Yeah. I mean, girls have crushes, and you're mine. I crush on you."

His eyebrows went up. "You crush on me?"

I blushed. That was embarrassing enough, but the other secret would've been worse. So much worse.

I ducked my head, shrugging. I kicked at a rock. "Like you don't know. Like you don't know a ton of girls like you, so whatevs. I like you, and I mean, do you want me to apologize for crushing on you?" I lifted my head, peering at him.

He looked confused and backed away.

My lungs could expand again.

"I—wait." His head cocked to the side. "So you were *following* me?" Even as he said it, I could tell he didn't believe it. I heard his tone. It was suspicious.

"No. I mean..." Crap. That wasn't as much of a distraction as I thought. Arrogant much? I tried to smooth it over. "I was going for a walk. I got lost, and then I saw you and I—" Fishbowl effect. My mouth was moving like a goldfish, and I was thinking. I was stalling. "What do you want from me? This is *embarrassing*."

I didn't need to act. My face was beet red. I was starting to sweat too. Gross.

He coughed, clearing his throat. "I saw you today. I saw you duck into your first-period class. Didn't realize it was you until later. You're in my fourth period. I watched you the rest of the day. You don't talk to anyone. No one knows who you are. I asked around."

My chest puffed up. Pride swelled there.

He looked taken aback, those eyebrows shooting up. "What? You feel good about that shit?"

I frowned, my chest deflating a little. "Wouldn't you?"

"Fuck no. You have no friends here."

That stung. I blinked a few times, trying to erase the feel of that invisible hand across my face. "Uh. Thank you?"

"No." He shook his head, his eyes becoming way too determined and way too focused on me. He moved closer again. His arm rested on the top of Maisie, and he was almost leaning over me. "What's your damage? I mean..." He leaned back, giving me a onceover. "You're hot." He motioned to my car. "You drive a chill car, so you're not hurting for money. What's your deal? You're just known as 'that girl' or 'she's in my class' and that's it. Someone thought your name was Colorado. What's your last name?"

"My name is Aspen."

"I know that much. Mr. Latham is a lazy fuck, but he still does roll call." He nodded at me again. "What's your last name?"

I hesitated another beat. "Monson."

He was quiet a second. I could almost see him connecting the dots before his eyes went flat. "Your parents are doing that documentary thing?"

I felt a jolt run through me, my hand jerking up and taking hold of my backpack strap. "How do you know about that?"

He was right, but they hadn't interviewed kids here. Only in Roussou. The people they were interviewing here were adults, people who wouldn't connect my parents to me. It was one thing I'd been adamant about—that they leave the high schools in Fallen Crest out of their project.

"My brother and sister go to Roussou," Blaise said. "I've heard all about the project."

Oh.

Oh, shit.

"So those rumors *are* true?" I asked. *Oh wow! Like, wowza wow.* "Is that why you moved here? To get to know your brother and sister? I heard they were twins."

"Jesus. Shut up," he hissed, backing away. "That's personal business." He looked around, his jaw clenching. "I did my due diligence with you. That's why I'm approaching you back here, 'cause trust me, I have no problem starting a scene. Started the day that way, and I could end the day that way. It's no skin off my nose. You got me?"

I sucked in a breath. He was scary when he was like this —scary *hot.*

"Yeah. Sorry." I lowered my voice. But it still seemed exciting to find out you have two siblings you didn't know about. Or I would've been excited about it. "What are they like? Who are they? Are you close to them?"

"Shut." His eyes got all big and mad. "Up. It's none of your goddamn business."

I winced. "You swear a lot."

"I don't care."

He looked at me like I was an alien, but that stuff didn't faze me. I was used to that. Hell, I preferred that. No one could figure me out that way, and this guy had come close.

I didn't like it.

I might need to up some stalker tendencies, but even as I thought it, it probably wouldn't do anything. I'd blurted that I had a crush on him, and he hadn't cared. He took that in stride. Then again, why wouldn't he? Most girls at school had a crush on him. He got laid daily, or he could if he wanted to.

Man, what would that be like? To know you could merely

look at someone and they'd do what you wanted? Sexually speaking. Would I want that? If I looked at him, gave him the eyebrow wiggle, and he'd follow me into a closet?

Wait.

Guys *would* do that for a girl.

Some guys would.

No. That wasn't right either.

Guys would do that, but then sometimes they talked trash about the girls they hooked up with. Though, maybe not him? I didn't remember ever hearing him brag about hooking up with someone. Girls bragged about hooking up with him, not the other way around. And he wasn't exclusive with Mara, but everyone knew Mara Daniels was a regular with him. He never said a word about it. That was from other people talking about seeing them.

And this morning, I'd heard what he said to Brian Strandling and what else he said to Zeke. Those words didn't seem like they'd come from a guy who'd hook up with a girl and then trash her for it.

I could feel a definite throb between my legs, and now I was staring at his lips and pulling on my hair, as if I could imagine it was his lips and what I'd want to do with them.

Tug on them.

Pull. Twist.

I was starting to pant.

"You're not normal."

I shrugged. "Life goals."

See? Stuff like that didn't faze me. Never had. Owen had always laughed at how odd I was. He told his friends— Pain laced my chest.

I got choked up and turned away, ducking so Blaise couldn't see my eyes.

I blinked back sudden tears.

I hurried forward, and Blaise had to move out of my way.

Then I was inside Maisie and starting the engine. "I have to go," I said in a rush before I closed the door. A second later, I was out of there, tears streaming down my face.

Not good.

No one, *no one*, got to see me cry. Ever.

7

BLAISE

The girl had issues. That was obvious.

I watched as she tore out of the parking lot, knowing she believed I thought she was psychotic. I didn't think that. She just seemed like a girl who didn't want attention. There was always a reason for that. No one grows up not wanting to be noticed; something had to have happened. But whatever it was wasn't something I had to deal with or think about. I'd confronted her, wanting to make sure she hadn't taken a video of Mara going down on me. I'd also wanted to feel her out, see if she was the type to blab about it, but she wasn't.

I'd thrown a ton of shit at her, and the only thing that cracked her surface wasn't something I said. I called her weird, and she deflected that as if it were air, but then something inside her broke through. I didn't know what it was, but again, it wasn't my issue.

I could walk away knowing there would be no collateral damage of her spreading rumors, but why did I care? It wasn't like people didn't know. A video would have been a problem. Then I'd have had to do damage to her, and there was something about her I didn't want to hurt.

I mean, she was hot, but just this conversation told me she wasn't worth it. No quick dip or taste. The girl had some severe damage.

And again, not my issue.

At all.

Why the fuck was I still thinking about this? I cursed, shaking my head clear and pulling myself out of whatever the fuck I was doing here.

Sick car, though. I wish I knew her better. I'd ask to drive it.

"Yo."

I looked over. Jamie and Oliver were heading across the parking lot toward me.

"What's your deal?" I asked as they approached. "Zeke ask you to keep an eye on me?"

They'd been like my shadow all day, and I didn't know what they were thinking. That made me wary.

They shared a look.

Jamie shrugged, crossing his arms over his chest. I was still standing next to the truck beside where Aspen had parked, and Jamie leaned a shoulder against it. "Zeke didn't ask us to do anything. We're just tired of how things have been here."

Oliver nodded.

Both seemed resigned.

Well. Fuck.

I shook my head. "We're almost out of here. It's too late to change anything. This ain't worth it for you guys."

Oliver grinned.

Jamie laughed. "Exactly."

I frowned. "What do you mean?"

He kicked up from the vehicle and shrugged, glancing back at the school, which was starting to empty of students. "Zeke might've done something if you'd pulled this at the beginning of the semester. You pushed back against him. He doesn't forget that shit—or he doesn't with us. You might be different, but you got pull. I mean, we're here. We've never backed anyone else, and he knew that's what we did today. We were backing you. He ain't going to do shit because it's almost the end of the year, but man, we got summer left. There's parties to be had, to throw, to crash. Zeke loves you, and he ain't ever gonna let you go."

I grunted. "That makes him sound creepy."

Oliver shook his head, shrugging. "No offense, but Allen *is* a bit creepy with you. He always has been. He really does love you, and not like he wants to fuck you. He's got unconditional, agape-type-shit love for you. He won't do anything to you, but us he might've fucked over. He won't now. We're heading into party season. He just wants to go along to get along, ya know?"

Party season. Summertime.

"I'm heading to New York."

They both laughed. "Then we're either all coming with you or you ain't going to be there long."

I studied them. Zeke had said the same to me a month ago, and my mom had laughed when I told her about my summer plans this morning. Why did everyone doubt that I was going to New York?

"I have to," I told them. "My non-bio dad is being an asshole to my mom. I need to go make sure he's not going to mess with her."

Jamie held his hands up. "Whatever. We'll come with you for that too."

"You know Allen's with you, no matter where you go," Oliver added. "You won't be able to get rid of the asshole."

And as if to prove his point, Zeke came out of the school just at that moment. I noted neither Brian nor Branston was with him, which meant he'd specifically told them to steer clear. He walked across the lot, slowing when he was within talking distance. He kept some space between us, eyeing Jamie and Oliver.

"Hey, man. What's the deal tonight?"

I let out a breath. I'd not realized I'd been holding it, but it didn't seem Zeke was going to hold this morning against me. "I'm supposed to do a family dinner. You up for helping me with some distracting?"

His eyes lit up. "Your sister-in-law going to be there?"

Jamie and Oliver started laughing.

I rolled my eyes. "Shut up, douches."

He was talking about my half-brother's girlfriend, who was not someone to mess with. My half-brother wasn't either, but Zeke already knew that. He'd gone against them earlier this year and gotten his car exploded because of it. He'd let bygones be bygones once he found out about my relation to them, but he knew things were dicey between my half-brother and me.

Zeke's grin turned wicked. "What about your sister? You think her boyfriend will be there? He's a nice little fighter dude to fuck with. Gets all hot and bothered if he thinks we're flirting with his woman."

"Don't fuck with Taz." Or her boyfriend, but I held that back because that would ensure Zeke would fuck with him. I was picking my battles here, and I was tired. Maybe that burst of anger this morning, whatever it'd been, had been enough for me? Got some of my demons out or something? Who knew.

"Yeah." Zeke laughed, rolling his shoulders back. He was settling in, which meant he was feeling good about how things were going between us. His grin was easy. "I'm down. I can distract anyone you want me to distract tonight. I love these family dinners. Drop the word *pussy* a few too many times and everyone's all up in arms."

I grinned. For a while, that'd been Zeke's favorite word. Pussy this, pussy that. Literally every other word was *pussy*. That'd been an interesting month.

"You want in too?" I asked the others.

"Hell yeah," Jamie answered.

Oliver nodded. "Count us in."

Maybe dinner wasn't going to be too bad. I'd never brought these guys to the house before, just Zeke.

I pulled my keys out. "I can drive."

Zeke got shotgun. "Have I mentioned how I'd love to make love to your G Wagon, B?"

"Fucking Mercedes too." Jamie whistled under his breath as he climbed in.

I shot them a look, snorting. "Right, because your BMW is so low class?"

Jamie just smiled. Cocky fucker.

8

ASPEN

I needed to camp. Stat.

Now.

I would break out in hives if I didn't get my camp on, and I had a plan formed before I'd driven Maisie all the way home from school.

School was mostly done for seniors. A few tests and a few papers to turn in, but we'd gotten most of our work completed a week or so ago. They had to have time to make sure we all had passing grades and could actually graduate. People were still showing up because they didn't want to piss off the administration, but I was different. No one really knew I existed, except Blaise now. And my biology partner. But neither of them would care. And neither might notice anyway.

When I got home, I pulled up the last of my remaining projects. I emailed the teachers, and within two hours, I had the final details for my last assignments. My plan was to complete everything. I made arrangements to take two tests the following morning, missing my slacker classes to get that done.

Since being here, I'd never caused a problem.

My grades were good: A's. I already had college set in stone:

Cain University. My parents didn't know that was my final choice. They thought I wanted to attend Hillcrest's sister university because so many of my Hillcrest friends were going there, but nope. I wanted to go where my brother had gone. Nate had found himself there. I knew things had been rocky in the beginning, but that smoothed out, and at Cain was the first time I saw him happy. I wanted to go there and understand.

But back to camping. Because camping would get me through the last weeks of school.

Camping would get me through the summer.

Camping let me breathe.

"Honey?"

I stilled, hearing my mom's voice at my door.

A polite knock came next, and I had to answer. My stomach was in knots, but I pushed back from the desk and walked over. My legs felt like wood.

My mom was on the other side, frowning, concern pulling her eyebrows together.

She wore a light summer dress, an artsy scarf wrapped around her neck with books on it, and her hair coiled up in a loose French twist. It was a mess of brown and gray since she was letting her last dye job run out. Minimal makeup, and she had on hemp sandals that wrapped around her ankles.

I already knew what mood she was in that day.

She was feeling an artsy/creative/loving/spiritual vibe. In these moments, she loved life and tried to be a beacon of light to everyone. This was the perfect time to make my request.

"Mom." My voice went all warm and happy, and I made sure to smile, radiating peace and tranquility.

"Daughter." A flicker in her eyes, and she tilted her head toward me.

She was on to me. She knew I wanted something.

Good thing I knew she wouldn't mind in this mood.

Right now she wanted to go to the desert and commune with

nature and take mud baths, all while dosing up on some really great pot. I never saw this side of her until she and my dad had their midlife crisis. Now this was a regular occurrence, and the vibes in the house were a lot more relaxed because of it.

"I want to go camping for my last week at school."

She didn't even blink. "Absolutely not." And damn, her smile never wavered either.

"Mom." I was getting serious now.

"Daughter." So was she. "It's your last year. You're not missing any projects or memories to go camping alone."

Well...damn.

"I've gotten permission to finish all my projects and tests in the next three days at school. And I can do it. I'll have everything completed and handed in by Thursday. I can take off on Friday."

Wait.

What was I doing?

I didn't want my parents to know when I graduated. I'd made up a fake email for them, so everything school-related actually came to me. I knew my grades for months before my parents remembered to ask. With their old-school way of thinking, no news from my school was good news. That meant I wasn't having problems, so they had no reason to worry about me. And straight As—a 4.2, with the new ranking system. School had always been easy for me. It was just the social scene that presented a challenge, but what parent actually waded into that world?

I needed to go camping.

I needed it like I needed to live. This past weekend was supposed to have fed my soul, but it hadn't.

I was going anyway. Regardless of what my mother said.

I made the decision right then and there. My projects would be done. My tests would be taken. If I didn't show up, no one would care.

I was doing it. My mom would never know anyway.

And so now I had to distract her. I moved in, wrapped my

arms around her, and buried my head in her shoulder. "I love you, Mom."

She stiffened for a second, then she melted. "Oh, honey." Her hand came up to the back of my head for a moment before she hugged me. "I love you too. So very much," she murmured next to my ear. "You know that, right?"

I squeezed her. "Always."

She sighed. "Come for dinner. Benny made Thai and your father is having a fit. You know he was hoping for tacos. Lord knows why. If he could, he'd have tacos every night of the week. Tacos and those damn cigars of his. I thought I got rid of the rest of them, but he snuck away to his editing shed. It's like he thinks we're oblivious that it's his he-shed more than anything." She paused, her smile turning tender. "You'll come for Thai with us?"

I nodded. "Of course."

Another hug, a soft squeeze of my shoulder, and she left, her hand grazing my cheek.

After dinner, I studied for my two tests and drew up a list for my camping trip.

I'd be back before she even knew I'd been gone.

9

BLAISE

B etween Zeke *and* Oliver *and* Jamie, Tasmin never stood a chance.

She came alone—no boyfriend and no brother with his girlfriend in tow. And I knew my half-bro well enough to know there was no way he would come without his woman or his friends. He had a tight group. I'd heard my mom complaining to Stephen one night that the only way they'd gotten my half brother to the first dinner was because Tasmin went behind his back to friend-guilt his girlfriend. She had come to support Taz. I don't know what happened, but he showed up with her, and then they'd all stormed off with Taz's boyfriend.

That'd been the pussy dinner. Zeke and I took off right after them, and that night had been a fun party.

I barely remembered it.

But with its smaller crowd, this dinner had passed without much needling or questioning or guilt tripping about why I didn't have a better relationship with *so and so*—just fill in the blank. At this rate, it was a rotating door. My mom was always disappointed that I wasn't closer to someone: Stephen, Tasmin, the brother who didn't give a fuck about me either, or even fucking Griffith, the non-bio asshole who'd raised me.

I got out unscathed, and then we went to Zeke's, where I spent the rest of the night in a drunken stupor. We passed a bowl around and played video games, just the four of us. No Brian or Branston, and I knew that was Zeke waving a truce flag. He knew I couldn't stand either of them, so I was happy.

The next day, I kept an eye out for Aspen.

There was something about her. It was bugging me. I didn't know what it was or why I was wasting my time, but I did.

I noticed she wasn't in any of her classes Tuesday morning, so I asked around. And then she was *back* in classes that afternoon, but I heard she was working on projects on her own.

Wednesday was the same thing. That day I heard she spent the entire afternoon in the library.

On Thursday, Jamie tapped my arm, nodding to Aspen as she hurried past us in the hallway. "Heard you've been asking about her."

"Yeah. You know stuff?"

"I know she got permission to finish all her shit this week. My mom is friends with one of the clerical ladies in the front office. They said the girl could officially not come to school any more as of tomorrow."

Well. *Crap.*

My chest tightened at that thought, though I had no idea why.

Jamie frowned at me. "Why you so interested in her? She's been a nobody all year."

My teeth instantly ground against each other. I hated that word, but I shrugged. "It's not what you're thinking."

He grinned. "You don't want a new BJ girl?"

I swore under my breath. "Tell me that's not what you guys are calling Mara?"

"Mara. Penny. Whoever. They all get on their knees at some point, don't they?"

I shot him a look, but he wasn't speaking with disdain or condescension. He was just saying it, like it was a fact. "You know it's talking like that that made me go at Strandling, right?"

He rubbed his chest. "You know I don't mean shit by it. I don't think less of those girls. They could turn it around and say we're all just fuck boys, because ain't that what we do? We service them too."

That was one way of thinking about it.

He frowned, straightening next to me. "You ever been in love?"

I frowned. "No, not like that." I'd never had a reason for that. I got what I needed without having to do the relationship. Some guys liked that, but it wasn't in the cards for me. I shrugged. "I suppose one day, maybe? But why, though?"

He shrugged. "No clue, man."

We went back to watching people pass us in the crowd. Many looked our way, but we were used to that. We were at the top of this school, so we got attention. It was the same way everywhere we went in town, and even if we went to other towns. We all looked like rich assholes. We walked like it, drove rich-prick cars, and there was an air about us—confidence, arrogance, whatever.

Entitlement.

Yeah. I could say it.

But while others thought that way, believed that way, I didn't. It was a shield for me.

And with that last thought, I'd had enough of school. "Wanna go to Zeke's and get wasted?"

Jamie smirked. "Can we bring some girls?"

I snorted. "Of course."

I was in the mood to fuck and forget.

10

ASPEN

I left on Thursday after school, and my parents thought I was
camping for the night. They'd be in for a surprise when I
didn't come back until Monday—if they noticed. You heard
that right. *Monday*. That meant Thursday night, all day Friday, all
day Saturday, and hell to the yeah all day on Sunday. I'd come
back Sunday night if I wanted to, but knowing me, maybe I
wouldn't.

I'd been like this before Owen died, but I'd *really* been like
this since he passed.

Maisie was packed, and I was almost out of Fallen Crest when
I pulled into the gas station. It was on the outskirts, right before
I'd hit open road. I could turn right and end up in Roussou or go
left and drive through Frisco. Those two towns made a weird
triangle with ours, but this time, my plans were somewhere
farther than Roussou. There was a small state park an hour past,
and I was going to try it out. There was a river I could camp
next to.

Plus, the redwoods.

I was super stoked.

After filling the tank, I went inside. I'd made my usual trip to the grocery store, so I had most of what I'd need, but this was a tradition of mine. I liked to stock up on coffee and gas station food on the way to wherever I was going, unless it was super close —those trips weren't worth the gas station food. I perused the aisles, my coffee in one hand and so far a bag of jerky in the other. I mostly liked the hot deli selections, and I know, they're gross on a good day. But Owen had always loved the stupid little pizzas and hot dogs, so who I was to turn up my nose?

"Yeah! I hear ya. I'll grab some—"

Crash.

Chest.

Hard chest.

"Oh, shit."

Hands came to my arms, steadying me.

I rocked back, blinking, dazed at whatever had just happened. It happened fast.

"Hey."

I stared up at concerned brown eyes, and a zing of lust seared me before I cleared my thoughts. That's when the burn of the coffee filtered through, and I opened my mouth.

A bloodcurdling scream came out.

"AHHH!"

I was burning.

My skin was melting.

I could feel the sizzle.

"Oh!" Blaise seemed to realize what was happening. He looked at my chest. "Shit! SHIT!" He grabbed my arm and dragged me through the gas station and into the men's bathroom.

"Ah! Not—"

"Shut it," he snapped as he turned the faucet on.

After that, I had no idea what was happening.

He ripped my shirt off. Literally. He grabbed the collar with both hands and tore it apart. Water was poured on me. I gasped, but it started to help. After that, he pressed wet towels over my breasts and down my entire front.

With a curse, Blaise took inventory. Some of the coffee had gotten to my pants. He went for my front button, but I caught his hands just in time.

"I got it."

"But—" His eyes went to mine, and he stilled.

But there wasn't anything in his face except concern and horror.

I blamed the haphazardness of the situation for what I did next, because if I'd been in my right mind, I would've pissed my pants just thinking about what I did. And that was, I cupped the sides of his face and lifted up on my tiptoes. My head angled as I zeroed in, and then my lips were on his.

Oooh. Oh!

Hmmm.

My lust amped up tenfold, and a buzz roared through my body.

I started to pull back, but he didn't allow it. His hands were on my face, and his mouth was on mine. He was demanding, pressing hard.

And whoa!

That first kiss had been a lot, but this one set me ablaze. An inferno started in my body, and I knew it had nothing to do with the third-degree coffee burns.

Holy cabana manna, this was—I'd never been kissed like this.

The door opened. "Dude? Wha—"

Blaise shifted. The door shut, and he moved us back. I felt him reaching to lock the door, and then he pressed me against it and his hands were on me.

His hands stroked my stomach, over my skin, and I had enough foresight to gasp for air as his fingers reached under my bra. I had a split-second warning before his mouth was back on mine. He popped the cups of my bra up, and his thumbs rubbed over my nipples.

I jumped as if he'd taken a live wire to me. I could almost hear the spark in the air, and my whole body washed over with pleasure.

I moaned, opening under his mouth, for him. His tongue claimed me, and I was lost after that. I'd like to think I'd been thinking during the first few minutes of our make-out, but when his tongue touched mine. I was done.

I was gone.

He could do whatever he wanted.

"Dude!" There was a pounding at the door.

Blaise ripped his mouth from mine, cursed, and shouted back, "It's busy!"

He'd turned back to me when his friend pounded on the door again. "Manager is coming. Get your girl covered."

The words penetrated our lust, and Blaise cursed under his breath. After that, it was a race. I had no shirt, so as I put my bra back in place, he tore his off and flung it at me. When I didn't catch it, he cursed and scooped it up. He pulled it over my head.

My arms shot through the sleeves, and he pushed me to the back stall. I had a glimpse of him raking his hand through his hair as he slammed the door shut, and I heard a key in the bathroom door.

This was so embarrassing. *So embarrassing!*

Blaise coughed, just as the door opened.

"Is there a problem in here?" a man asked.

"What? No problem."

Someone snorted.

Blaise's voice was strained. "I, uh, had a run-in with someone. Got coffee spilled on me. I was trying to stop the burn, you know?"

"Oh!" The man's voice changed. "You're okay?"

"Yeah. I'm good. All good."

Another snort.

"Well, are you..." A squeak of a shoe on the floor. The manager's voice sounded closer, "Are you alone?"

Blaise coughed.

The snort guy said loudly, "Holy fuck! I think someone's trying to pump and ditch."

"What?!" Then the manager was gone. I heard him run out. A second later, the snort guy started laughing.

"Ha-ha, dickhead." A door slammed shut, and Blaise came to the stall. He knocked gently. "It's all good."

I unlocked the door, letting it swing open.

Gah. I was melting and dying at the same time. His hair was messed up and looking seriously sexy, *and* not only did his chest look hella hot, but hello? Where had those grooves come from? They outlined his stomach perfectly, as if they were arrows, pointing right down to where I'd felt him grinding against me.

I gulped. And swallowed.

He'd been so hard. And big. Massively big.

I was back to my goldfish impersonation.

"You okay?"

My eyes snapped to him, hearing a little bit of pity. He knew what was going through my head and probably my body—well, most definitely my body, and I swallowed again.

"I'm just embarrassed," I whispered, hanging my head a little.

"I'm getting that, but you don't need to be. You know that, right?" He gestured to me. "You're hot, Aspen."

What all girls want to hear in a gas station after almost getting caught in the men's bathroom by the manager.

I sighed. "I know people saw."

Blaise tipped his head to the side, his hands sliding into his pockets. It only seemed to accentuate his six-pack. I groaned on the inside and wet my lips, because I was starting to salivate. One kiss from him had me hooked. He was like crack. My body was now fully on sexual conditioning response.

I just needed a look, and I was acting like a hussy.

"My buddy will help distract for us. Say the word and we'll sneak you out the back way."

"There's a back way?"

He nodded. "Yeah. Just past our door. You can go out that way, and I'll get whatever you were buying and meet you out front in a minute."

"Really?" That was sweet of him. I frowned. *Sweet* was not a word used to describe Blaise DeVroe.

He shrugged. "Tell me what you were buying."

I told him, and his eyebrows went up, but he didn't say anything.

I don't know if I was disappointed at the lack of reaction, but I was thankful after he stepped out into the hallway. A second later, I slipped out, and he indicated the back door.

I went through, remembering that I was still wearing his shirt when I stepped outside.

A staff person was on her smoke break, but she only looked at me before taking another drag.

I ducked my head, hotfooting it around her, then around the gas station and out to my car. A minute later, Blaise came out with his arms full. His friend was right behind him, and holy crap. I was embarrassed all over again because that friend was Jamie Conway, another one of the most popular guys. His reputation had skyrocketed this week after everyone heard how he and Oliver Ashlome had stepped up behind Blaise, defying Zeke Allen.

It was big news for FCA. Really big news.

I also noticed Blaise was wearing a gas station shirt. He'd turned it inside out. He smiled when he saw me grinning at it. He glanced down and shrugged. "I've always wanted Quick-Fill swag. I'll frame it one day and hang it over my bed." He winked before nodding toward the things he carried. "Did I get it all?"

Pizza. Two deli sandwiches. A hot dog complete with ketchup and mustard. My coffee. And my smoothie.

"You got it all."

He handed it over, our hands brushing, and I tried to ignore the sizzle that ran up my arm. A knowing smirk came over his face, but he was looking at Maisie—the backseat, to be more specific.

His smirk fell away. "Are you going camping?"

"Camping?" Jamie Conway stepped up next to us, gawking at my backseat. "No way." He smacked Blaise's chest with the back of his hand. "Forget Zeke's. Let's go camping!" He turned his eyes my way. "Where do you camp? Do you go a lot?"

Um... My heart sank to my stomach.

Blaise was thinking, and he was thinking fast. He was connecting the dots, and then he knew, and I knew he knew because he lifted his eyes to me. They were filled with accusations, but also—my stomach shriveled up—with pity. A whole bunch of pity. But also confusion. His eyebrows pinched together, but he wasn't saying a word.

Why wasn't he saying anything?

"You camp a lot?" Jamie asked again.

I flushed, remembering it was *Jamie Conway* asking me that question.

I bobbed my head up and down, my neck feeling stiff but also jumbled at the same time, like I couldn't get it right and my whole head felt loose. It was me. I was off-balance.

"I do, yeah. It's kinda my thing."

Jamie whistled under his breath. "That's cool. My older brother camps. He does this whole month-long trek, uses it to raise awareness and has a cam set up. It's pretty awesome. I joined him for a couple days, but I had to come back for football last year. How long are you going for?"

I opened my mouth.

No one had asked this many questions about my camping—

not even Miss Sandy, though she always wanted to know where I was going and how long I'd be gone.

"How long?" came from Blaise, and his tone wasn't so nice.

Jamie shot him a surprised look, but didn't say anything.

"I'll be out there a while."

"How long?" His eyes were hot and hard on me.

I pressed my lips together. What was going on here? I was so confused. "I dunno. A while."

As if catching on to something even I didn't know was happening, Jamie eased back a step, pulling away so it was just Blaise glaring at me.

"Word is you're done with school," he murmured. "You could take off until graduation."

Not helpful, *so* not helpful. But holy crap. How'd he know that?

I frowned.

"People are talking," he grated out.

Man, his eyes were not happy, not at all.

I swallowed over a knot, still not understanding what was going on. "I—I like to camp." It made perfect sense to me.

"Alone?"

Jamie winced, easing back another whole step. "Damn."

I gulped. "Are you mad about that?"

"You shouldn't be camping alone. How long, Aspen?"

"I..." No one cared. Why wasn't he getting that? Why was he caring? "I don't know."

"How. Long?!"

"I..."

"HOW LONG?!"

I jumped at his sudden shout, then heard myself saying, "Till Monday."

Jamie's eyes bulged out. "Oh, *damn*."

"Monday?!" Blaise stepped up, his chest almost rubbing against mine. The bag of food was still in my hand, but Conway stepped in and took it from me. He took the coffee too, and I watched it all go, only realizing once they were gone there was nothing between us.

He moved in, pushing me back against Maisie. His arms came down over my shoulders, and he had me trapped. His head lowered, his eyes intent on mine. "You were going to go camping for four nights?"

"I..." My mouth opened and closed. I was awash in so many feelings right now.

"Alone?!"

I was distantly aware of vehicles pulling up, people leaving the gas station, some going inside. People were filling up with gas, but then suddenly, a loud engine zoomed in and came to a screeching halt.

"Hey! Get away from her!" a woman shouted.

That all was clicking in the back of my mind, but mostly I focused on Blaise. Who was I kidding? I was *all* focused on Blaise. His mouth hovered just over mine, but at the sound of that voice, his entire body stiffened. It had already been tense, but now it bordered on a dangerous level of rigid.

His head snapped up. His nostrils flared

Blaise DeVroe was pissed.

And he was hot!

"Calm your fucking woman down, *brother*," he snarled over my shoulder. "This ain't her business."

Brother?

Fucking woman?

An icy dread blanketed me, and then all hell broke loose.

11

BLAISE

G oddammit.

Cross had to show up now? Right when Aspen's about to go off and camp alone for who knows how long? She said four nights, but Jesus. She finished school. She could be out there an entire week.

How long had she been doing this?

How many other nights had she gone camping? Been alone?

Where the fuck were her parents?

They just let her go out there? Alone?!

But now I couldn't get answers to my questions, because my brother was here and his woman was in my face. She yelled at me, tugging me away from Aspen, and all I wanted to do was grab Aspen, drag her into my Wagon, and peel the fuck out of here so I could be sure she wouldn't do something fucking stupid.

But first, *Christ.*

Bren—that's her name—was almost hissing at me. Her hands dug into my arms, and she pulled.

I turned to find Cross right there. "Get your woman off me, or you and I are going to have problems." I didn't have any patience today.

His eyes narrowed, but he moved forward, maneuvering himself between Bren and me. He began to pull her back. "Bren!"

"He's got his hands on her. Aspen, are you okay?" Bren looked around Cross, her eyes wide and alarmed.

Shit. She knows Aspen.

I looked down, and Aspen hadn't moved. The blood had drained from her face, and she looked up, meeting my gaze.

"What is happening?" she whispered. Her forehead dropped to my chest.

Thunk.

I felt something falling into place at the same time I heard it. And it wasn't her forehead. It was me, realizing something had just happened, and it moved me. I didn't want it to move me, but fuck it, I was moved.

Shit. Shit. Shit.

I didn't like this.

I stepped back, lifting my head, my eyes closed, and I cupped the back of Aspen's head.

What was happening here? She shuddered in my arms.

Ignoring the sudden silence around us, I bent down and murmured, for her ears only, "Do not leave. Please."

She nodded, her forehead not moving from my chest, and then I motioned for Jamie.

When he came over, I handed her off. "Put her in my car. Don't let her leave."

He nodded, taking her arm.

I sighed. "Babe."

Jamie paused, a grin starting.

"Keys," I said to Aspen.

Her eyes were still closed, her head down, but she dug into her pocket and pulled out her keys. I swiped them, nodding to Jamie. "Get her phone," I told him. "Have her text me." I wanted her number.

He nodded. A moment later, after she was in the car, my

phone buzzed in my pocket. Then Jamie locked the doors and sat facing us, his back to Aspen, blocking her view.

I sighed and turned to face my brother.

Cross was my half-brother, but we looked so much alike, we could've been twins. It had been a shock when I saw him the first time, and it was a second shock when I realized later that he knew about me. I hadn't known about him, not until I saw him with his group, facing off against Zeke. They'd been fighting—all of them, even Bren—because that's what they did.

His group of four loved each other.

They were tight, but not the kind of tight that was a show. They were legit tight, and he and Bren were a unit like I'd never seen in my life. He had it all, and as I looked at him now, I wanted what he had.

I mean, I didn't want his woman. She was gorgeous and all—a rock-tight body and dark hair—but she did nothing for me. But I did want friends that would step in front of a moving car for me, and that's what he had. Was that what I had? Maybe.

Zeke would do it. He'd said as much.

Maybe I was the asshole, taking what I had for granted?

Either way, this wasn't the time for these thoughts.

"Bren knows Aspen?" I asked.

Cross frowned, looking torn. He didn't talk to me. I didn't know if it was a rule, it was just the truth.

My blood had cooled, but I still didn't have much patience. "Don't make me say it again. I wasn't hurting her. I like her, so tell me what you know."

Bren moved around my brother, her eyes flashing a warning. "Yeah, we know her. She helped us out of a bind once. How do you know her?"

I settled back on my heels, taking a calming breath. My hands went into my pockets. We were communicating. Good. "We go to the same school."

She frowned, looking at Cross. They seemed to share a whole

conversation before she moved back, sighing and cursing at the same time. Then my brother stepped forward. It seemed he was the chosen spokesperson now.

His group remained beside their huge-ass truck, waiting to see how this ended.

Cross' hands went into his pockets, and I grimaced, realizing how much we looked alike. I pulled mine out, but didn't move. I just waited.

"We crossed paths with her once. She was camping." He indicated behind him with his head. "Bren was worried about her. She thought she might've been homeless."

I snorted. "She's not homeless."

He frowned. "You don't know—"

"She owns this car." I knocked on the hood of the *sickest* car ever.

His eyes widened. He hadn't been expecting that.

"And trust me," I added. "I know her parents. She's loaded."

"Oh." He nodded, accepting that, which surprised me.

I would've thought he'd want to argue just to argue. He seemed the type. Anything I said he'd have to go against, but maybe I was wrong on that.

"As long as you don't mess with her," he said. "Bren cares about her. And Bren cares about, like, five people. You get me?"

We shared a long, menacing look. But I got him.

If I hurt Aspen, for whatever reason, that would piss Bren off, and then he and I would have problems.

I was about to tell him to fuck off or that he didn't need to worry—I hadn't decided which yet—when another car sped into the gas station.

Cross stiffened. His friends straightened up too, and the tall one came over. "Dude." His eyes were trained over my shoulder.

Looking, I cursed. *Zeke.* But before I could even figure how I wanted to play this, since I knew Zeke did *not* get along with my brother, Jamie came hurrying over.

"Your girl's freaking," he said.

"What?" I looked, and Aspen's face was a white color that didn't seem good to me. I could see tears rolling down her face.

What the hell?

I remembered how she'd freaked before when she started to tear up. It'd been the one thing that broke her, and she got out of there immediately. Right now her eyes were glued to Zeke's truck, and as Zeke got out, frowning at us, I could see Mara and Penny climbing out too. *And* Brian and Branston.

"We can run interference, or I can let Bren handle your girl," Cross said.

My brother had assessed the entire situation as quickly as I had, and knowing his rep, maybe I shouldn't have been surprised.

Zeke meandered over, his gaze landing on Aspen's car. "Sweet ride, man. Whose is it?"

Shit.

His friendly, but cautious grin faded fast when no one answered. "Blaise?"

Aspen didn't want to deal with them. I could see that.

So I decided. I took her keys and gave them to my brother. "Get her out of my Wagon and drive her somewhere safe. Tell her I'll call as soon as I get rid of them." I hesitated, then added, "She doesn't like people seeing her cry."

Cross took the keys, his eyebrows shooting up, but he nodded. A second later, we broke away.

I turned to Zeke. "Can we talk inside?"

Jamie seemed to be on my same wavelength because he hollered, "Yo! I gotta show you guys something inside."

Mara and Penny had started to scowl, eyeing Aspen in my Wagon, but at Jamie's shout, they smiled. The guys brightened too, and they all went inside the gas station. Zeke watched them a moment before turning back to me. "What's going on?"

I motioned ahead. "Inside, man. Okay?"

He went with me, but slowly, and he glanced back over his

shoulder. As soon as we were heading toward the gas station, I sensed movement behind me. Once we were in, I looked back over my shoulder, and Cross and Bren had Aspen surrounded.

Good. I didn't know why seeing my friends had put her in a panic, but it had. I'd have to get that figured out as soon as I could. But first, damage control.

Zeke went to grab a soda and water before finding me again. "Okay. Your diversion worked. Whatever chick was in your G Wagon is gone. Want to tell me why you're wearing that shirt?"

I looked down. "You aren't pissed?"

He gave me an incredulous look, and then smirked. "Your problem ain't me. Daniels saw your chick." He whistled, shaking his head. "You got problems if you're hoping to get head tonight. I'm sure you could still pull out a finger bang, but not head." He flashed me a grin and patted my arm before heading to pay for his purchases. "Good luck with that, and just to be clear, we *are* partying tonight, right?"

I looked back outside. Aspen's car was gone now, and Cross' friends were coming inside. Bren and Cross were behind them. I sighed. That meant Aspen had taken off alone.

Zeke was waiting.

"Uh, yeah," I managed.

I locked eyes with my brother, but he didn't say or do anything. He stared back for a split second, his face a blank wall. Bren was the same as the other two loaded up on food and beverages before heading to the front to pay. My friends were in the same section. A few smartass comments were exchanged. It wasn't the first time this had happened, and I knew it wouldn't be the last. Bren and Cross hated Zeke, and they hated anyone who was friends with him. After the insults grew heated, the manager sent Cross' group packing.

"What a shock." The tall one whistled, rolling his eyes and grabbing his stuff. "The Roussou kids get targeted once again."

The manager's face grew redder by the second. He pointed at the door. "Out, or I'll call the police."

At the mention of the Fallen Crest Police, everyone snickered. The force was mostly corrupt, so they were laughingstocks around these parts.

Realizing his mistake, the manager yelled, "Someone get out! I can't have any damages to my property."

"Yeah, yeah. We're leaving," Cross said. He paid for his and Bren's items and disappeared out the door.

I had moved behind Jamie in line, still needing to pay for my gas.

Zeke stood beside me, watching them go. He shook his head. "Your brother's an asshole."

I agreed.

Cross had never once looked at me again. He and Bren climbed into the back of the truck as the other two took the cab. A second later, they barreled out of here.

I grunted. "Fuck him." And I meant it. He helped Aspen. He helped Bren. He didn't do that shit for me.

After we all paid for our stuff, Jamie came with me. The rest went with Zeke. Mara had stood beside me for a minute, and I knew she'd been waiting for a nod or some signal. I gave her nothing. I'd been making out with Aspen moments earlier. It felt wrong to do anything with Mara. And I knew she would've done anything I wanted, despite what Zeke said. That's just how Mara was.

After getting in my Wagon, I texted Aspen.

Me: You okay?

12

ASPEN

I was on my second night camping, and had some distance from the whole gas station debacle now, but I couldn't shake the Owens. Those are my blues, when I'm sad.

I'd freaked out at the gas station because of Blaise. He was so intense, so *right there*, so in my face. He cared. He actually, seriously cared, and I'd fallen apart. Then as I'd watched how he faced off against his brother, I was amazed. I couldn't believe *that* was his brother, because I knew his brother. I'd met his brother. I'd met his brother's whole group, and Bren. I remembered her. She was nice.

They'd been in the woods at a bonfire one time when someone called the cops. I helped them out, though one guy had been mean to me.

But back to Blaise.

Gah. Blaise.

The kissing.

The looks.

He'd been pissed that I spent time alone, but I hadn't had time to explain that I preferred to be alone. Some people are just loners. Since Owen died, that was me. Life was easiest this way, and I'd made my peace with it. I'd accepted it. I'd probably never date or have someone love me, and that was okay. For real.

But then there he was, getting angry—not *at* me, but *for* me.

I'd felt myself swooning all over again, and then Blaise's friends drove up. They were a splash of cold water. I saw Mara looking at me, and there was such sadness in her eyes.

Mara Daniels was gorgeous.

I knew she had a history with Blaise, current history, actually, and if she was looking at me like that, what hope did I have? I already was crushing on him, and now? Now I was gone.

Done.

Hook, line, sinker. Actually, I'd already been hooked and lined. I'd just sunk. Kerplop. All the way to the bottom of the ocean. There I was, falling for him.

He was so hot facing off against his brother. And his brother was hot too, but Blaise was hotter than hot. He had this golden, rich-prick aura around him that I knew shouldn't have made him hotter, but it did because it made him a badass too. Dangerous.

I shivered, remembering how it felt to touch him, be pressed up against him. And man, I had the Owens again because I couldn't go there.

But because I apparently wanted to make myself even more Owens, I pulled up the text messages.

Blaise: You okay?

No. No, I wasn't. But I hadn't replied to him.

Thirty minutes later:

Blaise: Can you let me know if you're alive?

Five minutes later:

Blaise: Seriously.

Two minutes later:

Blaise: You scared to text? Or should I start calling hospitals? I'll do it.

And to that, I had to respond.

Me: I'm camping. I'm fine.

He didn't reply for five very long minutes.

Blaise: Good to know.

I sighed, replying after that because I was a sucker for punishment.

Me: I freaked. It's hard to talk.

Blaise: I get that, but I was worried.

Me: I'm not used to people worrying.

Blaise: Well, that's fucked up. Even my non-bio dad who hates me would worry.

Me: That's...fucked up too? I dunno.

Blaise: It's cool. As long as you're okay.

I hadn't known how to respond to that, so I didn't.

Then twenty minutes later:

Blaise: Download this app.

Me: Okay. Done. Why did I do that?

Blaise: So I can find you if you stop texting me because a bear has eaten you.

Ooooh. A whole wash of warm emotions had come over me, and I'd choked back tears as I replied.

Me: Oh.

Blaise: Talk later. Have fun camping, now I won't worry so much.

Damn.

Damn!

Damn. That was nice of him.

I'd flicked away a tear.

Me: Okay. You too.

I hadn't asked what he was doing that night, and I hadn't asked all day long today. He'd sent a couple texts checking in, asking how my night was, if I was cold, what did I actually do when I camped... And because I didn't want to go deep and potentially depressing, I'd told him the surface stuff.

I read. I relaxed. I enjoyed the water.

But mostly, I felt close to my brother out here. Except on this trip. For some reason, on this trip, Owen wasn't being all Owen-y, and I wasn't feeling him with me. Instead, I was thinking about Blaise, remembering Blaise.

Blaise distracted me.

What was Blaise doing?

Was he partying?

Was he drunk?

Had he kissed Mara Daniels?

Had he done more than that with Mara?

I shouldn't have been thinking like that. We'd kissed. Once. We'd hooked up. Once. One time. There'd be no repeats, not for wallflower girls like me. We didn't get guys like that interested in us. But every time I thought that, I'd pull up our text messages.

If he didn't care, why was he texting me?

Blaise DeVroe was not a good guy. I mean, he was being a good guy to me, but he wasn't normally known to be nice, caring, or sweet. He was known to be blunt and a dick, and I'd seen enough to know that was accurate.

My head swam, all confused. What did this mean?

As if he knew I was thinking about him, my phone buzzed.

Blaise: I'm coming to hang out with you.

I jerked upright.

Me: What? No.

Blaise: Then you come back. Shit. Did you have to go camping so far away? That's over an hour drive.

My heart beat fast. My palms were sweaty.

Me: Don't come here. I camp alone. It's what I do. Alone.

Blaise: I'm tired of my friends and I want to hang out with you. Either you pack up and come here or I'm coming there.

I was going to have a heart attack. I felt my chest tightening.

Blaise: I don't have to stay the whole time, just for the night.

Blaise: Please.

Okay. Heart-melting moment here. I smiled before I realized I was smiling.

Me: Fine.

I frowned.

Me: That app really leads you to me?

Blaise: Yep. I'm only thirty minutes away. Buckle up, be there soon. I'm bringing booze.

Oh great. I didn't drink, like ever. He was violating my camping-alone policy, and if he brought alcohol, I'd probably succumb and have one, so there went my no-drinking policy too.

Me: You're a bad influence already.

Blaise: Tough shit.

Of course. Typical badass response. This shouldn't have sent me even deeper into my crush, but it did because I was just another stupid girl.

I couldn't wait for him to get here.

13

BLAISE

I was armed with food and booze. That's all you really needed when you went camping, right? Made sense to me.

I had gifts, and I wanted to get away from my life, at least for a night. I guess that was my theme, huh? Maybe Aspen and I were the same. I'd not seen another car in the last thirty minutes—this girl could define a new meaning of running away. Well, maybe not running because I knew where she was, but hiding? That was better.

Whatever the case, I wanted to make sure she was safe. That shit would eat me alive if it turned out she wasn't, not to mention that my brother's girlfriend would stab me. Literally. So besides the fact that I thought Aspen was chill in an odd way, I was coming out to make sure she was alive.

See? Good guy. Me.

I laughed to myself as I pulled up—my headlights finally hitting a tent and a campfire right before I turned the Wagon off —because no one could call me a good guy. No. One. Like, ever.

And that was enough thinking for me.

Time to get wasted. I hoped she was okay with that.

She moved toward me, and I could see her silhouette from the fire. Fuck.

She looked good.

She'd been hot before, but she was hotter, if that was possible.

And my dick was hard. Like, instant hard-on. That was going to be annoying.

"Yo." I groaned, stuffing that shit way way down. "I brought presents."

She was hesitant, but then came closer. "What presents?"

"You like sandwiches?" I tossed her the bag I'd gotten from a shop in Roussou, and she caught it, with a little surprised sound. "That needs to last tonight, and I can make a run for breakfast in the morning."

She weighed the bag, a small frown on her face, and I could see the shadow of it from the lights in my Wagon. It was cute.

Cute.

Jesus.

I was such a pansy.

I didn't like cute girls. I fucked hot girls. I banged model-types, though Aspen could be taken for a model. She had the height... I needed to stop checking this girl out. One kiss in a men's room, and I needed my head fixed. What was I doing?

Was it because of Mara? People had started to put us together like we were a couple, and I didn't do couples. I didn't fucking date girls. I screwed them, and that was it.

I'm honest about it. I'm not a total asshole. Girls know the deal with me upfront or I won't touch them. I've never needed to have a girlfriend, in New York or here.

I'd never wanted a relationship, but a flash of my brother and his woman came to my mind, and I paused.

No.

My chest was tight. I didn't want what he had. It was just because my life was unsettled. Everything had been tipped upside down, and I wasn't the kind of guy that handled not knowing shit very well.

"You okay?"

Aspen had drifted closer, her voice soft and concerned.

"Yeah," I barked, then flinched. "Sorry." I softened my tone. "Just stupid thoughts."

And because she was right there, and her green eyes looked all nice and gentle, and I remembered how she'd tasted in the bathroom, I cupped the back of her head. Her eyes went wide, but her lips parted, and that was good enough for me.

I bent down, my lips finding hers, but I paused there.

I didn't apply pressure.

I felt how stiff she'd gone, but then she melted into me. Her arms lifted. The bag dropped. I caught it and tossed it back into my Wagon, and her lips opened underneath mine. It was game *on*.

I'd only meant to have a quick taste, but this kiss was something else.

It was delicious and exciting. It was a promise of something more. My cock bulged, needing to be in her, but I just held her face, my tongue demanding entrance. She gave it, and I was in heaven. My tongue slid in, and this would be all I allowed myself —just this touch from her. When a chick opens herself up for you, it's like she's lifting a window for you to come in and escape the hardship of life, the cold out there. And you can't deny yourself the warmth. That's what Aspen was giving me. Her warmth. Her taste. And I wanted more.

I groaned, lifting my head. "I'm trying to be a good guy here, so I need you to walk away from me." When she didn't, I gritted out, "Right fucking now, Aspen."

She tore herself away.

I saw tears, and dammit—I hadn't wanted to hurt her, but I couldn't say anything. Not yet. I needed to get myself under control. I'd been two seconds away from slipping my hand between her legs and pushing her inside my Wagon.

She took off, back to her tent and fire, and I was the asshole visiting.

I should've left. Right now.

I shouldn't have brought my stuff to her front door. That's what I'd done. I wanted to get away from my life, from the non-bio dad who'd decided to make a surprise visit to town. Seems he was going to be gone all summer, and instead of just calling to let me know, he'd flown to California to deliver the news. He was at the house right now, sitting, talking with my mom and my bio dad, who was still sticking around. Who knew how long that would last, but the adults could have a night. Not me.

I could still go to New York to see my guys, if I wanted. I wasn't out here because of that. I was out here because I hadn't asked for a surprise visit from him.

Aspen was on to something. Just hide here.

Grabbing everything, I approached her campsite.

She had the tent up. There was a kitchen area, a picnic table. She had a hammock up. There were blankets inside the tent.

"Is that a chair?"

She sat, poking at the fire, and looked over where I was indicating.

"Yeah. It's a fold-out lounge chair." She glanced back at me, all shy-like, before averting her eyes. "There's a ton of cool camping gear out there."

I was noticing.

She motioned to one of the chairs, because now I could see there were two of them. "You can sit on that."

"Uh. Sure."

But first I went to the table and put down the supplies I'd brought, including a bag of ice. When she saw it, she got up and pulled something over. It looked like a trash can, but when she lifted the lid, it wasn't. I put the ice in there, feeling how cold it was.

"It's a solar-powered cooler. Neat, huh?"

"Yeah." I nodded. "You sit out here?" The place was lit up with her campfire and some lanterns, but still. "What do you do if someone comes up here that you don't want? There are men who search for campers. You know that, right? Like, they actually search out single women camping." I sat in the chair, but immediately stood again. "This is dangerous."

She shoved to her feet. "I've been camping for years. And I pick places that are off the trail. I'm not stupid."

"Bullshit."

Her eyes got big. Her face got red. "Excuse me?"

"I said *bullshit*. I drove right up to your spot. You can't hide—" I stopped and peered right at her. "Tell me you've never been scared out here by yourself. Tell me you've never had a guy poking around that made you uncomfortable."

She huffed. "Besides you?"

"Tell me that's never happened, Aspen. In all the years you've been this camping expert, you've never had an encounter with another camper that scared you?"

She didn't say a word.

She looked at the ground, and I knew I was right.

Fuck. *Fuck!* It had happened.

"When?" I demanded.

She rolled her eyes, shaking her head. "It doesn't even matter. I was smart. I got away, and it's never happened since."

But it happened.

It had happened once, and it could happen again.

My teeth ground against each other. "I'm not leaving you out here alone. You camp, I'm with you. Or someone else is with you. Enough of this alone shit."

Her head snapped up and her mouth fell open. "You—what? You can't do that!"

I snorted, sitting at the table and finding a cup in the bag. I poured myself a drink. "Watch me. I'll call for reinforcements if I have to." I leveled her with a look. "I know people who wouldn't like hearing about this. Don't forget."

She glared at me, collapsing back down. "You can't do that. You can't come in here and take all this away from me. You can't!"

Her chin wobbled.

Well, crap.

But no, I had to push past the guilt that was easing in. "Aspen, this isn't safe. There are big game animals that could hurt you too. I can't—this isn't safe. You want to camp, you need to have someone with you."

"You?" She snorted, but she wasn't looking at me anymore. Her head was down, and she was ripping a stick apart. Hell. She was shredding it, and then she threw the little pieces on the fire.

"Me or someone else you trust. I can't leave you out here. The man in me won't let me."

"The man in you needs to take several seats down."

Okay. I grinned. That was funny.

She glanced up, saw my grin, and smiled before she looked back down. "I've been camping for years. It's something I did with my brother."

Her brother.

I remembered—those movie producers were Nate Monson's parents.

"You mean Nate?"

She stiffened before looking at me. "You know about my older brother?"

I shrugged. "I just put it together. Zeke's obsessed with your brother's best friend, so I hear those names quite a bit."

The blood drained from her face. "You haven't said anything to him about me, have you?"

I shook my head. "You want a drink?" I grabbed for some ice in that weird trash can/cooler thing.

She shook her head, then stopped. "Yeah." She sighed. "You make me need to drink."

I grinned, handing her mine. "I'll take that as a compliment."

She took the cup, making sure to avoid touching my fingers, and I wiggled my eyebrows, letting her know I was aware of what she'd done. Then I gave her a cocky smirk and she flushed, pulling the drink away.

After I poured myself a second cup, I moved to the chair, but that didn't seem right. She was on the ground, so I eased down too, sitting close enough that my knee could touch hers if I wanted.

I sipped my drink. "I've not said anything to Zeke, but he's going to ask me. He knows I took off tonight, so he'll be up in my business, wanting to know where I went, who I was with—all that shit, just to warn you."

"And you have to tell him?"

I thought a moment. "Zeke can be a douchebag, but he's been a good friend to me. Doesn't feel right to totally lie to him." Alarm moved across her face. "But I won't say shit about your family. And I could give two shits who your brother is or who he's friends with."

"Oh." Her shoulders sagged. "Thank you."

I nodded, watching her lips as she took a sip of her drink.

My dick twitched, and I tried to ignore that.

"Good?" I asked.

She smiled and nodded. "Yeah." She went back to watching the fire. "Nate's not the brother I used to go camping with."

I watched her and sipped my drink. I could do this all night long, and it would be a great fucking night. This level of contentment was alien to me, but I wasn't thinking about that crap. I just listened.

"We had another brother—Owen..." She stopped, looking down.

A moment.

Her voice grew hoarse. "Owen and I camped together."

That was it. That was all.

Didn't need to read between the lines to figure out something had happened to Owen.

"That's why you go camping?"

She nodded, her tone tight. "I usually 'feel' him, if that makes sense."

I raised my eyebrows. "That frustrates you?"

"Well, this time I've not been feeling him. Does it make me crazy that I'm pissed about that?" Her voice took on a distant tone. "Camping's like air to me. I need it to... I just need it." Her eyes found mine, hardening. "You can't take that away from me. I won't let you."

I held her gaze, reading a promise there. It hit me that she could disappear. She could easily pack up and take off, and I'd not know where she was until she decided to show up.

Well, fuck.

That just meant I had to sneak another app on her phone, 'cause if it came to that, she'd delete the other one.

I nodded. "Got it." *Yeah, right.* She wasn't going camping alone, not ever again. Was I an extra asshole for worrying about her? Who were the assholes that knew she did this and let her go? 'Cause they were the real assholes.

But she seemed appeased and nodded, lifting her drink again. "Thank you." Then she frowned. "What are you doing out here anyway?"

I gave her a crooked grin. "Hiding. Same shit as you."

ASPEN

I JOLTED when he said that.

Hiding.

Yeah, I was hiding, I guess. I was hiding from school, from my parents. I was hiding from being alone at the house. But I wasn't *only* hiding. Who was this guy to come in and declare that I couldn't do it anymore? He was the dick I'd heard stories about, that's who. He wasn't God. He didn't get to decide these things about my life. He wasn't my dad or my brother.

I mean, yeah, we'd kissed, and those were some amazing kisses, but that was it.

Were we even friends?

I had no clue.

All I knew was I was confused.

I'd been doing my own thing and then *bam*, Blaise DeVroe was in my life in a big way. He was at my campsite. That was about as big as it got for me, and he was here, shoving his weight around.

I sighed.

I missed Owen.

Why wasn't I feeling my brother? It always happened when I went camping.

He'd abandoned me, and Owen was the one that never abandoned me.

I was nuts. That was the only answer for this. But I wasn't. I was fine. It was normal to do something you'd enjoyed with a loved one to carry on the tradition, and with the idea that they were still with you, just on the other side. I wasn't crazy for believing in that stuff. There were enough signs when Owen was around—like his favorite song coming on the radio or hearing his voice say my name.

"What are you thinking about over there, weird girl?" Blaise tossed a piece of bark at me.

I frowned, tossing it on the fire. "Don't call me that."

"Weird girl?"

"It's insulting."

"Okay." He smirked. "How about Hottie? Hottie with the legs? Legs?"

I tried to glare at him, but I kinda liked the names.

"What?" he mocked, grinning. "Want me to go with Colorado? Colo? Asp? That sounds weird."

"How about just Aspen?"

"Nah. I'll go with Colorado. Or I can go with Tree? Birch?" His grin turned wicked, and I could almost imagine the next word to come out of him.

I held up a finger. "If you dare call me a female dog, I will slice your tires when you're sleeping tonight."

He paused, holding my gaze, weighing my words.

"Shit," he muttered. "I think you'd actually do that."

"Don't mess with the Birch Lady."

And he was back to grinning. "Noted. I will forever fear the Colorado Tree Lady."

I grunted. "Damn right."

Then he laughed. "Man, you're a trip."

I smiled too, but his laugh abruptly stopped, and he pulled out his phone.

He swiped over the screen and sighed audibly. "I gotta handle this. My mom's throwing a fit." The screen lit up, and he hit a button, putting it next to his ear. "Mom."

A pause.

"I'm hanging out with friends." More silence, then a small growl. "Don't even start with that. Mom! Mom." He stood, his drink in one hand and the phone in the other. "I swear to God, Mom." He stopped, his head falling back to look at the sky. His voice rose. "I didn't ask him to come out here. I don't want him here. That douchebag's not here for me. He's here for you. He's sniffing around you, hearing you're shacked up with your real baby daddy. I'm the goddamn excuse, and I ain't dealing with it. Let's go back to New York. Let's pretend we're back there, and the same shit would be happening. You and him are fighting about stuff that's got nothing to do with me, and I'm gone. I'm not even in the house, and here you are calling me, trying to get me to come back, so you and him have a reason to be fighting. He doesn't want you, but he doesn't want to let you go either. It's called a toxic relationship. I'm eighteen. I've got my own money. You've got nothing to 'make me' come back, so I'm not coming. As long as he's there, I ain't." He stopped, listening again. Then his next words came out softer. "I know you're hurting. He cheated on you, but I knew he was going to decide he wanted another go with you. That's why I was going out there this summer. I wanted to see what he was going to do to mess with you. I can't imagine what Stephen is thinking, and Stephen seems like a decent guy. Don't let Griffith get in there and damage what you have with Stephe—" He stopped.

I could hear a female voice speaking on the other end.

He gave another sigh. "Mom. Mom, listen to me. No." A pause. "I'm not coming back tonight. I told you, I'm with friends. Yeah. I'll be back tomorrow. Don't let him sleep there, Mom. I mean it. If he's sleeping there when I get back tomorrow, I'm going to beat his ass. I'm telling you what I'll do."

They kept talking, but some of the fight had left him, and after a few more minutes where he was just silent and listening to her, they hung up.

He sat frozen for a second before turning and throwing his drink as hard as he could across the campsite.

"That was an excellent throw."

He barked out a laugh. "Shut—" He caught himself, raking a hand over his face. "Sorry. Bad habit." His shoulders heaved up and down. "I called him Dad all my life, thought he was my dad. Then my mom finally walked in on him after five years of cheating on her. She declared they were getting a divorce. We moved back here, 'cause she likes it here, and the new boyfriend starts coming around. The new boyfriend looks a lot like me. The new boyfriend, as I found out, was my *real* dad, so what do I call the asshole who raised me? Griffith? He ain't Griffith to me, but he's not my dad anymore."

He scowled, going back to the table and pouring another drink for himself. He looked over. "You want one?"

Did I?

I was almost done so I finished it and stood, taking my cup to him.

I handed it over, letting our fingers brush. I didn't look at him, but I could feel his eyes on me. They were smoldering, and I felt my body heating.

Then he pulled the cup away.

"So we've established that you're out here because you were hoping to be camping with a ghost."

I looked up.

That stung, but he was right.

That *was* why I was out here. He studied me until I nodded.

"And I'm out here avoiding talking to a guy that I don't even know what to call anymore because he ain't here for me. I'm just the excuse." He whistled under his breath, finishing my drink and handing it over. He picked up his cup and held it out. "Let's toast."

I frowned, but held my cup up to his.

"How about we toast to losing our virginity in a tent?"

I coughed and sputtered out, "What?!"

"Just kidding." He clinked his cup to mine and took a sip. "I'm not a virgin. Don't worry."

14

BLAISE

She lay in front of me, and all I wanted to do was touch her. That wasn't true. I also wanted to lift her shirt up, show more of that little bit of waist she'd revealed as she turned away from me. She wore tight yoga pants to bed, and I wanted to move in, slide my hand inside them, and push them down. Then I wanted to cup her ass, because I could see a glimpse of her thong—pink and dainty looking. I groaned to myself.

My hard-on had a life of its own.

It wanted me to move closer, grind against her... And whose fault was it that we had to sleep next to each other? Mine. What a fuck am I? Apparently, you needed more than booze and food for camping. You needed things like sleeping bags and blankets, and things to brush your teeth—not that I was really worried about that. I could slip away to the gas station back up the road and do my business there.

Aspen had suggested we share the sleeping bag. It was that or I had to sleep in my Wagon. California nights could get cold, so here I was, a little drunk, and Aspen looked wasted after her three glasses. She had at least a decent buzz happening.

That was then. This was now.

I was awake and sober. Painfully sober.

Fuck, man. Fuck.

That bathroom make-out sesh was back in my head, replaying over and over again. Every little moan she'd made, the way I'd cupped her breasts, stroked her nipples, and grabbed them with both hands. Who the hell wouldn't? She had a great rack, but now I was all sorts of regretting that because all I wanted to do was roll over on top of her, lift her shirt, and kiss those breasts while I slipped a finger inside her. Maybe two. Probably three. I wanted to wake her all the way up....

But I wouldn't. I was fighting a boner the size of the redwoods surrounding us, but I had to be a gentleman. Because apparently, that's what I'd signed up for when I decided I was going to be Aspen's friend.

Friend. God.

Gag.

I was not a friend to girls. I banged them, or at least I fingered them. Friends? Hell to the no. So why was I out here? I could've gone to Zeke's. He'd mentioned a rave in the desert, and I could've gotten lit up a whole different way. But I was here—in fucking boner rager agony—and Aspen was sleeping.

She was snoring. It was soft and cute-sounding, and there was that word again. *Cute*. I did *not* do cute.

"What's your damage?"

I grinned, hearing my words come from her. Guess I woke her up.

She flipped over to glare at me. "I can't sleep because I can hear how tense you are."

My grin deepened, and I raised an eyebrow. "You want to know my problem?"

"Yeah." She got settled, tipping her head to look up at me.

"Fine." I looked down. "It's not me that's tense. My rager is working double-time, and you're its techno music, if you get my drift."

She frowned, glancing down.

"I have a massive hard-on for you." There. I spelled it out.

She flushed, her eyes going round, but her lips curved up. She enjoyed this attention from me, and fuck me—that just made me want to torture her more. I was starting to live for her reactions, so I moved forward. I went slowly, giving her the option to pull away or stop me, but she never did.

Her teeth sank into her lip. I about jizzed my pants.

Cute.

Fuck.

She was all cute, and hot, and sexual, and I wanted to breathe her in, the more I was around her.

I rubbed against her, and she still didn't stop me. That felt good. That felt real *gooood*. *Reallly* good.

Her eyes closed, and she moaned, and that was it.

I slid a hand under her shirt, moving it up, and rolled her to her back as I loomed over her. I was grinding against her, and I felt her holding her breath as her legs opened a little bit more for me.

Hell yeah. I moved all the way over her.

This was going to go bad fast, but who was I to stop us?

I settled right between her legs, and I pushed in and up. She gasped. It was like touching heaven again. I hissed, needing to let some of the tension out, as my fingers discovered she had no bra.

No bra. Was that a sign? Who was I talking to?

My fingers found her nipple as I thrust against her. Her legs wound around my hips, and she began moving with me. Now we were getting it on, and I couldn't hold back anymore.

Dipping down, I found her lips.

Lust exploded in me. Shit, I wanted her. I wanted her so bad. This wasn't like with other girls. She was more somehow, and I groaned. I couldn't stop touching her. My lips opened over hers, commanding her, and she responded. She was so fucking good at that. My tongue slid inside to find hers, and as we kissed, I showed her how I wanted to be inside her in a whole other way.

I moaned. "You're amazing."

She didn't respond, but her body started shaking. She grabbed my shoulders and moved to clutch my head.

She wrapped her legs tighter around my hips and lifted up against me, grinding herself on my dick. I slid my hand under her ass, palming one of her cheeks and lifting her even farther off the ground.

Okay. Enough of this angle.

I shoved up, bringing her with me, then did some maneuvering until her legs were over mine, her arms around my head, my tongue in her mouth, and my cock trying to get through those hot yoga pants. I could feel her breasts rubbing against my chest, and this was officially the best camping trip I'd ever gone on.

I smoothed my hand down her side, working my fingers under her waistband, but I paused, giving her time to refuse.

I felt like I was going to explode, but I needed to touch her. I had to take care of her. Still, I waited, and when I didn't move fast enough, she took my hand, guiding me farther into her pants.

I grinned, nipping at her lips. "Hell yeah."

She laughed. "Shut it."

There she was, using my words against me. I was fast on my way to hard-core crushing on her, but then everything faded because my fingers were between her legs, and this right here was enough to let me die happy. There's nothing better than touching your girl, stripping her, and making her combust all around you. I was about to finish that job, and I sank a finger inside.

She grasped my shoulders, moaning against my mouth, and then she was moving with me.

I slipped in a second finger.

She rolled her hips, riding my hand like a pro, and this was better than my own climax. I kept thrusting, playing her body, pulling away from her mouth and going down to find her breasts. I ran my tongue around her nipple as she shuddered, her fingers raking through my hair.

Nothing better, ever, than having your girl writhing against you and knowing you're about to make her see fucking stars. I could feel her getting there; she was close. Her body tensed, her legs growing tighter around me. She was almost climbing me, and then, I felt her body snap. Her head fell back.

A guttural sound emerged from her, and she came all over me.

Best goddamn camping trip ever.

I held her close, easing her back down, because we were *so* not done. I nipped at her neck, giving her sweet, tantalizing kisses as she melted for me.

Then she came alive and her hand went into my pants, her fingers wrapping around me.

I pulled away from her mouth. "You don't have to do that."

She tightened her hold on me, just briefly, and she began to slide up and down. "Shut up, pretty boy."

She rolled me over, straddled me and sat up. I wasn't expecting any of this, but man, I loved it. I was loving this a whole lot, and then she made *me* see stars.

15

ASPEN

I had kissed guys before, but nothing like what happened with Blaise in my tent. No way, and I was embarrassed. But I also *wasn't* embarrassed, because he was so nice about it all.

This morning, he'd still been nice about it, waking me up with more kisses and those fingers moving inside me once again.

He never pushed me. Not once.

After I came, he kissed me on the lips and said, "I'm running to the gas station. Be back with morning coffee and donuts."

That was twenty minutes ago.

While he was gone, I went to the river to wash up. I changed clothes and began putting everything away. I knew Blaise would go back today, and I knew there'd be a fight if I tried to stay. So I was giving in, but it wasn't because of him. To be honest, I didn't know why I was giving in. Maybe it was because I couldn't feel Owen, or maybe I'd lost the desire to camp after last night.

Whatever the reason, I had most of my stuff put together by the time Blaise pulled back up in his Wagon.

He got out, flashing me a smile—a drink holder with coffees in one hand and a bag of donuts in the other as he came down the trail. He took in the near-empty campsite with a slight frown before setting the coffees and bag on the table. "You actually giving in on the camping thing?" He straddled one of the benches.

I went over and hopped up, my feet coming down just beyond his opened knees.

He lifted one of the coffees for me. I took it, our fingers sliding against each other, and we shared a look that made my insides sizzle.

"I figured if I didn't, you'd send up your brother and Bren."

He grunted. "Shit. I never thought of them. They'd be perfect. They're huge pains in the ass."

I hid a grin, sipping my coffee and almost groaning, it was so good. He unwrapped one of the donuts and slid it over to me.

Seriously sweet. Who knew?

"Can I ask about them?"

He smiled, picking up his coffee. "I'm fairly certain you know them better than I do. Maybe I should be asking you." His tone was teasing, but those words packed a punch.

"You don't know your brother that well?"

"Cross?" He frowned. "No, just that he hates me."

Oh. *Damn.* "He hates you?"

He shrugged. "Don't worry about it. It's not a big thing. I'm still hung up on finding out the whole daddy lie, you know?"

"Oh." I thought a moment. "Your brother was nice to me the night I helped them. He and Bren were. The tall one was okay, but the other one was kinda mean."

Blaise's eyes blazed. "What'd he say to you?"

"Nothing you haven't."

He scowled. "That pisses me off. I can be mean to you because I like you, but he can't."

"You like me?"

His scowl vanished. "I mean..." He shrugged. "I was thinking making you come last night and this morning kinda conveyed that message."

"Yeah, but you don't date." *Aw, crap.* Here it was. I hadn't meant to bring us here, but I guess I needed to know the parameters. Whatever that meant.

He got all serious, leaning forward. "I *don't* date. I mean..." Regret crossed his face. "But I can't say we're only friends either. I'm..." He expelled a ragged breath. "Man, I don't know. My last talk like this was with Mara when I said, 'I'd like to continue boning you, but if you need an exclusive handle, I'll walk.' She was fine with it, but you're not like that." He watched me intently.

My throat felt tight. He was right.

I *wasn't* like that.

I'd thought maybe I could be, but I couldn't. Knowing he'd been with me last night and this morning, and that he could be with her tonight made me want to die.

"I'm sorry, but I'm not that girl," I murmured.

"Well," he said softly. "Fuck me then." He leaned closer, his hand on my knee. "I don't want to be just friends."

"I don't want to be another Mara."

He flinched. "You're not. I don't know what this is, but I know you're not that."

Could he... What was he saying?

He looked away and pressed his lips together. "How about we shelve this? Come back to it later, and I promise not to touch anyone else until we know exactly what we're doing."

"Really?" *But what does that mean?*

He nodded, finishing his donut in one bite and standing. "I can't promise a relationship; I know that much. But I can promise you I won't touch anyone else right now. That's all I can give you. I'm sorry."

Well, damn. Seeing no other choice, I dipped my head in a nod. "Okay."

He raised an eyebrow. "Okay?"

"Yeah. Okay."

I was confused, but he wouldn't touch another girl. Okay then. I tried to smile. "Why am I suddenly terrified?"

"Fuck if I know." He picked up his coffee, finishing that too, and looked around. "Why don't you finish packing everything up, and just point me at things you want carried to your car? I can do that much to help."

So that's what we did.

I finished packing up what was left, and then pointed.

He carried everything to Maisie, and after I had a hard time getting something to fit, he took over packing her up too. His phone went off the entire morning, but he ignored it. There was one last coffee, and I was grabbing the last bag when I saw him duck into Maisie, putting it inside for me.

Then he held his keys in the air, grinning at me, and I felt all sorts of heat between my legs. He watched me come over to him, his eyes darkening as he looked me up and down.

He whistled. "You do camping good."

A stifled a laugh. That was funny.

"Thank you."

He grinned, bending down to press his lips to mine. "Wanna race back to Fallen Crest?"

Fallen Crest. I felt a sudden wave of nerves. "Uh..."

His grin faded. "What?"

"About Fallen Crest—when we get back there..." I swallowed over a lump in my throat. "What's the plan? Because your friends scare me."

He shrugged. "They scare me too."

"Blaise." I was getting frustrated. "This isn't a joke to me."

"I know." He tipped up my chin. "I pretty much gave you the one promise I can give. Can we see how things go? I won't let anyone mess with you."

I tried to ignore the sudden burst of tingles in my chest, but dammit—he was in there, and making me feel things I wasn't ready to feel. I never thought I would feel stuff like this, or have someone like him wanting to kiss me. And that's all he was giving me, I reminded myself. We were more than friends, and he wouldn't touch someone else, but relationships took more than that.

I'd have to go back to my same existence and what? Wait for him to show up? Make visits?

Then again, maybe that's what friendships were like?

"Okay."

His eyebrows darted up in surprise. "Okay?"

I nodded. "Yeah. I mean, I don't have friends in Fallen Crest. I'm out of practice for this stuff. All my friends at Hillcrest lived in the same building as I did, so it was different."

He frowned. "Okay then, I guess."

I'd started for Maisie when he caught my hand and pulled me in. His head dipped, and his mouth was on mine. A full minute later, he let me go, and my knees were shaking.

"That'll last me a while. I'll call later."

He'll call.

Okay then.

He'll call.

I could do this... Couldn't I?

But he said he'd call, so there was that. He was going to call.

16

BLAISE

Zeke answered after the first ring.

"Yo! Where the fuck you at, bro?"

I grinned. Always the same from him. For some reason, that settled me.

"Hey, I need a favor."

He belched into the phone. "Name it."

"Nice."

"Whatever. You missed the best rave last night." He whistled.

I could hear voices, but they were fading, and a second later, they were gone.

"Talk to me. What do you need?"

"Where are you?"

He belched again, then laughed. "We had tacos earlier. Guess the peppers aren't sitting right with me. But what do you need?"

"I'm not sure." I explained about my mom and Griffith. "If he's still there, I either need you to hold me back or be my alibi."

I could almost hear him smiling. "Yeah, man. Anything for you. You want just me or should I grab Conway and Ashlome too?"

I paused, but there was nothing else there. "Hey, Zeke—"

"Water under the bridge, B. They never really liked me, so it's all good. I can't fault them since, you know, I love you too."

There it was again, his unconditional bromance. "Right." I was such a dick. All the shit I'd thought about him in my head...

"Dude, I can almost hear your wheels turning, so shut the fuck up. Okay? So you want both or just Conway? Or just yours truly?"

Christ.

If Griffith were actually there, I would try to beat the shit out of him. "Maybe all three of you."

Zeke belched again. "On it. Oh, and Daniels was asking about you last night. Am I correct that your absence had something to do with the chick in the back of your very fine G Wagon?"

Crap. My stomach took a nosedive. "Mara was asking about me?" I was hoping to not deal with that whole scene, but I couldn't if she was going to push it.

"Yeah." He was quiet. "Should I avoid her?"

I barked out a laugh. "Nah, man. You don't have to avoid her; just pass on that I've got family drama happening."

Mara hated family drama more than I did. Her mom was diagnosed with histrionic, so those words would keep her away for a good week. She'd overheard one of my fights with my mom and turned into mist for almost a month. It was kinda nice, except her blowjobs were the best I'd had.

I wonder what Aspen was like on that front?

I felt a kick in my gut and looked down. Oh yeah. He was excited about that too—if we ever got there with her. She'd been excellent with the hand job.

"See you in a few."

"See you."

We hung up, and I stopped at the store before heading home. It'd take Zeke a while to leave his house. No one ever wanted him to go. Taking my stuff to the checkout counter, I wasn't paying attention when I heard from behind me, "Shit. That all for Aspen?"

It was my brother.

I tensed, then noticed the two packs in his hand. I nodded at them. "Those better *not* be for Aspen."

He paused a second, then looked away, but I caught the grin. "Fuck you," he said.

I smiled. "That's the point of those, brother."

The cashier looked at us, the previous customer done and departing. She reached for my box of condoms, saw me, saw Cross, saw what was in his hand, and blinked a few times.

Shaking her head, she ran the boxes over the register.

"Maybe this place could get self-checkout, hmmm?" I murmured as the screen showed what I owed.

"Uh, yeah." But her cheeks grew red as she looked from me to my brother and back again.

I flashed her a grin. "I know. I'm richer, but he's better looking." I whistled under my breath. "Which would you want at the end of the day, huh? What a dilemma, right?"

"I—" She gaped at me.

I frowned. "No offense, but I already got a girl like you that I might have feelings for. Next time, meet me first."

Cross cursed, shaking his head. "You are the biggest dick I know, and if you make a joke about your dick, I'll punch it. Happily."

I nodded at him, backing away and waving, the condoms in full view of everyone. "See you at home, brother." I winked.

The exit doors swished open, and I walked out. I could see Bren waiting in Cross' truck, and I smirked as I walked past. "Didn't know you two were into handcuffs and whipped cream. Right on."

I only noticed she was wearing a dress after I was past and almost to my Wagon.

I faltered. Crap. Maybe they were going on a nice date and I was being a dumbass making wisecracks?

The store's doors opened again, and Cross came out, his condoms in a bag.

He saw that I'd faltered and looked from me to Bren before his jaw firmed. He tossed the bag inside the truck through an opened window, and headed for me in two seconds. "What'd you say to her, huh?"

I narrowed my eyes at him. "Excuse me?"

He pushed against my chest. "You can be an ass to some girl I don't know, but when it comes to my girl, I tend to go nuts. Or don't you remember from the last time?"

My jaw snapped shut. "Yeah. About that last time..." I pocketed my condoms and shoved him back. He was surprised, so I was there again, harder the second time.

A door slammed shut. I could hear feet running over.

"He didn't say anything." Bren tried to push between us. "Fuck's sake, Cross. Stop."

I was rattled, though not because this was the first run-in I'd had with my brother. This was number three by now? We'd traded no punches the first time, and I hadn't hit back the second. This time, I felt my nice guy starting to fade. *And*, I still had Griffith to deal with.

I was rattled because I wanted to fight him. I hadn't thought I cared. I thought I could give two pumps about this guy, but I guess somewhere deep down I did, because I *really* wanted to knock his teeth out. How fucked is that? Realizing you might care about someone because you want to hurt them? Was that an indication of how truly messed up I was? Because being raised by Griffith was sure to do that to even the best kid.

I refocused and saw Bren talking to Cross. I heard the words *handcuffs* and *whipped cream*, and she glared at me over her shoulder. "He's just being a dick," she concluded. "That's it."

I started laughing.

"Shut it!" Cross yelled.

I laughed harder and showed him my teeth. "You got a nice set there. I'd like them better on the ground."

Screw it.

I wanted to fight.

Suddenly there was a screech of tires, and Zeke's truck raced our way. Jamie was out before it even stopped. "Hey, hey, hey." He stepped between us, frowning at my brother and me. "What's going on?"

Oliver was slower to approach, but he sidled up on the other side of our circle.

Zeke turned the engine off and slid out of his truck. It was a big-ass truck. He whistled, smiling crudely at Bren and Cross as he tossed his keys in the air, catching them and repeating as he came to a stop beside me. "Thought the fight you needed us for was at your house." He nodded at Cross. "You're exchanging that pussy for this pussy?" His eyes slid up and down Bren. "I'm so down for that. Winner gets your woman?"

I'd heard stories about my brother and his crew fighting. And I knew Bren had had a knife against Zeke's throat once upon a time, but he didn't seem to remember that. His words were fighting words.

The shit I'd been throwing out was just to get a reaction. At first.

If Zeke kept running his mouth, we really would be tossing down in a second.

I waited, breath held, for my brother to react.

"Enough!" It was Bren who decided. She shoved Cross back toward their truck. "Your brother was being sarcastic, but he wasn't mean. And his dumbass friend? Well, that's a fight for a different night. Come on. You and I have a date, remember?"

Cross didn't budge.

Unease shivered down my spine, but hell yes. I was so down for this. One big chaotic rough and tumble fight. Let's have this out. Finally. His eyes locked on Zeke's before they moved to mine, and whatever he saw in me, it changed him. A different look came over him, and he blinked, as if clearing his head.

Bren was successful in pushing him closer to their truck, but he braked and called over her shoulder, "Who are you fighting at your house?"

Right. I rolled my eyes. "What am I supposed to say? Your mama?" I gave him my middle finger. "It ain't any of your business. Go screw your woman."

His eyes went feral.

"NO!" Bren was firm. "I said no. Not him. Not your brother, because he might mean something to you later. Trust me."

Goddamn. "You're annoying, Bren."

She ignored me, still shoving my brother back to their truck. Once he was inside, she turned and addressed me. "You're a prick, but you're still blood to him, and I know him. That does mean something." Her eyes went cold. "Don't push him until you go over a line you can't come back from."

And with those kind words, she strode around to get in on the other side.

My brother flipped me off out the back as they drove off.

Zeke started laughing. "I was hoping to see some Bren fighting moves. That girl is hot." He turned to me. "Your house, right?"

Jamie let out a breath, his hand trembling slightly as he raked it through his hair. "We were driving to your place when he noticed the Mercedes here. We saw you and them, and it was perfect timing, huh?"

I narrowed my eyes. "You can't hang with me if you're scared of a fight."

Zeke started laughing.

Jamie's eyes widened, then cooled. "Yeah. Didn't know it was like that, but whatever. I'm down."

I doubted it. I could see why no one had made a move against

Zeke until now. They needed a fucking leader because they were followers.

I felt Zeke studying me and met his gaze. "Now can you see why I love you? No one else like you around these parts."

It was an odd thing for him to say, but I was understanding my "best friend" a little more each day. And it seemed odd, but right at the same time.

I sighed. "Let's go and hope Griffith isn't at the house."

"Can I call him pussy if we see him again?" Zeke asked.

I relaxed. "You can call him pussy as if his new name is Pussy DeVroe."

17

ASPEN

B laise never called, but he texted close to midnight.
Blaise: I'm sorry. Major family drama tonight. Non-bio dad refused to leave the house. I almost beat the shit out of him.

I sat up in bed, and a cold sweat came over me.

Me: Is everything okay now?

Blaise: Can I come over?

A zing raced through me, a flutter of excitement.

Me: Really?

Blaise: You're in the gated community, right? I know Tucker. He'll tell me which house.

Tucker was Mr. Carl's son.

Me: Tucker shouldn't let you go through.

Blaise: He won't unless you call and tell him to do it. Will you? Are your parents home?

I threw back my covers as I replied.

Me: Okay. I'll call. Tucker is supposed to put you on a list. My parents will see that list.

Blaise: He won't. I'll ask him not to. He works with my mom so he's cool.

I sighed and called the front desk for our neighborhood. Tucker answered. "Yeah. He's right here," he said after I explained.

"Can you let him through?"

I heard a beep in the background, and he came back on the line. "Are you sure about this, Miss Aspen? I know Blaise, and he's got issues."

"He's good with me. It'll be fine. Please don't put him on the list."

"I won't if you ask me not to."

"Thank you, Tucker." I hurried down the hallway and passed the front door. We didn't have the alarm on because my dad was in the back shed, where he was still editing. He said he worked out there, but we all smelled the cigars.

I waited at the side of the house until I saw Blaise's Wagon. He parked on the street, closer to the next lot, and walked back toward my house.

As he came up the driveway, I flashed my phone and waved at him.

He changed directions, coming toward me in the dark. "Nice. I've not snuck into a girl's house in a long time." He grabbed my hand and kissed my cheek.

I was momentarily stunned at that greeting, "For future reference, this is how you'll sneak in, okay?" I squeezed his hand as I led him through the side door.

"I like it. You're already my co-conspirator." He squeezed my hand back, and I led him up the back stairs to my room. "Can I tell you now how much I appreciate your ass?" he murmured. "It's the best ass I think I've ever seen."

"Shut up." I grinned as I tugged us into my room and locked the door.

"Ooh, a locked door too. Such a scandal."

"Shut up!" I took his head and tugged it down to mine.

I'd been wanting to do this since his text. No. I'd been wanting this since we left the campsite this morning.

Groaning, he deepened the kiss and picked me up.

I gasped as he walked us over to my bed. He eased me down and crawled over my body as I scooted up to the top. His eyes had darkened. "You are seriously gorgeous, Aspen." He ran a hand over my shirt, hooking it on my shorts, but he didn't do anything else. He only rubbed his thumb back and forth. I shivered, knowing what that thumb could do to my body. But he didn't do more.

Lying beside me, he cupped my face as we kissed.

He rubbed his thumb over my cheek the whole time.

Which felt nice. It all felt nice. My body was literally humming.

After a bit, I eased back, frowning. "Why aren't you putting the moves on me?"

He grinned, lying on his back. He slid one of his arms under me, pulling me against his chest. "I didn't come over to hook up. I just came over."

His other hand found my waist, rubbing back and forth over the stretch of skin showing there. He pushed my shirt up, but only moved over my stomach, back and forth in a slow and comforting motion.

"I almost got into a fight with my brother today," he said after a moment.

I tensed, shifting to angle my body so I could see him. His hand kept smoothing over my stomach. "About what?" I asked.

He shrugged. "Because I wanted to fight him. I don't even remember what it was about."

I rolled my eyes. "That doesn't sound like you at all."

He grinned, his hand darting up and tweaking just under my breast.

"Ow!"

But he covered my breast with his palm, soothing it before

going back to my stomach. "Sorry." He tensed, jackknifing upright. "Shit! I'm so sorry. I shouldn't have done that. I can't just grab you and—"

"Hey!" I sat up with him, catching his hands. I tugged on them, getting him to look at me. "It's fine. If it wasn't, I wouldn't let you into my house, much less my room. It's fine. I could lay down the law if I needed to."

His eyes clung to mine, a haunting agony starting to show there. "You sure?"

"I'm sure."

Then he relaxed, one muscle at a time, until he was lying down, his hand back on my stomach. After a bit, he started running it in a circle again. "Jesus." His lips found my shoulder, and he kissed me there. "I'm starting to realize how much of a mess I am. I am truly fucked up. I tried to fight my brother, and I don't even have a relationship with him. I called my guys to back me up in case I tried to fight my non-bio dad. I needed them to keep *him* away from me."

I frowned. "What happened?"

He snorted, a sound of disgust. "What always fucking happens with me. I mouthed off and kept going, purposefully pushing him until he wanted to flatten me. When we first came here, I thought I had everything handled. Then I found out about the dad situation, and now I'm just a walking asshole. The shit I said to Cross..." He shook his head, nipping my skin lightly before he sat up. "I shouldn't be here. I shouldn't bring this shit to you. You and me, we're moving too fast. I'm sorry."

He started to get off the bed.

My heart spiked in panic.

He was going. He truly was going to leave.

He paused, his hand on the doorknob, and looked back. "We shouldn't be friends even. I'll just fuck up your life."

"Stop!"

My heart splintered.

My stomach dropped to my feet.

That was enough. My voice unscrambled my head, and I darted off the bed. But I didn't go to him. He wanted to leave, and I wasn't going to physically stop him. That was beneath me, but when I saw he was waiting, I opened my mouth.

I didn't know what I was going to say until it all came spilling out.

"I need you. Okay?" *Oh my God. Did I actually say that?*

I blinked. I had. And there was more.

My chest ached. I didn't like to think about this stuff, but here it was. I balled my hands into fists. I'd never said any of this out loud.

"I barely know my brother. He's been so mad at our parents that he mostly stays away. He's almost a stranger, so then it was just Owen and me until..."

I couldn't.

I heard the car screeching. The red lights flashing.

The taste of blood.

Then nothing.

It was the feeling after the nothing that gave me nightmares, when I let myself remember.

I wasn't letting myself remember.

"Hey." Blaise stepped in front of me. "Hey." He wrapped me in his arms. "I get it," he whispered. "You don't have to say anything more. Trust me. I get it." He pulled back, looking down.

I wasn't at the edge anymore. He'd pulled me back.

"I am fucked up, and I'm guessing I'm contagious—making you think you're all messed up, but you aren't. You're good. You know that, right?" He said that like he was trying to convince me the sky was up and not down, and *I* was the moron for not believing him. Then he grinned. "You got a television screen in this house? Let's watch a movie." He looked around and made a *tsk*ing sound. "This massive place and no television in your room? So low-brow of you, Aspen. I'm disappointed."

"Shut up." I tugged him to the door and led him to the movie room. I was a little embarrassed. "There's a bigger one in the basement, but this one is just for me. They put it in on the off chance I might have friends who wanted to hang out."

My neck was hot. I knew my face was red, and I didn't know why. Blaise came from wealth too.

I motioned to the speakers. "We can turn it super loud and no one will hear us."

He looked around the room. The large screen encompassed an entire wall. There were couches spread out over the rest of the room.

He shook his head. "Man, no snack room? No attendant to walk the lane, check our tickets? Make sure we didn't sneak in? You're so poor."

"Stop it." I hit him with a pillow and nodded to the back. "The snack room is there, and before you make any more jokes, I actually talked my parents out of doing more than they did." This was embarrassing enough.

Blaise sighed as he grinned down at me. "Looks like we'll just have to hole up here in case there's a zombie outbreak. What? You don't have two pizza toasters? Just one? Talk about budget cuts. I can really see it in here."

I grinned, my chest loosening, and by the time we'd made a pizza and settled on the couches, it was well past midnight. When the movie started—a superhero one that wasn't scheduled to come out for another year—I got comfortable. This was one of the perks of my parents' job, but I was asleep not even halfway through it.

At one point, I woke to the feeling of a blanket settling over me. Then Blaise pulled me against his chest, and I closed my eyes once more.

"I'm not always this bad, Aspen," he whispered. "I promise."

He was almost perfect to me.

18

ASPEN

Blaise: Where are you?
Me: Still in bed.

It was Monday morning, just past nine, and I was tired. Not that I really had any reason to be, but I was. I was calling this an early vacation, since I was done with school. There was no reason to go, even though I wasn't camping after all. And since I planned to ignore my graduation (they would mail me the diploma, I checked), this was the beginning of my summer.

I'd been planning all these summer camping trips, but Blaise had ruined those for me. Not that I couldn't still go, but it would be different. I felt a slight panic thinking about that—thinking I might never want to camp alone again. No way. I'd still go. I'd start planning my next trip now.

Blaise: Come to school.
Me: No.

The phone rang a second later.

Blaise calling.

I answered, putting him on speaker and crawling out of bed. "What's going on?"

"I'm annoyed you're not here."

I grinned, running the water to wash my face. "I'm done with school. I've completed all my classes. There's no reason for me to show up."

"I'm your reason."

That felt nice, but I wasn't going.

He seemed to know that, because he sighed. "Fine. There are parties every day this week. Can I talk you into going to any of them with me?"

I'd dipped my washcloth under the water, but I paused and pulled it back. Turning the water off, I waited, my chest tight. He wanted me to hang out with his friends? I didn't people. At all. Blaise was becoming the exception.

"Hello?" he said. A bell sounded from his end and he cursed. "Shit. I gotta go. I'll call later, okay?"

"Okay." Thank God we didn't have to finish this conversation. "Have a great day."

"Yeah, yeah," he grumbled. "Fuck you."

I laughed, then ended the call and heaved a sigh of relief.

What do I do? I looked at myself in the mirror. I raised my eyebrow, digging at my reflection. *Huh?* I asked myself. *What do you do when you're falling for the popular bad boy and you're completely out of your league?*

I was an introvert. I was socially awkward. My only positives were that if you put me in front of a professional photographer, I photographed well, and my parents had money. That was it.

But my life wasn't even a problem for me to complain about. What was I doing?

There was a knock on my bedroom door, and it pushed open. Miss Sandy walked in with her housekeeping cart. Seeing me, she jumped back.

"Ahh!" She sagged back against the door. "Miss Aspen! You scared me." She took in the still-messy bed and my desk with an open bag of chips and my computer on it. My closet spilled clothes on the floor, and Blaise had left a blanket and pillow on my couch yesterday.

"Miss Aspen?" She seemed mystified.

So was I. Blaise had showed up Saturday night and then hung out most of the day yesterday, so the room was messy. He'd gone home when his mom called saying she wanted him to be there for dinner. I'd gotten a few texts late last night, so I knew he hadn't stayed at his house. He was at Zeke's, and he'd sent a picture—just him and Zeke playing video games all night. He hadn't needed to reassure me, because I didn't take him for a liar. The only thing he owed me was not to touch another girl until we knew what was going on between us.

But it was kinda nice to get the text too.

"Sorry," I told Miss Sandy, surveying the mess.

"No." She patted her chest, frowning. "Why are you not in school?"

Graduation was next Sunday. I just needed to play this so they didn't start wondering about it—not until it had passed. "I'm not feeling well," I lied with a smile.

"Oh no." She crossed the room, putting the back of her hand to my forehead. "You don't feel like you have a fever, but one never knows." She motioned me toward the bed. "Shoo, shoo. Get in bed. I'll bring you everything you need."

She hurried around the room as I crawled back under the covers. She picked things up, straightening the room, still doing her job. I had to smile at that. Miss Sandy, always the professional. When she came to one of Blaise's shirts, she paused.

I groaned, realizing what it was.

The emblem on the shirt was a marijuana leaf making a sexually suggestive hand motion.

I knew that *now*.

She rotated swiftly to me. She put the shirt on the bed, then picked it back up and folded it, placing it on the arm of the couch. She looked at me, and I waited, biting down on my lip.

Sandy hadn't come in yesterday.

Blaise had been here most of the day and no one knew. My mom had emailed me and come over once, knocking on the door to ask if I wanted to go with them to dinner in Los Angeles. They were going there for business and would be gone most of this week. I'd declined the dinner invite, and Blaise had left shortly after that for his own family dinner. He'd thought it was a hoot, standing behind the door while my mom was on the other side of it.

I'd just rolled my eyes at him because I'd already lost probably three years of my life, worrying he'd be caught. My mom wasn't known for coming in and being motherly, but there had been times when she decided we needed a mother-daughter talk.

However, lately she'd seemed distracted, and I'd used that to my advantage. I wasn't sure why I wanted to skip graduation, and I didn't want to focus on it long enough to find the reason. I just knew once it had passed, I would breathe easier.

"Would you like tea for your morning breakfast?" Miss Sandy asked.

That's it? That was all she was going to say?

I didn't know if I was disappointed or overjoyed, but I nodded. "Yeah. That'd be great. And could I get just some egg whites?"

She paused in the doorway. "No toast this morning?"

I usually grabbed my own food, but since Miss Sandy thought I was sick, I knew she'd prepare a tray.

I tried to give her a smile, and I suddenly had a feeling she knew I was lying. "I'm good with just tea and the egg whites. Thank you, Miss Sandy."

"Of course, Miss Aspen." Her smile was tender. "You feel better, okay?"

I nodded and blinked back a tear as she shut the door. I collapsed into my bed, feeling like the worst person in the world. I hated lying, but this was graduation week. I needed to stay firm. I just had to.

I picked up my phone and took a picture of Blaise's shirt, sending it to him.

Me: You left a memento. Miss Sandy found it.

Blaise: Aw, shit. Sorry.

Blaise: Who's Miss Sandy?

Me: Your future worst nightmare.

Blaise: That sounds ominous. I'll probably love her. Later.

HE TEXTED, informing me that Zeke was having people over to his house if I wanted to join. I told him about the sick lie, and that I was committed. I was hoping to have the flu all week. He wished me good luck, but said maybe he'd come to get sick with me.

I laughed, tossing the phone away, and went back to planning my next camping trip. Blaise was in my head, though, so I tried to use extra caution about ensuring my safety.

My mom called twice. Once before dinner, letting me know they were meeting my brother and some of his friends, because apparently Nate was in LA for some reason. Then she called back after dinner to tell me everything he was doing, that he was living with one of his best friends and talking about starting a company with his buddies.

I listened to her, my knees pulled up to my chest, and reached out to turn off my light. The moonlight still lit the room pretty well, but it felt right to me.

Hearing how Nate was doing, that he was doing well, was like a dagger to my heart.

I didn't know why. I think it was my mom's tone.

When the accident happened with Owen, it set everyone in the family on a weird course. It took us a long time to heal. But that healing had been the catalyst for them wanting to make things right with Nate. Life was short. My mom had started her hippie new lifestyle. My dad enjoyed his cigars more, and they'd changed their work focus. Instead of producing, they were directing more, which I knew they enjoyed.

Having Nate as part of the family had become a big thing for my mom.

She wanted him back in the fold, and she was trying. She and my dad were both trying, and I think things were better, but this was my older brother. He seemed to enjoy life away from us, and who could blame him?

Whatever.

It was all good.

I was happy my mom was happy, and I could hear in her voice that she was.

She said Nate had asked about me. "And of course I told him how great you're doing in school—4.2 GPA, highest honors, and you're never in trouble. Oh, and I told him how you're still enjoying your little camping trips." She sighed into the phone. "Oh, honey. He looks really good. He seems happy."

That's all my mom wanted.

"I'm glad for that, Mom," I told her, keeping the tears out of my voice.

"You're such a sweetheart. How'd I luck out getting you as my daughter?"

Then she needed to go because a producer was calling her, so we hung up.

The camping trip didn't seem as much fun after that.

I texted Blaise, but he didn't respond.

I didn't expect him to. He'd said he'd be partying at Zeke's for most the night, so when it got to be around midnight, I got ready for bed and crawled in.

Ten minutes later I snagged his shirt and put it on.

19

BLAISE

Aspen was hiding this week.

I knew that's what she was doing, because I was doing the same—except from my family. I didn't know why she was hiding, but I would find out. I was waiting for the right time to push for some answers, 'cause I'd gotten to know her a bit. The chick was a steel trap when it came to her family. I, on the other hand, needed to learn how to shut my mouth, so I was practicing.

My friends and I were at Manny's this afternoon, a popular hangout pub/diner place. The owners were cool, and as long as we didn't get into fights and kept ordering food, they let us chill here. The back room had pool tables and other games, but it was currently filled with Roussou kids, so our group took over the front section.

This was day three of partying.

Monday had been at Zeke's. Tuesday, we went cliff diving. Not everyone dove, but I loved that shit. That's mostly all I did, and I was almost thankful Aspen turned me down when I asked her to go. I was able to dive to my heart's content and not worry about her being worried for me.

Now it was Wednesday, and it was turning into a full day at Manny's. Kids from Fallen Crest Public were here too, but I didn't pay attention to them. I had my boys, and I was holding true to my promise to Aspen. Until I knew what she and I were doing, my hands would stick to her and her alone. I was counting down the hours until I could head over to see her. I hadn't been there since Sunday, and Sunday night to Wednesday is a long fucking time.

I was jonesing for some Aspen time.

I was also jonesing to leave Manny's since the Roussou kids were getting rowdy. I saw two of my brother's friends across the room, so I knew it was a matter of time before Cross and Bren showed up.

"Yo." Zeke held up his hand, waiting for my fist to pound it before he slipped into the seat next to me.

I'd been nursing a mixed drink for the last hour—not that it was a mixed drink when I'd ordered it, but it became mixed at the table.

"What's up?" I asked.

Zeke had been cool all week, but I knew he was curious about the Wagon chick. That's what he was calling Aspen. I was prepared for that line of questioning when he threw me for a loop.

"Is your sister still good with that boyfriend of hers?"

Wait.

What?

"The fuck is that your business?"

I might've said that a bit more harshly than needed, and Zeke knew it. His knowing grin turned smug, and he nodded toward the parking lot.

"She's coming up with her friends, and she's solo. Your sister is hot. She's going to get noticed."

I was perplexed, but that was all he said. He slid back into his seat, but then leaned over again. "Oh hey."

What now? I was still thrown by the sister comment.

"If you slide out of here before I see you again, I'm organizing a trip on my dad's yacht. We'll leave tomorrow after school, skip Friday since it's a useless day for us, and come back Sunday morning."

"Graduation is that afternoon."

"I know." He flashed me a grin. "It's a really long end-of-the-year party. I think we're due, right?"

"A yacht, huh? We have a limit on how many are invited?"

He cocked his head, side-eyeing me with a way more smug smirk than I wanted to see on his face. Ever. I was about to tell him to drop it or I was going to wipe it off him when he broke out smiling. "How about we do you, me, and your mystery girl, and I'll make sure Conway and Ashlome don't have Daniels as their plus one."

"How many, Zeke?"

That meant they'd invite Penny, Ria, or one of the other girls in that group—all of whom had nails and were mean as hell.

I didn't like what he was doing. I knew his dad's yacht could only comfortably sleep eight. He was forcing me into a situation where I had to bring Aspen or go on a trip without her, and I didn't want to do that.

"I won't come unless I know who else is coming."

"Come on." He groaned, tipping his head backward.

Penny and Ria were heading over, and I knew this conversation was a waste. "I'm out."

"What?" Zeke's mouth dropped open before he caught himself. "You're being a bitch, man."

I was reaching for my wallet when I heard that. I was in his face in a heartbeat. "Don't you fucking speak to me like that."

A sudden hush fell around us.

Zeke's eyes went hard, and a mask slammed over his face, but he didn't move.

I was breathing on him, but he didn't lean back.

His words were low, and I heard the warning in them. "Don't do this, bruh. You're disrespecting me."

"You did this." God, I wanted to tap his chest, but I refrained.

That was my crazy side, but I wasn't one of his bitches, and according to him, that's why he liked me.

"And you're continuing to do this," I added. "You don't think I know what you're doing? A yacht trip, and I'm supposed to bring my woman when you know the other girls will rip her apart? You think I like being in that place? Being put there by my 'best bud'?"

He was quiet a moment. "Your woman?"

My what?

I blinked.

He threw me a crooked grin, the air around us suddenly easing up. "You called her your woman."

Well, fuck. I did.

I growled. "Don't put me in that spot."

I'd known Zeke since first grade. We'd moved when I hit fourth grade, but I came back every summer to spend time with him and his family. I knew his little sister. I knew his mom. I knew his dad was a dick, but who didn't have one like that? This asshole Zeke was not the guy I remembered from the last time I'd seen him, which was two summers ago. He'd come to spend time with me and mine in New York, and it'd been a fun month—a full fucking month. We'd spent that time on my non-bio dad's yacht.

I got the significance of Zeke inviting me, but I still didn't appreciate the parameters of the invitation.

He let out a sigh. "Fine. How about we do the trip after graduation, and instead, we go on a two-day bender at my house?"

"Yeah, man." I tossed my cash onto the table, made sure the passing server gave me a nod, and turned back to him. "But if you ever call me a bitch again, you and I will be trading blows."

Then I let it go and walked past him.

I was overdue for some Aspen time, even though I knew I was

leaving behind a seething friend and more waves than I wanted to create at this place—not Manny's, but in Fallen Crest.

I was just past the first row of outdoor tables and circling to the right side of the parking lot when I heard a voice behind me.

"I'm surprised it's taken a whole semester for that shit to start."

I groaned, not even stopping. "Not today, Cross."

He was alone, and he blocked me before I could get to my vehicle. His gaze focused over my shoulder, and he scowled at whatever he saw.

"Taz's boyfriend tried to go it alone," he said. "It didn't work. He needed a crew to back him up. That's what we did for him."

"Well, gee. Thank you for the history lesson I didn't ask for. I've got to be going now."

I made a move to walk around him, but he blocked me again, stepping to the side.

He threw his keys up, catching them, but his eyes were still locked over my shoulder. He began to grin. "He never thought it through."

I narrowed my eyes. "What are you talking about?" I turned to look at what he was seeing, and even I was surprised.

Zeke stood at the edge of the tables, a cup in his hand and his jaw in a firm scowl. He looked ready to march over and beat us down.

Cross laughed low. "He hates the thought of me. I bet he never considered that you and I might get along one day. Why would he? We can't stand each other, but he doesn't know what you and I both know." His eyes turned my way, growing more wary. "We're stuck with each other for the rest of our lives. You ain't stuck with that prick."

I wanted to rub my hand over my face with my middle finger. I refrained. "You getting to a point? Because I'm about at the end of my patience."

"No point. I just liked stopping you to talk and making your boy all jealous. He came to one of our parties and leered at Bren. Turnabout is fair play, and I'm going to love screwing with him. He hates the thought of losing you as a friend." He paused, frowning. "Why does he got such a hard-on for you anyway? I saw your confrontation, and we've been hearing, even in Roussou, how you're starting to challenge him. Your boy is a bully. No way is he going to let this go for long, and what then? He gets all his boys to beat you up?"

I stilled.

What the hell?

Was he...?

Yeah. He was.

I winked at him, knowing it'd piss him off. "So that's what you fuckers are nervous about? That my best friend might give me a beatdown and what? You'll have to rally for me? 'Cause we're brothers?"

Cross clenched his jaw. "'Cause Tasmin would never forgive me if I let that go, and yeah, I've been to war with your school already. I want an easy summer with my guys and Bren. That's it. You getting your ass beat by your crowd won't bode well for us."

I rolled my eyes and patted his shoulder. "Then you're off the hook. I get my ass beat, don't worry. I won't be calling you for vengeance. I've got a whole group of boys in New York who will gladly hop a flight out here to have my back. Unlike you, I don't have just three people to back me up." My tone turned mocking. "I have ten times that amount."

With that, I got in my Wagon and pulled out.

My words echoed in my ears, and I tightened my hold on the steering wheel.

My words had sounded good. They'd sounded confident, but they were empty. I might be able to wrangle up a group to have my back, but that wasn't the point. Zeke wasn't the bad guy Cross thought he was, but he wasn't a great guy either. That's where I understood him when no one else did, because he and I were the same.

We weren't *all* bad.

There were pockets of good in us.

Or maybe that's just what I told myself as I turned my car toward Aspen's house.

nock, knock!

Keys and phone in hand, backpack on, I paused in my room. I'd been about to head to the store. There was a new camping security system I wanted to check out before buying.

"Yes?"

Miss Sandy opened the door, a frown on her face.

She'd been frowning most the week. I was sure she was on to me and my whole "sickness," but she'd never said a word. She kept doting on me. I got hot packs, warm washcloths, and tea. I got bowls of chicken noodle soup, boxes of Kleenex, cough drops, medicine for nighttime, and medicine for daytime. You name it, I got it, so I was feeling all sorts of guilt. But my parents were still in LA, so I only had a few more days until I was in the clear.

"Miss Sandy! Hi."

Her eyes traveled over my jeans, sandals, and tank top.

I was busted.

But after a small sigh, all she said was, "There's a young man at the gate asking to come see you."

I frowned. A young man? Blaise? "Oh."

It was daytime, so he would've gotten Mr. Carl at the gate. That meant Tucker truly hadn't put Blaise's name on the list, which was cool of Tucker, but not so cool now.

I bit my lip, tugging at one of my backpack straps. "I'm feeling better, so I was going to go to the store. I'll just talk to him out there."

"We should tell him to wait?"

I nodded. "Yeah." I slipped past her and hurried down the hallway. "See you tomorrow, Miss Sandy. I'll be back later, and I might be worn out, 'cause I'm probably not back to a hundred percent." *Cough, cough.*

I was such a shitty actress, which was ironic, considering my parents.

Then I was down the stairs, through the kitchen, and out to the garage. My parents had taken my dad's vehicle, so my mom's was still in the first stall. She always got the first stall because she said if she brought groceries home, she needed close access to the kitchen.

I couldn't remember the last time she went grocery shopping, but it was what it was. She got the first stall.

I headed past the next three empty stalls to Maisie.

When I got to the front gate, Carl pointed me over to the side.

Blaise's G Wagon was parked and Blaise was waiting beside the road.

He jogged over, and I tried not to ogle, but *damn*, he looked good.

He tapped on my window.

I rolled the window down. "Hey. I was headed out anyway and figured it'd be easier this way. Miss Sandy didn't seem too approving."

He nodded, his hands going into his pockets. "Where are you going?"

I hesitated, but this was me. I had to be me. "There's some

new camping gear at Holliston. I wanted to check it out, see if they had the new security system."

He frowned, his head tilted to the side, and I sighed on the inside because even that looked good on him.

"Let's take Maisie back, and I'll drive," he said.

"What?"

"Come on." He tapped my window again, grinning—and my word, there was a dimple there. A dimple, folks. A dimple!

"I'll follow you through, and then we can hang out." His eyes darkened. His grin turned wolfish. "I need some Aspen time. Badly."

I frowned, a little kick of concern tightening my throat, but I nodded.

He jogged back to his car, and I pulled around to explain the plan to Mr. Carl. He gave me a tight nod as his gaze looked back at Blaise. When we got to the house, I pulled Maisie into the driveway and hurried down to the road.

Blaise had brought his Wagon around, so I slipped in on the passenger side.

That's when the nerves hit me.

I liked riding in Maisie, and getting in Blaise's Wagon, I got all tongue-tied. This was a boy that had kissed me, made me explode, and I was in his vehicle. He was driving, and we were going to hang out. Was this an appropriate time to confess that I'd never been on a date?

Would he look at me weird?

Because I felt weird. I felt all sorts of *what the hell am I doing?* Blaise was so out of my league.

"Did you come from a party?" I asked.

He turned toward the gate, easing slowly so Carl could open it for us. "Huh?"

"What'd you do today?"

He glanced at me, then did a double take, his eyes narrowing. "What's up with you?"

My stomach tanked. "What?"

"What do you mean *what*? Something's up with you. You're looking at me like my fingers have not been inside of you and I'm not sitting here hoping my dick will follow one of these days. Just spell it out."

Jesus Christ. Forget my stomach tanking. He just brought his foot down hard on my stomach. I felt squashed, then the anger started in.

"You're such a prick! You can't talk to me like that."

"Like what?" Both his eyebrows were up, but so were the corners of his mouth. He tried to hide his smile with his hand. "I'm being honest. I want to bang you. Badly. Most girls would love hearing that from me."

"Well—" I jerked forward, but then I stopped.

I *did* like hearing that.

I leaned back in my seat, grumbling, "You made me feel squashed, and now I'm, like, loving what you're saying? How messed up am I?"

"Huh." That was all he said as he moved his car to the side of road. We'd just cleared the gate and turned the corner. As soon as the Wagon was in park, he grabbed the keys, tossed them to the dashboard and he was on my side. He buried his head in my neck. His hand pushed behind me, smoothing down my back, nestling between me and the seat until he could cup my ass. "Jesus," he groaned. "Do you not get how much I want you?"

I was starting to get it, and I was shocked at the suddenness of it, but this hug felt nice.

It felt really nice.

I melted into my seat as he murmured into my neck, "You have these long legs that I daydream about winding around my waist. Your rack is honestly perfect for me, and not to mention just you." He wasn't doing anything except rubbing my ass, but my body was burning up. An inferno built between my legs, and he just kept talking, stoking that fire. "You're unbelievably sweet.

And pure. And chaste. And you're smart. And you're kickass because you do your own thing. You're funny in a cute way, and I love how you'll be biting your lip, and then I'll say some smartass comment, and you burst alive—like a bomb or something—and then you're all about putting me in my place and trying to make me a better person."

He eased his head back, his eyes finding mine, and the seriousness in them took my breath. "Whatever the fuck this is between us, it's not just taking *you* by storm." His eyes fell to my mouth. "I called you my woman today."

My heart pounded. "You did?" I felt the drumming in my sternum.

He nodded, his voice hoarse. "Yeah, and I never took it back. I didn't even want to, because fuck—I want you to be my woman. Will you be my woman?"

My mouth opened and hung there. Not even a full week ago, he'd been saying he couldn't do a relationship. I didn't have time to voice my thoughts before he groaned and pulled away.

"I'm sorry. I know I'm all over the place. A week ago, I didn't want to date anyone. Five days ago, I promised you I wouldn't touch anyone—but nothing else—and I've spent the night with you twice, plus most of Sunday. Today, I had to force myself to stay away from you because I know once I'm in your presence, I won't want to leave, like, ever. School is going to suck tomorrow, and now I've sprung this on you? I'm sorry. I really am."

Oh.

My.

God.

I couldn't talk. I couldn't think. I could only feel, and my heart and vagina were throbbing in unison. I was one giant, aching organ, needing to be touched.

I had never experienced *anything* like this.

This guy had just said some of the most honest—a bit crass at times—and extremely romantic things to me, and I could only gape.

Then I lunged for him. My hands found his head, and my mouth was on his.

Someone growled (that was me) and he said, "Hell yeah."

He moved his seat backward and brought me over to straddle him. I went right to grinding on him, and his hands moved inside my shirt. His fingers found my breasts as our tongues began a dance together.

I was buzzing for him.

My vagina was singing a melody.

I just wanted him.

"Shit, babe," he whispered against my mouth, but I soon shut him up.

He was quiet for a long time, and I was blind with emotion. It pulsated through me. Need. Want. Desire. And when I felt his fingers moving inside of me, I hissed like I'd just gotten water after seven days of thirst.

It felt so fucking good.

I rode his hand, and he groaned, moving me until his fingers were so deep that I threw my head back, my hips blindly answering that need to explode. And then I did, and I was a mess. I came apart, literally. I started crying on his lap.

"Hey. Hey." He ran his free hand over my face, sliding my hair from my cheeks. His voice was so soft and tender, crooning to me as if I were a broken baby bird. I couldn't handle it. A whole other burst of sobs erupted from me, and he cursed and undid his seatbelt.

Yeah. That'd all transpired with his seatbelt in place.

"Come on." He lifted me in his arms, guiding me to the backseat.

I climbed back there and waited in a corner until he was next to me. He scooped me up, bringing me back to his lap, and he folded himself around me, kissing little kisses under my chin.

"What's wrong?"

I kept crying, but the part of my brain that was still operating knew he hadn't gotten off, and I reached for his jeans. I started to unzip them, but he grabbed my hand with a soft chuckle.

"If you think I'm going to let you touch me when you're sobbing, think again. I'm not that kind of guy." He nuzzled my neck and pushed some more of my hair back. "Come on. Tell me what's going on. Who do I need to beat up? I'll do it. I'll even call Bren to help. I think she has a woman crush on you. She's pretty fierce about you not being hurt."

I stopped crying, his words surprising me. "What?"

"Yeah." He grinned, his eyes darkening. "Cross warned me, said Bren only cares about five people. And if I hurt you, she's going to slice me."

"What?!"

"You didn't know? She's scary. Zeke's got a hard-on for her because she's so scary. He actually likes when people challenge him."

Oh God. Now he was talking about his *best friend*! Anxiety spiked my pulse, and he felt it. He smoothed his hand up under my shirt, laying it over my heart. "What's this about?"

I shifted on his lap, trying to slide off, but he tightened his hold.

"Tell me," he nudged.

I opened my mouth. What was I going to say?

Then I just blurted it out. "I have self-esteem issues."

He frowned, his head resting against the seat. "Everyone does, don't they?"

I shook my head, focusing on his chest. I couldn't look him in the eyes anymore. I grabbed his shirt, fisting it. "Not like me. Not like... I hide from people, but it's not because of them. It's just easier for me to handle life that way."

I was horrified. I'd never actually thought about *why* I did things. I just did things. And yet I'd just explained it out loud.

With Blaise coming into my life, things weren't making sense anymore. I couldn't stay like this if I was going to have him in my life. It wasn't fair for him, for anyone.

I needed to make myself better.

"I went to therapy." I looked up, and I almost fell apart, seeing the somberness in his gaze. "When my parents sent us to Hillcrest, I had problems. I don't really remember everything I did, but they said I was dealing with some attachment issues. Then Nate left, and those issues came back, but I didn't tell my parents. The only person who knew was Owen."

"How old were you when that happened?"

I was too young. "Seventh grade."

There was more, more that I didn't want to talk about.

I sagged on his lap, resting against his chest. I felt his fingers sliding through my hair, smoothing down my back.

I spoke into his shirt. "I have problems believing people want to be around me. And, something else happened."

Blaise went rigid.

I didn't like talking about this, but he had to know. He had to know to understand.

"Aspen?" His voice was so soft.

It was my undoing.

"Aspen, what happened?"

I couldn't look at him. I kept looking at at his shirt. It was safe there, no judgement there.

"Aspen?"

"It's nothing like what you're thinking." I looked up. I had to. He had to see.

His eyes grew soft, matching his voice. "I don't think you know what I'm thinking."

Yeah. True.

"There was a teacher once. She—uh—they told me later that she was unhinged. I don't remember her like that, but she was *my* teacher." This was hurting. Seriously hurting. "She, just, she started asking me questions about my parents, personal questions. She asked about Nate. She asked a lot, and then one day, my parents pulled me from Hillcrest. I went to a school in Europe for a while."

His eyebrows dipped. "Why Europe?"

"They told me later that she had made threats against me. She was trying to get money from my parents. I got sent away when it started. There was a whole investigation launched, and she was fired, but she was popular with the other students. They blamed me, and when I came back, it didn't go away for a long time."

God.

That hurt.

My chest felt ripped open.

Saying those words, hearing them, I was embarrassed.

"Hey." He leaned back, tipping my head up. His eyes were fierce, his mouth set in a determined line. "The teacher thing is messed up. You know that wasn't your fault. Right?"

I nodded. "I know."

But the effect didn't go away.

He sighed. "You're not saying, but I can only imagine what the others said to you, and I'm sorry. I'm *really* sorry you went through that." He cupped the side of my face and leaned forward, his forehead resting against mine. "I can't speak for what happened to you in the past, but I can speak for now. I will be a dick. Okay? Like, full disclosure here. I know I will be a dick, because I just am. I will try not to be. I never want to hurt you, but it's my default setting. So far I'm not that guy with you, and I will always try to be better. I'm sure I'll slip and the D will come out. Having said that, I'm an honest dick, so if I skate on you or leave you and you're feeling your stuff about me, ask me. Okay? I will be honest. You never have to worry or wonder where I am. I'm brutally honest, though maybe that's a good thing with you and me, huh?"

I grasped his wrist. My heart pounding harder, more sure. "Do you promise? You'll always be honest?"

"I will, even if it hurts you. I'll be honest."

He wasn't telling me pretty, fake words. He wasn't saying he'd always be there for me. He wasn't saying he'd never leave, but honesty was big. I could work with honesty. I could handle the truth, no matter how much his answer might hurt.

I breathed out a shaky breath. "You can't ghost me."

"I won't do that. I promise. Call, text, and if I'm able, I will respond. I can promise you that much."

I nodded. "Okay."

His thumb traced my bottom lip. His other hand had remained between our bodies, resting just inside my jeans, and now he began tracing under my thong. He had me squirming within a beat, and he grinned, leaning forward to nip at my lips.

He groaned. "I think I'm obsessed with your body."

I let out an abrupt laugh. He'd said he'd be honest. But I could handle that, and I stopped thinking, closing the distance until my mouth was over his. He maneuvered himself to lie on top of me, and I liked it.

Oh yes. I liked this a whole lot.

21

BLAISE

This was ridiculous. I was a horny guy in heat, like, twenty-four-seven.

I couldn't even take my girl—and I couldn't believe I was already calling her that—to dinner at a restaurant.

I wanted to touch her all the time.

I wanted to kiss her all the time.

I wanted in her pants super bad, but I was also enjoying just giving her lots of orgasms.

We did actually make it to her camping store later, and I loved that she was looking for a security system, because that meant she was thinking of my concern. But I was also distracted every time she made a sound.

She was cute.

Every new item she saw, she fell in love with, and my dick tried to grow into its own zip code. Every time she smiled, even when she was confused by something, she was adorable. She looked amazing walking around in those tight jeans, her simple tank, and I knew how those nipples tasted and felt. I could see they were hard for me, and every time I saw another guy checking her out, I gave him the look I reserved for people I wanted to murder. She couldn't figure out why no store attendants came over to help her. They were all dudes, and they weren't stupid. They saw how I wanted to rip their heads off.

Smart little fuckers, they were.

I was trying to be a good guy. I could've pulled her back to my Wagon, driven her somewhere, and had her moaning for me, but nope—a full date. That's what I wanted to give her. So after the store, we went to dinner.

And I was in agony.

She was currently rubbing my lap under the table, and this time, she knew the torture she was putting me through. She soaked it up, and I wanted to soak her up, but that would be later. When I leaned over and whispered that promise to her, she blushed, and I kept hearing this weird *thunking* sound in my chest, like something twisted up in me was falling into place.

It scared the shit out of me, but not enough to end this date. Never enough for that.

After dinner, Aspen wanted to go to a bookstore, so we hit one up. We held hands. And she showed me the romance book aisle. Her favorite.

I noticed she tended to go for the pretty covers.

I picked one of those up and read the back. It was about a school shooting. Serious shit, but she kept going back to it and then putting it on the shelf again.

I bought it when she went to the bathroom.

She squealed when I gave it to her, and I wanted to eat her all the way up, but now we were stopping for ice cream. We found ourselves a table, which was good because I didn't think I could walk. She licked her cone and seemed oblivious that I was mesmerized. I had to scoot down when some guys from our school walked by, because my hard-on was trying to lift the fucking table.

"Babe." I leaned forward, trying to think of my grandma. "You gotta stop torturing me. My balls aren't blue anymore. They're fucking black."

Her eyes got big, and I swear, that made her even hotter. I needed to find new words for *lickable, tasteable, fuckable, hot, cute,* and *adorable* because those weren't enough to describe her.

A date.

We were dating.

I'd asked her to be my girl, and she'd climaxed her response.

I was dating someone, and I wasn't letting her go.

This shit was getting serious.

A girlfriend. That was next.

Or were we already there?

"Blaise."

Did I have a girlfriend? Was I her boyfriend?

The panic I thought I'd be feeling wasn't there. What did that say about me?

"Blaise."

"Hmmm?"

"Blaise!"

I jerked out of my thoughts, finding Aspen giving me a weird look. "What?"

She pointed to the side, and I looked.

Aw, crap.

Zeke stood there, wearing the biggest shit-eating grin. My first thought was to punch him and wipe that smirk off, but the second was *shit, shit, shit* because Zeke wasn't alone.

Our entire group of friends had decided they wanted ice cream.

22

ASPEN

Zeke Allen leered at me. I hated it.

"Hey, buddy." His leer turned even smarmier, and he shoved in beside Blaise and leaned forward, his arms resting on the table. "You and me have not officially met. I'm Zeke."

I opened my mouth, but no surprise, nothing came out. I'd tried getting Blaise's attention, but he'd taken that moment to get lost in his thoughts. Otherwise I could've warned him when I saw Zeke's truck turn in to the parking lot. He'd parked next to Blaise's Wagon and gave it a long look before heading inside, a confused frown on his face.

And Zeke's truck had been just the first.

Four more vehicles pulled in after it, and now the entire front section of the ice cream shop was overrun with Blaise's friends: Penny, Ria, Deja, Kit. The guys that came with them. They'd all entered, the girls giving me nasty looks. I saw Mara for a moment, but when she saw me, she turned and left.

Hurt had flashed on her face, and a part of me felt bad. But the other part was terrified because this group was the nightmare of every book nerd out there.

Blaise let out an aggrieved sigh, raking his hand through his hair. "No," he growled, and it seemed to shock everyone. Even Penny cast him a cursory look. Zeke looked mildly amused. He lifted an eyebrow, waiting.

Blaise shoved him out of the booth.

"Come on, man." Zeke's arms fell open. "We gotta meet her at some point."

Blaise gave him a dark look, taking my hand and pulling me out. "Not today, *bruh*."

He led me through the group, back to the front of the restaurant.

"You can't keep doing this," Zeke called.

Blaise stopped, his hand gripping mine. His body stiffened as he turned back slowly. "Excuse me?"

"You keep starting shit and then leaving. That's not how it works with me." Zeke sounded almost charming, but there was an edge in his eyes.

It sent shivers down my back.

Blaise laughed an ugly laugh. He did not look like he was having the same shivers. He was looking like the one who gave those shivers to others. "That's not how things work with you? Who the fuck do you think you are? You ain't Ghandi."

Someone snorted beside us.

A dark cloud came over Zeke's face before he caught himself. Then that eerily charming smile returned, and he shrugged. "I'm just letting you know how it is. That's all. We miss hanging out with you."

"I'm really sick and tired of the cloak-and-dagger warnings, Zeke. You want to throw down? Let's throw down."

Just as I thought Blaise was going to break my hand, he loosened his hold. He pulled my hand into both of his and began rubbing.

Zeke watched the movement, and there was a flash in his eyes. Sadness.

I frowned, biting the inside of my cheek. Why?

He shook his head. "You know what? Never mind. We're good. I was just pissed about earlier."

What happened earlier?

Blaise relaxed and tucked my hand back in his, moving forward. He and Zeke did a man hug, thumping each other on the shoulder. Blaise said something to him no one else could hear, and Zeke nodded, holding up his fist.

Blaise met it with his own before leading me out.

The crowd moved aside for us, but I felt their attention on my back like I was a target, strung up like a bullseye. My knees were weak when we got to the parking lot.

Blaise stopped, turning to me. "You okay?"

I nodded. "Yeah."

He kissed my forehead, leading me to his Wagon by the hand. He opened my door, and I climbed in, his hand on the small of my back. He got behind the steering wheel, backed out, and without any discussion, turned toward my house.

He was quiet until the last intersection before my house. "Can I sleep at your place?"

"I assumed you would."

He grinned as the light turned green, but went straight instead of turning left. "I like that." He nodded ahead. "I want to grab some things from my house, so fair warning. You can stay in the vehicle if you want. I'm sure Douchebag Dickhead will be there and my mom too." His jaw tightened. "Why she doesn't kick him out and make him stay in a hotel is beyond me. I don't get women sometimes." Then he muttered after a beat, "Maybe I just don't get moms."

For some reason, that broke my heart.

He turned into a neighborhood I used to know.

I watched the houses, remembering how Nate would take Owen and me to see his friends. Blaise slowed, pulling into a driveway.

"This was the old neighborhood," I told him. "My parents thought about buying a house here, but when the gated community started, they went there instead."

"Yeah?" He turned the engine off, watching me.

I nodded, looking down the street. "My older brother knows people who live here."

Blaise gave me a somewhat sad smile. "Yeah. I know."

"You do?"

"I've met a few of them."

"You have?" I felt a knot tightening in my throat.

"My brother's girlfriend ran into this one lady. She's kinda nosy, but in a nice way. Anyway, she's been over to the house. She and my mom are friends, and I'm pretty certain she knows your brother and his whole group."

My tongue felt so heavy, lying on the bottom of my mouth. "Really?"

"Yeah. Malinda Decraw." That sad smile remained on his face. "She'd really like you."

Oh. I blinked back tears.

Blaise pulled the keys from the engine. "Let me slip inside and grab some stuff. I'll be back super quick. Okay? You can stay here."

I was distantly aware that I nodded to him, and he disappeared inside.

When was the last time my brother drove this road? Did he drive past Blaise's house? What house does Malinda Decraw live in?

Was she inside now?

I could taste the tears on my face.

～

BY THE TIME BLAISE RETURNED, I had stopped crying, and when

he got into the car, I tried to give him a smile. I meant to reassure him, but he saw through me.

"What are you feeling?" he asked.

He'd said he would always be honest, so I figured he deserved that too.

"Numb."

He didn't respond at first, but he started the engine and took my hand. He held it the entire drive back.

He parked in front of my neighbor's house when we got back to my place. No one was around when we went inside. It was too late for Miss Sandy or Benny to still be here, and my mom texted earlier to say she and Dad were staying in Los Angeles through the weekend.

My whole mission to avoid graduation had been for nothing. They wouldn't have known anyway.

I should've been relieved. I wasn't. I was something else instead.

I didn't know I was crying until Blaise's arms were around me.

When he started to get into bed, I stopped him. I tugged him to the movie room instead.

We turned something on. He held me. And I tried not to cry.

I mostly failed.

But he held me the rest of the night.

23

BLAISE

Something was seriously wrong with Aspen, and it was becoming clearer that it was her family.

I hated it. I hated every part of how she'd cried herself to sleep in my arms last night. I'd been breaking apart, but I couldn't do anything except comfort her.

Still, I was pissed.

And I was up early while she remained tanked. I eased out from under her. *Fuck this.* I was taking matters into my own hands. This was different. Aspen was different.

As I looked through the house, I got more and more angry at the empty walls I saw. There were no pictures of her, of her brothers. There were no family photos. There were no plaques on the wall. No trophies.

No handmade stupid-ass trinkets.

Nothing.

This house was a show house.

There was nothing personal here.

There were no marks on the doorway from the kids getting taller. And it was a new house, I got that, but seriously—a few pictures at least?

I was perusing the kitchen when the garage door opened and an older lady came inside. She startled, a scream came from her, and dropped the bag in her hands.

I waited it out. I'd made myself a cup of coffee, so I lifted the mug and took a sip.

A second later, she spat out, her eyes narrowed and promising all sorts of way to gut me, "Who are you?"

I narrowed my eyes right back at her. "I take it you're Miss Sandy."

Some of her fiery promises faded, but her eyes only turned wary. Her nose wrinkled and her mouth turned down in a pinch. "You're the marijuana shirt guy."

I grinned. "I am, and it's no longer my shirt since Aspen's been sleeping in it. She wants it, she gets it."

I hadn't meant that to sound dirty.

I coughed, clearing my throat. "Let's talk about Aspen's parents, shall we?"

A whole different look came over her then, and she took a step back.

Awareness.

I saw it trickle in, and by the time we were done with our chat, there was a bit more on her face. I, however, was ready to bash something. More specifically, I was ready to roll heads.

"Thank you," I managed to tell her at the end.

My coffee was long done, and I hadn't refilled it. I didn't need the caffeine. I was hyped up on a whole bunch of other emotions.

When I turned to head back upstairs, she called after me.

"You care for her."

I nodded.

The truth of that surprised me. I hadn't expected it. But I couldn't stop it. I didn't even want to anymore.

She nodded back. "Good."

That was it.

That was my meeting with the infamous Miss Sandy, and I'd been right. I liked her.

And I didn't care if she liked me or not. She would, eventually.

Everyone liked me, *eventually*.

Aspen was the only thing that mattered, and I was going to wake the entire neighborhood up, because she deserved to matter to everyone.

24

BLAISE

"Hey."

I was just putting my stuff in my locker when Zeke came over. Shutting it, I turned to him. "Hey."

He grinned, leaning against my neighbor's locker. "You don't sound too enthused."

"Would you?" I waited a beat, adding, "If I were doing the shit you've been doing?"

He flinched. "Yeah, man." He raked a hand over his face. The hallway was full of students. Quite a few watched us, and I didn't like it. I was used to the attention. We got it almost everywhere we went, but we were getting more.

They were all waiting, seeing if Zeke and I were going to throw down.

I wanted to give 'em all the middle finger.

"Look, let's walk and talk?" he said. "Yeah?"

I nodded. We started down the hallway.

Anytime we needed to hash something out, we went to the football field. I'd be late for my next class, but that was fine. I only had one project due this week, and it was my last class of the day.

Zeke laughed as we headed out the door, flipping everyone behind us the middle finger. "Hungry-as-fuck gawkers."

We were on the same wavelength.

Zeke waited to speak until we were past the groups hanging around outside. Once we'd crossed the parking lot, he put his hands in his pockets, hunching forward. "So."

I could hear how uncomfortable he felt. That made me feel a little better, just a bit.

"I, uh, I don't really know how to start this." He laughed with a hitch.

I'd never heard Zeke sound uncomfortable. This was a first in our friendship.

"I do."

He sighed, angling toward the bleachers. "Why am I not surprised?"

I smiled, and my shoulders relaxed a whole lot. "Why are you such a dick?"

He snorted. "You're calling me a dick?"

"Yeah. I'm not a dick like you. I don't control and intimidate and do that sort of shit. I don't make others fall in line and do what I say."

"I disagree with that."

I growled. "We gonna talk this out or just go right to punching? I'm down with either."

He eased away. "I've no doubt you're good with throwing a punch. I've seen you do it."

Now that I thought about it, I had intimidated Brian when I shoved him against the wall. And I'd told Jamie he couldn't hang with me if he was scared of fighting. So I guess in that way, I was as guilty as Zeke. Well, fuck me then.

But I hadn't hit anyone except Brian that one time. I'd wanted to throw down a few times, but I always refrained, which was a good thing. Me fighting was not good, ever. Everyone knew my brother could fight, but no one knew my rep. I'd left that back in New York and been thankful to escape it.

"Why do you think I've never called your bluff about fighting?" he asked quietly.

I sneered at him. "The dick part of me wants to say it's because you're a pansy." His eyes went flat, and I smirked. "But the part of me that's trying not to be that guy has no clue." A beat. "So why not?"

"Because I know how you are. I know you're not bluffing about fighting."

Well, shit. "You've seen videos?"

"I've seen it in person."

I frowned, shooting him a look. "When?"

"When we were in third grade."

"What?"

"Why do you think I love you so much?" He shook his head, stupefied. "I was getting my ass beat by two fifth graders. A sixth grader was in on it too, and then suddenly out of nowhere, you came barreling in. You kicked their asses—and you were in third grade with me. Those guys had been bullying me since first grade. You show up, and after one afternoon, they never messed with me again. You did that."

I wanted to roll my eyes. "You're telling me that because you were bullied, you turned into the biggest piece of shit?"

He barked out a laugh. "No. I'm telling you that I saw what you could do when you were a third grader. I sure as shit know you ain't bluffing. Fuck, brother. Half the time I think you're salivating over the chance someone *will* call your bluff, but no one will. We all know it ain't a front."

"You could organize a group. Get the drop on me."

He snorted, shaking his head. "And then what? We'd have to kill you to keep you down. You'd heal and come back and fuck every one of us over. And while you were healing, I know that brother of yours would come around. His crew too."

Maybe. "So why are you such a piece of shit with people?"

He cursed. "Can you drop the dick attitude right now? I'm here for peace and resolution. I won't want that if you keep insulting me."

I nodded. "Yeah, right. Sorry."

Now that he'd mentioned it, I remembered that day. I remembered that whole year, and those guys had picked on Zeke every single day. Before school. During recess. During lunch. After school. I finally had enough, and that's when Zeke became my best friend. He became my shadow, and I never lost him after that. The reason it started had just faded from my mind.

"I'm a hothead," I told him. "And I'm a prick, and I'm pretty messed up about my family. None of that's a good recipe."

"I get that." He nodded, moving to sit next to me on the bleachers. He leaned forward, resting his elbows on his knees. We faced the empty football field. "I may be a lot of things. And I'm not proud of what I became while you were gone, but you're back. I remember how it feels to know no one's gonna mess with me with you at my side. It means something to me." His tone grew hoarse, and he looked away. "Since you came back, I've remembered that I wasn't such a bad guy before. I just morphed into him when you left. It sucks, and I gotta learn how to not be this guy, but it's hard. It's a lot of work."

I grunted and held up a fist.

He hit it with his own.

"You and me both." *Works in progress.*

He studied me a second. "That chick helping you?"

I nodded. "I think so. I'm not a dick when I'm around her."

"So you going to finally tell me her name?"

I smirked. "Like you don't know. And no, I'm not officially telling you."

"What?" His eyes flared. "Why not? I'm your best friend."

Yeah, I supposed he was. But I couldn't risk it.

He knew. I knew he knew, because Zeke was like that, but

with me not telling him, the gates were still closed. He couldn't go fanboy over her brother's best friend. That'd be weird and awkward, and a scene I didn't want to deal with.

"Not yet." I watched him from the corner of my eye, gauging his reaction. "You gotta trust me. It's too new."

He settled. "I get that, but you know I know, right?"

"Don't." I scowled. "*Don't.*"

He frowned. "Why? 'Cause of the girls?"

He knew why, but okay. Let's go with the girls instead.

I shrugged, stretching my legs out. "Partly. And partly because I care about her and it's new to me too. I've never given a shit like this about anyone, including you. It's unsettling."

I was tired of all this personal sharing.

"Why do I feel like we should throw down anyway?" I asked him. "Just for old times' sake?"

Zeke's smile was blinding. "Right. I get it. We're still dicks. Don't worry."

"Speak for yourself. You've become a pansy."

"Hey." He rounded on me, his face twisted before he saw I was joking.

But was I?

He punched my shoulder. "Don't call me that again."

I laughed. "*Pussy.* Your favorite word."

He scowled, but started to laugh. "Yeah. I love that word. Did you know there was a chick from Roussou telling people she and I were dating? We hooked up a few times, but that was it."

I shook my head. "I was the one who you told that, and I'm not surprised." Though, to clarify, I didn't know she'd been telling people she was dating him, but I was the one who gave her a name since Zeke just recognized her face and would drag her off somewhere private when he saw her. He'd never taken the time to remember her name. It wasn't an altogether uncommon scenario for him.

"I'm sure you've had five girlfriends this year you know nothing about."

He cursed softly. "That's not something I'm proud of."

No, it shouldn't be. And I wasn't proud of my own indiscretions.

I sighed. "We might've turned into assholes for a while, but we can be better."

"Yeah."

If anyone had told me I'd be sitting on these bleachers, having this conversation with Zeke, I would've punched them in the face.

But here I was.

And we were having this talk.

And I suddenly felt like I really did have a best friend.

I swore. "No one can know we talked like this to each other."

He shook his head vigorously. "Hell no. Either of us talks, and the other can punch him in the dick, without pants."

Sounded perfect to me. "Deal."

We were heading back and through the empty halls when Zeke slowed up.

"Shit." He cast me a worried look. "You gonna handle that okay or you want a distraction?"

I thought he'd seen Aspen at first, that she'd come to school, and I got excited. Then I saw Mara loitering by my locker and my chest deflated.

I shook my head. "Nah. I got this."

It was time, and judging by the look on her face, she knew it. Zeke headed out, but I focused on Mara. She looked as if she'd rather be anywhere else, but she was in front of my locker for a reason.

"Hey."

She closed her eyes, shaking her head. "Jesus."

I chuckled. "Sorry."

I waited. It didn't seem like my place to start this conversation.

She leaned against my locker, folding her arms over her chest, and she looked away. "So you're dating her?"

"Yeah."

My response was quiet, but honest. I'd always promised honesty.

She blinked a few times, her throat moving.

"And you care for her?" Her words came out strangled.

Fuck. More honesty. "Yeah." She had to know. She deserved that much. "She's mine, Mara. She's just... She's mine."

A tear slipped down one of her cheeks. She wiped it with the back of her hand. "Okay." She nodded, blinking to keep more tears from falling. "Okay. I'm probably going to sleep with Zeke to get back at you. Full disclosure."

I laughed. "Okay."

Her eyes narrowed. "You're supposed to *care* if I do that. Fuck you. I can see now that you don't." Her voice rose. "But if *she* did—"

A burst of anger lit in my stomach, and she saw it.

"Yeah." She nodded. "Yeah. I see that now. You'd go apeshit if Zeke touched her."

I sighed. "What do you want me to say? We were never exclusive. I told you that. I never promised anything."

"I kept myself just for you. We *were* exclusive on my end. I did that for *you*."

The bell rang, and we had a nanosecond before the hall was flooded. Piss-poor timing.

"I never asked you to do that."

"You wouldn't have touched me if I hadn't. And I know you liked that I kept myself for you."

The doors opened, and people streamed out.

Mara didn't seem to care. She shoved me against the locker. Someone gasped, and then the whispers started, the buzzing rose in volume as word was already getting around. This shit would be all over social media in two seconds, and I saw the first camera snapping our pic. Someone else was out and out recording us.

I flipped it off. "Take it down or I'll bust that phone to pieces."

The guy's eyes bugged out and he quickly deleted it. He was gone in the next second, scurrying off through the crowd.

Mara glared like she wanted to kill me. "We're going to make her life hell. *Full disclosure*," she sneered. "I'm the nice one in the group. Not anymore. That girl is going to wish she was dead by the time we're done with her."

I saw red and started for her.

Someone screamed beside me, startled at how quickly I'd moved, but I caught myself, holding back.

"Don't," I warned, and I was *real* serious. "Don't you *dare* hurt her."

"She's a loser, Blaise. What are you doing falling for her? Claiming her? *You're* a loser." She gave me a onceover, but she'd lost her heat. She didn't mean what she was saying, and then she was just crying. "I hate you. I hate you so much."

"Mara." I reached for her, but I didn't know why. To hold her? Comfort her? I couldn't do either.

"No," she choked out, turning and pushing her way through the crowd.

I hung my head. "Fuck!"

25

ASPEN

I was sweating bullets, my phone next to me.

Blaise was in school for the last Thursday of the year, and I was sitting in my room. I wished I could talk to him.

Was this dumb of me? A stupid idea?

What sister was nervous about calling her brother? I mean, that alone made me a freak, right?

It wasn't that Nate didn't like me, but he was older than me. When he went back to Fallen Crest, he'd been angry, and with reason.

Owen and I had understood it even back then.

Nate had been close with his friend, and then Mom and Dad pulled him away. If someone pulled me away from Owen, I'd—well, maybe that wasn't a good comparison.

But anyway, Nate and I had always gotten along. When I saw him, he was kind. He said all the things a big brother should say. He asked me how I was, teased me about dating. He asked about school. He asked who my friends were. And those questions were all easy to answer, but they were surface questions. Nate and I never went deep. I never felt like I had a right to ask him about his life, so I sat back and let Mom do the talking. What if he told her the kinds of things I told him? What if he wasn't fully truthful because he didn't want Mom and Dad to actually know how he was doing?

He had reason not to trust them. I got it. I wasn't honest with my parents either. It was easier for them to think everything was fine, and for the most part, everything *was* fine.

I mean, really, what was my problem?

I had anything I could ask for, except maybe friends.

Having Blaise in my life was opening my eyes. It was as if I'd been living in a room with the shades drawn, the windows closed, and the light off. And I didn't know it. I hadn't known there was a world with lights on, the windows open.

Now I wanted things I'd never had before, like friends. How did I get some? Were they worth it? Or maybe not? Maybe they'd just leave too?

This made me feel like a dramatic, angsty teen because yeah, yeah, everyone leaves. That's how life works. The world goes around and relationships start and end, but saying that to taunt myself and actually living it were entirely different things.

Blaise had chosen me. He'd broken through the walls I had up, though I didn't feel like I'd really had the chance to build them with him. He was just in, and that terrified me.

But I couldn't do anything about it now, except ride the wave as long as I was on it. When he would leave, I'd crash and hope to survive it. Because that's what was going to happen. He would leave. I wasn't being dramatic. I was being realistic.

I wasn't the girl for a happily ever after. I never had been. I'd always known that.

Happily ever afters were for girls who were, I don't know, love-able—liked by people. They weren't freaks. They didn't have damage. They didn't go camping alone for days, weeks, and one time a full month by themselves. They thought that was crazy and ridiculous.

When I woke from the accident, I hadn't just mourned Owen.

I'd mourned the life I'd thought maybe I had a chance at having. He died, and I knew my shot at being normal went with him. People left me, so whatever. I needed to deal with it.

Right?

Right.

Still, I was fully aware that I shouldn't have been scared to call my older brother.

"Just do it, Aspen," I said out loud. I could do this.

My hand shook, but I couldn't keep going this way.

I hit his number and waited, sitting with my knees pressed against my chest at my desk. It wasn't the most comfortable, but it helped me feel safer. I felt like disappearing.

"Hey!"

Oh my God, he answered.

"Nate?" I coughed, my voice coming out shaky.

"Yeah. Aspen? What's up?" I could hear voices on his end, and then he cursed. "You haven't called me in forever. Wait, is everyone okay? I just saw Mom and Dad. Are they—"

"No!" My hands were clammy. I hadn't thought about him jumping to that scenario. "They're still in LA—for work, I think. Or maybe they were staying for a benefit."

"Oh." He sounded relieved, and the noises behind him disappeared. His voice came back clearer, louder. "So what's up? It's not every day my little sis gives me a call."

He sounded cheerful, like he meant it.

I cried with relief. Why had I been nervous? Nate had never been unkind to me. Ever.

"I..." Still shaky.

I was such a freak.

I coughed again. "I was just calling to call. You know. Um..." I picked at the edge of my desk. "Mom said you were in LA?"

"Yeah. I'm here visiting some people."

Cool, cool.

So cool.

Um. . . "So, uh, are you still in Boston?"

His tone shifted, growing softer for some reason. "Yeah. I'm still in Boston. I'm living with a friend who's in law school. You remember Mason Kade?"

"He's not the one in law school."

"No, no. I'm living with his brother, Logan. We were all in a house with Mase and Sam, but that didn't last long."

"The NFL guy and the runner?"

He laughed. "Yeah. Sam's the runner."

Mom was right. He did sound happy.

"You're at Fallen Crest Academy now?"

"Uh-huh, yeah."

"How's that going for you?"

"It's okay. I mean, we're basically done for the year. I'm done for the year."

"Right." He grew quiet. "Owen would've graduated this Sunday. Right? Your guys' graduation is the same as Roussou's, isn't it?"

I frowned. "How did you know that?"

"Know what?"

"When Roussou was graduating?"

"Some good friends of mine, Channing's little sister goes to Roussou. She's graduating this year. Actually, I'm coming back to Fallen Crest not this weekend but the next one. Heather's throwing a party for Bren—"

"Bren?!" I jerked upright.

"Bren Monroe. Do you ever hang out at Manny's? Her brother's girlfriend is the owner."

Bren.

Cross' girlfriend.

Blaise's brother's girlfriend.

Bren, who had come to my defense at the gas station, who I had helped hide at a party one time. She was *connected* connected to my brother.

Did she know?

"Aspen?" Nate asked, his voice faint and soft again. "You still there?"

"Yeah." My voice was raspy, and I hated it.

Why was this bothering me?

"Does she know you?" I asked.

"Who?"

"Bren."

There was a moment of silence on his end.

"Do *you* know Bren?" he asked.

"Does she know you, Nate?" I whispered. "Please, just answer that."

If Bren knew my brother when I barely did? That thought ripped me apart.

"No, Aspen." He sounded alarmed. "Do you know Bren?"

Silence.

"Aspen?"

"Not really." I barely got that out, sinking down in my chair. Could I disappear? I wanted to disappear.

"Why are you being weird about this?"

"No reason," I said quickly.

Please let this go.

"I'm not getting a good feeling here. Why is that? What's going on? Are you okay?" he asked. "You never call me. Mom said you're doing great, but..." He cursed. "Mom and Dad are in LA this weekend?"

He already knew that.

"Owen would've graduated this year."

His voice grated against my ears. He wasn't getting it, and then I started to get it... Had Mom never told him?

I was supposed to graduate this year too.

I had been bumped up a year because my birthday was in late May. I was never too far behind, but never quite in sync with my class. Most were turning eighteen. Most were starting to feel like adults, and I had just turned seventeen two weeks ago.

Another way I'd never been normal.

I thought Nate knew, but it happened when he wasn't talking to the family. It could've been overlooked and forgotten to fill him in because it was so normal when he started talking to us again.

I had to stop this conversation.

I didn't want Nate alarmed. I didn't want him calling our parents.

"You're going to be alone the day Owen would've graduated, aren't you?"

It was too late. He was going to call them.

"Don't say anything. Please."

"Aspen."

I could hear his disapproval, but even worse, I heard his pity.

I couldn't stand his pity.

"Please. If you call Mom and Dad, they'll come back. I don't want them to do that. It's fine."

"No, they won't. They'll understand."

He truly didn't know. That was okay, though. That was better.

"You don't get it, Nate. I can't go there." I couldn't sit in those chairs. "I can't wait for the moment when they would've called his name." *When instead they'll call mine.*

He was quiet for a long, long time.

I waited, scarcely able to breathe.

"Okay," he finally said.

My hands shook. My arms trembled. My knees were boneless.

"Thank you."

"What are you going to do instead? You shouldn't be alone, Aspen. I get not wanting Mom and Dad there, but what about your older brother? I can fly back. I can come early. It's no problem. I have a buddy I can see in LA during the week too."

I opened my mouth to tell him no, but then I thought about it.

Blaise would be graduating that day. Blaise was popular. There'd be parties galore for him.

If Nate were here with me, Blaise could go without me, and he could party. He could come to me that night.

So, why not? "That actually sounds good."

"Yeah?"

"Yeah." I felt tears on my cheeks. "I'll see you on Sunday?"

"I'll book a flight and let you know when I'm arriving. We'll do brother-sister stuff all day. Sounds good?"

"Sounds great."

"Okay. Love you, Aspen. I mean that." Another beat. "We should do these calls more."

"Agreed." I smiled, and we hung up not long after that.

Well, go me. This was progress.

I think...

26

BLAISE

I t was the end of the day, and I'd just turned in my last project.

Tomorrow was a skip day for all seniors, so we were done. I never kept anything in my locker except what I needed for class, and all those notebooks had been tossed. I could grab a pen and not come back till Sunday for graduation.

"Heard about your showdown with Daniels." Zeke fell against the locker next to mine.

I frowned at it, realizing someone must've used it, but I'd never seen them. Then a guy stopped, looked at Zeke, and turned to go.

"Hey," I called after him.

I didn't know the guy. He was smaller, and wearing the old uniform, though it wasn't mandatory anymore. He looked at me, but didn't come over.

I gestured to Zeke. "That your locker?"

The guy swallowed, his Adam's apple bobbing up and down. "Yeah."

"You need in there?"

"Uh..." He tugged at his collar. "Yeah."

I smacked Zeke on the shoulder. "Move. The guy needs to get into his locker."

Zeke's eyebrows rose, but he moved to my other side. He leaned around me as the guy cautiously came forward to open his locker.

"Sorry. I didn't know."

The guy stared a moment before stammering, "Yeah. Cool. Yeah." Then he ducked inside his locker. He grabbed two things and dropped one of them. He scooped to grab it, stuffing it into his pocket before I could see what it was, and slammed his locker shut.

He started off, but stepped back. "Hey. Nice knowing you. You're going to Cain next year?"

I frowned. "What? No. I'm going to Columbia."

He seemed confused by that. "Really?"

"Uh. Yeah?"

He shrugged. "Okay. Well, have a good one then."

Zeke and I watched him go. He glanced back over his shoulder a time or two, his eyes getting big until he put on a burst of speed and turned the corner.

"That's the first time you've seen him all semester, isn't it?" Zeke said.

"Yep."

He barked out a laugh. "Classic." He punched me in the arm. "Columbia? For real? Fucking come to Cain. Everyone's going to be there."

"Everyone? If you're hoping to entice me, you're falling short."

"Oh." He fell silent. "Well, I'll be there. Why Columbia, though? Who's there?"

Well, shit. I hadn't thought about it until now, but that could be the reason Griffith was in town. "Non-bio dad has roots there. I was accepted last year. I'm a legacy for his fraternity too."

Columbia was one of the best schools in the nation, but Cain wasn't bad either. It was a DI school like Georgetown.

"I thought you were going to Grant West."

"Nah. Cain all the way." Zeke ducked his head a little, glancing away.

If my best friend had ever been self-conscious, I was thinking this was it. He looked five.

He shrugged, shifting on his feet. "You know my mancrush on Mason Kade. Gotta follow in his footsteps." His head jerked up and he yelled, "Strandling! What the fuck, man?"

Brian passed our hall, talking to a girl. He looked up and gave us a nod. Saying something to the girl, he motioned toward us, and they both raised a hand, separating.

"Who was that?" Zeke asked as Brian approached. "You going to bring her to the party tonight?" He turned to me. "Party tonight. That's why I came over. It's not at my house. We're trying out a new place. You going to bring your woman?"

I ignored his question, eyeing Brian. "Hey, man."

Brian had steered clear of me since our throw-down, but he nodded back. "Hey. Uh, about the—"

Zeke was all smiles, grabbing Brian's shoulder and squeezing it. He started to do the same to me, got a look, and lowered his hand. "It's all good. Water under the bridge."

Brian looked at him. "What I was going to say, is yeah. It's all good. Sorry I was a dick. Sorry I've been a dick, like, all year."

Zeke's head inched back. "Whoa. What's got into you? That's a different tune than you were singing last week."

Brian looked down before rolling his shoulders up and back. "What do you want me to say? I was pissed, but it's the last day. Things are different."

He was out of Zeke's shadow.

"You and Branston are heading to Seattle, right?" I asked.

"Yeah. Our grandfather donates heavily, so we got two spots

easy. There's an Alpha Mu chapter up there. We had a call from them. They dropped your name, said you were joining their chapter in New York?"

I felt a strangled laugh come up my throat.

"Why'd they bring my name up?"

He seemed nervous, grabbing the back of his neck. "I don't know. He knows one of the guys in your house. They were having a conversation and got to talking about legacies."

"But why'd *my* name come up?"

Brian avoided my gaze.

"Dude, just say it."

Zeke pointed at me with his thumb. "He really is all about the honesty. Be as blunt as you can, and he'll probably want to hump you."

I laughed. "Just say it."

He exhaled. "Okay. There's talk about your dad—"

Zeke coughed. "Non-bio dad. Or Daddy Dickhead. Either term works."

"—your non-bio dad and how he's got some controversy heading his way. Rumor is that twelve women are coming forward in a lawsuit against him."

"You serious?" I wasn't surprised. Note that.

"Yeah. I'm sorry, man."

Zeke frowned at him. "Lawsuit about what?"

"Sexual shit." Brian's eyes darted to me. "I guess it's bad, and they're considering dropping you."

I could follow the bouncing ball. "Shit." I shook my head. "They're trying to push me off on another house, aren't they?"

Brian shrugged again. "I don't know. They asked me about you. I told them you're not like that. I vouched for you, if you wanted—"

No. I knew. I *so* knew.

I turned to Zeke. "Start looking for a house."

He stared at me. One blink. Then he smiled. "Are you serious?"

I nodded. "No fucking way am I dealing with that asshole's problems."

"I was going to pledge. You?"

I saw all the plans Zeke was making. We'd be fraternity brothers, roommates, the whole nine yards. "No."

"What?" His smile fell.

"That was my plan last year, but not now. I'm not going the fraternity way."

"But..." Zeke swallowed. "We can't be roommates then."

"Dude."

He looked like he was about to cry.

I patted him on the shoulder, holding it there a second. "It'll be fine. I can get my own place."

"Yeah, but..."

"You gotta make sure you can get in the school," Brian said.

I gave him a cocky smirk. I wasn't valedictorian or salutatorian, but I was in the top seven. Plus, Cain had already reached out, offering a soccer scholarship. I'd just said no because of my non-bio dad's history with Columbia. Those plans had all been made before the divorce, before everything, and I hadn't thought to change any of it.

I hadn't thought much about next year.

I liked Cain. I felt good about the decision.

"Wait. Where's your girl going next year?" Zeke asked.

Oh.

Maybe not?

I WAS DRIVING to Aspen's after school when my phone rang.

The ring came through my sound system, and I glanced down.

Marie calling.

I hadn't been looking forward to this call, but I'd assumed it was coming. I'd been dodging the house all week while non-bio was there, and graduation was in three days.

I hit accept. "Hey, Mom."

"I want your ass home now. Enough of this. I'm done, Blaise. Do you hear me? Done!"

"Did he tell you about the lawsuit coming against him?"

She was silent.

A full five seconds, and then a sniffle. "What are you talking about?"

I gritted my teeth. "Is he there right now?"

She was silent again.

"Am I on speaker?" I turned the wheel, heading north.

"No," she said tightly.

"Then walk away from him. Pretend to hang up and go to the bathroom."

It sucked that we had to lie like this. He'd helped raise me all my life. She said he'd always known about me, that I wasn't his son, but he'd chosen to marry her anyway. He chose to adopt me. Then he used her money, invested it well, and hit it big with a product. He moved east, taking us with him, and after that, our lives blurred.

I grew up.

Sports. Parties. Privilege. Everything that life entailed.

Until he derailed it. Until he got caught. It wasn't even that he cheated, because I knew he'd cheated long before she caught him. She knew too. I was the one who told her, but she hadn't believed me. She hadn't wanted to believe me, and I knew she felt guilty about that. It was the reason I got away with so much shit, but my mom wasn't a bad mom. She was just caught up in her own guilt, her own shame, an ex that had crushed her spirit, and the potential for a new family, because Stephen was a good guy.

He was also a fucking patient guy, but then again, I'd not been around. I didn't know how he'd been handling having Griffith at the house all week.

I heard her saying, "Okay. See you soon. Love you, honey." A shuffling sound.

Static.

Her voice from a distance. "I have to pee."

He said something.

I gripped the steering wheel, hearing his tone. I couldn't make out the words, but he was griping about something.

"I know. I will," my mom said. "Hold on."

More static.

More shuffling sounds.

The sound of a door squeaking. A click, then a buzzing.

Her voice came back, hushed, but clearer. "What lawsuit?"

I told her about my conversation with Brian. "I'm sorry, Mom."

She hadn't interrupted, not once. She'd always been good like that. She'd listened through the whole spiel, and now there was silence, only sniffling coming from her end.

God. I couldn't— I saw a gas station and swung in, parking at the far end and turning the engine off. I hit the lights and slumped back in my seat.

"I'm sorry, Mom." It was worth repeating.

"Twelve women?" Her voice sounded so tiny, strangled.

"That's what he said." I pulled the keys out and held them in my hand.

She cursed softly into the phone. "You know if that many women are coming out at once, there are so many more who haven't come forward. This is going to be—"

"No, Mom." A knot was in my throat. I shoved it down. "We don't live out there anymore. We don't run in those circles. You are not to blame for his mistakes."

"He asked about money. Jesus Christ! Money, Blaise. That's why he's here."

Yeah...

"I'm going to—I don't know what I'm going to do, but I hate him. I shouldn't be saying this to you. You're our son—" More sniffles. "I'm so sorry, Blaise. I kept you for myself all these years."

I sucked in my breath.

Jesus. *Now* she said this?

"I lied—"

I couldn't. One confrontation at a time.

"Mom!" I stopped playing with my keys. "I am not *his* son. I am *your* son. I'm not his. I know you see the good in him and always have, but you need to see him clearly. Once and for all, Mom. Please."

I waited.

More sniffling, but she was listening.

I wanted to break him, bone by bone. I wanted to mop the floor with him, using his body to push all of his blood to the drain, and then I wanted to drag him outside and leave him there to rot. But I wanted to get through to my mom first.

It was pivotal.

"He married you for money, and he got lucky, hitting it big. But, Mom, *Marie*, he was never a good husband or a good father to me. Ever. He's cheated on you since I can remember. My friends told stories about their moms having fights with their dads because of him. That was in fifth grade! He's never come to any of my games. He only cares when I don't have straight As. He gave me *one* talk when I was younger, and that was to keep my dick clean, always use condoms, and ask their ages. That's the only fathering he's ever done with me, and I know it's because you made him. I heard you arguing."

"You did?"

I closed my eyes. She was hurting. That meant I was hurting.

I lowered my head. "Yeah, Mom. I always heard you guys fighting."

"Oh, Blaise. Honey."

"Mom..." I had to ask. I couldn't tell her what to do. She was my mother, but Marie always did what she thought was best, whether it was the right thing or not. "What do you want to do?"

Her answer came back swift and heated. "I want him out! Now! I want to march back there, take a shovel, and make my kitchen red."

I was almost proud, my chest swelling. I also knew where I'd inherited the violent streak from. "Mom, let me call Stephen."

"No, Blaise! Sweetie, this isn't for you to handle. I'll handle your fath—I'll handle my ex-husband."

I paused, debating, and then I lied. "Okay."

"Okay?"

"Okay. You said you'll handle it. I trust you."

Totally lying.

"Oh. Um...okay?" She was silent a moment. "Wait. You're done with school, aren't you? Wasn't it your last day today?"

"My last project, yeah."

"Are you celebrating with Zeke tonight?"

I hadn't told her about Aspen. Now was a good time to do so, but it didn't feel right. She couldn't afford to be distracted from dealing with Griffith and getting him out of the house, out of her life.

"Yeah, I'm heading to his house now."

"Okay. Can we, uh, I'd like to celebrate the graduations—all three of you kids. Your brother and sister, and yours. Do you think we could, maybe, have a family dinner?"

I hesitated. "Let's talk this weekend about it."

"Okay. Yeah. Okay." She sounded a bit more upbeat. "I love you, honey. So much."

"I love you too, Mom."

She took another moment, and I knew she was gathering her strength. Once she hung up, I dialed my real father for the first time ever.

He answered right away. "Blaise! Hi. Is everything okay?"

I heard voices where he was, and I knew he wasn't at my mom's house.

"The asshole who adopted me has been at our house all week."

"What?"

Good, and not good. He didn't sound like he knew. That meant my mom hadn't told him, or told him the whole truth.

She was good at that.

I was blowing her up, but I didn't care. "He's claiming to be there about me, but he's not. I'm not going to tell you the real reason, that's for her to tell you, but my mom needs help. I can't go there. I go there, and I will put him in the hospital. I'll give him a reason to sue us or arrest me." I really wanted to do that. I wanted it so bad. "He needs to get out of that house and away from her permanently. He needs—"

"Blaise."

Fuck. He sounded calm. Why was he calm?

"I'm already on my way. Don't worry. I will take care of this."

Then he hung up, and I sat there wondering if I'd done the right thing or not.

A second later, my phone rang again. It was an unknown number.

I hit accept. "Yeah?"

Cross' voice came over the speaker. "My dad just took a call from you and tore out of the restaurant. What's going on?"

I was silent.

Tell him? He'd go there, and fuck, but I didn't want him to deal with it. That was my family, not his. I didn't go to *his* house. I didn't get involved with *his* mom.

But what if Stephen needed backup?

I made my decision.

"It's none of your business." I hung up and called Zeke.

"Yo!" His normal greeting, always happy.

I put the keys back in and started the engine. "I need backup at my house."

Not even a hesitation. "When?"

"Now."

He burped. "On my way."

I peeled out of the parking lot.

27

ASPEN

After my call with Nate, I went walking on the hiking trails north of Fallen Crest.

I stepped through a clearing in the trees, and a feeling sparked in me.

It was unsettling.

It was alarming.

And I turned to look out over the place I'd never considered my home. For some reason, maybe it was a gut feeling, one of those hunches, but I knew.

Something was wrong.

Something was going to happen.

28

BLAISE

I pulled in at the same time Zeke came up, three more cars behind him. He'd brought friends. Brian jumped out from his passenger side, with Jamie and Oliver coming out of one of the other two trucks. The last vehicle was my brother's, and he wasn't alone either. His entire crew was with him. I only had time to throw him a glare before heading to the house.

We could hear shouting, and then I was inside.

"No! Stephen!"

The sight was not what I was expecting.

Griffith DeVroe used his fists. Often.

I never wanted to think I'd been beaten as a kid, but now that I was older, I knew I had been. He'd hit me, punched me, used his belts on me in a way that was abusive. My mom never knew. I'd been ashamed, and he'd threatened to fuck around even more on her if I told.

All that was rolling through me as I entered the house.

But it wasn't Griffith beating the shit out of Stephen in front of me; it was the other way around.

Stephen reared back, roaring, and threw another punch.

"You." *Punch.* "Get." *Punch.* "The fuck." *Punch.* "Out." *Hit, hit, hit.*
"Of this house!"

He stopped, his chest heaving.

He was in a suit, his tie thrown over his shoulder. There was
blood on his hands and at the corner of his mouth, and he had a
nasty looking bruise around one of his eyes. Griffith had gotten a
few hits in.

My mom was in the dining area, her hands covering her
mouth. Tears streaked over her face, which was deathly white. I
cursed, heading for her.

Stephen was shaking Griffith now, and my non-bio dad wasn't
a small guy. He was two hundred and eighty, almost all muscle.
Stephen was half his weight, but trimmed up.

Crap. Maybe I'd gotten my violent streak from him too?

"You are scum for what you have done to your wife and son,"
Stephen bellowed. "My son! Mine! You will leave their lives and
have nothing to do with them. You hear me?" He turned and
tossed Griffith across the kitchen.

He started for him, but Cross shoved through the
crowd. "Dad!"

Stephen jerked back, looking around. He blinked a
few times.

I crossed the kitchen, intending to go to my mom.

She saw me, and her eyes filled with tears. "Oh, no."

I hardened. She didn't get to cry anymore, not over this
asshole.

Stephen fell back a step. "Cross!" Then he saw me. "Blaise."

Griffith's functioning eye opened, hearing my name. I saw the
old asshole come back to him. Hatred filled that one eye, and the
fucker who used to put his fists on me thought he could do
it again.

"You little piece of—"

"No!" Stephen roared, going for Griffith.

I got there first. My hands went down, fisting his shirt, and I lifted the fucker to his feet. A good punch of adrenaline eased the strain.

"Don't!" I roared in his face. "Don't you say another word. You're going to do as he said." My arms started hurting, so I shoved him against the wall. He tried to swing, but I ducked and kicked out his knee.

He crumpled after that.

He was done.

It was all over his face—he loathed me. He wanted to hit me.

I laughed, kneeling next to him. I'd ceased caring who was going to hear me the second I walked inside my home. "You beat me, you miserable piece of fuck."

I heard a gasp behind me.

"You locked me in closets when she wasn't around. You threatened me. You threatened her. You used your belts on me. Those days have been gone for a while, but I have evidence."

His eyes widened.

"I kept a diary. I wrote it all down."

I felt dead inside. I let him see that. I let him see what he'd done to me.

"You *never* broke me. Ever. And if you think you're going to go to the authorities and make some bullshit claim against my real father, I'll come forward against your ass. Look behind me, *Dad*. All these guys are witnesses. Not one of them will back you up. Not one."

His eyes shifted, and they narrowed.

They closed.

When they opened, I knew I was looking at a beaten man, in more ways than one.

I leaned down. "I know about your lawsuit."

His eyes shifted again, blinking, then focusing on me. I couldn't name the emotion I saw there. Maybe it was panic? I was beyond being able to read him. He was just an abuser—that's all I could see.

"I don't know what those women have on you, or what they'll get you charged with, but you will not do a goddamn thing to pull myself or my mother into it with you. You are alone. You got it? Alone. You'll not utter her name or my name once during the entire process, or you will have worse things to deal with. There's no statute of limitations for child abuse in New York. Remember that."

I stepped back, and Zeke rushed in.

He'd been standing right behind me, and he went around to grab one side of Griffith. Brian took his other side, and the two of them dragged Griffith from the house.

I knew Zeke would call one of his dad's private service cars. The driver would take Griffith to a hospital, and he would stand with him the entire time, pretending to be there for him, but he'd act as a spy.

And I knew this because Zeke was my best friend. He glanced back just before hauling Griffith out of the door. His eyes met mine, and his chin went up.

I nodded back.

I might not have my brother's crew, but I had Zeke.

"Blaise," my mom whispered.

I turned.

Tears streamed down her face, and she looked stricken.

"I never knew."

I saw the emotions crossing her face, and I shook my head. "I never wanted you to know," I said, my voice rough. "I never wanted anyone to know."

"Baby." More tears. She bit her lip, and that reminded me of Aspen.

I wanted my girl, but that'd have to wait. I lifted my arms, and my mom stepped into them. She broke down, clutching me.

I knew, in the logical part of my mind, that this wasn't my fault. I'd been the victim. But I'd chosen to keep it hidden from her. So in a way, it *was* my fault too. I was the cause of my mom feeling this pain, and I hated myself for it.

Then again, I usually hated myself. This was par for the course.

ZEKE HAD DONE EXACTLY what I'd known he would, and he'd come back in after the car took Griffith away. He gave me the numbers for the driver and guard that'd be with Griffith until the hospital released him, and then he asked what I wanted.

I told him to take off, and he nodded. "I'll see you tomorrow then."

He left with the rest of the guys.

After she broke down for the fourth time in my arms, Stephen had taken my mom into the bedroom. They'd been in there for two hours.

I didn't know why I was waiting, but I was. I moved to the back porch.

Maybe I'd been waiting for this moment, though I wasn't at all happy about it, now that it had arrived.

Cross stepped out on the back porch and sat in a chair beside me.

"He—"

I stopped him. "Get lost."

"The fuck?"

I turned to him.

I didn't give two fucks about anything.

"Get lost. Not your life. Not your problem."

He sat there for another beat, and a disgusted laugh ripping from him. He shoved up, shaking his head. "Fucking prick." He crossed the patio, and a second later, he was gone—he and his friends.

Good riddance.

I waited another hour.

It was dark by then.

It was cold by then.

I saw nothing, and I felt nothing.

I'd read that once you finally share your deepest secret, you're supposed to feel free. That was bullshit. It had just imprisoned me further. I was pinned down, experiencing it all over again—every emotion, every memory. Now I would wait, holding my breath while everyone who'd heard my secret had the power to further hurt me or give me nothing in response.

There was no freedom.

There was no love, or healing, or warmth.

A victim.

I was a fucking victim.

I'd never said the words, but I knew that's what I'd been.

I hated him because he'd done this to me, and I hated myself, because I *wasn't* a fucking victim.

No. I just hated life.

I hated fucking life.

Then there was movement at the door. I heard it slide open.

I didn't look, but I knew it was Stephen. He was the only one still operational. My mom was probably passed out by now.

"Did she take a valium?" I asked the darkness.

He was quiet as he crossed to take the chair his real son had sat in earlier. He eased down slowly. I heard a crinkle and looked over. He had an ice pack on his face. "Yeah."

I nodded. "She'll be out till tomorrow. You'll have a full night's sleep."

"The fuck I will," he said.

I turned to him.

His eyes burned. "I just learned one of my sons has been physically abused. You think I'm going to sleep tonight?" He shook his head. "You must have no clue how much I love you."

My stomach clenched.

"How much I fell in love with you the first time I saw you," he added.

My chest clenched.

"The second I saw you, I knew you were mine."

I closed my eyes.

"I was livid with your mother, but that's not for you to deal with. You're done with that. You got it?"

I looked at him, not understanding.

"I told you I had it tonight. You didn't have to come."

I opened my mouth.

He shook his head. "Cross told me he called you. He told me what you said, and I don't know if that's why you came, but I'm here. This is my shift now. While I'm glad all this is out, and your mother and I know what happened to you, making sure Griffith doesn't talk isn't your job. Do you get that?"

I just stared.

"You beat me, you miserable piece of fuck."

I'd ceased thinking once those words left my mouth.

Stephen leaned forward, the chair squeaking under him, and he rested his elbows on his knees. "There's a lot to process, but are you going to be okay for the night?"

My entire body was locking down, but I managed a slight nod. "Yeah." I flinched internally, hearing how monotone I sounded.

"I have a girl," I told him. "I'm going to go see her."

The air seemed to shift around us. He stood, slowly. "Okay. I'll hold it down on this end. You go be with your girl tonight." He walked to the door, limping slightly, and paused. "If I have to tell you every day that I love you for you to accept it, I will."

I looked at him.

His eyes were clear, gazing at me steadily. "I mean it. I love my children. *All* of them."

I didn't know how to take that, so I didn't respond.

He went back inside, and after another five minutes, so did I.

I didn't call Aspen.

There were text messages from her on my phone, but I would read them tomorrow. I just wanted her, and fifteen minutes later, I pulled past the gate and drove to park in front of her neighbor's house.

I called her.

"Blaise?" She sounded tired.

I started to tell her I was here, but the words froze in my throat.

I realized my hand was shaking. That was odd.

I tasted salt, and I frowned, touching my face.

I was crying.

I'd cried before, but I'd always known I was crying.

I hated crying. It was weak.

That's what he would have said if he saw.

A gurgling sound bubbled up from my throat. What the hell was that?

"Blaise?!" Aspen sounded alarmed.

I hadn't meant to make her sound like that.

I hadn't meant for her to find out about any of this.

I'd just meant to go to her, crawl in bed with her, and hold her. That's all I wanted.

But I couldn't talk. I couldn't get any words out.

I hung up, hating that I'd hung up on my girl, but I couldn't talk. What point was there, then, to see her? I was useless to her. I was worthless.

But I couldn't bring myself to leave, so I sat in my Wagon and stared ahead, not seeing anything.

It might've been a minute later, maybe five. But there was a tap on my window, and then I saw Aspen.

She was biting her lip, her eyes all worried, and I hated that I'd made her feel like that.

But I was paralyzed. None of this made sense to me.

She opened my door. She reached inside. She unclipped my

belt. She took my keys out of the ignition. She grabbed my phone, and then she took my hand.

I was led inside, and we both crawled into bed.

She wrapped her arms around me, and someone was crying.

I wanted to believe it was her.

I knew that wasn't true.

29

ASPEN

I woke up to the feeling of lips pressed against my neck. He swept my hair to the side, the movement a caress. His arms around me, his legs entwined with mine, he was tasting me. His hand skimmed down my side to my hip, then slipped under my shirt. He rubbed my stomach, moving in slow circles, and I knew where he was going.

I strained against him, lust and need throbbing inside of me.

I felt him against me, rolling his hips, grinding slow.

I gasped, my head pressed to my pillow as his fingers found my breast. He held me in the palm of his hand, and his thumb caressed my nipple.

I'd never thought about dating. It wasn't that I didn't like boys. I did. I crushed hard on them, but I worried they wouldn't want me. It had settled firmly in me and taken root, holding me down. Then Blaise happened, and I was still trying to catch up.

I was still trying to catch up, but this morning, even if I'd been considering remaining a virgin, that was gone. He'd been destroyed last night. I didn't know what had happened, but I would. Until then, I'd just hold him.

And this morning, I was going to love him.

I wouldn't say the words, but that's how I felt. I knew I'd been falling.

It was done. I was over the edge.

I was his, for as long as he needed me. I was his.

I was resolved. And feeling that surety, I took his hand and guided it between my legs.

It was as if that was the last permission he needed.

His kisses grew more insistent. He thrust hard against me, pushing aside my underwear and sinking in. He curved his fingers into me, thrusting in rhythm from behind.

The pleasure was building.

Climbing.

I'd never, ever, thought this would happen to me.

I'd never thought someone would care for me like this, would need me, would come to me when they were wrecked.

Love and the need to protect him, care for him, made everything so much stronger. Clearer. I reached behind me. I needed more of him.

I didn't care about anything. Only him. Only this moment. Only us.

I couldn't reach him, so I pushed at my underwear, pulling it down as the throbbing overwhelmed me. It pulsated through me.

He paused, his mouth at my ear. "Are you sure?"

I nodded. "Yes. *Please.*"

He groaned and leaned up, his mouth finding mine.

He turned us, moving more slowly. Gentle. He held himself above me, and the look in his eyes broke my heart, but in all the right spots. I was shattered, moved beyond words, because whether he knew it or not, I saw love shining back to me.

I reached up, cupping the side of his face, and pulled him down to me. His lips melded to mine, and it was like the last turn of a key in a lock. He reached over the side of the bed, pulling a condom from his wallet. A second later, I felt myself open, almost magically, even as he slid inside of me. There was pressure there, the barrier, and he paused, a soft curse slipping from him as he kissed my neck. Then he thrust through, breaking it, and sank deep into me.

He held still, holding me fiercely.

He turned, nuzzling my throat before lifting to my mouth. "I didn't know. I didn't think."

I shook my head. "The pain's almost gone." And it was.

He waited, letting me adjust to him, and when I began to move my hips, he moved slowly with me. He let me set the pace. As pleasure overtook the pain, I felt amazed. I hadn't known this would be what it felt like.

It was so good, and it was with Blaise.

I wound my arms around him, my fingers sinking into his skin, as if I could climb out of my own to be even closer to him.

He thrust harder, rubbing against me, and then it was *only* the sensations. I was almost fevered, needing more and more.

"Fuck, Aspen." He moaned, a hand to my hip as he lifted himself, only to sink farther inside of me. He hit a deeper angle and pushed me over the edge, my body trembling and jerking with my orgasm. Waves and waves hit me. I rode them out, loving them, as Blaise waited until I was done.

He held himself still, watching me.

I looked back at him, knowing this morning had changed me. It wasn't just the sex. It was more than that—last night, realizing I loved him, and yes, this morning too. All of it swept through me, overloading my body, but I knew he needed to finish.

I reached up, pulling him back to me. I kissed him, tasting him. "I'm okay."

His arms flexed, still holding me. "Yeah?"

"Yeah." I ran my hands down his back to his hips, and I lay back, my hips rolling against his. I wrapped my legs around his waist.

He groaned, his lips pressed hard against mine, his tongue

slipping inside and tasting me as he began to move inside of me again. This time was for him.

He thrust slowly, gently at first.

Then as I continued to be okay, he went harder. Deeper. He held me up, his hand under my ass, as he pounded harder. I moved my legs higher around him, and with a primal growl, he reared up and went deep two more times before his body jerked.

After a moment, he collapsed onto me, and I savored it.

I held him as his body shook. Trailing a lazy hand down his back and side, I waited until he looked up at me. He reached for me, and we kissed. It was tender at first, but then grew more demanding, commanding.

He lifted his head, his eyes black as he studied me for a beat. "I don't deserve you."

I think my heart broke. "Blaise?"

He shook his head, pressing a kiss to my forehead before he pulled out. "Let me clean up, get rid of this." He stood, taking the condom off, and went to the bathroom. It was then that I felt the stickiness between my legs and winced, also feeling some soreness.

I reached down, pressing lightly. I hadn't thought about this when we were in the middle of it.

Blaise came back a moment later, carrying a washcloth.

His face was gentle as he sat beside me, moving my leg. "Let me see."

I did, but it was different now. I felt self-conscious.

As if he could sense it, he shook his head. "Don't feel that. You are perfection, Aspen. Don't let anyone make you think otherwise." His words came out fierce as he put the washcloth between my legs. It was warm, soothing.

He cleaned me, and I relaxed back into the bed.

"Feeling better?"

I nodded, my eyes closed.

"You're going to be sore. I'm sorry."

I opened my eyes, seeing the worry in his. "Hey, I didn't tell you."

He looked tormented. "I knew. I mean, I didn't, but I should've known. I should've asked."

I sat up, taking the washcloth from him, and I scooted down, my legs going around his waist, my front against his side. I tipped his chin toward me. "It happened the way I wanted it to. If you think a girl doesn't think about the conversation to tell the guy she's a virgin, you're an idiot."

He stiffened, but the corner of his mouth lifted. "Yeah?"

"Yeah. I didn't *want* to have the conversation. This was how I wanted it to happen. Thank you for not being mad that I didn't tell you."

His hand flexed over my leg. "I'm not a complete dick."

He wasn't a dick at all, not to me. But I didn't tell him that because I knew he wouldn't believe me, not yet.

He grinned, his hand rubbing over my leg. "Wanna shower together?"

"What?"

"Shower."

My eyes went wide, and he laughed. "Come on." He stood, taking my hand. "You're going to be too sore for anything, but this is the fun part." A pause. "The other fun part." He drew me to him, then moved behind me, his hands at my hips.

In the bathroom, he held me back as he turned the water on, testing it.

When it was warm, he maneuvered us into the shower. He was pressed all up against me, and he was right. As he drew soapy lines down my body, it was a whole lot of fun.

30

BLAISE

F uck. I could've stayed here forever.

After the shower, we both got dressed, but there was a whole lot of touching, tickling, and laughing. I couldn't get enough of Aspen. I was starting to think I never would, and that thought should've terrified me, but I wasn't going there. Not now.

We snuck out for breakfast, and when we came back, Aspen told me to park in the driveway. I carried the coffee and bag of muffins as she led the way. We went through the garage and into the house, and that's when I met Benny, the chef.

He was a nice guy, maybe in his forties, and he doted on Aspen. Miss Sandy was there too, giving me a tight-lipped look. I was thinking she knew I spent the night. I just flashed her a smile and she huffed, looking away.

Aspen was becoming a lifeline to me.

No way I could pull back, not if I wanted to keep breathing. And yeah, there was a prickle of alarm in the back of my mind.

I shouldn't have needed someone like this. It wasn't healthy—for me, but mostly for her. To have a guy like me come into your life and need you as much as I needed her? That couldn't be normal, or good for her. I didn't want her to feel like she was drowning in me. Ever. But we could deal with that later. We sat at the table and had our breakfast.

Benny and Miss Sandy joined us. The lawn guy came in later, sitting close to Benny, and it kind of seemed like these three were more Aspen's family than her own.

That shit wasn't right. Not at all.

Miss Sandy might've guessed my thoughts, because she gave me a pointed look. But I ignored her. After breakfast, Aspen wanted to be lazy, so we headed up to her movie room. She grabbed a journal. I lounged back, watching sports, and she sat next to me, writing.

I drew circles on her back as her leg pressed against mine, and this right here was heaven.

I never wanted to leave.

I knew she wanted to ask about what had happened with me last night, but I wasn't ready to go there. She gave me space.

But it was pressing on me.

I was on borrowed time. Eventually that world would interrupt us.

My mom had taken a valium to sleep. *Fuck.* Every time an alert went off on my phone, I tensed. So did Aspen. She was reacting to me. When my phone finally rang, a part of me was okay with it.

It was time to get this shit over with.

It was Zeke calling.

Aspen saw the screen, but my hand stayed on her back.

"Can I take this here?" I asked.

She looked over her shoulder to me, biting her lip. She nodded, a strand of hair falling over her face.

I reached up to tuck it behind her ear as I lifted the phone and pressed *accept*. "Hey."

"Hey!" Zeke's voice boomed. "I'm surprised you picked up. Thought for sure you'd be MIA until Sunday."

I cringed. "Nah. I'm here. What's going on?"

"Wondering what you and that fine woman of yours are doing today. The boys called, asking to meet up. The party didn't happen last night." He offered no explanation, just kept on going. "So instead of having it at the field, I was thinking maybe we could meet up—put our heads together and see what everyone's in the mood for today."

My hand pressed against Aspen's spine. I didn't realize until she shifted, but then I jerked my hand back. "Sorry."

She frowned. "What?"

"Nothing." I put my hand back, and she leaned into it, relaxing, but she was eyeing me. That same strand of hair fell down over her face.

"What?" I asked her.

"That to me?" Zeke asked.

"No." I pulled the phone away a little. "You okay?"

Aspen watched me, chewing her bottom lip until I ran my thumb over it. "Oh. Sorry." She laughed. "I don't even realize I'm doing that."

I nodded, waiting. She had something to say.

After another couple seconds of silence, I smoothed my hand over her back again. "What is it, babe?"

"Babe?" Zeke asked, but he was a lot quieter than normal.

She looked down, as if she felt shy. "He can come here."

I frowned. "What?"

She sounded surer. "He can come here, if he wants. You two can have your meeting here."

This was big.

"You sure?" I asked quietly.

She nodded. "Yeah. Ask him if he's had breakfast. I bet Benny would love to do a whole spread if he didn't."

I relayed the message and Zeke boomed, "Hell to the fuck yeah! I'm going to meet your babe, and I ate, but I'll eat again.

This boy never says no to food. Shoot me the address, and I'll be over in two pumps in a virgin."

Fuck's sake. "Really, dude?"

"What?"

But Aspen was grinning when I hung up, and I texted him the address.

Aspen pulled her phone out. "Carl? A Zeke Allen is going to be arriving later this morning. Let him through, please."

She nodded after a moment. "Thanks."

I waited until she hung up. "You sure about this?"

She nodded, relaxing back against me. "Yeah. He's not going to be mean with you here, and he's your best friend." She reached over, running her hand up and down my leg. "Does he know what happened last night?"

I tensed. I didn't want to tell her. So she was going to ask someone else.

My voice was a bit hoarse. "Yeah. And yes, you can ask him. I'll tell you more later, but I'm okay if he tells you what he heard."

"He was there?"

I nodded. "He was there."

Her eyes held mine. "Okay."

She climbed off the couch, heading to let Benny and Miss Sandy know about the impending arrival.

I lay back and cursed. Ready or not, my two worlds were about to collide.

31

ASPEN

"This place is *lit*! Holy pussy shit."

"Zeke," Blaise warned.

"Sorry, but wow." His mouth hung open, and he hadn't even stepped into the garage yet. We were still standing in the driveway.

This was a surreal moment for me. I never thought I'd have people over.

Owen was the one who made friends, and I'd thought his were mine—until after. Then it just seemed too much work.

Now I was getting the point. Kinda. But this was also surreal because it was Zeke Allen.

He'd been the most popular guy in our school until Blaise came.

I talked to Miss Sandy and Benny. Both were under strict instruction not to mention my last name. Blaise was worried about Zeke's freak-out meter. I'd told them not to discuss what my parents did for a living—because again, freak-out meter.

I mean, he might already know but why bring it up? Why make it something when it might not be something. If that even made sense?

He finished gawking at the front of the house, and when he turned to me, his eyes warmed. "Hello there."

Blaise introduced us, a hand to the small of my back.

Zeke looked me over before throwing Blaise a smirk. "I can see why you're keeping her to yourself."

Blaise's hand pressed harder to my back. "Yeah?"

"You are one fine piece of as—"

"Dude." Blaise glared.

I felt myself blushing. "Thanks?"

Zeke grinned.

Blaise put his hand on my hip to propel me back inside. "Aspen, you do not have to thank a guy for telling you that. Any other guy who said that would be hitting on you with your man right next to you. That's not cool."

Zeke followed us. "But not me. That's me giving my approval. I can tell you're nice, and you're going to take care of my boy for me."

I almost stumbled, those words were so unexpected, but Blaise caught me. I looked up, and he was smiling. Five minutes in, and I was beginning to see why Blaise liked Zeke.

I never could before.

Zeke proclaimed almost the same sentiments when he met Miss Sandy and Benny, though fortunately he didn't comment on their looks. And Blaise had given up trying to censor his friend.

After we sat to eat the breakfast spread or to watch Zeke eat, he leaned back and lifted his chin. "So, man, what's the word? What are we doing today?"

My eyebrows lifted. Not one word had been spoken about what had happened with Blaise last night, and Blaise had been tense. I knew he'd been waiting. With this question, he relaxed. His hand had been gripping the back of my chair, but it eased down and he shrugged.

"I'm thinking that's up to you."

Zeke nodded, eyes falling to the table. "Yeah." Then he looked back up. "Anyone called you today? Your family or...anyone?"

Blaise's hand stalled on my leg. "Nah, man."

Zeke went back to studying the table. "You turned your phone off after my call?"

Blaise's jaw clenched as he leaned forward. "The phone's on. If you got something to say, say it."

Zeke didn't blink. "That piece of shit needs to go to jail."

My stomach dropped. I froze in my chair.

"He put his hands on you," Zeke added. "I've got a big fucking problem with that. I don't know if your girl knows about this—" His eyes slid my way, an apology there. "But I'm your best bud, and I fucking love you. You'd be okay if someone did that shit to me?" He nodded at me. "To your girl?"

Blaise's fingers gripped my leg. He wasn't hurting me, and he pulled me in closer.

I looked over.

He wasn't looking at Zeke. And his jaw kept clenching, unclenching, and clenching again.

A wave of sadness pierced me. I felt a tear fall, but I let it go.

My voice was hoarse. "You were beaten?"

"No," Blaise hissed.

"Yes," Zeke said at the same time. "'*You beat me, you miserable piece of fuck.*'" He paused. "That's what you said. Locked in closets. He threatened you. He threatened your mom. He used belts on you." He leaned forward in his seat, his voice dropping low. "If you don't think those words are going to be permanently engrained in my memory, you're a fucking moron. You saved me when I was kid, and then you went home and were beaten on by an adult, a parent." He placed a fist on the table. "Make that fucker pay."

I closed my eyes.

I couldn't.

Belts? Locked in closets?

Wave after wave of sadness sliced me.

My entire chest felt like it was caving in.

An adult did that to Blaise? My guy! The guy who held me, made me feel loved, who had started to show me a world I never thought I'd see, much less walk in?

I wanted to kill this guy.

"It was your father? Who did that to you?"

Blaise jerked toward me, and he stiffened even more. "Aspen."

Zeke watched me. After a moment, he grinned. "I like you."

I glanced at him, but stayed focused on my question. "Your father? Your non-bio dad did that?"

Blaise didn't answer, but his eyes were bleak.

Zeke answered, "Yeah. His non-bio dad."

I shoved my chair back.

"Where are you going?"

I picked up my phone. "My brother. He knows people who can hurt that man."

Blaise muttered a curse. He shoved his chair back and took the phone from my hands. "Aspen, no."

I looked at him. "He needs to hurt. A lot."

He smiled down at me, his hand on my hip. "I know, and he will, but I gotta make sure he doesn't hurt my real dad."

I waited. "Your real dad?"

"My real dad beat the crap out of him last night. He was whaling on him when we walked inside."

Wait. "Really?"

He nodded, sliding my phone into his pocket. "It's all good. I won't let him hurt anyone else I care about, but *he's* hurting today. I bet he can't even piss standing up."

That made me feel better. Some of the tightness eased. "Good. He shouldn't piss standing for the rest of his life."

Zeke lifted his fist. "I *really* like you."

Then it hit me what Blaise had gone through. There were

pieces and holes, but I was putting together what had happened last night.

And he'd come to me.

He came to *me*.

I wanted to cry.

"Aspen." Blaise's voice came out thick. He was feeling it too.

I pressed my forehead to his chest, grabbing ahold of his shirt. His fingers slid through my hair.

I slid my arms around his waist and held on. After a moment's hesitation, Blaise wrapped his arms around me too. We held each other, ignoring the world around us, or just Zeke since it was only him here.

Blaise leaned down to my ear. "Later I'm going to show you how much your reaction means to me." He pressed a kiss to my forehead.

I looked into his eyes.

They blazed with an emotion that made my throat swell.

I didn't dare name it. If I did, I'd fall even harder, faster. And I was scared of what I already felt.

"I wish Owen could've met you," I whispered.

"Babe." His face transformed with such tenderness and warmth. He cupped my face with both hands and lowered his head, his lips finding mine.

Yes. Owen would've liked him. He would've liked him a whole bunch.

THE THREE OF us hung out the rest of the day.

Blaise suggested the pool, so we swam for the next couple hours. Miss Sandy brought out swim trunks for both of the guys. I went up to my room to change. I pulled out a one-piece and a bikini, laying them both on my bed.

I couldn't decide.

I'd normally grab the one-piece, but Blaise was here, and I wanted to look good for him.

It wasn't until Miss Sandy knocked once on the door, stuck her head in, and said, "The bikini, Miss Aspen," that I made my choice.

She came in and disappeared into my closet. After I changed in the bathroom, she held out a cover-up for me. I took it, feeling sophisticated for maybe the first time in my life.

She took my hand and whispered, "I like your boy very much, even if he did stay the night."

I nodded, fighting a blush. "Me too."

"We'll bring lunch out to you and your guests," she said as she retreated. "They're already enjoying the pool."

"Miss Sandy."

She paused, glancing back.

"Thank you."

She nodded, her eyes blinking a few times. "Of course, Miss Aspen." She started to leave, but looked back once more. "It's nice to hear laughter in the house again. It's been a long time."

Oh. Now I was crying.

I took a deep breath, pulled the cover-up on, slid my feet into sandals, and headed downstairs. She was right. It'd been a long time coming, and I was going to enjoy this moment.

Who knew when I might get another one like it.

32

BLAISE

I t was nice to spend the day with Aspen and Zeke. My girlfriend and my best bud were getting along. Zeke didn't bring up the party again, and I was grateful. That would've made Aspen tense. I didn't want to put her in a situation she wasn't ready for. Having Zeke here was a big deal, and I thought he might have realized that.

He brought out a soccer ball later, his head cocked to the side. "Yeah?"

It'd been a while since I played.

I wanted to. Instantly. The feel of kicking it, moving it forward, moving it with me, running alongside it as if it were a part of me—that all came back to me in an instant.

I wasn't known for soccer here. I was enjoying that. It was a break from another thing that came with New York. The pressure. The extra attention.

I got attention here, but it wasn't like anything I got in New York.

I was enjoying that, and Aspen. I glanced over. I hadn't talked to her about soccer yet. She had no clue, and right now, I kinda liked the confusion there. But damn. Zeke knew what he was doing when he brought that out. Just seeing it in his hands and I wanted to rip it from him, herd it, keep it to me, and that feel of running the length of the field, kicking it in, almost nothing was better. Well, sex was, but I was really missing the feel of scoring a goal especially when it was after a tough battle.

Zeke couldn't compete with me. If I gave in—fuck. Who was I kidding?

"Give it to me."

His grin turned cocky. "Come get it from me."

There was a section of grass on the other side of Aspen's dad's man-shed.

Zeke led the way, swaggering over there like he could hold his own against me. He knew I played. He knew how well I played, but I was thinking that he had forgotten.

He was about to be reminded.

He turned, dropping the ball with his hands going to his hips. He was going to say something, maybe lay out some rules, but I was already there.

One touch and I pulled the ball from him.

"Hey!"

His legs closed. He thought I was going to kick between them, but I didn't. I merely reached out, my toe on top of the ball, and I tugged it to me. That's right. It was mine, not his, and I flashed him a grin, knowing he'd pick up on my sentiment.

He scowled. "Not fair."

I laughed, starting to run with the ball. "If you think I'm playing with a handicap against you, no fucking way." I urged it farther down the grass, nudging it with the side of my foot. The inside. The outside. I bounced it back with my heel, stopping, rotating, jumping around it, and when Zeke got closer, I flipped it in the air, my knee bouncing it beyond him.

I was toying with him.

He knew it. I knew it. I caught his grin. He was loving this too.

My legs were tingling. There was a pull in my gut. My foot was aching, needing more and more. Harder. Faster.

I played with Zeke, easy keep-away game until the ache was too much for me to ignore. The grass wasn't long enough. There was space on the side of Aspen's house and kicking the ball farther, I pushed off. I left Zeke in my trail, handling the ball between myself. I moved it up and around, jumping, spinning. I stopped it, the back of my heels imprisoning it and I flipped it up and over to the front of me. I loved doing that. I caught it in the crook of my calf and knee, then tossing it to the grass and moving it forward once more.

Jesus.

I got lost, playing, pushing myself.

Challenging myself.

I forgot time.

This was how it was with soccer. I needed a worthy adversary. I needed to let out my pent-up tension. I needed to be forced away from it. I needed to go back in, stealing it, knowing that victory. Relishing that victory.

I was salivating all over again.

Yeah. I was ready for soccer to come back. Only another month and I'd have to start training, then another month after that and I'd be on the field again. I couldn't wait.

I stopped, sweat pouring down me, and a burst of applause came from the sidelines.

Aspen and Zeke were both there.

Zeke was wearing that knowing smug look. Aspen's eyes were big, dazed, and her lips had parted. I recognized the look. I was feeling it too, and there was a whole other urge I had to fight off because I really wanted to grab her, tell Zeke to piss off, and drag my girl upstairs.

"Long time coming, man."

I grunted, reaching out and Zeke hit his fist to mine.

Yeah. Long time coming.

"I didn't know you played soccer."

I shrugged. "I'm kinda on break, so I haven't talked much about it."

She frowned a little. I saw the questions, but then she nodded to me.

We headed back, my hand slipping into Aspen's.

As if there'd been a conversation about it, both Zeke and Aspen didn't bring up soccer again. Instead, we showed Zeke the movie room and he was stoked. (His word.)

There was more I hadn't known about.

Aspen showed us the tricked-out basement. There was an even larger theater room down there, which her parents used for their work. She'd mentioned that before, but it was cool to see it.

There was also a gaming room, which had a pool table, air hockey, table football, and a basketball-shooting game. Benny and Miss Sandy kept bringing down snacks and drinks, so we hung out in there most of the day. Zeke and I had reverted to being little boys, and we were in game heaven. Aspen played too, laughing at us, and I couldn't help myself. Any excuse to touch her, and I took it.

When Zeke went to the bathroom, I had her pinned in the far corner in a heartbeat. She moaned, and we were both panting when Zeke returned and cleared his throat. "Dude."

I flashed him a grin, raking my hand through my hair.

He rolled his eyes and challenged Aspen to an air hockey game.

Before they began, he made a point of telling me to go for a walk and think grandmotherly thoughts.

I shot him a cocky smirk, but did as he said. When I came back, they were both laughing.

"I've never seen my dude so happy," I heard Zeke tell her. "You're the reason for that."

"Yeah?" Aspen replied.

I had to smile. She sounded nervous and hopeful all at once.

"Yeah."

Ping.

Someone just scored.

"Don't hurt him, okay?" Zeke added after a moment.

Ping!

"That goes for you too," Aspen responded, her tone chilled.

Zeke grunted. "Man, I really like you. Have I mentioned that?"

I heard the soft thud of the puck on the table.

"You sure you went to FCA?"

They began playing. *Slap. Thud.*

Another ping.

"Since the fall," Aspen said.

"Huh. Are you like a silent assassin or something? How'd I never see you?"

I could hear her smile. "Because I'm a silent assassin." *Slap, ping.* "I win."

I took that as a sign and walked back into the room.

Zeke shook his head, standing back from the table. "Your girl kicks ass at air hockey."

Aspen's grin turned shy. "I used to play with my brother a lot. We had these at Hillcrest."

Her brother. *Owen.*

I made a note that it was time to push her about him. She was ready.

Crossing the room, I moved to stand behind her, and put an arm against the table on either side of her. She was trapped, and I looked over her shoulder to Zeke, who was shaking his head. The walk hadn't helped me, not even a little bit.

"What's the plan for tonight?" I asked.

He gave me a look. "You tell me."

Zeke could easily go party. I could read that from him, yet he was here. He was worried about me, and I wanted more time with both of them. Just them. I straightened, pulling Aspen back against me. "Let's get food and booze and watch a movie here."

Zeke flashed a cocky smirk back. "Sounds perfect."

WE'D JUST HEADED out in my truck when Zeke said, "I like her."

Aspen had chosen to stay behind, but we were going to Roussou for the pizza she wanted. It was supposedly the best, and she wasn't having it when we suggested any place in Fallen Crest.

So, we were driving to Roussou.

"Why didn't you tell me about her brother?" Zeke asked.

I slowed, pulling up to the gate. I nodded as Carl waved, and I pulled through.

"Because…" *Fuck.* What could I say here? "Because I don't know much. She doesn't talk about Owen that often, and I don't know what happened. I've not pushed her."

"I'm not talking about that brother," Zeke said. "But I'd like to hear about him too."

It took a second.

I clued in and glanced over.

Holding on to the handle above his door, he lifted an eyebrow. "Yeah. *That* brother." His mouth set. "Why the fuck didn't you tell me?"

Shit. "You know?"

"We watched a movie. The account said *Aspen Monson.* That house? Your girl said she moved to town in the fall. I know those directors moved to town at the same time."

I nodded.

I gripped the wheel. "It's new with her and me. I'm not used to giving a shit about someone, and she's got some…"

Zeke relented, his hand dropping from the door handle. His head rested against the headrest. "She's got some hang-ups. I get it. And you were worried about me going all fanboy? You think I'd push an angle to use your woman or something?"

I gave him a look.

Zeke's face got hard. "Dude. Seriously? I don't give a fuck about them. They ain't you. They ain't someone who's made you smile. I can be normal, you know." He cursed under his breath, looking out his window. "I mean, I get it. The reason I like Mason Kade so much is because you took off. Mentors and shit—I don't have one. You anchor me. No one anchored me when you were gone, but the idea of...how not to be? Mason Kade provided that. It's why I look up to him so much. That make sense?" He cursed again, looking embarrassed. "Look, whatever. You don't have to worry about me. It's cool who she is, but that's it. I know you heard us, and I meant what I said to her. As long as she takes care of you, I won't be a dick to her."

"Got it. Thanks." My voice felt strained.

This had quickly gotten to be too much talking, too much sharing. Both of us cleared our throats. I expected a comment about someone's pussy to break the mood, but instead I got: "Daniels hit on me."

I expelled some air. "I forgot about that situation."

"I handled it. I won't touch her. I wouldn't do that to you, but she's rallying. You gotta know that."

"I forgot. I've had my own crap, you know?" I turned onto the highway that'd take us to Roussou.

"I know."

We drove in silence.

We were ten minutes out when he asked, "What are you going to do?"

"She said she and the girls were going to go after Aspen. So I guess keep Aspen away?"

"We got three months of summer. I don't want to not hang out with my best friend."

I didn't want that either. "I'll figure it out."

He nodded, and we finished the drive in silence.

I'd never been to the Roussou pizzeria, but the place was busy when we pulled in. Inside, Roussou students were everywhere, and conversation stalled at the sight of us.

"Should I call the guys?" Zeke lowered his voice.

Seeing who had gathered around a table in the back, I wasn't sure.

"Nah," I told him. Fuck whatever was going to happen. If we busted heads, fine by me. I'd not let myself think much about last night, about what my brother and his friends had found out, but screw them. I wouldn't let myself walk scared, even if we were in their town.

I went to the counter and put in Aspen's order.

The girl was taking it down when suddenly her head popped up. "Is this for Aspen Monson?"

I almost bugged out. "Yes, and keep it down about her name."

Her eyes got big. "Oh! Oh. Sorry. I—no one else orders that pizza. Cilantro, mozzarella, caramelized onions, Roma tomatoes, and pineapple aren't ordered everyday. With an egg in the middle of the pie." She looked me over and then moved to Zeke before telling us our total. Once I paid, she printed off my receipt and handed it over. "I like Aspen. That's all."

I eyed her, putting the receipt in my pocket. "Who are you?"

"Ava, but Aspen wouldn't know me. I've just been here when she picked up her pizza."

Oh. Well. Then I was fine with this Ava girl.

"Yeah. She's cool."

Ava handed the order to the guys in the back and returned. She cocked her head to the side. "Are you her boyfriend or something?"

Zeke barked out a laugh.

Her eyes grew noticeably unfriendly.

He just laughed harder.

From the side, I heard a voice. "Ava, it's cool."

Ava looked. I looked.

Bren, my brother's girlfriend, stood glaring at us. "He actually cares about her." She raised her chin, her eyes cold. "And he better be good to her, or I'll slice him."

I smirked back, noting Cross behind her. "Keep your woman in check, *brother*. She's showing her fangs. If she keeps at it, I'm going to think she's jealous. Wouldn't want to start thinking she wants to be me or have my hands—"

I was interrupted by a fist across my face.

And that's why I'd said it.

Maybe I'd started to get the itch when Aspen said her favorite pizza place was in Roussou. Maybe the idea had begun to form then and grew as we drove. Or maybe it was just always there, nestled under my chest, waiting to come out every time I saw him.

Either way, I welcomed his punch.

I loved it.

He hit me, and I reacted, wrapping an arm around his waist. I dragged him outside, the doors bursting open, and then it was on.

There was yelling around us.

At first there were hands trying to drag us away, but this was more than a school rivalry. We were brothers, and we hated each other, and I think this was something we needed to do.

After a bit, a circle formed around us. Bren and their friends held Zeke back.

Cross and I were trading punches.

I was relishing this moment.

He hit me. I hit him.

He threw an uppercut, so did I.

After the sixth punch, he realized what I was doing, and he started to falter.

I was grinning like a madman, and I loved even that. I rushed him, tackling him to the ground.

He didn't know anything about me. He didn't know who'd tucked me in when I was younger. He didn't know I played soccer like a goddamn badass. He didn't know where I was going to college or that I felt almost as much loyalty to Zeke as he and his friends did to each other. He didn't know any of that shit.

And he didn't deserve to know.

I was done with him, and even though the sky was starting to spin and I tasted more blood than I wanted to, it was time to knock his ass out.

I twisted, prepared to take out his knee when I heard a sudden yell, "Hell no, you don't!"

That's when I felt a shove from behind. I went down, and when I looked up, some guy was there—some big motherfucker, and he reared back.

Well, fuck.

Then I saw nothing.

~

ASPEN

THEY SHOULD'VE BEEN BACK by now. It was almost nine. I paced.

I was a mess, and I didn't like this. The pizzeria was not that far. After calling Blaise's phone twenty times, he finally answered.

"Oh my God! Where are you?" I shouted.

I shouldn't shout. I needed to calm down.

I heard a voice, but it wasn't his. "Who is this?"

"Who are you, and where is my boyfriend?" I demanded.

The person on the other end sighed. He sounded older. "Your boyfriend got into a fight with his brother."

"His brother?"

"Yeah. Look, you're not going to lose it if you come here, are you? We don't want another fight to break out. We're having a hard time keeping him and his brother apart."

What?! "Where?"

He told me the address, and I wrote it down. "Okay. I'll be there soon."

"Hey, uh—maybe bring a new shirt for him or something. There's a lot of blood."

My stomach clenched. I swayed on my feet, but *new shirt*. Got it. Check. The blood? I'd think on that later. "I will."

I hung up, and I didn't think about where I was going, or who I was going to see. Those would've been my normal concerns. I wasn't alarmed as my GPS took me out of Fallen Crest and toward Roussou. The pizzeria was in Roussou. I'd expected that.

But I didn't expect to find myself parking in front of a bounty hunting office.

I looked over the vehicles parked outside, clenching Blaise's marijuana shirt, which I'd started to sleep in. It was the only one he left at my house.

I lingered on a distinct Hummer.

Oh, crap, crappier, crappiest.

Maybe it was a different Hummer. I really, really hoped so, because I knew he'd recently gotten a new Hummer.

And this one looked new. It looked brand new.

Was it...?

I quelled my nerves and walked past it, ignoring the Massachusetts license plate. I was trying to tell myself it wasn't *him*, but then I walked inside.

There were guys everywhere.

I heard shouting from the back. Blaise's voice, and laughter after.

There was a big mammoth guy, and a shorter mammoth guy. There was a guy with a scar on his face. A lean guy with tattoos all over him was coming out of a room in the back. He had his arms crossed over his chest.

I heard the tattoo guy saying, "Only you, Matteo." He laughed, and one of the mammoth guys grinned at him.

I turned, and despite all my hoping and wishing, there he was.

The guy who I knew owned the Hummer outside looked over.

He saw me, kept going, then did a double take. He jerked forward. "Aspen?!"

Damn.

I heard Blaise in the background. "Who did he say?"

And I said, "Hi, Nate."

33

ASPEN

O h, boy. I was not ready for this.

The tattoo guy gave Nate a sharp look, but my brother was coming toward me. "What are you doing here?" he asked.

The tattoo guy came with him, but the rest stayed back, and I was thankful. There were a lot of guys in here—a lot of big guys, and they all looked scary. Time sort of slowed down as Nate approached, and I saw movement from a back room.

"What the fuck?" Blaise demanded.

He'd come out of a room, another guy trying to hold him back.

The breath left my lungs.

I swayed, gulping. His face was a mess of bruises. There was tape over one of his eyes, around the side of his eye, and still more at the corner of his mouth. The other side of his mouth was all black and blue. His shirt was bloody. All of it. There might've been a dry end or a corner, but for the most part: dark blood red.

That was my boyfriend, all broken.

He saw me, and a fire lit in his eyes.

"Aspen," he gasped.

Cross' head popped out of another room. He saw me and disappeared back into his room.

"Aspen?" Nate said.

The tattoo guy turned to look at me. "We talked on the phone?"

Nate frowned. "You did?"

I ignored them as I watched Blaise leave his room. He stalked past the guys to take my hand. He took the shirt in his other hand.

"Let's go," he said.

"Hey!"

"Hold up."

"I don't think so."

A chorus of voices rose in protest.

"Aspen, wait." Nate focused on my hand in Blaise's. His jaw clenched. "The *fuck* is going on?!"

Blaise tugged me after him, opening the door. "Let's go."

"I said *hold* up!" That was the tattoo guy.

He reached out toward me, but Blaise growled and blocked him.

"Don't grab her," Blaise said, putting a firm hand on my hip. He turned his back on everyone and gentled his tone. "Let's go."

I glanced at my brother, but Blaise opened the door, and we were outside.

"Aspen, wait. Please," Nate called. He jogged after us.

The tattoo guy remained on the doorstep, his arms crossed. That's when I noticed he was gorgeous. But he seemed older, and I had a guy, so it didn't really matter. But if I hadn't been with Blaise, then *whoa*. You know?

As if reading my mind, the tattoo guy grinned.

"Aspen!" Nate barked. "I can just follow you home. It's technically my house too."

I cast a look over at Blaise. Nope. No room for compromise. He had to go. He couldn't stay. I could see that in the way he kept clenching his jaw. A vein stuck out in his neck, and his hair was crazy, like he hadn't been able to stop raking his hand through it. That wasn't a good sign.

I called over my shoulder, "Find me there. Until then..." I motioned to Blaise as we cut over to where Maisie was parked. "I gotta go."

At the car, I unlocked the doors and looked back. The tattoo guy was still watching.

Nate was at the edge of the sidewalk, his hands on his head. He looked perplexed.

I waved. "It's nice seeing you."

He held his hands in the air in a WTF motion, and then dropped them as I slid inside, shutting the door.

Blaise pulled off his very bloodied shirt and tossed it on the seat, dragging the one I'd given to him over his head. He tugged the hem down as he got inside. A second later, Maisie pulled out into the street, and we were off.

Blaise hissed, flexing his hand. He folded his bloodied shirt and wrapped the dry ends over his knuckles. He pulled it around to tie it in a knot and leaned back, breathing out a curse.

"Shit! My phone." He patted his pocket and relaxed. "Oh. Monroe gave it back after you called and said you were coming."

I cast a sideways look. "What happened back there? I thought you just went to get pizza."

His eyes closed with another soft curse. "I'm sorry."

I waited.

"I messed up."

"Blaise," I said gently.

"What?"

My hands tightened on the wheel. "Tell me what happened. Please."

"Yeah." His head rested against his seat. "We went to the pizzeria, which is a popular place for Roussou kids, by the way."

I hadn't thought of that.

"We walked in. Ordered our stuff. The girl at the counter recognized your order and mentioned you."

That was shocking. And interesting. "What'd she say?"

"That she thought you were cool, but she didn't like me." He grimaced. "She also didn't like the thought that I knew you, was ordering for you."

"What?"

His smile didn't reach his eyes. "You better get used to it if we're going to last. I look like a dick. I walk like a dick. I act like a dick. I am a dick, to almost everyone except you." He thought on that. "No. I am a dick to everyone *but* you. People clock that, and they're going to worry."

I kept driving, but looked over every now and then.

He studied me intently, his words soft. "You're good people, Aspen. I'm not."

Jesus. And then he said things like that...

I felt my tears rising. "Shut up."

"Aspe—"

"Shut up!" I gripped the wheel with both hands. I wanted to squeeze it in half. "Just stop talking like that. Stop it."

Then I waited.

I kept gripping the wheel, my heart pounding in my chest.

I clued in.

He was silent.

I glanced over. He grinned. "I stopped, but it's the truth."

I cursed under my breath.

His phone started ringing, and he pulled it out, hissing again from his hand. "It's Zeke." He hit the button and put it on speaker. "You're on speaker, Zeke."

"Who else is there?"

"Hi, Zeke," I said.

He was quiet for a beat. "I'm glad she's there. You tell her what set everything off in the first place?"

Blaise had his eyes closed, shaking his head. "No, man."

Zeke laughed. "Aspen, babe, you must have, like, unicorn glitter in the air around you or something. Everyone goes to bat for you—people who don't even know you. Monroe. The pizza chick. Who's next? Hell, I might start worrying about Blaise's intentions, and I love the guy."

"*What?*"

Blaise opened an eye, saw I was not happy with this conversation, and said into his phone, "I'm good. I gotta go."

"Hey! Don't hang up," Zeke rushed out. "Don't know where you are, but I grabbed the pizza. I'm at my house if you want to drop by. I made sure no one touched your girl's pie. It's in the back kitchen."

That's when I heard the music blaring from Zeke's side. Funny. I hadn't noticed it before.

"You want to grab your pie?" Blaise asked.

My first response was *what fucking pie*? Blaise had been in a fight—how was pizza important? But then I took a breath, counted to ten, and realized my stomach was growling. I shrugged. "I could go for some pizza."

Blaise's eyes warmed. "We're on our way," he told Zeke.

"Yessss. See you in two pumps, yeah?"

Blaise hung up, putting his phone in the divider between us.

He rolled his neck and touched the side of his mouth. "Fuck. That hurts."

The tattoo guy had said they were having a hard time keeping Blaise from his brother. Cross had been in the other room, and his face had been bruised too. I'd been in too much shock over Blaise's face, but I was remembering now.

I didn't like what I remembered.

"You fought your brother?"

"Yeah," Blaise said meekly.

"Why?" *Over me?* That made no sense.

"Like I said, the pizza chick didn't like the thought of you and me. Bren came up—"

"Bren? Your brother's girlfriend?"

He nodded. "Bren came up and actually vouched for me."

This was *so* not making sense.

He looked away, sighing. "I don't know. Cross came up, and the stuff from last night's still bothering me. I got mad just seeing him, and I mouthed off. I said shit I knew would piss him off."

"Who threw the first punch?"

He was quiet for a moment. "He did, but I said shit he had to hit me for. I started the fight."

"Because he got time with a decent dad while you got beat up by a guy who wasn't your dad. That's why."

Hold up. Hold up a freaking minute...

I'd heard my voice. I knew those words were mine, but I hadn't thought them. They were just there, and they were *a lot*.

I bit my lip. "I'm sorry."

Blaise made a gargled sound.

I looked over to see his mouth open, and he stared at me. He blinked and shook his head.

"You're right."

I didn't know what that meant, but I felt bad. "I'm really sorry. I shouldn't have said that—"

"No," he croaked. "No. You're right. I saw him, and it was too much. I just wanted to destroy him, you know?"

Not really.

"I wanted to wipe that smirk off his face using the pavement. I wanted to smash his face in. Like, fuck him." He sighed again. "Aspen, I don't know where or what you're going to college for, but you need to go for counseling. It would've taken me a year of therapy to figure that out."

"I'm going to Cain, but I'm undecided on a major."

"Cain?"

I nodded. "Yeah." We'd never talked about this. My heart started beating fast. My palms felt sweaty. "Where, I mean, where are you going?" *Please don't say across the country. Please don't say on another continent.*

His grin spread. "I was going to go to Columbia."

Crappy, crappy, crap. That was in New York. That was across the nation. Wait. He said... "*Was?*"

He nodded. "I sent an email to Cain this morning. They offered me a soccer scholarship a while back, but I turned them down. Things changed recently."

My chest squeezed. My hands got sweaty all of the sudden. Did I dare hope? "Yeah?"

"They emailed me back this afternoon. I'm in. They gave the scholarship away to someone else, but they're going to do their magic and get me in and on the team."

"Are you serious?" I might have been hyperventilating.

"I'm serious."

Who does that? Sends an email in the morning and hours later gets into school?! Cain was not an easy school to get into, either—although it had been for me.

"I saw you play, but you must be some soccer star."

"I am," he confirmed, gloating. "We didn't talk about it, but that's why I didn't show up here till February. I wanted to finish the season at my old school."

I remembered watching him.

He loved it. That was obvious, but it'd been more. It was as if he was doing what he'd been born to do. The whole afternoon was special, but when Zeke brought the ball out, I watched Blaise. He couldn't take his eyes off it. It was like it was a part of him and how dare Zeke be holding it instead? Then he merely took it from Zeke and the rest was something I knew I'd never forget.

It was special. A moment that Blaise was letting us in, letting us see him, and he wasn't hiding. He wasn't giving attitude. He was ferocious and hungry. I had felt the power from him as he tore off, leaving Zeke behind. It'd been about him and the ball, no one else. When he stopped later, he was panting, but so had I been.

A dark excitement curled through me, leaving tingles in its trail.

I was near breathless now. I couldn't wait to see him play again.

The lights of Fallen Crest were nearing, and I needed to get my head on straight. So much was making it spin. I took a breath. One thing at a time.

I had no idea where Zeke's house was.

Blaise gave me directions, and as we got close, I could see it lit up like Christmas in Times Square. Cars and trucks lined his driveway and both sides of his street.

Zeke was having a party. Why hadn't I realized that over the phone? Zeke and *party* were almost interchangeable.

Blaise got quiet, observing me as I parked and then just sat there.

"I can run in and grab the pizza," he offered. "You can stay here."

My chest squeezed even harder.

He knew I had issues. I'd told him some of them, but I hadn't told him the rest yet. We both had things we needed to work through.

I looked at him. "This thing with you and me?"

"Yeah?"

"Are we... Are you...?" What was I saying?

He leaned toward me. "Are we what?"

I couldn't say it.

I felt things for him, emotions I didn't dare share. I didn't want to scare him away, and I was still scared of it myself. But if we were going to...you know...*be* something, I should brave a party for him. A normal girlfriend would do that. A normal girlfriend would set aside her issues and go be with her poor beat-up man as he went to see his best friend.

I could be a normal girlfriend.

Right?

Blaise was still waiting, so I forced a smile. "Nothing. Let's go inside."

Yeah... I had a feeling I should've stayed in the car.

34

BLAISE

My face hurt. My hand hurt. Walking even hurt, but we were going to get that pizza for Aspen. I was doing it, no matter how much my body told me to sit down, roll over, and fall asleep for a month.

I held her hand as we walked, and my head pounded to the music before we even neared the front door.

The door burst open, and I was blasted with pain.

I stopped, groaning before I checked myself.

Two guys paused in the open door.

"Dude!" one of them said. "You're our fucking hero, man."

Jesus Christ. I didn't even know this guy.

"Yeah." I offered a small smile back, but I ground my teeth. My head wanted to split in half. I kept walking.

"Don't touch him!" Aspen jerked her hand from mine to block the guy.

I twisted.

"He's hurt," she hissed. "He was in a fight."

He stared at Aspen with a blank face, his hand in the air. He'd been about to hit me on the shoulder or back. His blank expression switched to nervousness.

He lowered his hand, stepping back. He saluted me with the beer in his other hand. "Sorry. Just had to come out and congratulate you. Any guy that lasts a round with Cross Shaw, only to be knocked out by one of Monroe's bounty hunters, is legendary in my mind." He touched his beer to his chest and took another step backward.

"Yeah, man." Aspen took my hand as I clipped out, "But don't touch me or her."

I gave him another look and let Aspen tug me toward the house.

Zeke was holding court in the back section of his basement. He had a bar in the corner, and everyone had congregated around him. There were a couple pool tables, and couches in all corners of the room. The sliding doors had been pushed open, and the party spilled out around the pool.

The music was going to give me a migraine.

"Yo." Zeke reached for a beer, but paused. He leaned over to the back of his bar and came out with a bottle of whiskey. He opened it as he made his way to us. "You got sprung, huh?"

He handed it over.

I took a drink for the impending migraine.

Zeke nodded to Aspen. "You drink? If you don't, I could make something virgin for you."

I paused, checking his tone and look, but there was no hidden innuendo there. Zeke was truly offering to make something non-alcoholic for Aspen.

My chest swelled.

He was rolling out the carpet for her. He'd done it at her house, but doing it here in front of everyone, he was giving her his stamp of approval. That would go a long way with everyone else.

Aspen stepped close to me, resting her head against my arm. "You know what? Give me a beer. Never been a big drinker, but maybe it's time, huh?"

Zeke's grin was almost blinding. "Right on." He nodded before going back behind the bar.

I glanced down. "You sure? You don't have to. I'm in pain. I needed something to dull it, but I'll quit in a second so I can drive back, if you want."

"Drive Maisie?" she said incredulously.

She was adorable.

I wanted to taste her pouty lips. I *needed* to taste them.

"Uh, whoa." Her eyes went wide and darkened. She'd felt my sudden response.

I caught the back of her neck and leaned down.

Moving my mouth to her ear, I whispered, "I want you grinding on me tonight. I want to watch you as I slide inside of you, and I'm going to make you come three times for me."

Her knees folded.

I caught her. Her hand pressed to my stomach, fisting my shirt. "Oh. Okay. Yes, please."

Adorable. Fucking adorable.

"Seriously, guys. Keep the hot and heavy till later," Zeke said, returning from who knows where. "Daniels is here, you know?"

That was a cold shower. It worked on Aspen too, because she jerked away from me.

I caught her right as she was about to run into Brian, who held three beers by the necks. I tugged her back, focusing on Zeke, who was handing a beer in a glass to Aspen.

"Cheers." He held his drink up.

I clinked it with the bottle of whiskey. Aspen joined us, and as she drank, Zeke asked, "So now that I've been an ace host and the beverages have been distributed, what happened?"

"You tell me." I frowned. "I woke up in the back of Monroe's bounty hunting office. You were gone."

He rubbed the back of his neck, watching the crowd around us.

Not me. I ignored everyone but these two.

"Your brother's girlfriend stayed back to handle the pizzeria staff. I don't know why. She seemed to know the girl we were talking to, but they wouldn't let me come. Said I'd escalate the situation. Your boy had one of his goons with him, though. What happened?" His eyes slid to Aspen. "How'd you hear? I didn't have your number, and his phone was still on him when they took him."

Her eyes got big.

I smoothed a hand down her back, keeping her close. "Channing Monroe called her."

"Hmmm..." She held up a finger, finishing her drink. "No. I called your phone. He picked up and asked who I was, then told me to come down if I thought I could help the situation."

I felt a kick from that one. I'd been mouthing off to Cross, hoping to incite him again.

Zeke read my face and started laughing. "You are such a dick. People say I'm a dick, but you're worse."

I frowned. "Come on."

"No, no, no." He backed away, bowing. "When someone comes along that's scarier than me—and you've earned that especially lately—I acknowledge it."

I rolled my eyes, and he motioned us to follow him.

Holding Aspen's hand, I moved us through the crowd. She kept close, her other one rested on my back. It was a light touch, but she was with me. And I liked it. I liked it a lot.

Glancing around as we walked, I realized almost who all was here.

"You invite Roussou people?"

Zeke tossed me a grin over his shoulder. "Why not? I don't discriminate. Besides, things are cool with me and Gambin again." He gestured toward a guy across the basement.

"Huh."

Gambin was one of the athletes from Cross' school, and seeing me, he separated from his group. He followed us into the den connected to Zeke's bedroom. It acted as a gaming room. Zeke used it for his smoking room too, but tonight, only two guys were inside.

"Out." Zeke jerked his head toward the patio doors leading to the pool.

The guys were passing a blunt, but they looked up, saw us, and scrambled. I didn't recognize them.

"Finally." Zeke sank down onto one of the couches.

Brian sat on his other side.

We were here for pizza, but the whiskey had helped my headache a little. And I wanted to relax, have my girl with me in my scene. I went to the far inside corner of the couch and sank down. When Aspen made a move to sit next to me, I leaned back, pulling her onto my lap.

"Blaise."

She stiffened, but I molded her against me. I leaned back and closed my eyes. *What a fucking night.* I felt her fingers touching my face, gently, as she inspected my damage. But everything had already been cleaned and bandaged by one of Monroe's bounty hunters.

I opened my eyes and saw Zeke watching us as Gambin came in.

"Making sure all my teeth are there?" I asked Aspen.

I'd meant to tease her, but it came out a bit more gruff than I wanted. I put my hand on her thigh when she tensed. "Sorry. I must be in more pain than I thought."

She nodded, biting her lip.

I lifted my hand to touch her mouth. "Not that."

She let it go and breathed out, her body relaxing against mine. She rested her elbow on my shoulder, her head cocked to the side. "Do your ribs hurt?"

I frowned. Cross hadn't hit me there.

I shook my head. "Nah. We were trying to mess up each other's pretty faces."

She smiled. "Okay. That's good then."

God, she was beautiful, soft golden hair. She had lips I wanted to do dirty, dirty things to, and her body was ridiculous—tight, toned, and perfect everywhere.

My dick was already hard with her in my lap, but thinking about what I wanted to do to her tonight, fucking painful.

Aspen felt it, and her face flushed. She laughed, burying her head in my neck.

That felt nice too.

Zeke caught my attention, jerking his chin up. He wanted to talk.

I leaned in and asked Aspen, "You want to participate in our conversation or just relax in my lap?"

Her eyes were dark, and I knew she was thinking lusty thoughts, so I wasn't surprised when she lifted a hand, touching the bruise on my lip before she murmured, "Just kinda wanting to relax."

I nodded and moved her to the other side. Her back was to the room this way, and I pulled her legs up to rest next to us on the couch. One hand held my whiskey and the other curved behind her. I rested my head back.

This was the life.

When Aspen had settled, her head pressing to my shoulder, I gave Zeke the signal.

He was fighting a smile, but stopped. A full-on shit-eating grin spread over his face. "Fuck. Never thought I'd see it, but it's here."

I smiled back.

Gambin leaned forward.

A couple other guys had come in, but they held back. There was another couch on the other side of Zeke, so we had a tiny bit of privacy. Good. I was on edge. I wouldn't have handled that well. Although Aspen somehow made everything okay.

Jesus. What was my problem?

What was I becoming? I'd never needed a girl to calm me down, but Aspen was suddenly that person for me—more and more every time I saw her. How long ago had I told her I couldn't date her, and now I needed her touching me to get through a room? It was unreal, but I wasn't a moron. I wasn't going to fight it. I was going to hold on to her, keep her as long as she would stay.

Because that was the situation.

She was going to go away. Eventually.

Not today. Not tomorrow, but some day, and it was for the very reason Zeke had been teasing me about. I was the biggest dick here. I'd been physically abused, and that shit had happened for a reason. It was like Griffith knew there was bad in me, and he needed to beat it out.

I grunted, the sound low in my throat, because he'd failed. It was still in me, just pushed down far enough that it only came out in pieces. Aspen was my salve. I was a blistering, angry wound, and I needed her covering me to dull the pain, just a little.

Always fucking angry. What a shitshow I was.

"B." Zeke moved his foot, nudging mine and motioning.

Gambin watched me, an intense look on his face.

"What?"

Aspen stiffened at my irritation.

I took another shot of whiskey and ran my hand down her back until she was soft again. She nestled into me.

"I was asking how things are with your brother now?"

This cocksucker. He had a sly look in his eye, like he knew something I didn't. He had an angle. That's what it was, and hell no. That was personal shit.

Aspen raised her head to watch me.

She knew I was ready to blow, again.

"Who are you?" I asked.

Zeke's eyes got big, and he fell back into his couch, smothering a laugh.

Gambin straightened. His face got hard, and if he could've thrown a punch, he'd have made a show about threatening it. But the guy was weak. He knew it, as we had a whole stare off, and he flushed before lowering his head, because he could tell I knew it too.

I wasn't some rich, pretty punk.

"You don't have to be a prick," he said.

"But that's what I am." I flashed him my teeth. "I don't know you. Who the fuck you think you are, asking about my brother and me? It ain't your business. And go run your mouth, I dare you. Let's see if you have a mouth to run by the end of the night."

The room fell silent.

The bass from the music filled the space, but after staring at me, measuring me, Gambin clenched his jaw and turned to stalk off. Two guys that had been lingering by Zeke's bed followed him. Lackeys.

Brian whistled under his breath, moving over and kicking his feet up on the coffee table in front of him. "That was cold."

"You know if he sees your brother in Roussou, he's going to start something," Zeke added.

I snorted. "That'd be dumb of him. It's just me here. Cross has his whole crew."

"The fuck?" Zeke glowered at me.

"What?"

He shook his head. "It's not just you. Christ. When you going to get that through your skull?"

I knew what he was saying, and I forced myself to calm down. "Yeah. Thanks."

Zeke expelled a harsh breath, but he smiled. "Damn straight. Finally."

Brian lifted his chin, tipping his drink toward me before he took a drink.

"So *are* you and your brother okay?" Zeke asked.

I took a pillow from the couch and flung it at him. It hit him square in the face and bounced to hit Brian, who snagged it. When Branston, who I hadn't noticed before, started laughing behind him, Brian threw it at him.

"Fucker."

Branston caught it and put it behind him in the chair. "Hmmm. I could fall asleep like this."

I surveyed the group, noting two people missing. "Yo. Where's Ashlome and Conway?"

Brian stilled and shared a look with Zeke.

"What?"

They didn't answer, not right away.

Zeke's shoulders lifted for a moment. "Conway's with Daniels tonight."

Brian pointed up. "There's a whole group upstairs. All the girls are there."

Zeke's grin was wry. "I've been cut off as long as I hang out with you."

His words hit me, and I began to laugh.

Mara was trying to ice me out from the guys by using sex against them, the lack of sex.

I shook my head, still laughing. "You going to do it?"

Zeke scowled. "What the fuck?! Did we not just go over thi—"

"You going to give up pussy for your best friend?" I held on to Aspen as I leaned forward. Her arms wrapped around my neck. "When I know you get so much pussy from Roussou that you don't even know you're banging a Roussou chick until I tell you."

Zeke chuckled. "Oh. Yeah. Well, you know. FCA pussy is golden or something."

I rolled my eyes. "Mara's an idiot."

"You know it won't work."

I nodded. It wouldn't work, but I knew it wasn't the only plan she was going to implement. She'd soon learn I didn't care who was sliding between her legs, and that'd piss her off. And Zeke wouldn't toss me away. Take my friends from me? I really only had one. But I had to admit, since they were here this evening, not upstairs, Brian and even Branston were starting to grow on me.

"Ashlome and Conway are weak," I said.

They never stood up to Zeke. Now they were up there, boning my last girl.

I was ready to leave.

Mara would eventually hear that I was here. She'd come down. She'd see Aspen on my lap, and she'd probably have a foursome to get back at me. I liked Mara, and I cared enough about her to want her not to do that. She'd regret it later.

And if she took the fight to Aspen, I didn't know how to stop that.

I wasn't sure Aspen knew how to handle that. Mara wouldn't come alone. She had the other five in their group.

"Stop worrying," Zeke said, indicating Aspen. "Make up with your brother. Have his girl come around. Those chicks won't fuck with your girl. They ain't dumb."

It... I had to stop and make sure I'd heard what I heard. And I had.

I scowled at him, but there was no heat. There was merit in Zeke's suggestion. Bren Monroe was a fighter. She fought dudes. She could more than handle the girls.

"One mistake in that scenario," I said after a moment.

"What's that?"

I held Aspen close. "No way am I hanging out with my brother this summer. He doesn't get my summer."

Aspen tensed and lifted her head. She was watching me, and for once I avoided her gaze. I didn't want her to see inside of me, and I knew she would. I felt stripped raw in front of her. Then she caught my chin and made me look her in the eye.

Her eyes were fierce.

I tried to look away.

"Hey." She leaned in, resting her forehead against mine. "He doesn't get anything else. It's not like that. You got a brother. That's what you get." She lifted her head, bringing her mouth to my ear. "And you got a dad. A *good* dad."

See? Straight to the bone.

I closed my eyes, looking away, but I stroked the side of her face. Rubbing a thumb over her cheek, I looked again, and she had paused—literally in the palm of my hand—the sight moved me. I started to melt. I didn't know what it was, like that whole thudding feeling I'd felt a week ago, when something clinked into place.

It was deep.

It was strong.

It was life changing.

And it scared the piss out of me.

I let out a sigh. "Maybe we should go?"

Her eyes dropped to my mouth. "That sounds good."

I groaned as she stood, and I moved right behind her. I had a hard-on to hide, though every jackass in this room knew what I was sporting. My hands remained on her hips, and I let her lead us out of the room.

"You taking off?"

Zeke held up his hand as we passed him.

I met it with mine. "Catch you later?"

"Yeah."

Aspen kept going, so he watched us as we moved through the room.

"Party tomorrow night?"

That would be Saturday night before graduation, and when Aspen almost stumbled over a step, I remembered there was a situation there. But I'd wait to ask, like I was waiting on addressing the issue of her parents. Timing had to be perfect.

"Let's talk tomorrow," I called over my shoulder.

He nodded. "Got it. Have fun."

Aspen started out into the hallway, but I caught her hand and moved ahead. Guess my dick was going to lead us.

"Don't do anything I wouldn't do," Zeke called.

My hand squeezed Aspen's. "That's virtually nothing."

His laughter sounded behind us as I took her out through his patio doors and skirted around the far side of his pool. It saved us from going through the house, but we still came around the side of his house as a group walked up the driveway.

They saw us and stopped. Whatever had been said, whoever was laughing, all of it died.

"Good grief, Blaise," said the girl closest to me. "What happened to you?"

I grimaced and drew Aspen in front of me. I used her shamelessly as my shield. I was desperate. Ducking my head to her shoulder, I nipped her skin before grinning at my sister. "Your twin thing must be off, Taz."

Aspen faltered again, almost falling back, but I manhandled her. I hurried her past my sister's friends. She was there with girls who I knew had fucked Zeke, and a couple other guys too. I recognized her boyfriend, and he was throwing me definite shade, but I didn't care.

"Blais—hey!"

I guided Aspen down the driveway.

Taz followed me to the street. "Jerk face! Stop."

I chuckled. My sister was learning how to talk to me. This was better than the other bullshit she'd tried.

"Not now. I got somewhere to be." I turned around, taking Aspen's hand. I kept walking backward, so Aspen kept going too. "I need some alone time. You know how it is." I gestured to her boyfriend. "It's nice to see you two crazy kids worked it out, huh?"

The guy was full-on scowling at me now. He crossed his arms. The other guy with him gave him a cautious look.

Taz stopped, her hands in the air. "I've called you, like, twenty times over the last month. You never answer."

A strangled laugh left my throat. She had no idea.

"What happened to your face?"

We kept going.

Taz stood on her tiptoes, as if that would help her. "I deserve to know, you know!"

I felt an asshole statement coming. I tried to squash it, because Taz had always been nice to me. She was eager for a relationship. But I couldn't stop my mouth. "Yeah. Call your real brother first. Then we'll see what you say."

I saw the flash of hurt in her eyes at the same time I heard Aspen gasp.

But then we were into the street, and I maneuvered Aspen in front of me so I didn't have to see *another* person who could love me learn that they shouldn't.

35

ASPEN

I waited until we got into Maisie. Then I waited as Blaise cursed that he'd forgotten the pizza and ran inside to grab it. He was back five minutes later, and I knew he'd accomplished that by being rude. There was no way he could've walked through that house without people trying to talk to him, so he must have shrugged each and every one of them off like a bad rash. That was his way, I was learning.

I waited as he got in and I drove back to my house. (He said he was fine, and he seemed fine, but I still wasn't sure who I trusted to drive Maisie right now.)

I waited as we went into my house and up to the theater room with its snack room kitchenette. I kept waiting as Blaise heated us each a couple slices of pizza and led the way to my room.

Then he took a big bite of a slice, tossed the plate on my desk, and reached up to pull his shirt off.

That's when I asked.

"When's my turn?"

"Hmmm?" he asked. He pulled his shirt free, his eyes wide as he finished chewing what was in his mouth. "What?"

I shifted back on my heels.

His eyes dropped as he noted my movement, my posture.

That's what he did. I was learning that too.

He saw everything. He watched everything, and then he decided what he wanted out of the situation and went about creating whatever that was. If he wanted sex, he'd go sensual now. If he wanted a fight, he'd say something mean—though he never did that with me. Not intentionally. So I waited to see what sort of Blaise I was about to get. I wasn't sure I was ready to be his adversary, not yet, but I knew it would come. If we remained on this course, we'd butt heads. Every couple did. The resolving of it would tell me what we had.

I wasn't a dating expert, but I'd read books—romance, textbooks, cognitive behavioral therapy handbooks. I'd done quite a bit of that. But I also knew things because while I'd had my brother, he and I had had a damn good relationship.

Then he died, and I was alone, and now I had Blaise.

I was also learning that I never wanted to be alone again.

Blaise still hadn't said anything, but he eyed me like I was a wounded animal that could strike any second.

"When are you going to turn on me?" I asked.

His eyes went flat.

I lowered my head. "When are you going to push me away?"

He stepped back.

"When are you going to decide you don't want my love in your life?"

Because that's what he was doing with his family—with all of this.

His jaw clenched.

I'd pushed his button. "There it is. You don't like what I'm saying."

His eyes cooled. "Didn't take you for a dick."

I raised my head, not allowing him to look down on me. I watched him the way he'd watched that Gambin guy at Zeke's party, only he'd done it sitting down, with me on his lap. He did it like a professional.

I was so out of my league. I shook my head, easing away from him. "What am I doing?"

"What are you talking about?" he asked.

We'd just switched roles. I'd been on offense, and I'd intended to see it through. He was worth it. So what was I doing now? Backing away? Running off? I flinched, hearing Blaise's own words in my head, *"You running?"*

Probably. Because that's what I did. I didn't stand and fight.

Concern colored Blaise's expression.

"You care about me," I said.

His head tilted. "Yeah. I thought I'd made that pretty clear to you." His eyes darkened. "Is that what this is about? You don't know how much I care about you?"

Yes.

But no.

My chest hurt. My skin felt stretched.

I felt a storm coming. My pulse sped up.

A panic attack was imminent.

He couldn't see me like that.

"He's seen you like that already."

Really?! I sucked in my breath. Now I heard Owen's voice?

I could hear my brother laugh. *"You didn't really need me before. Don't run. You chose him. No more running."*

I'm not going camping anymore, I decided then and there.

He just laughed.

"Aspen?"

Right. Blaise was here. He was alive. He wasn't a voice in my head.

I could be so crazy sometimes, so what the hell? Owen was right. I'd chosen him. I needed to commit, so here goes nothing— or everything.

"Owen wasn't my twin," I said.

Those words were not what he'd been expecting. I read it on his face. His mouth went flat, but he didn't say anything.

"But everyone thought he was," I continued.

My chest tightened again, like something was sitting heavy on my throat. I had to push through it, ignore it. That was my panic rising.

I coughed and plunged forward. "I'm smart. I don't know if I told you."

He nodded slowly. He was listening. He was with me.

"Like, I'm almost genius-level smart."

"He doesn't respect modesty. Be bold."

Fuck off, Owen!

"Be proud."

I sucked in my breath, feeling tears rising. Damn. He always used to do that to me.

"I *am* genius-level smart. Like, they wanted me to skip a grade." I winced. "Or two." Then I hurried. "But I didn't let them. I mean, I went up one grade..." I wasn't explaining any of this the right way.

So not a genius.

I tried to backtrack. "Here's the thing, I'm young."

His eyes clouded over. "How young?"

"I turned seventeen three weeks ago."

I was a sixteen-year-old senior. Har har. Laugh at the little genius girl. Now let's all throw popcorn at her so she can break down and we can feel better about ourselves.

I braced myself—it was always the same response. Always.

But nothing came.

I'd even closed my eyes, preparing myself. For nothing.

I opened them and Blaise was just staring at me, except the clouds weren't in his eyes any more. They were all over his face. He was almost glaring. I hadn't expected that reaction. Though, maybe I should've? We did have sex. Were you supposed to explain all your hidden secrets before climbing into bed with each other? Probably.

I was going to suck as an adult. I couldn't even get this teenager stuff right, and I only had one year left. Well, not really. I was off to college. That was adulthood. Kinda.

"That's why you don't have friends?"

"What?" I squeaked out.

His face was livid. I thought I was reading that right, but his tone was tender. "You don't have friends, Aspen. We've talked about this. I knew you didn't know anyone at school, but I thought there'd be someone. Old friends from your last school. A cousin maybe? There's been no one."

Crap.

So many craps.

"I..." had no idea what I was doing anymore. What was the point of me starting this? "I thought I had friends." Then Owen died. "I realized I didn't later."

"What happened?" Blaise was quiet a moment. "Where are your parents?"

God.

Right there. He'd dug right in, right to the bone.

My throat burned.

I didn't answer.

"They aren't here. We're graduating in two days. Where are your parents?" He spoke so softly, so kindly.

I hated it.

Fine. *Let's do this.*

It was time, right?

"It used to be me and Owen. Nate left us while we were at Hillcrest, but I had Owen. He had friends. I didn't, though I didn't realize that until later. I'd *thought* they were my friends. Owen was the popular one. I never was. I was a year younger, but in the same grade, and when people know that, it makes a difference. They look at you differently. You're not one of them."

I could've told him some other stuff about when they found out you were smarter than they were, but I didn't have the energy at the moment.

"Kids can be cruel," I said in summary, my words faint even to my ears. "Owen died last summer."

The screams.

The music.

The brakes.

The screeching.

The metal being hit.

"There was a car accident," I told him. "There was nothing salacious about it, just a run-of-the-mill car accident."

"No car accident is run-of-the-mill," he rasped.

True.

"No drugs. No drinking," I clarified. "Owen was driving me and two of his friends. They were in the back. I was in the front." Here was the hard part.

I didn't want to feel it, so I started closing myself down.

One wall at a time.

"You gotta tell him, sis. For you."

"Owen and I were fighting over the music."

"I don't want to listen to rap," I'd told him.

He'd laughed. *"Whatever. Driver picks the music."*

"I changed the music because I was being stupid," I explained.

"No sad shit, Asp. Come on!" He'd still been laughing.

"We started a little wrestling match, shoving back and forth, and then…"

"Look out!"

"We were going around a curve, and there was a car coming toward us. It was in our lane."

"Oh shit!"

"Owen yanked the wheel, and time slowed down. We missed the car, and it was so weird because I could see them perfectly as we passed. It was a lady, and she'd been reaching back to the seats behind her. She didn't even see us coming, but they did. She had two little kids in their car seats. She saw them see us, and she was starting to turn, but it was done by then."

"Aspen," Blaise breathed.

My throat was so tight, I could barely swallow. I could barely talk.

"Owen held my hand as we hit the metal guard rail on the ditch. The doctors think that's what saved my life, but we don't know. Owen died on impact. One of the guys in the back was tossed from the car, but he ended up being okay. It was a miracle for him, and the other guy just had scrapes and bruises."

I was completely numb, just the way I liked it in moments like these.

I whispered, "I was in the hospital for two months."

"And no one visited you?" His voice came from right behind me.

He had migrated closer. I could feel his heat now.

I found myself leaning back, and one of his arms curled around me, resting low on my hip.

I nodded, my head moving against his shirt. "His friends never came to see me. I thought maybe it was the hospital not letting people visit, but that wasn't the case. My mom and dad were there almost every day. Nate visited too. The days kinda blurred together."

The after.

I turned in his arms and tipped my head back to look at him.

"That's why my parents came back here. They were worried about me the first semester, but now they're on this whole kick to make things right with Nate."

Blaise's other hand came to my hip, holding me against him.

His eyes searched mine. "Why aren't your parents here this weekend, Aspen?"

I felt a rock in my gut.

"My parents aren't bad parents. They're just... They're worka-holics, and when they get into a project they're passionate about, they're really into it."

"They forget you."

I heard his condemnation, and I moved back.

"It's not totally like that."

"It's exactly like that."

I shook my head. "No, it's not. They've just been gone this week. At the beginning of the year, they were here every day. I couldn't move in this house without my mom or dad on me, asking how I was, talking to me about my counseling sessions. They were *overly* in my life, so when they got the green light for this new project of theirs, it was a relief. I could go to school again and pretend to be normal."

I sighed.

It was now.

Now or never.

"I miss my brother. I miss him so much that *after* the acci-dent," a deep breath, "I wish it'd been me. Not him."

I turned.

I closed my eyes, folded my head, tried to disappear in on myself.

The after.

The after when I wanted to disappear and be with Owen.

"Aspen," his voice was so soft, so tender behind me.

"I'm better, but it's a lot. It's why I wanted to be invisible at school, why I was proud of having no one. It's better to have no one to lose than to have that one get ripped from you, and wish it'd been you instead."

"Aspen." His hands came to my shoulder, stepping up behind me. He folded me against him, just holding me. "Do your parents know?"

I shrugged. "Told my counselor. I don't know what she shared with them."

It's done, sis.

A tear fell.

I said, leaning back against him, letting him hold me, "I don't know Nate that well. Our family is so distant."

He was quiet, so I looked up.

His mouth was pressed in a flat line.

He had to understand.

I pulled away, turning to him. "I'm not going to our graduation ceremony."

His eyes flared, and he opened his mouth.

I shook my head. "I can't be there. Owen was supposed to graduate with me, and he won't be there. And no one here knows him. No one knows me. My parents have forgotten about graduation, and I want them to keep forgetting. I'm going to tell them next week after it's all done, and I know they'll feel bad. They'll want to throw me a party, but it hurts too much. Owen was my best friend, and I... I don't want to celebrate these things without him. It's too hard. It's too painful."

There.

That was it. That was all of it.

I could wait now.

Would he understand? Would he push it?

I hoped he wouldn't.

I didn't have the energy to argue anymore.

Blaise sighed and brought his forehead to rest against mine. "Babe, that's why you *have* to celebrate these things. I don't know your brother. You've barely talked about him, but I've got a strong feeling he would want you to walk across the stage."

No, no, no.

I tried to pull away.

His hand tightened, and he moved even closer, his lips just above mine. "I don't care how you slice it in your head, if he loved you, he'd want this for you." A beat. "He would want you to do it *for* him."

36

BLAISE

I woke the next morning, and I had to make decisions today. Hard decisions.

I wasn't excited about any of it.

Aspen had her head tucked into my arm, and she was hugging me like an octopus. I grinned. So cute.

But damn.

I needed to be an asshole today.

After she talked last night, we went to bed, but we'd only cuddled. I wanted to know more about Owen, more about all of her family, and once she'd opened the dam, the rest came flooding out. I don't think she dozed off until around five in the morning.

It was now nine-thirty, and if I was going to do what I was going to do, I needed to get to it.

Pressing a soft kiss to her forehead, I eased out of bed. I grabbed my clothes, went to one of the guest bedrooms, and used the bathroom there to clean up. My head was killing me. My neck was stiff. I didn't even want to look in the mirror, I knew there'd be bruises there I didn't want to see.

Fuck. I was sore.

I popped some painkillers and headed for the kitchen. Coffee was needed like I needed an IV bag.

I was checking my phone, heading to the main level when I heard a door open and shut.

I couldn't remember if Aspen had said what days Miss Sandy and Benny had off. Was it the weekend? Or just Sunday? I knew they weren't usually around that day... I also remembered her brother Nate was in town. And he'd promised to meet her here.

Walking into the kitchen, I realized that time was here.

He was pouring some coffee when he noticed me.

"Well..." He turned, leaning a hip against the counter. "If it isn't the punk kid who took my sister away from me."

I smirked.

I couldn't help it. It was a reflex.

"Right. Because me staying in that environment would've been cool for who again? You?" I shook my head. "By the way, where the fuck have you been all Aspen's life?"

His eyes narrowed, and his glare turned icy. "You might want to watch the attitude. I've squashed assholes bigger than you."

"You think I care about that?"

I didn't know much about Nate Monson—he was best friends with Mason Kade, and Zeke talked way too much about that guy, so mostly I'd tuned him out. I'd gotten the gist. And that gist was that he and his friends could handle their own against a lot of enemies. They weren't afraid to piss someone off, and they weren't afraid to fight.

Right.

Respect there, but I didn't give a fuck in this situation.

The more I'd listened to Aspen talk last night, the more furious I'd become.

This fucker. He and his parents—all fucks.

"Graduation is tomorrow," I growled.

His nostrils flared, but that was only his reaction.

"She's gotta go. She has to do it for him."

He still didn't say a word.

I snorted. Whatever. This guy was going to help Aspen make a mistake she'd regret.

Fine. Moving on 'cause I had more. I had a whole bunch more.

"Your parents know Aspen hasn't been in school the entire last week? I've slept here more than I should've been without one of them knowing, and guess who has noticed? Sandy. Guess who hasn't told the people who should be told? Sandy." Yeah. I was saying shit I shouldn't be saying. Aspen would be so pissed at me, but I was seeing red.

I was seeing the girl she must've been after her car accident.

I was hearing her words in my ears.

"...I wished it'd been me, not him."

"...why I was proud of having no one."

I was gritting my teeth.

Anger, furious and blistering white-hot anger was racing through me, boiling my blood.

"It's better to have no one to lose than ... wish it'd been you instead."

"She needs her family. She needs to not be proud not to have anyone."

His jaw was clenched. He was scowling at me.

I forced myself to stop, because crap, I'd said too much. I showed her hand, my girl's hand and she could be royally livid with me if she wanted.

I prayed she wouldn't. I hoped she'd understand.

"When's it my turn to get pushed away?"

I winced, hearing her words against me come back again.

Never, I vowed. I'd never push her away. I'd hold on, hold on as long as I possibly could keep her.

I had to get out of there or I'd say more and anything I'd say now would not be beneficial for my relationship.

"She's smart, you know."

I turned back.

He looked down his nose at me, holding his coffee and leaning against the counter as if he hadn't a worry in the world.

He took a sip, speaking like I was dirt. "She's smarter than you'll ever be. She's the genius in the family."

"I'm aware." I flashed him a hard grin. "Smarter than both of us."

He grunted, but his mouth twitched. "Look, she'll be tortured if she goes to that ceremony tomorrow. And I get why she didn't want our parents to know. She and Owen were close, like, really close. It's the only reason I was able to leave them, 'cause I knew they'd have each other."

Anger sparked in me. "But that's not a thing now, so where the fuck have you been all year?"

He went still, eerily still. "You might want to watch your tone with me."

"You might want to clue in about your sister. She's been alone all year."

His nostrils flared again, and his head lowered.

He thought he could pin me down? Make me scared?

He'd never dealt with me.

"She's got no friends—had no friends," I continued. "And where is her family? Miss Sandy. Benny. They're her family. They're the ones who've met me. I've had meals with them. They know how I like my coffee." I lifted my chin. "And you're a special class of brother if you think she should skip her own graduation because of the brother who's go—"

"What?" he suddenly demanded.

I paused.

I'd gone too far.

His voice came back low. "*Her* graduation?"

I paused.

I frowned. "Yeah. Her graduation. She graduates tomorrow." Then it fell into place. *He didn't know.* "She was moved up a year. She told me last night."

His hand jerked, spilling coffee over his shirt.

He didn't move. He didn't seem to notice the coffee.

"She's graduating tomorrow?" He looked down. "When?"

Dude. "Tomorrow."

He looked back up. "Not the graduation, dipshit. When did she move up a grade?"

I opened my mouth...

And Aspen answered from the doorway. "The year after you left us."

Damn. Regret seared through me, and I turned to her.

Her eyes weren't on me, though. They were on her brother, and they were full of pain.

"Aspen." I moved toward her.

She held a hand up. "You told him I don't have friends. You told him everything. That wasn't your information to share."

I held still.

I had.

If I held still long enough, could I turn time backwards? Could I take that back?

"I'm sorry."

She shook her head.

I'd fucked up. Big time.

"I already knew," Nate said.

"I've always been like this." She turned to him. "It's why they moved me up a year. You left, and I was having... I don't actually think it was about how smart I was." She looked away, hugging herself. She looked like she wanted to disappear. "They moved me up a year so I'd have Owen."

Nate coughed, his voice sounding strained. "Aspen. I didn't know."

She lifted a shoulder. "To be blunt, it wasn't your problem. It was Mom and Dad's." She bit out an ugly laugh. "It was my problem. No one else's. I should've... I should've dealt with it a long time ago." She rocked back and forth, biting her lip.

I recognized that look.

"Tell him about *after*," I said.

Her shoulders went rigid, and she shook her head. "Don't, Blaise. Don't push that." She swung back to me, and I could see a ghost in her eyes. "I lost my parents. I lost my older brother. I lost my best friend. I've lost everyone in my life. What can you say about that? You've got people in your life. You lost an abuser, but you gained two siblings. You gained a new father. Do you know how many times I'd die for that chance again? To have Owen back?" She wiped away a tear. "You have no idea, and you keep pushing them away. Stop. I've cyberstalked your brother and sister. They're both really cool people. I met him, and he was kind to me. There aren't a lot of kind people out there."

Yeah.

I knew.

Because I wasn't one of them.

Pain radiated through me, and I couldn't do a damn thing to take away hers. Nothing. I was fucking helpless as I watched the girl I loved cry in front of me. And some of that pain was my fault.

Love.

Shit.

Yes. Love. Loved. I loved this girl.

Mine.

"Aspen."

"Stop." She turned away. "I'm good for the day. I know you probably have parties you want to go to—"

"Don't do that." I moved toward her.

"Watch it," Nate said.

I ignored him, standing right behind her.

"Aspen."

She wouldn't look at me.

"I'm sorry I spoke about you to your brother. I know it doesn't mean much, but it's because I care. It's because..." My chest was so tight. She still wasn't looking at me.

I dropped it.

I didn't want to tell her when she was like this, when she was hurting. Those words weren't meant to put a Band-Aid over a wound. They were more. They meant *more* to me.

She meant more to me.

This girl, who was curled in on herself and looking like she wanted the world to swallow her whole, had the power to gut me. One look from her. One touch from her. One word from her, and I could be on top of the world or ready to dive into hell—all for her and all because of her.

"Hey." Her brother straightened from the counter. "Let's, um, let's table this for now. Your name is Blaise?"

I jerked my head up. "Yeah."

He looked suddenly tired, and he ran a hand over his face. "If you don't mind, could I have some time with my sister?" He watched her a moment. "It seems like we have a lot to discuss, things I need to make amends for."

Aspen's head fell.

I wanted to take her in my arms.

I wanted to take her away from here, back upstairs, somewhere private. I wanted to kiss her, make her feel good, but fuck —I'd felt helpless before. There'd been a lot of dark times, and this was one of them. And I should've had the words to make it better. I didn't.

When Aspen didn't say anything, I went to her.

"I got things I want to say to you too."

She drew in a breath, her teeth clenched.

I pulled her close and pressed a kiss to her forehead.

My chest was full, tight. There was something I wanted to say, but I didn't. I didn't know if I could.

I left.

37

ASPEN

"Nice guy." Nate grinned at me. "He's got a bright future ahead of him."

I swore at him. "Like you were any better?"

He let out a sputtering laugh. "I think I just met myself."

I shrugged. "He's got reason to have that attitude." I moved around the kitchen island, pulling out a mug. Nate stepped aside so I could pour some coffee. "You had attitude too. Remember that?"

He eyed me, taking a sip of his coffee. "How old were you then? How do *you* remember?"

I grinned, pulling out some creamer. "I idolized you and Owen. I remember everything you guys did."

He groaned. "I'm actually embarrassed."

I laughed lightly.

It felt good.

It felt...right. And that was weird.

I sipped my coffee. "Why'd you come early this weekend?"

He shrugged, hiding a yawn behind his mug. "I decided to come early." He was quiet a moment. "I didn't know you'd moved up a grade." His eyes lingered on me. "Why didn't you tell me you'd be missing your own graduation?"

I scoffed. "You're right, Nate. I *must* be the genius in this family if you can't figure that one out. You would've said something to Mom and Dad, and you all would've made me go."

"Well, yeah. I mean, I agree with your boyfriend. He told me before he realized I didn't know *you* were graduating this year. I agree with the punk." Nate scowled. "Owen would want you to do it, and you know that. It's why you didn't say anything."

He didn't get it.

No one did. Even Blaise.

Especially Blaise.

Owen would've understood.

"I'm a loser."

"Aspen." Nate put down his mug.

I moved away, turning away. "No. I am. I mean, I just am. Girls either didn't like me—even in elementary school—or they only liked me for Owen. You and he were popular. I wasn't. I've always been 'off' from the mainstream, you know? School was where Owen succeeded socially. Not me. That wasn't for me, and I don't want to go tomorrow because Owen should've been there. And there would've been cheers for him, party plans. And it wouldn't have mattered to me that none of them were my friends, because they were Owen's. None of those people will be there tomorrow. I'm the loser, and I'll get polite claps. And that'll hurt, because I'll feel like I didn't live up to his memory. Like I was supposed to fill his shoes or something, like I should get all the cheers for him, you know? Does that make any sense?"

Nate was quiet a beat. "I'll cheer for you."

I snorted. "A pity cheer."

"No," he barked. "No, Aspen. Not a fucking pity cheer. You're my sister, and I've been an asshole absent brother. Jesus. I'm sorry. I'm so sorry, but your boyfriend is right. You should go tomorrow, and I don't care who cheers for you and who doesn't. I will. I know your boyfriend will, and based on the two wonderful meetings I've had with him, I've got a feeling he's going to make *everyone* cheer for you."

I grinned because he would. That was a Blaise thing to do.

"But it's not—"

"Owen would want you to. That's really the only answer you need. You have to, for him." His voice dropped, growing hoarse. "I know we're not that close, and that's something I want to change, but you have to know that I only left you and Owen in Hillcrest because it was you *and* Owen. You two always had each other. I knew you guys were good as long as the other was around. And when he died last year—I don't know." He rubbed his hand over his face. "I've been so involved in other people's families that I've forgotten my own. I forgot you. I'm sorry for that."

Well...

That was nice to hear.

I almost felt like yodeling, that's how nice it was. I never yodeled.

"Wanna go camping with me?" I asked on a whim.

He laughed. "Wait. You're serious?"

I nodded. "I really like camping."

Nate's lips pressed together. "I'm not a big camping person."

Oh. I looked down.

He sighed. "Fuck's sake. Really? Camping?" He gestured out the window. "What about your boyfriend? He thinks you're pissed at him."

I grinned. "He kinda threw me under the bus. He can sweat a little."

Nate's eyes narrowed. His top lip began to curl. "He doesn't seem like the type who wants to sweat about hurting his girlfriend."

"He'll get over it." I shrugged. "Nate. Too much talking. More camping. Let's get a move on. You owe me for all these years of forgetting about me."

He groaned. "Why do I have a feeling you're going to throw that in my face a whole bunch more?"

"Because I will." I was smiling so hard now. "Until you no longer owe me."

He bit out a laugh, but he didn't gripe the entire time we were packing Maisie.

I wasn't really going to make my brother camp with me, but he didn't need to know that. We would drive out to a campsite, and he could set everything up. I'd make him hang out with me for a bit, and then I'd text Blaise where to come.

Nate could go back to town, and I could spend another night with my boyfriend.

And then, tomorrow afternoon, I'd do what they all wanted.

I'd graduate for Owen.

But I didn't want to dwell on that just yet. I had a day of camping first.

38

BLAISE

I figured since Aspen was dealing with family, I should too.

When I swung into my driveway, my mom's Prius was parked outside, and so was Stephen's car. There was another car too, but I didn't know who it belonged to.

I heard voices as soon as I went inside, but when the door shut behind me, they quieted.

A chair pushed back over the floor.

"Blaise?" my mom called.

"Yeah." I didn't want to deal with this.

My mom came down the hallway. "Hey." She seemed tentative. "Hi. How are you?" She started to reach out, but paused. "What?! Your face."

I winced. "No. I'm fine."

"But—"

"I'm good, Mom. I'm fine."

"Blaise."

"Mom. Seriously. Not now." I gentled my tone. "Okay?"

She stared at me, her hands wringing together. Then, she stepped close and gently pulled me in for a hug. "Oh, honey. I'm so sorry."

It seemed like an eternity had passed since that night. She acted like she hadn't seen me in months.

I hugged her back. She was my mom.

As soon as she felt my arms, she started crying.

"Oh, God. Mom."

She gave me another big squeeze before she stepped back. She tried to wipe her tears all dainty like, as if she could absorb them without messing up her makeup.

I shook my head, grabbing a Kleenex. I dabbed it against her face. "Hold still."

I cleaned her up, and she laughed a little when I was done. "You've always done that for me—kept your mother looking good and sane."

I grunted. "Ship's long gone for that, Mom." I gave her a look. "For both of us." I started to move past her.

"Hey." She blocked me. "Where've you been?"

"We talked about this. He was here."

"I know, but he's not anymore, and you've still been gone." She frowned and moved closer, dropping her voice. "Is there— are you in trouble?"

"What? No. I'm not in trouble." *For once.* "I'm fine. Just been partying a lot. That's all."

"He has a girlfriend," said a voice from behind her.

Seriously?

Taz had come to stand by the fridge in the kitchen. She gave me a smug look and tossed her hair back. "And he's been fighting with Cross."

"Honey."

I ignored my mom and glared at my sister. "Snitch."

Taz just grinned, moving back into the kitchen. "Come and eat, brother. You're late for brunch."

I gave my mom a look. "Brunch?"

She ran a hand down my back before giving me a firm pat on the shoulder. "Your sister brought her boyfriend over."

"Yeah." Taz took a bowl of biscuits to the table as I entered the kitchen. She set it down and filled her glass with orange juice. "We're talking about graduation parties. I'm having one for me and Cross, whether he wants it or not—and whether he knows it's happening or not."

Stephen sat next to my mom's chair. Sure enough, Taz's boyfriend was sitting at the table too.

"Come on, Blaise. Sit." My mom made it sound like I didn't have a choice. "You owe me two weeks. The least you could do is have brunch with us."

I needed coffee. With whiskey.

I held up a finger and disappeared into the kitchen for a moment. I couldn't find the whiskey, but I grabbed the brandy.

Taking my drink, I went back over and sat.

"It's nice that you didn't ask Zeke to brunch," Taz said.

I had my phone in my hand under the table. I smiled at her. "Uh-huh."

Me: Brunch. My house. Asap.

My phone buzzed two seconds later.

Zeke: On it.

Taz gave me a look. "You just texted him, didn't you?"

"Uh-huh." I gave her a closed-mouth smile, sipping my coffee. I needed more brandy.

"Uh, so..." My mom folded her hands together, resting her elbows on the table and smiling brightly at everyone. "We're only missing Cross and Bren. Then we'd have a full table."

My phone buzzed again.

Aspen: I'm making Nate go camping with me. I'm not mad at you. I'll call later, okay?

A whole buttload of tension left my body. I almost felt light-headed.

Me: Okay. I meant what I said.

Aspen: Come camping tonight.

Me: Tell me when and where, I'll be there.

Aspen: I will.

Taz cleared her throat. "Hello? Excuse us, Blaise. Are we boring you or something?"

The world felt right again, so I grinned and sassed back. "You don't know me well enough to think of me like that, so that makes me think your real brother's given you that complex, not me." I gave her a dark look. "Stop putting your brother issues on me. I'm not your twin's replacement."

Her boyfriend started coughing and shot me a look.

I smiled at him too.

His name was Race, and he seemed like a decent guy. He came from money, and he was part of Roussou's underground fighting ring, but that was all I knew about him.

"You're a dick," he told me.

I shrugged. I was. It'd been a dick thing to say. "Honesty. It can be a weapon."

My mom looked down, her eyes closed. I could almost hear her counting for patience.

And Stephen just looked at me. His eyes were clear, no judgment, nothing clouding them.

So why not? "I have to ask, Stephen. Did you divorce your wife in the hopes of starting a new family with my mom and me?" I gave him a questioning look. "Because you missed the boat with us. I've met your other son. You're better off with him."

"Blaise!" My mom's chair scraped against the floor, and she grabbed my arm, yanking me out of my seat.

I was more surprised than anything.

I went with her, and she dragged me to the back hallway, toward her room. Deviating to the basement, I jogged down the stairs and veered into my room.

She trailed me. "I don't understand why you're always so mean. That man upstairs stood up for you—"

I gave her a scowl, rifling through my drawers. "I don't need anyone standing up for me." I grabbed a bag and began filling it with clothes and shit. "And if he hadn't beat the shit out of Griffith, I would've. Learned how to fight back in New York out of necessity, Mom. You were just usually too baked out of your head to notice."

Toiletries.

What else would I need for tomorrow?

A suit.

Crap. Had I even brought any suits from New York?

I headed for the closet.

She followed me, standing in the doorway. "I was not baked out of my head."

"You were—stoned, wasted, drunk. Does it matter? I don't blame you." I tempered this with a smile as I put my hands on a suit I hadn't remembered I even owned.

Shit. Would I actually need this? I should take it, just in case. I moved past her, tossing it on the bed and headed back to the closet.

"He was abusive. He was verbally and emotionally abusive to you, and he was verbally, mentally, emotionally, and physically abusive to me. That's the way the cookie crumbled. It was life. We dealt with it. You divorced him, and now he's out of our lives. So yay you, Mom. You did stand up for me. You don't have to have any guilt there anymore." I grabbed a bunch of clothes and paused to pat her shoulder, giving her a wide smile. "Thumbs-up, Marie."

"Fuck you," she hissed.

I was being a dick, such a dick, but I was numb to it.

I wanted distance.

I wanted away.

I wanted Aspen, but I couldn't have Aspen so I'd pack, go to Zeke's, and get wasted. When Aspen called, I'd get a ride to her or I'd sober up so I could drive to her, and then I'd be okay again.

"What is wrong with you?" my mother asked.

I smirked. "Lots. We know this."

She sucked in a ragged breath, and I saw the tears.

Hell. I hated when she cried. I really hated it.

I tried to tune her out, but I heard her say, "I am sorry, Blaise."

I paused, not seeing what I was stuffing into the bag.

She kept crying. "I didn't protect you from him, and I'm sorry. I'm so sorry, for everything. I wanted you for myself. I was scared Stephen would take you from me. I'm..." She hesitated. "I went to see a therapist this past week."

I stood there, holding whatever was in my hand, and I didn't move.

I didn't dare move.

"It felt good, talking about everything. I'm going to go again. I actually—" A sad laugh came from her. "—have it set up for the next six months. She thought I needed that many sessions considering what we left behind, you and me."

I closed my eyes.

"Stephen's the one who suggested her. He said he went to see her right after he left his ex. He said Taz is thinking about seeing her too."

She was going to take a knife and drag it across my chest. I was just waiting...

"I can't control you. You have your own money. You're eighteen. You have more power as an adult now than I ever felt I had, so I'm not going to try to be your parent. Not now. I messed that up by staying with him for so long."

I knew tears were still sliding down her face. But she sounded strong. She sounded resigned.

I'd never heard my mother sound like that.

After a moment, she shifted gears. "Taz said you have a girlfriend?"

My eyes opened, and I looked down. I'd been holding a pair of socks. Snorting, I tossed them aside and rifled through the bag. What the hell had I even thrown in here?

"What's her name?"

None of your business.

What the hell else did I need?

"Where'd you meet her?"

I dropped the bag and turned around. "I'm not talking about her."

"Okay. Yeah." She tried to smile, but those tears.

I hated when she cried. Cursing, I hauled my mom into my arms.

She sniffled, tensing, but I cradled the back of her head, and that was enough. She dissolved in my arms.

I didn't know if that was right or not. It was what it was.

I waited until she had stopped crying. Zeke would be here by now. I pulled back and smiled down at her. "Cheer up, Mom. You got a pain-in-the-ass son who will someday not be such a pain in the ass."

She laughed, flicking the last of her tears away.

"And it seems you have a good guy upstairs." I bent down, resting my forehead to hers. "I will try to not be such a dick."

Pulling away, I studied her.

"You like Taz, huh?"

She smiled, bobbing her head. "I do. She's a good girl, just lonely. I can understand that."

A bit of my wall crumbled. I didn't like thinking of my mom as lonely.

"I think counseling will be good for you, Mom."

Her eyes turned sad, and she eased back a step. She cupped the side of my face. "You're such a handsome boy. I got lucky having you. Real lucky. Despite the things you say, you've always taken care of me when I needed it."

I batted away her hand. "Okay. Sentimental shit is my cue to leave."

She reached up and held the sides of my face. "Let me say this. I know you are hurting. I know I can't help you with that, but I also know you persevere. That's your trait. You're always strong, and you always get through whatever it is you're dealing with. And I can't take credit for that. That's you. That's all you, and I want you to be proud of that."

Her eyes flicked to the ceiling and back to mine. "As for them, and the changes in our lives, it'll all work out. I just want you to keep working on you. And whoever this girl is, I can tell she's good for you. I've always seen fragments of the man you'll become, and lately, I've been seeing more and more of them. You will become a man I'm proud of, and I know this because you're already a son I'm so proud of." She hugged me tightly. "So proud of you."

I let her hug me.

"Mom, I can't be a dick with you being a Pinterest hologram and saying all this cheesy shit." But I grinned as I straightened a strand of her hair.

I loved my mom.

I might be a massive dick, but everything she'd said was right.

I pressed a kiss to her forehead and whispered, "Love you."

Zeke was standing in the hallway just inside the back door when I came up from the basement.

His face lit up when he saw me. "Bruh!"

"Let's head."

His face faltered. "Dude. Brunch?"

"I'll pay."

"Dude." He grinned again, and we left.

I tried to tell myself I wasn't being a pansy when I pulled my phone out later and texted Taz.

Me: Congrats on your graduation tomorrow. I'll come to your party if you want me there.

39

ASPEN

Nate kept trying to talk me into letting him rent a camper. He was allergic to tents, he'd explained, but not campers. He loved campers. The whole time was like that. Nate making a joke. Me laughing. Then we'd descend into silence with awkward looks.

I didn't know my brother. Not really.

I knew this, but knowing it and experiencing it were two different things.

It was sad, to be honest. I wished I knew him. I wished I knew him how I knew Owen.

I sighed at one point. "I miss Owen."

Nate had been on his phone, but he looked up and without a word said, he put it away. He leaned back. "I wished I knew Owen how you knew him."

I'm here, dudes.

I grinned. "Some days it's like he never left, and some days it's like he never existed. He was my only friend."

Nate's eyes closed. "Aspen."

"He was funny. He was fun. He was reckless sometimes. He was cocky. He was the popular guy at school. So many girls liked him." Giving Nate a more intense look, I said, "He was like a mix of you and Blaise together."

Nate's mouth turned in, and he was trying to contain his grimace. "Thanks?"

I laughed. "No. Owen was the best of all of us."

Sure. You wouldn't have said that if I was alive. Now I'm dead, and all things are holy Owen.

I grinned, knowing that's what he would've said.

"Aspen." Nate's head was hanging low. He wasn't looking at me, and if he hadn't said my name, I wouldn't have thought he was even talking to me. His tone was far-off, distant. Soft. Regretful. He added, "There's going to be a time when you're going to be mad at me, mad at Mom and Dad." He looked up, his eyes keen and sharp. The regret was there, more prominent. "You *can* be mad. You can be furious with them, and me. I know that's not how you usually roll. Sometimes I think I got all the anger in the family, but I just—you have every right to be angry at us. And when you feel that, you can call me and chew me out. It's deserved on my end, and if you want to chew out Mom and Dad, I will be there. I will back you up. Fuck." He shook his head. "I might do it myself because they deserve it. I missed out on you and Owen. I really missed out on Owen, and I'm--" He choked off, blinking rapidly. "I'm just so sorry."

The words weren't just for me. I knew it in my gut. I felt it in my bones.

You hearing this, Owen? Those words are for you too.

I'm hearing this. Dumbass doesn't know I'm still around. Haunting his pasty buttcheeks.

I snorted, hanging my head down.

"What?" Nate was half grinning, half frowning. A confused look in his gaze.

"It's nothing. Just, if Owen were here, he'd probably say he's haunting your pasty white buttcheeks."

You left out 'dumbass.'

Nate laughed, tipping his head back. "That actually makes me feel good. I think he would like a few of my friends."

"Yeah. Probably."

It was later that night when I let Nate off the hook.

Blaise pulled up, and my brother was so relieved. It was almost comical.

He couldn't leave quickly enough.

Hugs were given. Promises were made to see each other the next day, and that's when I told him that I was going to attend the graduation ceremony.

Nate looked like he was about to cry, but he gave me one more hug, hit Blaise on the shoulder with a threat to keep me safe, and then he was gone. After that, Blaise and I got ready for bed.

We crawled into the sleeping bag and he went first, telling me about his mom.

I told him about my time with Nate.

Blaise nodded. "You deserve that."

Then he kissed me, and there wasn't much talking after that.

I wasn't shocked later the next afternoon when they called my name at graduation that there were *two* roars of cheering—one from where my brother sat with some of his friends, and the other from where Blaise and Zeke sat. Both stood up and hollered, but Zeke ran up and down his aisle, getting everyone to do the wave.

I started crying.

I met Blaise's eyes, and his smile had been so gentle, that I swear there'd been a whole hiccup in my chest.

Then there was the very, very eerie feeling I got as I took my diploma.

The hairs on the back of my neck stood up, and a shiver went down my spine, but I wasn't scared. That shiver wasn't a bad shiver. It was in awareness, and it spread through my entire body.

Owen was here.

He was walking beside me. He received the diploma with me, and he stayed with me the rest of the ceremony. And as much as I hated to admit it, Blaise and Nate were both right. Owen had wanted me to do this for him, and because of him, but that was all I could handle. I was technically the valedictorian of our class. I'd been informed on Friday, but when the principal asked if I wanted to be recognized as the valedictorian, I turned him down.

I'd only moved to Fallen Crest my senior year, and I didn't want to do the speech. Whoever was salutatorian and the third in line deserved it more than I did. They had likely attended Fallen Crest Academy all their lives, and they'd been competing heavily for the top two spots, according to one of the secretaries in the front office who liked to gossip. So I was good with that.

Coming to the ceremony was plenty for me, and afterward was the best part.

I met Blaise's mom, who started crying. And I met Stephen, Blaise's real dad, but after a quick hug, he had to leave. Roussou's ceremony was starting in thirty minutes.

Then Zeke came over and picked me up in a big hug. He twirled me around, and I felt the entire world watching us. Blaise scowled at him, but there was no threat in it. He tucked me under his arm, and the two started trading joke insults.

Nate came over with two friends in tow. One was a big, muscular guy named Matteo. The other was a girl who introduced herself as Grace.

Zeke was beside himself, his eyes all wide and bulging as he turned into a bumbling choirboy.

Nate had told our parents, and it was then that Mom and Dad came over.

Mom was crying. Dad looked like he'd shed a few tears.

He was right. Blaise was right. It was right to have them here.

As much as I didn't confide in my mother, she was my mom. She was Owen's mom too, and as soon as she hugged me, she broke.

This day wasn't about me—that's the thing that hit me.

It was about my family, because we all loved Owen. We'd all lost Owen.

My mom started to pull away, but I held her tight and whispered, "He's here, Mom. I can feel him."

That set her off again, but eventually she pulled back and blinked at Nate.

"I just want all my babies happy."

"Mom." Nate opened his arms, and she went to him. They had their own moment.

My dad caught me up in a hug, and I introduced my parents to Blaise. Their reaction could only be described as cautious. Blaise didn't seem to care. Nate thought it was funny.

Slipping my hand in his, I rested against Blaise's side.

His arm came around my shoulder.

In this moment, everything felt good. Everything felt right.

So why was I worried?

40

ASPEN

We were parked in his Wagon at the recently reopened Fallen Crest drive-in.

Blaise's mouth was on my throat, and moving south. I was about to burst out of my clothes, not to mention my seat.

"Blaise."

I had about three seconds before my mind shut off and I wouldn't give a crap where we were. So I needed to disentangle his arms—and more importantly his mouth—because we were *so* not somewhere that we could move this where we wanted to go.

It had almost seemed a joke when a local business owner had announced his plan to reopen the drive-in, but it'd been up and running for the last two weeks, and based on the number of cars around us, it was proving to be popular. The grand opening had been a week after our graduation—same as the night Blaise's mom had talked him into letting her have a graduation party for him.

It'd been a rocky event.

Marie wanted to go big and bold, and Blaise only wanted Zeke and me there. After a few exchanges, Marie had compromised. We were still getting to know each other, but I liked her. The guest list ended up being Zeke, Brian, Branston (all guys I was starting to get to know and becoming more comfortable around), Stephen (who was lovely), Taz (who I adored instantly), and Taz's boyfriend, Race. He seemed intense.

The last two weeks had been interesting for my family.

Nate had stayed almost the entire week after graduation, because his friends were all coming in the next weekend. So that meant my parents were around the entire week, and since meeting Blaise, my mom was like a dog after a bone. Blaise had attended three family dinners, two family breakfasts, and every time he picked me up, he had to come into the house.

"Pick me up" was a relative concept, because Blaise was still sneaking into the house and sleeping over.

We'd slowed down on the sex, but there'd been a lot of nights of sweaty moans, and a lot of me cursing about why he wanted to slow down. Yes, *he* did. Not me. I was like "get in me now," and Blaise was all, "no, we need to slow down. I have to show you how much I care about you."

For a badass boyfriend, he was ridiculously careful with me.

I knew I loved Blaise, but I hadn't expressed that to him. I started bringing it up, but each time I did, he began kissing me, and I ended up trying to get him to climb into my pants. He'd refrain, and I'd want to curse him.

I was starting to get a complex, about him.

So, I was both surprised and not surprised that he was putting the moves on me now.

We were at the drive-in. And probably he wasn't planning to follow through, because he couldn't, so why was *I* trying to be the responsible one here?

Screw that.

I turned and climbed onto his lap.

He leaned back, his eyes surprised, and I grinned as I straddled him.

His hands went to my legs. "Hey."

Yeah. Turnabout is fair play.

"Hi." I moved forward and began tasting his throat.

"Jesus, Aspen." He groaned.

I grinned, moving down his throat to his chest.

He took deep gulps of air, his hands kneaded my hips.

"You like this?" I asked.

He groaned.

Yes. He liked this. He liked this a whole lot. I could feel him between my legs, and I ground down on him.

I heard a swift intake of breath before he grabbed the back of my hair. "Woman," he warned.

I ignored him. I lifted my head, my mouth finding his just on the end of that warning, and he was gone. He cradled my face in his hands and took over the kiss, commanding me. His tongue slid inside, and I met it with mine.

I loved when we kissed like this.

I loved it even more when I felt him inside of me in other ways, and grabbing his hands, I guided one between my legs. "I want you," I whispered against his mouth.

He tensed, still cupping my cheek with his other hand.

He was trying to clear his head, trying to think clearly. I knew the signs by now, and I wasn't having it. Pushing against his chest, rubbing over him, I reached down and unbuckled my jeans.

"Fuck, Aspen."

He moaned, and his hand tunneled inside.

I lifted up, just slightly, and then his fingers were there.

I sank down, and we both paused at the feel of him inside of me.

Thank God his windows were tinted—a graduation gift from his mom. And that was a fleeting thought before I began to ride his hand.

This. Right here.

Blaise loved making me come. He loved kissing me, he loved

moving down there, his tongue slipping inside, and every time I would shatter in his arms. But in the last two weeks, that was all he'd done for me.

I'd touched him as well, taking him in my mouth a few times, but it was driving me insane. He had avoided telling me what was going on with him, and tonight, I vowed as I moved over him, tonight was the last night I'd let that continue. I *would* get answers.

He tugged down my tank top and found my breast.

Yes. *Oooh.* That felt good

Yes. I would get answers. I would.

But—oh my God!

I was there.

Almost there.

He felt so good.

Oh!

Oh holy hell!

Then, with a different flick of his fingers, I almost screamed and erupted at the same time.

His mouth latched over mine, silencing me, and I shuddered in his arms.

Why had I waited so long to experience that?

I was addicted to Blaise. And his wonderful hands. And his cock. Yes, totally addicted. I'd go through withdrawals if he ever stopped touching me.

I rested against his chest, his hand smoothing through my hair, and fell asleep.

~

"YEAH, DUDE."

Voices woke me up.

I blinked a few times, clearing the fog.

Still on Blaise's lap, I now had a blanket over me. My head

was turned toward the passenger seat, and he was talking to someone out the driver's window. *Zeke.*

"The girls are waving the white flag," he said. "We've not been hanging with them for the last two weeks, but now they've heard we're going dune buggying, and they're all about being 'friendly bitches.'" Zeke started laughing. "So how 'bout it? You and the missus ready to brave the girls now? Pen promised they'd be nice, and you know she speaks for Ria and Deja. Kit's too smart to mess with things. She's going to Cain next year with us. So it's just Daniels, and seriously, that girl's been sexing it up between Conway and Ashlome. I don't think she wants to admit that you don't care she's banging two of your buds."

"We're not really buds anymore."

"Yeah." Zeke got quiet. "I hear ya. So what do you think?"

Blaise stroked the back of my head.

"I'll talk to her. I know you're actually friends with Penny and Ria. This hasn't been fair to you."

Zeke snorted. "Screw that. Pen still hits me up on the phone, and it's not like I haven't had pussy for the last two weeks. That Monica girl has a big throat." He laughed. "Though, she thinks we're still dating. Might do good to let her see me with Penny again. Pen doesn't let any girl think they own me."

"Yeah. I'll talk to Aspen."

"I know she'll be good about it. Your girl is a good one. She wants what you want."

Blaise's arm tightened around me. "Yeah. Maybe."

There was a thump on the door, and Zeke said, "Okay. Get back to your woman. Get her home; she looks tired. I'll hit you up with time and details tomorrow."

The window whirred up. "You think your parents will freak if you sleep at my place?" Blaise asked.

I lifted my head, still feeling drowsy. "Nate flew back to Boston. My parents are deep in edits for the docu-series, so no. But we should stop at my house so I can grab some clothes and make it look like I slept there when Miss Sandy checks my room tomorrow."

I tipped back and smiled up at him. "How'd I get so lucky to have you care about me?"

His eyes darkened. He traced every inch of my face with his eyes, and my body warmed, tingling with each second that passed. "How about we go to my place and I'll further explain how much I care about you?"

I sat up, my mouth just over his. "That sounds perfect."

As we kissed, I renewed my vow: *answers.* I was going to get them. Plus, I knew he had condoms there, though I'd been on birth control since I was fifteen to regulate my periods. We'd had a whole conversation about that. He wasn't a guy that looked queasy when talking about that stuff. I liked that a whole lot.

"When's the trip?" I asked as I slid back over to my seat.

He glanced sideways at me as he pulled out of the drive-in lot. "I knew you were awake that whole time."

"It's Mara, right? Her friends too?"

He was silent for a beat, then shrugged. "Yeah."

"What are you worried about exactly?"

He grunted. "Them being assholes to you. Isn't that enough? They're catty bitches."

I angled my body toward him and rested my head against the seat. "But isn't that my problem to deal with?"

His hand flexed over the steering wheel. "What do you mean?"

"It's a girl thing. You can't take that on for me."

"They're bitches."

I hid a grin. "That's my problem to handle. You can't control everything."

He swore under his breath. "I can damn sure try. Those girls aren't nice. They're mean. I've seen how they tear into someone. They're vicious."

"Like you have?"

Another jaw clench. "It's not the same."

"Why not?"

"Because it's not you. I don't care about anyone else. What are you doing here? You want me to let those girls go at you? You nuts?"

"No." I laughed. "And I brought you up because no one could control what you say or do to people. And those people either fight back or they don't."

"Babe, I annihilate people. I don't ever want you to be on the end of that from anyone."

"Well, while that makes me feel good, you know people are going to be mean. It's the world out there. And if you think I haven't had to deal with mean girls, you've got your head in the sand."

"The fuck?" He shot me a look. "Who was mean to you?"

"Girls at Hillcrest. They didn't like that I started setting the curve in our classes, especially when I wasn't supposed to be in their grade. Some girls targeted me when Owen didn't want to date them. He was like you, you know." My smile turned sly. "Not promising anything and actually sticking to that, even if the girl got mad, thinking she could trick him into dating her. He wasn't as blunt as you are, but he was honest." I thought a moment. "I think that's why I like when you're blunt."

"Aspen." He took my hand and pulled it back to his leg. He entwined our fingers. "I'm never bluntly honest with you."

My throat tightened at that. "I wish you were, and you were in the beginning."

He glanced over, slowing for a stoplight. "You want me to be a blunt dick to you?"

"Not a blunt dick, but you can be honest. Bluntly honest. I respect that. You have no idea how many people say nothing through lies and pretty words. I hate that stuff. Loathe it."

His gaze dipped to my mouth. "Noted. Does that shit turn you on?"

I barked out a laugh, my throat loosening again. "Maybe. I don't know."

"Jesus." He leaned over. "I think we need to further explore this conversation at my house."

"Yes, please." My lips grazed his, and he applied pressure, starting the swirl of goodness and pleasure in me even as he pulled away.

The light turned green, and he eased forward.

We didn't talk the rest of the drive.

We pulled up at his house after a stop at mine, and his mom's car was parked outside. She never used the garage. There was another vehicle there, and I had learned over the last two weeks that it was Stephen's car.

We could hear laughter as we entered.

Blaise reached behind me, shutting the door and locking it.

"Blaise? Honey, is that you?"

"Yeah, Mom," Blaise called, his hand moving to the small of my back. "Me and Aspen."

The TV silenced.

A chair squeaked.

She came around the corner a second later, smiling warmly. "Hi, Aspen." She took in the bag Blaise held for me, her smile slipping a little. "You're spending the night?"

"Yeah," Blaise answered.

He wasn't asking, but neither of us moved, so we were asking, in a way.

Marie blinked a few times. Her voice came out raspy. "Oh yeah. That's fine." She cleared whatever emotion was pulling at her face and smiled. "I know you like coffee, but do you enjoy donuts, Aspen? I can run to the store and grab some in the morning."

I waited, expecting Blaise to answer for me.

He didn't.

His mom seemed surprised by that too.

I nodded. "Yeah. I'd love that."

I wasn't like Blaise. I was kinda in love with his mom. She'd only been kind to me. She also seemed broken in a way—like now, when she was holding her breath, as if preparing for Blaise's harshness. It didn't come, and she blinked again.

She nodded, her smile growing wider. "Aces. I'll do that then."

Blaise groaned. "Okay, Mom. We'll be downstairs."

She held a hand up, waving. "Do you—do you need anything tonight?"

Blaise eased in front of me, herding his mother back and out of the way.

She backtracked.

I followed.

We went through the kitchen, and I looked over. The television was still paused in the other room. Stephen sat on the couch. He lifted his hand in a wave. "Hello, Aspen."

"Hi."

He didn't greet Blaise. Blaise didn't look over at him.

"Mom, I'll handle it. I'll come up if we need anything."

"Okay, but it's not too late. I can order pizza. Maybe I'll do that? I'll do that. Just in case." She reached for her phone.

Blaise took the phone out of her hands, but he did it gently. "For real, Mom. Don't order food for us. If I get hungry or Aspen wants something, I'll make something here. You don't need to order anything."

"Are you sure?" She looked around him to me. "Aspen, what's your favorite food? I feel like I should know this by now."

I opened my mouth.

Blaise shot me a look, but it was tempered by a slight, crooked grin. "Don't tell her. She'll order it tonight no matter what I say."

I smiled. "Okay."

Marie swatted Blaise's chest. "Oh my gosh. I'm sorry—"

He took her hand, his smile gentle. "I'm fine, Mom. For real. Aspen's favorite food is pizza from a place in Roussou, and I won't let her tell you the toppings because I know you. You'll drive there to pick it up, and we are good. I promise." He pulled her to him, giving her one of those forehead kisses I'd learned he reserved for me and his mom and no one else. "Enjoy your night with Stephen. We will be fine. Promise."

He took my hand and led me past the dining room. We went down to the basement, and Blaise asked over his shoulder, "All that said, do you want pizza?"

I laughed. "I'm good. You know how much I had for dinner."

A burger, fries, *and* a shake. I was still stuffed.

"Good." He let go of my hand, nodding toward his bedroom. "I'll grab some water for us, just in case. You want something else to drink?"

I shook my head, heading inside and going right to his bathroom.

It might seem silly, but I loved this part.

I loved getting ready for bed, knowing I'd be sleeping with him soon. I loved everything about it—dressing for bed, sliding under the covers, him crawling in beside me as he switched the lights off. Then he would pull me into his arms, and if I woke during the night, he was still beside me.

I stared at myself in the mirror.

That girl was alive. She was glowing, and there was happiness in her eyes.

I almost didn't recognize myself.

I knew some people would be upset that Blaise and I were sleeping together, but those people didn't get it. They didn't understand how much we'd already been through, suffered. This was a moment in time for us—or for me at least.

A blip in my life when I wasn't alone, when I had a partner with me.

I didn't know how long it would last.

I didn't know if it would last, but I'd been alone before Blaise. There'd probably be a time when I would be lonely after him, so

I was going to focus on the now. I wasn't going to think about what others would approve or disapprove of. They must have had great lives if they had time to judge mine. And good for them, but that wasn't my reality.

I just wanted to be with him. That was it. And if that brought heartache, I'd survive.

Blaise was my respite. And I hoped, beyond hoped, that this didn't end up being only a small blip in my life, but that was worry for the future.

For now, I got ready for bed and smiled as I felt the excited butterflies in my stomach. They were always there when Blaise was around, or even if I thought of him, and that was a good sign.

That told me I was living. I wanted to do more of that.

I slid under his covers and waited.

41

BLAISE

This wasn't a good idea.

Why had I thought I'd hold back at my place when hers was becoming like torture to me? I was an idiot.

She was settled over me, her mouth moving on mine, riding me. *Goddamn.*

I loved this feeling. I loved this girl.

She could ask me for almost anything, and I'd try to make it happen—anything to make her happy. But I'd been holding back from sliding inside of her. It'd been a looong fucking two weeks. I was nearing the end of my control, though.

What had I been thinking? That the idea of my mom and Stephen upstairs would help me hold back? Yeah. Nothing was helping my restraint, and Aspen was on a mission. Like I hadn't known what she wanted when she straddled me at the drive-in. She'd been working to get my dick in her.

Shit.

Such a fucking crass way to think of it when it was the girl I loved, but at this moment that was all I could think: Dick. Inside. Her.

Now.

Those four words, and in that order.

I almost gasped as she pulled her mouth away from me, sliding down my body. "What are you doing?"

We'd been making out for two hours straight. Two long and intensely pleasurable hours, but I was going to blow. I didn't want her mouth on me when that happened. That was for later, when she was older. *Jesus.* She'd been a virgin, and I'd thrust inside, almost unable to hold back and be gentle. I'd been shaking from the effort, but I never wanted to hurt Aspen. Ever.

Her mouth was on my stomach now, and she pulled my boxer briefs down. That wasn't helping me.

"Oh, whoa, Aspen." I reached for her.

"No." She actually batted my hands away.

"What?"

She ignored me, and oh God, my dick was out. She touched me.

I almost seized, my head throwing back.

Holy fuck. That felt so good. Insanely good.

This wasn't—her mouth closed over me, and I was gone.

Helpless.

She could've asked for my bank information, and I'd have given her the password.

Hell. Hell. Hell.

Oh man.

She sucked like she'd been sucking me all my life.

Whoa. *Shit*. I wasn't going to last long—not like this.

Growling, I sat up and yanked her away. Her mouth popped off in surprise, her eyes wide, but then she saw what I was doing.

She was clean. I was clean. She was on birth control. We'd had a long conversation about that. I wanted to make sure everything was fine with her, but this time, condoms weren't even a thought for me.

I moved her over me, and she opened her legs.

I pulled her down and sheathed inside of her in one continuous motion.

We both froze at the contact.

And then, her hand against my chest, she began moving over me.

Aspen had learned a lot in the last few weeks. Her hips moved back and forth, riding and working me over like *I* was the novice. She watched me, toying with her lip, and I knew she was about to tease the fuck out of me.

She slowed.

I growled, reaching for her hips.

"No." She laughed, stopping completely.

"Aspen." I growled again, this one sounded more savage than I'd intended, and I closed my eyes, trying to calm down. My breaths came at a rapid pace. She was making me lose control.

"No. This is for me," she said. "All me."

I groaned, but damn, this was what she wanted.

And when she came, it was the best fucking thing I'd ever seen.

My girl was stunning.

But now it was my turn, and grabbing one of her tits, I flipped us. She squealed in surprise, but gentle had gone out the door when she took me in her mouth. I rode her hard, and it wasn't long until I felt her come for a second time in my arms, and I let myself go right after her.

My lips found her throat, and I kissed her.

What the fuck did I ever do right to get her?

IN THE MORNING, after we showered together, she trapped me.

She'd been touching me, kissing me, and I took her over the counter. I was weak. I was whipped.

Then, as we were both dressing, she said, "I want to know why."

I knew what she was asking. She wanted to know why we hadn't been having sex the last couple weeks.

I didn't want to talk about it. I hauled a shirt over my head, yanked it down, and shrugged. "I don't know."

I started for the door.

"Oh no." She raced for it, getting there fast.

I glared at her, but she was cute. Hella cute.

She stuck her lip out, trying not to smile at me, her hands on her hips. In a tank top, no bra, and cute shorts with a bow on them, she was not giving me the intimidating look I knew she was trying for.

I reached down, slid my hand inside her shirt, and cupped her breast. She gasped, her eyes closing, and I leaned into her. She pushed back against the door, and I nuzzled her just under her chin. I'd learned it was the spot I liked the best. If I kissed her at just the right angle, her entire body would shiver in my arms.

I murmured over her neck. "Knowing my mom, she probably has an entire spread upstairs waiting for us—complete with homemade lattes and gourmet cappuccino, if that's a thing."

She shivered, just as I knew she would, but she pushed me away. "No. I want to know."

I sighed. "Aspen."

"Blaise." She grabbed my chin, yanking me down to look at her.

There was a lot of glaring.

"I want to know," she said again. "Honesty—I deserve that, and you know it."

Damn. She was right. But I still didn't want to.

I did anyway. "We're moving fast, and you only told me two weeks ago how old you really are."

My words even sounded stilted to me.

Her hand fell, and I saw the hurt flare in her eyes as she looked away.

"Hey."

She stepped out from my arms, ducking behind me.

I whirled with her. "Hey."

She hugged herself. "You weren't thinking like that when you touched me last night and this morning."

"I'm a guy, but I'm trying here. I'm trying to be honorable."

She frowned, her eyebrows pulling together. "Honorable?"

"You're young. I'm a really big dipshit. I just—I'm too selfish to walk from you, and I'm not going to. But I don't want to... I don't know."

"What?"

Hurt her?

Harm her?

Ruin her?

I felt like I was going to do all three of those things, but I couldn't deny her. Never that. That'd be like ripping my own heart out.

"I'm just trying to do the right thing here. For once in my life."

Her eyes narrowed. She chewed at her lip. I hated when she did that, because then I wanted to chew at her lip. She shook her head, slowly. "Well, stop. That's stupid."

I laughed. "That's stupid? Trying to do the right thing?"

"Yeah." Her hands came to my waist and her fingers tucked into my jeans. "We're together, right?"

"Fuck yeah." This girl had such power over me. I cupped the back of her neck, unable to hold back the surge of possession I felt. She was mine. Mine to protect. Mine to care for. All mine.

A smug-but-happy look pulled at her mouth, and her eyes twinkled. "Then stop with this bullshit of holding back from me. I don't like it. I actually detest it."

I lifted my head. "You detest it?"

"I like your honesty. The problem is you think being honest is being mean. You don't get that being honest is actually being kind. If someone else doesn't want that truth, that's on them. That's not me. I respect honesty, whether it hurts or not. Be honest with me. Don't change because you assume I can't handle it."

Crap. She was right.

"Okay." But *fuuuck*. "Are you sure?"

"Stop." Her fingers moved deeper in my jeans. "Got it?"

"Got it."

She yanked me back to her, her mouth already angling up to meet mine.

It was a little longer before we went up to breakfast.

L ater that day, I sat in Blaise's Wagon, waiting.
That seemed to be the theme for the day.
We went to Zeke's, and waited.
We drove to the parking lot, and waited.
We waited even longer.

Then we went to a camping place, and waited. Or I waited. Blaise got out, going inside with Zeke and a couple of the other guys. So far eight other vehicles had joined us.

Then Blaise came over with Zeke, and both stared at me long and hard.

"Yeah?" Was the world ending, and they didn't know how to tell me?

Blaise closed his eyes, tipping his head back.

Zeke's grin was wide, and he clapped Blaise on the back. "So, your boy and I had a discussion inside. Guess what we decided?"

Blaise's eyes opened and they were bleak, seriously bleak.

Zeke was loving this. "We rented another camper, for guests."

"Guests?"

Blaise shook his head, cursing.

"The girls coming with us are bitchy," Zeke explained. "That's just how they are, and you're coming with us, so I talked Blaise into getting some allies. Guess who we invited?"

I waited again. "Who?"

He nudged Blaise, who answered, "My siblings are coming, with their entourages."

Entourages? "Who are they?"

Zeke pounded Blaise once more on the back before turning to walk away. "This should be fun," he called over his shoulder. He whistled all the way back to his truck.

Blaise got in, and we waited once again.

"What's happening?" I asked.

"There's a spot we can go dune buggying not far from here, but Zeke and the guys want to camp. We rented campers for everyone, and now we're waiting for my brother to show up with his group."

"You don't want them to come?"

He shrugged, sighing. "I don't know. It's...it'll make Taz happy, I know that much."

What was I missing here? "Why would you need allies if these are your friends?"

"For you."

"What?"

"You mentioned meeting my brother and his friends, remember?"

"Yeah?"

"Well, Bren still has a hard-on for you. Figured you could do to have some backup."

"Oh." Warmth spread through me. "You did that for me?"

"Taz and Bren are not actually bad people to hang with. I'm more worried about Cross' two other friends starting fights. They can be dicks."

I snorted. "Then they'll fit right in."

Blaise grinned at that, and that made me grin back.

We ended up waiting an hour before a large truck pulled in,

with another truck beside it. Cross hopped out, heading over to Blaise's window, and Blaise rolled it down.

Cross stopped, looking past Blaise to me and giving me a nod. "We're here," he said. "Bren wants to do this."

Then four large campers and one smaller one pulled out from behind the main building. Each had its own driver.

Blaise nodded toward them. "We rented one of those for your group. The rest are for us."

"Okay, but what's the setup?" Cross watched the campers roll by.

Zeke's truck started off, picking up the trail behind the last camper. He slowed, saluted us with two fingers, and proceeded forward.

"None of us has the license to drive those things, so their drivers are taking them out. They'll get them set up. We'll use 'em for the night or two nights, and they'll come back to get them. You guys are here for—" Blaise motioned to me. "Thought maybe Taz and your girl wouldn't mind a camping night with their men?"

Cross' eyes skimmed over me, narrowing slightly.

It was eerie how similar these two were. Besides their looks, I could see both were smart, both were alphas, and I was pretty sure both were not to be messed with.

"Food? Water? Booze? That shit?"

Blaise shrugged. "We'll stop at a store somewhere."

Cross nodded and let out a silent sigh. "You remember us?" he asked me.

"Hi! Yeah." I waved.

Blaise's mouth twitched, but he looked down at the steering wheel.

My greeting had come out a bit too excited. But this was Blaise's brother, and this was a big deal. A mundo deal. And yeah, he was almost as hot as Blaise. The two together? *Lethal.*

"You remember my girlfriend? Bren?"

I nodded, trying to keep it cool.

Blaise's shoulders were starting to shake, just slightly.

"Yeah. Bren. She's nice."

Now Cross' lips were twitching. "Uh-huh. Yeah."

I just smiled. That seemed the best option here.

"Okay." Cross stepped back. "We'll follow you guys, but I can't guarantee Z and Jordan will play nice."

Blaise's eyes darkened. "Just keep to your side of the campsite, yeah?"

Cross' face grew frosty. He didn't answer, just walked back to the large truck. He climbed into the backseat, and I got a glimpse of his girlfriend inside.

I sucked in my breath. I'd forgotten how beautiful she was.

Blaise raised his window, eased the Wagon around, and we began to leave the lot. We were the last besides those two other vehicles. The others had followed Zeke.

"Who are Z and Jordan?" I asked.

"My brother's moron friends."

I jerked forward. "Wait! I remember them. The shorter one was a dick to me, asked if I had problems or something."

"What?" Blaise turned to look at me sharply.

Oh, crap.

I felt the air in the truck roll with danger. Tension.

I swallowed, leaning back. A shiver went down my spine. "It was nothing. He just, well, he asked if I had problems socializing, and I do actually. I don't think he meant it to be mean." I lowered my voice, "You asked the same thing, Blaise."

He bit out a hard laugh. "Yeah, but I give a fuck about you."

He didn't bring up the topic the rest of the drive, but when we stopped an hour later for provisions, he glared at the shorter guy that got out of the truck with Cross in it.

Zeke noticed too and nudged Blaise. "What's up?"

"I'll tell you later," Blaise said under his breath, moving forward into the store.

Zeke glanced at me in question.

I hesitated. "The shorter one was kinda mean to me once. I might've mentioned it without thinking."

Zeke's eyes got wide. "Right on. Looks like we're having a rumble tonight."

Blaise had disappeared into the store, but I grabbed Zeke's shirt, holding him back. "What do you mean?" A *rumble* didn't sound good. It made my stomach churn. Really not good.

Zeke shook his head, a wry grin on his face. "Yeah, I'm sorry to break this to you, but your boy is protective. He's going to call out Zellman, but knowing Blaise, he'll probably try to do it a smart way."

Oh God. "What does that mean?"

Zeke shrugged. "I don't have a clue, but don't worry. Blaise makes everything better. That's what he's like deep down. He settles things. It'll be fine."

That *so* didn't settle me.

43

BLAISE

By the time we got to the actual dune buggying site, we didn't have time to go out.

We pulled in time to camp for the night. That meant we'd stay a second night. That was all good, but even though my brother was set up on the complete opposite side of the campsite, I still felt an itch under my skin.

Every time I saw him, it doubled in size. And it was worse now that I was actually trying to be civil.

Aspen. All this shit was for Aspen.

The dune racing was for us—but the girls, my brother, that was all for her.

As soon as we pulled up, we assigned the campers. Aspen and I got the smaller one since I didn't want anyone perving on her while she was in bed with me. Bren and Taz came over right away. They followed Aspen toward the camper, but I had a word with Bren before she went in.

Once Taz ducked inside with Aspen, I nodded to where my brother and the other two dipshits stood. "Aspen told me what the pipsqueak said to her in the woods."

Bren narrowed her eyes. "Pipsqueak? Really?"

I scowled. "If he says one disrespectful thing to her, all bets are off. I'm coming for his ass. You and my brother can lay down against me. I don't care."

Her eyes stayed narrowed. "Why are you telling me this?"

"I'm letting you know. That's all."

"Fine."

Taz and Aspen came out, and Bren stepped back from me. I morphed into a nice guy, grabbing Aspen's hand and tugging her over for a soft kiss. I flashed Bren a warning look before the three of them headed off. My eyes swept the campground and found Cross staring right at me.

I wanted to raise my middle finger.

Stomping down my inner asshole, I kept my hands in my pockets.

I needed a drink.

"Yo." Zeke came from next door, carrying rum, a bottle of Coke, two cups, and a bag of ice thrown over his shoulder. We had set up a table just outside my camper, and he put everything down. "You look ready to tear your brother's face off already."

He began pouring, and I reached around, taking the bag of ice.

I filled one cup, and Zeke rotated them.

I put ice in the already poured cup and set the bag back down.

Zeke took his drink, sitting by the table, and cupped his hand around his mouth. "Conway, you and your pussy friend get to make the fire."

Conway and Ashlome glared at us.

"What the hell?" Conway threw up a middle finger.

Zeke leaned forward, waving his own. "That's what you get for doing what you've been doing the last two weeks. Like there wasn't going to be a comeuppance? Fucking crazy if you thought that."

I loved my best friend. A lot.

Both guys transferred their glares to me before stomping off.

Zeke leaned back, holding his cup up, and I met it with mine. "*Salud.*"

Zeke nodded, taking a slurp from his. "You think cops come around with drug dogs?"

I froze. "You didn't."

He laughed. "No, but I kinda wish I'd brought something— something soft, you know?"

I could only shake my head. "No way."

"You used to."

"That was before I had Aspen."

He let out a sigh. "Never again?"

My answer was firm. "No way. Not unless she leaves me one day."

"Shit, B. You're talking like you're married."

Married? No. But I needed her. I knew it. I leaned forward, my drink in hand. "I'm not going to go to a dark place or anything. It isn't like that."

"I know. If there's anyone who could survive the worst of the worst, it's you."

"Yeah." *Fucking Griffith.* I hated him.

"You talked to your brother at all since that night?" Zeke asked.

I glanced over, not answering.

Zeke was watching their trailer.

The girls were making Aspen laugh.

My chest loosened a little, seeing that.

"It was a good call inviting them," he noted.

I sucked air through my teeth. Yeah. I hated admitting it, but he was right. I grunted in response.

Zeke laughed. "Yeah. This is going to be a fun night. I'm not even here for the dune racing."

"Shut up."

He laughed louder.

I wanted to shove his chair over, but I didn't. See? I was growing.

AFTER THE FIRE WAS GOING, Zeke and Brian got the grills going.

Penny and her girls had helped get the food ready to go, and I was at the table, loading up a plate when I glanced back.

Daniels was right behind me.

She had her own plate, with a hot dog on it and nothing else. She never had been a big eater.

"You didn't have to invite two watchdogs to stand guard over your girlfriend," she said.

I picked up my drink and headed back toward my camper.

As I sat at my table, Mara followed me. She sat down where Zeke had been sitting earlier, putting her plate on the table.

She wanted to have this talk.

Fine. Let's talk.

"What do you want?" I asked.

Air escaped her in a burst, and she rolled her eyes. "God. For you to give a damn?"

"I did, before you threatened someone I care about. It stopped then."

She studied me, a flash of pain tightened her face before she squashed it. She lowered her head. "Yeah. I'm seeing that, but do you really blame me?"

"Yes."

Her head snapped back up.

I knew I was cold, but she'd threatened Aspen. What'd she expect? "She's blameless, and you know that. And I never lied to you. I never promised you anything."

"But if I had slept with someone else, you would've stopped touching me."

I inclined my head. "Yeah, and that was on you to choose. You knew I didn't want to date you. Before Aspen, I didn't want to date anyone. I wasn't lying about that. How you chose to respond is on you." I lowered my voice. "You've been fucking two guys thinking I'll give a shit about it? That's stupid and reckless, for you."

Her face twisted, and she started to cry.

That got me. Regret sliced through me, because I did care about Mara, but I didn't care enough. That was the problem, and she knew it. She just didn't want to accept it. But Ashlome and Conway? Neither of those guys was going to make her his girlfriend.

"Mara." I sighed, but I couldn't touch her. I wouldn't, and not just because of Aspen. It was for Mara too.

"I just didn't—" She stopped.

We'd been friends. We'd been more than friends, but I'd said all I could. The rest was for her to figure out. There was physical cheating, and there was emotional cheating. Letting Mara lean on me now would be giving her something that should only be Aspen's. And it would also only prolong her pain. This conversation was done, and she sensed it, looking up at me.

I shook my head.

"You're such an asshole," she hissed before fleeing.

She left her plate behind.

Zeke headed back over, sat in her spot, and eyed the plate. "You think she's coming back for that?"

"Have at it."

He popped it in his mouth in two bites, then grinned around his chewing. "Nice and plain, but grilled to perfection. I'm going to watch her, see if she leaves any more food around. Can't have the bears getting it." He winked at me.

I grinned, but just slightly. "I'm always the bad guy."

"Nah." He hit me with the back of his hand, a distracted pat. "You're just *usually* the bad guy. Everyone knows you're doing what's right with Mara. She's got issues. You came, and she saw a guy who was strong enough to help shoulder some of her problems. You told her you weren't that guy, but she chose to ignore that for a semester. That's on her, and everyone else here knows that." He paused, raising his cup to the fire, and then indicated my brother's group. "Except them. They don't know any of us." He grinned at me. "They think we're rich pricks." He belched and added, "Which we kinda are."

I grinned. "My brother's family isn't that bad."

"Nah. They just ain't in our league." He leaned forward. "So whatever. We'll be the bad guys. Not like we're not going to get that all our lives."

He had a point.

We sat in silence for a while.

"Are you going to get wasted tonight?"

I shook my head. "I can't. I'll start a fight if I do." I wanted to be sober for Aspen.

"That's too bad. I was hoping for some entertainment."

I grinned, but my hand shot out, punching his arm. "Asswipe."

"Dickhead."

"Dickwipe."

"Dude. Something other than *wipe*. Please."

I thought about it. "Fucker."

"Nice." He gave me an approving nod. "Sticking with the classics. Right on."

ASPEN

I WAS DRUNK.

And giggly.

And stumbling.

I swear, that table had not been there two seconds earlier.

Bumping into it, I almost fell down and dissolved in laughter.

Hands caught me, righting me.

Yes. I'd forgotten they were here too.

I looked up. Bren and Taz. They were wonderful. I didn't know why Blaise didn't like them.

Bren's hand tightened around my arm, and she tried not to smile. "You, uh, don't have to share all your thoughts."

Um...

Had I?

Taz laughed on my other side. "I don't know. I appreciated her giving us drunk GPS directions as we walked across the campsite."

Right. I had done that. Drunk GPS...

We neared my camper, and I felt a smile on my face. "This is my place! This is where I'm sleeping."

"We're very aware. The whole campsite is now aware."

I had no clue who said that, but I didn't care.

Blaise stood from his chair.

"No!" I launched myself at him.

He caught me, like I knew he would, and I curled up in his lap.

"I love you." An alarm sounded in my head, but I wanted to get this out. "I love you, and I've known for a while, but I didn't share." I frowned. "I don't know why I kept that to myself."

He was frozen, his eyes latched to mine as a strangled laugh came from him. His hand curled around my leg, and he grasped me tighter as he sat with me on his lap.

"Uh, thanks," he said over my head. "I got it from here."

Bren took off right away.

"Bye, Bren!" I yelled, waving.

She was only four feet away.

Taz was still laughing. She'd been laughing at me most of the night.

And she wasn't leaving.

Yay, Taz!

She sat in a chair next to our camper door. She nodded toward me. "You sure you're okay with her?"

"I'll be fine."

I peered up at Blaise. He sounded sad. Why'd he sound like that?

I didn't like that.

Blaise was sad a lot of the time. He was sadder than most of us, to be honest.

"Okay." He patted my arm. "You don't have to say that with everyone."

Taz covered her mouth, trying not to laugh. Why now? She'd been laughing openly most the night.

"This is live television," she said. "I would sign up for this subscription."

"Shut up." But Blaise grinned.

Oh good. I could relax.

I laid my head against his shoulder.

He wasn't so sad now.

"Oh my God," he muttered under his breath.

"Yep. She's certainly all yours."

He shook his head. "So, uh, how are things with the boyfriend?"

I heard a shocked laugh. "What is this? A Blaise who's actually asking me a conversational question? How scandalous of you and your anger problem."

His hand curled around my waist, shifting me against him.

"You're here. I'm here. She's about to fall asleep. And I actually don't want to rip your brother's face off his skull, for the first time all day."

She laughed. "Progress. I'm impressed."

Blaise groaned, and it relaxed me further.

"Just a conversation with my little sister."

"Ha. Younger than you by a month, dickhead."

"Yeah. Our dad was a busy guy that year."

Silence, then a sputtering laugh. "I can't believe you said that."

"It's true."

"Yeah."

Blaise sighed, and I fell asleep.

44

ASPEN

pounding headache woke me in the dark, and I jerked around, then immediately regretted it. Hitting a body, I cried out.

And I couldn't see.

I had no clue where I was.

Wait.

That body turned over, and arms swept me in.

I relaxed, recognizing those arms.

I burrowed into Blaise and whimpered. "How drunk did I get?"

"Really drunk." He held me a second. "I need to turn the light on. Cover your eyes."

Why? Why to the light?

But then it was on, and I turned my face toward the pillow.

Oh, God. No.

What had I been thinking? I hadn't. That's what I'd been thinking. Nothing.

I'd been sitting there, enjoying Bren and Taz, and enjoying the camaraderie of the guys. They were funny. They'd told stories the entire time, but I mostly enjoyed the ease they had with each other. I only felt that when Blaise was around Zeke, but no one else. He didn't trust anyone.

Then I'd started drinking, because I wished I could have him come over with us, but I knew he wouldn't, and the more I drank, the sadder I got, but the drunker I got too.

"Here."

I opened my eyes to find him holding a glass of water in one hand and two pain pills in the other. Thank God. I really loved this man.

Swiping both, I swallowed the pills with the water, and then I had another problem. I had to pee. And my breath was horrible.

Holy—he'd let me go to bed like this? Embarrassing.

"Bathroom?" I croaked, one eye closed and the other opened just the tiniest bit to see his answer.

He chuckled, climbing out of bed.

I tried not to notice how good his shirt and boxer briefs looked on him, because it was cold out, and we were camping, and I had a splitting headache, but I did. Because he was hot. That's all.

He padded barefoot past the kitchen area and opened a door. He reached inside and a soft light turned on. "Here."

I loved him. I loved him so much.

I slipped inside, and a second later, he knocked on the door and shoved my bag inside. I loved him even more.

I didn't change clothes, but I pulled out some better for sleeping and tossed them on the table in the main area. Then I shut the door and went back to rifling through my bag. Toothbrush. Toothpaste. I needed all the cleaning things I could find, because who knew drinking could make you smell?

After cleaning up a bit, I stepped back.

Leaving the light on, I didn't want to look at Blaise. I knew he was back in bed, and he was probably watching me, and for some reason, acknowledging that would've made me feel self-conscious. So I ignored him as I quickly changed clothes. Then I tossed my bag aside and went back to turn the light off.

"Leave it."

"Really?"

He nodded, looking at me from his pillow. He seemed exhausted. There were soft lines around his eyes and mouth. He had a sleepy look to him. "I'll turn it off later."

"Okay."

I padded back over, and he held up the covers.

I slipped in, but then he lifted me and rolled me to his other side, so he was between me and the door.

I squeaked in surprise, but then relaxed and *really* relaxed. He'd been warming my spot for me.

Man. I *really* loved him.

I settled in. Camping was awesome.

"How was your night?" he asked.

I searched his eyes, wondering if there was more to that question, but he seemed genuinely interested.

"It was nice, actually."

He propped himself up on an elbow and reached for my hand, twining our fingers. He looked at our hands, his finger sliding against mine. "You seemed like you had a good time with them."

"I did."

His eyes lifted, held mine. He smiled, though it was slightly sad. "You can talk about my brother. I won't get mad at you."

"Okay." So I did. "Zellman apologized for being slightly mean to me before. He said he didn't mean it the way it came out. Jordan's nice, and they're all funny. I really like Bren and Taz. Thank you for inviting them."

He nodded, his eyes falling back to our hands.

"And I liked your brother," I added after a moment. "He's nice."

His eyes lifted back to mine. "Good." He laid down on his

pillow and turned toward me. He pulled me to him, our legs tangling. Then he said softly, "I know my brother is a good person. It's half the reason I hate him. If he were a bad guy, I wouldn't feel like a shit person."

I held my breath.

His eyes fell to my mouth. "I'm jealous of him. That's why I hurt him so bad."

My breath caught in my chest. "Because of your dad, right?"

He shrugged against the blanket. "Not totally. I think just the whole situation. I've seen their mom, and she's nice too. I mean, I get why she and Stephen didn't work. They don't seem to fit, but they tried. They tried for their kids. That's respectable."

I cocked my head up. "Your mom's nice."

He looked away. "My mom's damaged. So am I. *He* did that to us."

Oh.

Oh God.

I closed my eyes and a wave of fierce protection, fierce love, fierce everything for him rolled over me, almost drowning me. I sputtered with the need to clasp him, anchor him, take away his hurt. But I couldn't. That stuff was deep inside.

He had put it there.

"Blaise..." I reached up to touch the side of his face.

He caught my hand, pulled it to his mouth, and pressed a kiss there. "You told me you loved me tonight."

I sucked in my breath. *Oh God.* I had.

The night came back to me in parts, but I remembered sitting on his lap. I remembered babbling, a lot.

"Blaise."

"Did you mean it?" His eyes caught mine. There was a yearning there.

I nodded. "Yes." It left me in a whisper. "I love you."

He didn't respond—not right away.

Then he nodded. "I love you too."

"You do?"

Poof. The headache was gone.

Or, kinda. I smiled.

"I do. I love you." His eyes moved back to my mouth, and he pulled me even tighter against him. His leg hitched higher, rubbing.

My breath quickened.

I was feeling the love. Or, I was feeling something down there.

"I want to have slow sex with you."

Oh, dear Lord. "Okay," I whispered.

Grinning, he moved over me, his mouth found mine, and he did what he'd said.

I was pretty sure slow sex was code for making love.

45

BLAISE

I headed out before everyone else, needing wind and speed.

There were four things in my life I now loved: my mom, Aspen, soccer, and ATV racing. The place called it dune buggying, but it was more riding an ATV up and down a large beach. This early in the morning, I had the entire place to myself.

The guy drove my ATV up and double-checked my gear, and then I got the go-ahead to light this place up. I did.

I was an adrenaline junkie—had been for almost forever. Cliff diving. Jumping out of a plane. Bungee jumping. I was up for it. But this morning, I wasn't doing it to escape my non-bio dad, which was usually the case. I wasn't trying to hide from a household I was trapped in and not giving a fuck if I died or not. This morning felt different.

It was like a goodbye, in an odd way.

That way of life was done, and I knew it was because of Aspen. It was time to let go of some of my haunts. Griffith couldn't hurt me anymore. He couldn't hurt my mom either, but the other shit was my brother and sister. They were here. They didn't have to come, and they'd stayed to their side of the campsite last night.

I had to let that shit go too.

I didn't have to let them in, but Taz would weasel her way. She already was. Our conversation had been stilted on my end, but she'd been laughing the whole time. She knew I was trying, so I'd gotten an earful about her and her boyfriend—more than I wanted. She enjoyed torturing me with it. When she'd started to get into their sex life, I said goodnight.

She laughed the entire way back.

But it had felt good.

Sitting with her, talking to her, that felt good.

I kicked on some more speed, the wind and ocean whipping past me. I braked, and the ATV flipped around. There was a small dune above with a path going up and over it, so I gunned, heading for it and past it.

This shit.

Going fast.

Doing tricks.

Defying the odds.

It was exhilarating.

I used to love defying serious injury, but even the injuries never really bothered me. Griffith never messed with me when I was laid up with a broken arm or leg. The more serious the injury, the longer he stayed away. That was my time, my choosing.

In those moments I'd controlled what pain I felt—rather than enduring it from him. Because fuck him.

I'd wanted to murder him, so many damn times.

I didn't think that want would ever leave me. It was another haunt I'd carry probably all my life. But on this run this morning, something was changing. It was bittersweet.

I raced up and down. I drove up the cliff, jumping over it, wet sand spraying everywhere behind me.

I wouldn't stay out here when the others came. It wouldn't be as fun, and most of those guys didn't know what the hell they were doing. They'd just drive up and down the beach. They didn't understand the fun of pushing, fearing what you were about to conquer, not knowing if you actually would or not, and then if you did—the elation that you'd defied gravity. There were always bigger challenges, more odds to overcome, and one day you would lose. If you were scared of that, you didn't have any place on the trek. But if you accepted the inevitable, you could never lose.

But anyway, I was done with this stuff.

I had people I wanted to stay alive for now. That had hit me hard this morning—waking up and smelling the air differently, feeling the heaviness of the morning sun, knowing people would hurt if I died. It made me scared. Today was my last time. Not that doing adrenaline-junkie shit had been my life goal or a career or anything. But if an opportunity came up, I took it.

No more.

This was my last trip, my last weekend. My last time.

Eyeing a higher rise, I headed for it. That was my last trick for the morning. After that, I'd go back and hand over the keys.

I could hear other ATVs farther down the beach now.

Driving up to the peak took a little while. I had to gun the engine a few times, but I got up there. I was higher than everyone else, high enough to see where we were camped, and I saw a lot starting to move around.

Another ATV drove down the beach, coming right for me.

I waited, watching it.

It was bypassing all the ridges and trick spots, heading straight for me.

Just below me, it paused, and the driver leaned out, looking up.

Even with his protective gear on, I recognized my brother.

He leaned back in and the ATV shot beyond me. He was coming around, starting up the path to where I was waiting. After a moment he pulled up right next to me. He raised his head in greeting.

I didn't respond, just watched him.

He cut his engine and leaned back against his seat, waiting for me.

We were totally alone. The others had remained below.

Fine. I was Mara déjà vu here.

I turned my engine off.

"I figured we should talk," he said.

I grunted. No shit. "What do you want to talk about?"

"You done hating me?"

Yep. Right for the jugular. I didn't answer.

"I saw you talking to Taz last night. She was glowing when she came back."

"Maybe you should try talking to her too." I eyed him, resting an arm over the wheel.

He glared. "What's that mean?"

"She's lonely, dickhead. Fucking talk to her. Give her the time of day."

"Like you do?" he shot back.

I shrugged. "You knew about this fucked situation before I did. You were digesting it the day I saw you for the first time. Fuck off if I'm not handling it the fastest rate I could."

Maybe it wasn't the right thing to say, but it was the truth. And right now, that's all I had. I didn't know what else was going on with me, but finding out about Stephen, then finding out about Cross and Taz had thrown me for a loop. A big loop.

I still didn't know if I was right again.

But I was getting there.

"They were separated."

I looked over. Cross wasn't looking at me anymore, and his hands were tight on the wheel in front of him.

"My mom told me that recently," he added. "I thought it was an affair, but it wasn't. Not really. My mom and dad were going to get a divorce. I'm guessing they'd been struggling for a while. She told him she was pregnant before your mom did. That's why he and my mom tried again."

Shit.

This sucked.

My insides felt scraped, like an ATV had been joyriding over *me*.

"Did you talk to your mom?" he asked. "Find out why she lied to you?"

Yeah. Right. Like I was going to tell him how that conversation went? "You first."

His face clouded instantly. "Why are you like this? I'm trying. I've been trying—"

"I tried first. Remember that?"

He stilled. "Yeah."

And I *had* tried. When this first came out, I'd approached him twice. He wasn't receptive either time, and since then, well, forget him. That'd been my motto, and that was around the same time my anger had started to bubble up. I'd been pissed, then angry, then livid, and I'd been running on furious ever since. I was trying to get back to the pissed level, but it took work. A lot of work.

"I'm sorry I was an asshole to you first," he said, still not looking at me. "Can we, just...I don't know. This is hurting Taz, and I didn't get it until last night. It made her night that you talked to her for a while. Seeing that, I started thinking differently."

I wanted to gut myself. With a plastic knife.

But...

"You were nice to Aspen last night," I told him. "Thank you for that."

He let out an abrupt laugh, shaking his head. "I bet that killed you to say." He pulled his helmet off, and he was grinning. "It wasn't hard. She's a nice girl. Got no clue how the fuck *you* ended up with her, but it is what it is."

I knew that. At this point, I was certain everyone knew that. I didn't need him to say it. But whatever.

This felt weird. Uncomfortable.

I was sitting here, on top of a cliff, having *a talk* with my brother.

I still hated him. Except I didn't, actually. Not really.

I rolled my eyes. "Lay off your dad."

He turned to me. "How's that your place to say?"

I looked right at him. "Because he beat the shit out of the guy who used to lock me in closets. He's there for my mom. You have a good dad. Don't take that for granted."

We stared at each other, neither backing off. Eventually he sat back, and his shoulders dropped. "I'm supposed to go easy on my dad because he didn't beat my ass? You kidding me?"

I shrugged. "He was unhappy. You do shitty things when you're miserable, but trust me, you got the better dad."

"Whatever," he snapped, looking back out at the beach. "I'm sorry for your shit, what you—never mind."

I felt a kick at his words. We both knew what he meant, and yeah.

That was enough said on the topic.

Some other ATVs were starting to come our way.

None of them seemed to know what they were doing— driving around, jerking and awkward. Someone was going to spill.

Cross shook his head. "I saw you before. There's a ridge down there, and I knew it was you. You're good at this stuff."

I didn't answer, but he wasn't waiting for a response. "Someone's going to flip their ride and get impaled." He laughed. "We'll have to take 'em to the hospital."

I grunted. *Probably.* Everyone liked to show off until they were in the back of an ambulance. And I was betting it'd be one from my group.

"I heard you're going to Cain," he said after a moment.

I frowned. "Who'd you hear that from?"

"Are you?"

I nodded. "I'm going to be on their soccer team."

He cocked his head. "You play soccer?"

Another nod. "I rock at soccer."

He didn't reply, his face an impartial wall, but I was learning to read my brother. He was surprised, and a little impressed, if I was getting him right.

"Listen," he said. "I don't know if I'll talk to you again all summer. But we're doing a party at the end of August. The four of us are renting a house. We're doing a preview party for that project Aspen's parents are working on. You're invited."

"You're asking now to get Taz off your back, aren't you?"

He jerked up a shoulder, shoving his helmet back on. "Maybe."

I laughed. He was. And I knew I wouldn't see him the rest of the summer. He'd live his life with his friends. I'd do mine with my friends. On the off chance we did see each other, we wouldn't talk. That's what this was about—setting a tentative peace. But no matter what we said today, we both still had issues to resolve. And those issues didn't really have anything to do with each other.

And I didn't want to deal with those right now.

I drew in a deep breath and reached forward, turning the engine on.

There were two ATVs right underneath us. I could jump them both if I had enough momentum.

Not saying another word, I began backing up until I had enough space.

It was like Cross knew what I was doing, because he waited, watching me.

I gunned my engine, shot past him, and flew in the air.

There were screams from beneath me, but I cleared both with a little extra distance. I left a wave of sand raining down, and I laughed, loving that.

After that, I headed back.

I wasn't surprised when Cross wasn't too far behind me.

We turned in our rides and gear, and oddly, we walked beside each other back to the campsite. We didn't say a word, but it felt nice.

I'd admit that to no one.

46

ASPEN

By Saturday night, the trip was winding down. Blaise had gone out early in the morning to ride, and later in the afternoon. I'd realized he enjoyed doing that stuff when no one else was around, but he'd said he was going to take me out in the morning.

I hadn't been sure what to expect from this trip, but it was fun.

While Blaise was gone, Bren and Taz had come over and sat with me at our camper. When he came back, he and I went inside. He'd held me while I read until Zeke came over, and then Blaise had gone off with the guys. They'd taken a trip to town and came back with more food and booze.

A few people had started drinking early in the morning, but once the guys came back, party mode got cranked up a notch. The music blared, they fired up the grills, and the drinks were flowing.

Now it was the evening, and Blaise was drinking while I sat on his lap. We'd moved from in front of our camper to join Blaise's friends around the fire. Bren and Taz stuck with their group, and they were laughing a lot. Taz sat on her boyfriend's lap, and Bren sat close to Blaise's brother. The other guys were eyeing a few of the girls on our side of the campsite.

At one point, I saw Mara Daniels break away from the main group, and I sighed, figuring maybe this was the time for our showdown.

I knew it was coming. Everyone had been waiting, or they had been in my head, at least. People watched whenever Mara came close to where Blaise and I sat. Blaise would stiffen too, until she moved to a different group. Then he'd relax. The other girls in her group had left me alone. I'd gotten a few dirty looks, but that was it.

Whatever Blaise had done, it had worked to warn them off.

But still, this was my fight. He couldn't take this on for me. As I saw Mara head over to a camper by herself, I slid off Blaise's lap.

He held me in place. "Where you going?"

I rested my hands on his chest. "I've got something I need to do." I pushed off of him.

He started to stand, and I shook my head. "No. You stay. I need to do this alone."

He growled. "I don't like this, Aspen."

I snorted. "I don't care." I gave him a smile and leaned down, brushing my lips over his. "I have to do this. Let me."

He scowled, but stayed where he was.

"Keep him back," I told Zeke.

He laughed. "Yeah, right. Good luck on that one."

Blaise's scowl shifted to his best friend.

Zeke shook his head.

I headed around to Mara's camper, but when I looked back, I wasn't alone. Her girlfriends were right behind me.

Penny raised her eyebrows. "You think we're not going to rally around our girl? Blaise warned us off, but it's different when you're the one seeking her out. All bets are off."

Well then. Lovely.

I eyed them. All four gave me varying hostile looks.

Then I heard a scrape behind me, and saw Bren and Taz walking to join us.

Penny raised her head. "This doesn't concern you, Monroe."

Bren snorted. "It's a chick fight. Of course we're coming to have Aspen's back."

Penny's gaze turned wary. "We don't fight like you do."

"I hope not, but if you do…" Bren's grin was a slight bit evil. I liked it. She added, "I got no problem wading in."

Penny looked past her. "And if you do? What then? Your crew will come? We're girls."

"So let's keep this just girls." Bren shrugged.

The camper door opened, and Mara stepped down, taking everyone in before her eyes fell to me. Her demeanor was frosty, and she didn't waste time. "Get the fuck out of my way."

I readied myself, rolling my shoulders back. Chin up. That's what you do when you're about to fight, right?

"I'm giving you your shot," I told her, already bracing myself because I didn't really know how this worked.

She frowned. "Say what?"

"I'm right here. Blaise gets tense every time you walk by us or get near us, and I don't know… I figure this is coming, so go for it. I'm here. Take your shot. If you want to hit me, do it. If you want to say something to me, do that instead. I can take it. I'm ready."

Her eyes narrowed.

A brief image of a snake winding up, raising its head for an attack flashed in my mind… Maybe this wasn't such a good idea.

But I still added, "I'm kinda tired of waiting, to be honest. Time keeps moving. Feelings will fade, and you might not get your shot later, so strike while the iron is hot. Right? That's the saying?"

Someone snorted behind me. I wasn't sure which side it came from.

"You're an idiot," someone else muttered.

Again, I wasn't sure, but I was betting that wasn't Taz or Bren.

Mara rolled her eyes. "I don't have anything to say to you."

What? I frowned. "Why not?"

She shook her head. "Are you always this stupid? I'm leaving you alone. Take this and shoo, bitch."

But... That's not how this was supposed to happen. "I don't get it. Aren't you supposed to lay into me or something? Make me bleed? Cry, at least?"

"Why?" Her eyes flashed, but they looked hollow, empty. It was gone in the next breath. "My problems aren't yours. Blaise never lied to me, and it ain't your fault he fell for you and not me. It's my fault I didn't keep him."

I had no clue how to process this. This was really not going how I'd prepared myself for. I had psyched myself up for a *fight* fight. "But—"

"Dear God." A hand took my arm and pulled me back. Bren frowned at me. "She's trying to be a good person. Leave it alone."

I swung my head back to Mara. "I don't get this."

"What the fuck do you want from me?!" she screeched. That was more like it. Her hands formed fists and she came at me, but only took a few steps before stopping. "You are rubbing salt in the wound by doing this. Back off! I have shit to deal with, and it has nothing to do with you. This ain't a television show where I'm the mean girl and I'm going to write *whore* and your phone number in the bathroom or something. *Bitch. Whore. Slut.* Is that what you want from me? For the last *fucking* time, I got my own shit to deal with, but I'm not a bully. I never actually planned on doing *anything* to you."

"You told Blaise you were going to do something to me."

A bitter laugh rippled from her. "I wanted to hurt him. Threatening you hurts him. That's all I wanted. You helped me in the beginning of the year. Do you not remember?"

"I did?"

She laughed again. "I needed an answer on a test, and you moved your shoulder. You knew I didn't know it, and you let me see your test. That one question helped me keep a passing grade. It meant a lot to me."

I was pretty sure I hadn't done that on purpose.

"Oh." I eased back. "Yeah."

Someone stifled a laugh behind me. This time I guessed it *was* Taz or Bren.

Mara waved, dismissing me. "Just go away. You got the guy. Stop rubbing it in by doing stuff like this. It's barely manageable watching him fawn all over you, treating you like you're made of glass or some shit. Want to do me a favor? Get away from me. That'll help."

And with that, she was done. She swung around, grabbed a bottle of wine, and stalked off. Her girls went with her, and I watched them move past the guys, giving them a wide berth too.

Taz stepped up. "That was refreshing. For once, no one came to blows."

"I'm kinda disappointed," Bren said. "But relieved at the same time." She looked at me. "You okay?"

I nodded. "Is it wrong to feel bad for her?"

"Nah. She's hurting. That's obvious. But she's trying to do the right thing by not taking it out on you. Steer clear of her. That's the kindest thing to do now."

She was right.

Taz gestured to their side of the campsite. "We're going to do s'mores. You want to hang for a bit?"

I looked over my shoulder, my eyes meeting Blaise's over the campfire.

I nodded in their direction, and he looked over to where his brother was.

I was trying to convey that I was going over there, but that's not what happened. His shoulders went rigid, but he nodded and stood. He said a few words with Zeke, grabbed some of the booze we'd been drinking, and came around to where we were standing.

Bren went stiff next to me. "What are you doing?"

His tone was cool. "Not starting shit." He nodded. "She likes you."

That must've been enough, because Bren and Taz turned back, and their entire group watched us come. All were silent for a second until we settled.

I sat at their table, with Blaise beside me at first.

Then as the conversation started, as Blaise remained quiet, just sitting with me, and the guys started to relax. Conversation flowed, and after a full hour, they were laughing and telling jokes. The s'mores were yum. Blaise gave me an extra one of his, but for the most part, he was content to remain quiet, sipping his drink.

Later on, Zeke, Brian, and Branston moved their chairs so they were closer to where we sat, but they remained at their own bonfire.

Then Blaise moved, grabbing one of the bigger lounge chairs. He settled in and pulled me down onto his lap. And that's where we sat the rest of the night.

Blaise held me while I laughed with his brother and the rest of their group.

It was nice.

It was progress.

47

BLAISE

The next month didn't unfold the way I wanted it to, nor how I expected it to.

I'd thought July would be fun and filled with lots of Aspen sexy times. I'd looked forward to lazy mornings, rides in the car with my girl, and cuddling and more in the evenings. I was going to get a van and get it tricked out for camping—maybe with a wide moonroof so we could cuddle under the stars. Romantic crap like that.

Guess what happened?

Her brother happened.

Nate went apeshit on her parents while she was camping with me. I don't know his motivation or the reason for his timing—since he'd seemed to keep it together at her graduation and the weeks after—but he ripped their asses a new one.

Aspen's parents were now woke, and trying to be the world's greatest parents instead of the neglectful asses they were. That translated into an entire month where I didn't see my girl.

They whisked her off for trips all over the damn world: Europe, Singapore, Australia, a brief stop in Brazil for sentimental reasons (don't ask me; I haven't a clue why), and then off to some cabin they used to own in the mountains. It was supposed to be huge, and Aspen had been rallying to get me to come, but they'd been there the same weekend I had to go to Cain to look at apartments.

That was the other thing that happened—my plans for next year.

Soccer training started in early August, so I needed to get there and get situated. That also meant a conversation with Zeke about his true living aspirations. He wanted to rush a fraternity, but at first I'd thought he and I could get a place, and then if he rushed, that was fine. I'd have the place to myself.

But Zeke backed out, and it wasn't because he didn't want to start out living with me. He got *his* ass reamed by his dad. That seemed to be going around.

A cop friend had been at the house, recognized the smells coming from Zeke's room, and informed Zeke's dad that if his son didn't clear out his room, he'd be returning with drug dogs. Zeke got the wake-up call of all wake-up calls.

He lost Daddy Dearest's funding for college, so as of end-July, Zeke wasn't sure if he was still coming to Cain University or not. And it wasn't a bluff. He'd lost everything—his trucks, his room (he'd moved into a closet-sized bedroom on the same floor as his parents, and no one was happy about it) and all their house staff got a month's paid vacation.

Zeke was the new household staff.

Turns out, his dad *did* give a shit, and Zeke had had no idea how much. So he was currently cleaning their house, not partying, and also working as an intern at his dad's company to earn money for college. His dad had made it clear he didn't give one iota if Zeke missed a year of higher learning or not.

So that's where Zeke was, and that's why I'd ended up getting an apartment by myself as close to Cain's soccer complex as possible. I already knew Aspen wanted the dorm experience. She'd said she wanted to embrace what college was really about.

That was cool with me.

She'd meet people in her dorm, but I knew I'd be driving over to pick her up most nights and bringing her back early in the morning after my soccer runs.

So here I was. I'd not seen my girl all month, and my best friend was now a question mark.

This sucked was a gross under-exaggeration.

"This place is gorgeous, Blaise."

I glanced back as my mom came through my new bedroom door. She went straight to the window.

"Oh wow. Look at that view."

I looked. The view wasn't anything great. It was the soccer field, which was going to be my home until January, but if it awed her, who was I to take that away?

"The place looks good." Stephen came in next, not overly impressed, but still supportive. He nodded. "Smart. I can see why you picked it."

It had no amenities, but I didn't need them. I'd be using the college's, and the rent was high enough that there were serious renters here. The management office said I was the only college student in the complex, and that made me happy. I preferred *going* to parties, not hosting them or living around them.

"They said a lot of professors live here, and some post-doc students," I told my mom and Stephen. That translated to *non-party people* in my mind.

Stephen gave me the same look he'd been giving me for the last month. I wasn't sure if it was respect, but maybe more of a re-assessment.

I'd been around nearly every night—except for the few nights Zeke's parents had okayed me coming over to play video games. I was one of their only "approved" friends for him. Brian and Branston were out, so it was all me. I was actually the good guy in that situation. I'd also gotten serious about training, because I knew once Monday hit, and practices started, I'd be in sore shape.

Stephen had never seen me during soccer until this last month. I got *real* serious about my sport. Growing up, training had been another time Griffith mostly stayed away from me. Maybe because I was with coaches a lot, and he couldn't get away with his normal punching since bruises would be visible. But ever since I was little, soccer came around and he took a hike, for the most part.

That was another reason I loved the sport. It'd been my only escape.

"How much is the rent?" Stephen asked.

Yeah. Neither he nor my mom was going to be privy since they weren't paying. I had a trust fund from Griffith. He hadn't taken it away, and we'd been assured by a lawyer that he couldn't. I also had money set aside for me from my grandfather, my mom's dad. She came from old money back east. When we went back to New York, that old money got even older, if that made sense. There'd been a fund for me, but it just grew. Though, I didn't want to have to touch my inheritance from my grandfather, not if I didn't have to.

And until then, I wasn't going to sweat about it.

I grinned at Stephen. "It's high enough that most college students can't pay it."

His mouth twitched, and he nodded. "Got it."

My mom turned back from the window, a smile on her face. "So, have you heard from Aspen?"

I raised an eyebrow. "They're heading back to Fallen Crest this weekend."

Her smile faltered. "The same weekend you're moving here?"

I nodded, my throat tight. I missed my girl. *A lot.*

Fucking parents.

My mom and Stephen shared a look, but I knew what they were thinking.

The timing was suspect for sure, but I didn't know what podium her parents could stand on. They'd been reserved about me at first, but somehow that took a turn for the worse. They really didn't like me now. When I asked Aspen if she knew why, she hadn't a clue. They weren't sharing with her or me, so I was guessing maybe they were just being hypocritical.

Aspen said they were repeating history, thinking I was a bad influence. I didn't know what she meant by that, and she didn't seem inclined to explain. She started cursing, swearing they couldn't control her once she got to college, and I'd lose her for a while on one of those tangents. I learned to pick my battles.

Her parents weren't going to get between us. I wouldn't let that happen.

But, they were Aspen's parents, and they were giving a shit about her, and since I was trying to be a better person, I refrained from raising hell in the Monson household.

I also didn't mind in one sense because they were *caring*. They were doing their job.

Didn't mean I didn't dream sometimes about going in and rocking the boat. Or that sometimes I wanted to upturn it, fling them into the sea, and only offer a paddle if they got off their high horses.

I mean, I felt that way when they picked their weekend to come back to Fallen Crest.

Still. Good guy. I was trying here.

I shrugged. "They can't lock her in an ivory castle once she gets here."

Stephen studied me. "You know, your mother knows people who know the Monsons. We could talk to someone if you wanted us to pull some strings."

I shot him a look. "You think I need your help to see my girlfriend?"

His face went blank. "No, of course not."

He turned away.

Marie's eyes narrowed, resting on him before turning to me. "I have friends. I have connections. I can say one thing to Malinda

Decraw-Strattan, and trust me, she could turn the Monsons'
world upside down."

"Don't, Mom," I growled.

This was going from decent to nasty in a heartbeat. We were
past the unpleasant level, skyrocketing past it.

"But why?" She stepped toward me, gesturing to Stephen.
"Your dad—"

"HE'S NOT MY FATHER!"

I'd been quiet.

I'd been silent when I first found out about my real father.

And maybe it wasn't totally the father thing. Maybe I was
more pissed about Aspen's parents than I wanted to believe, but I
was here.

My control snapped.

I didn't know why. Well, that's a lie. I knew, but now she was
better. Mom was getting better. She wasn't so broken now, and I
wasn't alone.

"Hey!" Stephen turned back.

"No! You too—shut up."

"HEY!" He surged for me.

I locked down, flinching, but putting a wall up.

I couldn't help myself.

Griffith had come at me with punches. He'd rain down on me
until he got a good punch in and I saw stars, and then he'd ram
my head into whatever was closest—the wall, the corner of a
piece of furniture. It didn't matter.

When I went down, the kicking started.

I was instantly ready for an attack, and they both saw it.

Stephen froze, drawing in a breath. Horror flared over his
face. "Son."

"Honey," my mother whispered.

I was cornered.

I needed an out.

I looked, but Stephen was blocking the doorway.

He saw where I was looking and drew in another ragged breath before swinging wide, out of the way. "I'm not going to hurt you. I just didn't want you to disrespect your mother."

I laughed, and even I winced at the sound coming from me, 'cause that was no laugh. I didn't know what it was. It was heinous. It was harsh. It was empty.

It was tortured.

But I made the sound anyway, and I couldn't stop. I shook my head, moving out of the room.

The walls were closing in.

The ceiling coming down.

The floor rising.

I was going to get crushed.

I had to get out.

Get out, get out, GET THE FUCK OUT!

"Honey."

I heard her behind me, but there was a rushing sound in my head.

I could see out the living room window into the parking lot, but I wasn't really seeing shit.

I was seeing him.

Swinging at me.

Towering over me.

I closed my eyes. I couldn't handle it.

But then it got worse. I drew in a sharp breath, and I couldn't breathe.

There was no more air.

I could feel it—kicking, hitting. And I could hear him—the taunts, the threats, the mocking. That fucker liked to tear me down in every fucking way possible.

The burns.

I could smell it. My skin.

Fuck.

I hadn't smelled that smell in years. He only did it once, stopping because she caught me, seeing it. I lied, said it was a bully from school. He'd stopped doing it after that, seeing how pissed she got, how she tried to make me identify him at school.

But the scars were still there.

It was like he was still fucking with me. He was still in my head. He was still contaminating my life.

He could still take everything away from me.

"Blaise!"

I reacted.

I didn't mean to.

Later I would understand that I'd been in a flashback, but in the moment, a hand touched my arm, and I turned.

I ducked. I grabbed the hand. I twisted, and then my fist was in his face.

It was Griffith I saw. It was Stephen I hit.

The screams didn't penetrate, not at first.

Not until Griffith was on the floor. Even then I kept swinging.

My knuckles were red.

That got to me first.

They were red and bleeding, and I stumbled back. *That wouldn't be good, not for my first day of practice.*

That thought gutted me.

I started laughing, and I fell to the ground.

I pulled my knees up, my elbows resting on them, and lowered my head to cry.

When was the last time I'd cried?

"Stephen!"

My mom's voice filtered in, and I turned...I looked...I saw.

I felt nothing now.

I took almost a clinical assessment of the scene.

He'd been beaten to a bloody pulp. My mom went to him, and he pushed her aside.

His eyes were on me, or the one eye that could see.

Fuck.

Stephen pushed himself up. He crawled to me.

I watched him, detached from myself. What was he going to do? Try to hurt me? He was *crawling*. But then he moved to sit next to me, and he reached around me.

I tensed.

I was ready.

He could do it. He could hurt me. I deserved it this time.

He touched my shoulder and pulled me close—my head to his shoulder, his hand cupping the side of my face.

We sat like that.

No way.

I was frozen.

I was in shock.

I had no idea where my mom had gone.

This whole thing had happened in the blink of an eye.

I hurt him. Stephen. Not Griffith.

I'd hurt someone the way Griffith hurt me.

I was like him.

"I'm him," I muttered.

"No, Blaise. You're not." Stephen shook his head, hissing from the pain. "You thought I was him, and you defended yourself. I shouldn't have touched you. I should've read the signs, and I didn't. I am sorry."

No. I pushed him away, scooting over at the same time. "That's fucked up. I just beat your ass, and you're apologizing to me?"

"Blaise." He started for me again.

I scooted farther.

It never occurred to me to get up, to stand to my feet.

He kept moving over, and I kept scooting away, kept shaking my head.

I stopped when I hit a corner and couldn't go any farther.

He kept coming, though.

Finally, I folded in on myself, cowering, trying to hide.

I couldn't hide.

I couldn't disappear.

"Blaise."

He was still here. Why wouldn't the fucker go away?

"Blaise, you've been through trauma."

He was still touching me, a hand to my head.

I wanted to shove him off, kick him away, but I didn't have it in me. I was done. The fight was gone.

He could beat me now, and I wouldn't raise a finger against him.

I heard crying —my mom. I recognized her voice.

And where was I?

Not a closet, or a room at the New York apartment.

I was in *my* apartment.

I was under the kitchen table, backed into the corner between the wall and the fridge.

Shit. How had I gotten in here?

"Blaise." Stephen had crawled under the table with me.

"What are you doing under here?" My voice didn't sound like mine. It was different, a stranger's. I didn't like it, instantly hating what I heard in my tone.

Weakness.

Stephen stared at me a second. "You came under here, so I did too."

"Why?"

That shit didn't make sense to me.

"Because you're my son." He said this like it made perfect sense. "Because you're hurting, and I'll heal from this—and I know you'll never do it again—but you're still hurting. Blaise." His hand went to my ankle. "You need to see a counselor for what you've been through."

"I have." None worked. They all twisted shit so it seemed like my fault.

He gave me a look like he knew things about me I didn't, and I hated that too. Who gave him that right?

"You saw therapists *he* paid for. They weren't real professionals. It will help you, I promise."

Promises meant nothing to me. They were just words, just something meant to manipulate, give you hope, and they were a weapon to take that hope away.

Promises could crush you, if you let them.

"No, thank you."

"How about this?" His tone grew more assertive. "You see a therapist or—"

My nostrils flared. This was more like it.

"Or what?" I taunted. "You're going to press charges?" I felt a cruel smile on my face. I felt it inside of me. "Surprised it took you this long to get to the threats." Threats I understood. They're what made the world go 'round.

Stephen seemed at a loss for a beat. Then his shoulders fell. His jaw slackened. He looked defeated. He looked sad. "I was going to say, if you don't get help, you'll do this to someone else. You could do this to Aspen."

I felt a jolt.

The world spun.

Direct hit.

The fu—no. I was the *fuck*.

He was right.

Dear God.

I couldn't hurt Aspen. Ever.

He nodded, his shoulders lifting. "That got in. Good." He blinked back tears. "Good." He crawled out from under the table.

I stayed, because if I could've, I would've stayed under that table forever.

I heard him cross the room and tell my mother, "I got to him."

Whatever that meant.

48

ASPEN

My phone woke me, and it took me a second to realize the time.

It was four in the morning.

Shit.

Blaise calling.

He hadn't called last evening, and we always did a video call. I looked forward to it every day, but he'd texted saying he'd call me later because something had happened.

My heart raced as I grabbed my phone and scooted up in bed. "Hello?"

"Hey."

Oh God.

He didn't sound good.

"What happened?"

He was silent a second.

"Blaise?"

His voice was strained, so strained. "I beat the shit out of Stephen today."

"What?" I hadn't heard that right.

I was about to laugh. What kind of joke was this?

But then he said it again, dull this time, as if he flipped a switch and turned himself off. He sounded like a robot.

"I beat the shit out of him."

I'd heard right. This wasn't a prank. "Are you—"

"I'm not going to bullshit you. I'm laying this out clearly. When you come here, I don't think we should see each other."

My mouth fell open.

I felt as if he had beat the shit out of *me,* a complete sucker punch to my throat.

I couldn't—*what?!*

He continued, as if this was a business call, as if he was telling me my services were no longer needed. "I was having a flashback from Griffith, and Stephen touched my arm. I rounded on him until he was bleeding on the floor. Then I crawled under a fucking *table* and tried to hide."

Now I heard emotion. I sagged with relief. He wasn't totally gone.

My boy was still in there.

"I'm fucked up, Aspen. I—if I did that to him, I could do that to you. What if I'm in a flashback and you touch me? That can't happen. If something happened to you—" He broke off for a moment. "I'd never get over that. Nothing can hurt you, especially me. We can't—I gotta get myself together. I'm dangerous right now."

"Oh." My heart was still beating, but it was in someone else's hands. His hands. "Blaise."

"I miss you so much, so fucking much, but this shit in my head—I have to get it out of me. I can't hurt you, ever."

Damn him.

Damn him for making me love him even more.

"You're going to therapy?" I asked.

"I'm going to, yeah. Mom and Stephen left earlier. I'm at the apartment, and I have practice in an hour. I've not slept all night. I knew what I needed to do, but it's taken me all night to get the courage up to call you."

"Babe."

He laughed. "Guys don't like being called that."

"Shut up."

He sighed. "I deserve that."

I wasn't going to cry.

I wasn't.

I wasn't...I was crying.

Dammit.

I tried to keep the tears out of my voice. "Are you breaking up with me?"

He fell silent for a minute. "I don't want to." Another beat. "But that's selfish, isn't it?" His voice sounded stronger, but still bleak, if that was possible. "To keep you tied to me when I can't be around you? You're coming to college, and I know you're excited. That's not fair to you. I'd be holding you back."

Okay.

I heard him, and he'd made up his mind.

So okay.

I'd gone without him for a month.

I could handle another month, and that's all I would give him —except he didn't know that.

"You don't see anyone else."

"What?"

I was firm on this. "You don't fuck anyone else. You see a therapist, and that's it."

"That's it? What are you talking about?"

"I'm talking about you breaking up with me to fix yourself. So I'm giving you parameters. You cannot fuck anyone else. Got that?"

He was quiet again, then, "Yeah. No problem."

"You need to fuck, you call me."

"What?"

I was on my knees now, and almost yelling. "Agree to that!"

"Fine. Yes. If I need to fuck, I'll call you. But doesn't that—"

"Agree to that!"

"Yes! I agree. If I want sex, I'll call you. Of course I'll call you. I'll want to call you all the time. This—I don't *want* to do this, but I can't risk hurting you."

"You go to soccer and you kick ass at soccer, and then you have therapy sessions. Every day."

"Every day?!" His voice shrank to a whisper.

"Every day. You want to break up with me to get fixed? Then you fix yourself. Every single day. I am not fucking around with this. I want you. I love you. I am already aching for you, and then you wake me up and say this to me? If you're breaking up with me for this, you do the work. Soccer and then therapy." I barked orders into the phone like a drill sergeant. "Intensive therapy. Get it done, and then I will make everything right for you again. You got me?"

He was silent.

"You got me?!"

"I want to fuck you so bad right now."

I closed my eyes and fell forward, my head hitting the bed. "Agh."

"Can we video chat? Right now?"

I wanted to, but then it'd be even worse. More torture. I couldn't. I couldn't do that to myself. Or him.

I choked out, "One month. You got me?"

He groaned. "One month."

"Do the work."

"I'll do the work."

Oh, heart. Melting.

My knees shook.

A whole month? My heart was being squeezed out of me, but no. We could do this.

"Aspen?"

My hand squeezed my phone so tight. "Yeah?"

"I love you."

Yes. A whole month. That was it. "I love you too."

.

49

ASPEN

J uly had been long.

August was longer. I think because there was more at stake, and because college lay ahead of me at the end of the month. Until then, there was more family time. Nate was around a lot, but August still seemed endless.

No calls from Blaise. No texts.

He was serious, and I was serious.

I was also going insane.

I missed him.

I wanted him.

I cried for him.

I bargained in my head so I could contact him.

But no.

In the end, I didn't reach out, and he didn't either.

If he wasn't doing the work, I was going to kill him.

That was my new mantra, and it was getting me through the month—that and listening to Nate call my parents every night and ream them out for things he'd been holding in since his high school years. Guess he needed a couple weeks to process, but them forgetting my graduation had been like the dam breaking with him.

He got mad, and then he got furious, and then he'd started sharing. I loved it.

Our parents wished he'd stop sharing.

I didn't.

50

BLAISE

"I'm going to admit that when you first called and requested daily appointments, I thought you were insane."

I sat in my therapist's office, across from her, and she was laughing.

"I've never had a client request daily appointments for an entire month. It was a miracle I could even shift my schedule around to accommodate you. And then to have you actually show up for all the appointments?" She shook her head. "Usually the problem is clients who don't show up." She stopped laughing. Her hands folded in her lap, over her pencil skirt. I'd been envisioning Aspen in that same outfit. She didn't dress like my therapist, but the skirt? Hell yeah. Put some glasses on her, maybe give her a ruler, and she could bark orders at me any day of the week.

My therapist sat up straighter.

Her name was Naomi. She was recently married and had moved from Washington down to Cain. I knew all this because her husband was the one who spoke to her for me. After Aspen's *command*—fucking hot command—I did my research.

Naomi Ferrer was new to the area and setting up her private practice. She had the acumen, because I saw her degrees online, and I'd guessed she'd have the most open calendar for what I wanted.

I'd called and made my request. She'd turned me down flat.

Then I found out her husband was one of the professors at Cain, and he was a soccer enthusiast. That's when I approached my coaches. I'd been hesitant, because shit like this wasn't usually discussed on the soccer field, but my coaches had supported me. My head coach said they'd rather have a guy getting his head cleared than a hothead who could be a danger on the field. That made sense. One of them spoke to Dr. Ferrer's husband, and he got her to change her mind. She was even amenable to my soccer schedule, which came in handy because we'd had three matches before classes started next week.

"I'm impressed with you, Blaise," she told me.

I nodded. "It's a good thing you didn't know me a few months ago."

"You've made progress. I was initially worried about the emotional duress I'd be putting you under daily, and the ethics of that, but you handled it. And you did it well, and again, I'm impressed. For an incoming freshman, you're setting up a phenomenal foundation to build upon. But..."

There was always a *but,* I was finding.

"You still have not confronted your mother about why she wasn't honest with you all those years. That's a problem."

We'd been through everything else.

Eye movement desensitization and reprocessing therapy— EMDR. That'd been enjoyable (insert heavy, heavy sarcasm). But the post-traumatic stress crap I dealt with *was* better. Someone could touch my arm when I was in the middle of a flashback— and I'd had a few more over the month—and I could check myself.

I now recognized the state when I was in it, and I was also hopeful that eventually, the flashbacks would stop happening.

For now, though, I could navigate my way out of them using the tools Dr. Ferrer had taught me.

That was all I wanted. It meant I wasn't such a danger, but my head was still messed up. Sometimes I felt like the more therapy I got, the more crap we dug up, and the worse I got. That had lasted until this week when, surprisingly, some of that shit had started to lessen.

Dr. Ferrer said I could slow down my therapy, but she wanted to see me for another six months. Turns out, a childhood of abuse and trauma really fucks someone up.

"I have a guess as to why you haven't confronted your mom, but I want you to tell me your thoughts. Because you do have them, right? You have some idea, don't you?"

God, I missed Aspen.

Right now. I wanted her here. In my arms.

I wanted to hear her voice.

"Blaise."

"What?" I hadn't meant to wander off. "Sorry."

"It's fine, but I would like you to answer my question."

I didn't want to answer, and not because I didn't know. I'd thought about this; I just didn't like saying it out loud. That made me feel...more raw, if that was possible.

More exposed.

I was getting tired of this daily shit.

Every day I felt exposed, vulnerable, emotionally stripped, and then every night I had to regroup from practice *and* from counseling. Aspen wanted me to do the work, so I was, but it was *hard*. The hardest thing I'd gone through... No. That wasn't true.

Surviving *him* had been the hardest thing.

That's when I knew I had to answer.

"Because if I confront her, I will hate her."

Naomi shifted in her seat, her mouth tightening. She didn't seem to have expected that answer.

"That door is shut right now, but I know it's there," I continued. "I've been angry at everyone except her. Been wanting to tear into everyone, hurt them, except her, and part of that is because she was all I had growing up. I had no one else—and yeah, I didn't fully have her either, but she's my mom. He broke her too. She didn't know the extent of what he was putting me through. I hid it. He hid it. She hid from herself, drinking. Then this shit that he wasn't my real dad came out, and I was relieved. I was thankful. But..."

I rubbed my hands over my face. "I try to sit and think about the 'what if.' What if she'd told me? What if she'd told Stephen? I don't know who wins going down that path, so I don't. Nothing can be changed. I survived. I used to think I was like him, that I was the lowest piece of shit on this earth, but I'm not. This— doing this shit, keeping focused with soccer, having Aspen in my life—I'm not him. I won't be him. And I don't know, a part of me is grateful I attacked Stephen, because I have that clarity now. I didn't have that before. I couldn't have that before, so maybe I should yell at my mom. I don't know. Is that the right thing? Lash out at someone who was hurting right alongside you? Lose the one person I had during all that hell?"

I shrugged, no longer seeing my therapist. I didn't feel the chair I was in. I wasn't aware of the room around me. I had no concept of time or day or anything. I just saw my mom after one of the last times he'd ripped into her.

"She was crying so hard. The words he said to her, no one should ever hear those words. But he said them. And she took it, and I realized she'd been taking it for years. Fucking years. And she was still standing too. So I don't know. I honestly don't. I have enough bad shit inside of me. I don't want to let myself think further about the 'why' of her putting me in that situation. If she knew what we'd end up in, I don't think she would've done it. That's obvious. She would've told Stephen she was pregnant, but she didn't. She told *him,* and he loved her, or that's what he said, and I have to think it hurt her something fierce to go with him, to

decide to keep quiet about everything. We've never talked about
it, but I know it eats at her. And I know she'll tell me. She'll have
to, and I know she's sorry, and I know she'll apologize for lying to
everyone, but... I don't know. I'm still healing. She's still healing,
and we're not there yet. We will be one day. I have to believe that.
But I'm tired. Of all of it. I'm tired of being a dick. I'm tired of
lashing out at people. I'm tired of hurting people, but I also know
I'm still me. I'm still an asshole. I know I will say shit to hurt
people, and I hate that now. I don't know. Who am I to judge her,
you know? Who am I?"

Naomi leaned forward. "Her son."

"She said she's in counseling."

She nodded, leaning back. "She is. I asked you earlier if I
could reach out to her therapist. You both signed waivers so we
could talk, and your mother has made progress as well. Great
progress. I'm aware that your biological father was in counseling
too, as was your half-sister."

I nodded. "Yeah."

"It's an intense situation."

I laughed, the sound hollow.

"I heard everything you said, but I don't understand why you
won't ask your mother. I want to push you to do it, but I'm trying
to respect you and meet you where you are, so help me. Help me
understand."

It was goddamn simple.

"Because if I do, I open that door to all the other demons in
there, and I'm not ready. I'm not ready to hate my mom, and I
know that's what will happen. If I hate her, he wins. That piece of
shit won't ever win and get between my mom and me. I won't let
him. I won't lose her."

She drew in a breath, as if seeing me in a different light. She
nodded. "Okay. I got it now." Another slow bob of her head. "So
when you're ready, you'll ask her. And Blaise, you won't lose
her. Ever."

My throat swelled up. It was an irrational thought. I could recognize that, insight was a bitch, but it was there. I'd treated my mom like crap the last few months, but that would've been different.

I slumped further into my chair. "Or when she's ready, she'll tell me."

"And until then—"

"He can't win," I told her again. "He *doesn't* win."

"Got it."

"Good."

Because that made one of us.

I didn't get it. I didn't know if I'd ever get it.

51

ASPEN

I was excited, but sad and also nervous, all at the same time. It was move-in weekend. That meant I'd found my dorm, and my room. I'd met my roommate and my floormates. I'd met my resident advisor. And even though I already knew the campus and had done a tour last fall, I got my schedule and walked through all the buildings. My parents were with me. Nate came too. But shortly after we arrived, he disappeared. He said he knew a few people who had remained local, so off he went.

He'd wanted to show me the house he used to live in when he went to Cain, but I already knew about it. It was now rented to Blaise's brother, Bren, and their group of friends. They'd had a shindig there last night, and I knew Blaise had gone with Zeke, who—according to social media—had found out two days ago that he was attending Cain after all.

I wasn't sure what had happened there, because I'd thought he was going here all along, but he seemed happy in his post. I was glad Blaise would have him here too. There were other pictures with both Blaise and Zeke in them, but I was trying not to think about it. Blaise had said he wouldn't fuck anyone else, and I had no reason not to trust him, so I was trusting him.

I also knew he'd had a soccer match earlier today, and the girls were going to be a thing. Just going to the bathroom on campus, I'd overheard girls talking about the soccer team. "I know football is always a big deal," one had said. "But I swear, we've never had that hottie on our soccer team before."

Blaise had said he was a big deal in the sport at his other high school, and it only took an email for him to get into Cain because of soccer. I mean, I saw him play and he'd only been kicking the ball around by himself so I got it. I understood the excitement.

This was a preview of what was to come.

Nervousness, excitement, and sadness chased each other through me once again. Could I be overthinking things? Maybe.

I just missed him.

"So..." My roommate turned to me, a wide smile on her face.

I'd just come back up after goodbye hugs and kisses with my parents. Nate had texted that he was still around and would see me for brunch tomorrow before heading off, but until then, here I was. Back in my room. Saturday evening—nowhere to go and maybe a guy I should be calling, but I kinda wanted him to call me. But he didn't know I was even here, so I was being a little irrational, and I didn't care.

"So." I smiled back at my roommate.

Her name was Jade, and she seemed super cool. Straight black hair that hung at her chin. Dark eyes. An angular shaped face that could've stepped off a Bravo television show. I knew some girls might've hated her, but I'd never been like that.

I'd been around models before, so I could instantly read who was going to be catty and insecure. Jade wasn't like one of those girls. There was a laid-back aura about her.

Her closet door was open, and once I closed the door to the room behind me, she wheeled backward on her desk chair. She had a bottle of Jameson in one hand and a bottle of rum in the other. "What's your drink of choice, roommate?"

Seriously. So awesome.

I smiled. "Rum and Coke, please."

"Hell yeah!" She stood up, lifting the bottles over her head, and went to the fridge.

I went over and hit my playlist. "Settle Down" by Chaptabois filled the air, and soon both of us were bobbing our heads to the beat.

We were on our second round when someone knocked on our door.

"Come in!" Jade called.

The door opened, and two more girls I'd briefly met on our floor came in.

We introduced ourselves again. One was a shorter Latina girl, and that's how she introduced herself. She stuck her hand out and said, "I'm Veronica, and I'm Latina. I have an accent, and I'm not going to tell you where my family is from, because I'm from Texas, and that's it, girl. Got it? We'll move forward from this, and all you need to know is that I'm a hella good time. Also, I don't do nicknames. My name is Veronica. Not Ronnie. Not Rica. Not Ver. Veronica. Got it?"

"Got it." I nodded and smiled. I liked this one already. "I'm Aspen."

Then she melted. "Oh, man. One look and I know you're the sweetest and shyest girl ever. You remind me of one of my sisters, Crystal. Heart of gold."

Instant friends.

The other girl was her roommate, and she had sleek, reddish hair, blue eyes, and a ton of freckles. Hers was one of the most arresting faces I'd ever seen. Her name was Angeline.

"We heard the music and guessed you might be our kind of girls." Veronica sat on my bed, since it was nearest.

"You want drinks?" Jade asked.

Veronica boomed, "Hell yes."

Angeline cringed, but then shrugged. "College."

"That's right, girl." Jade pointed over her shoulder since she was at the fridge already. "We're in college, and classes don't start till Monday."

After Veronica got her drink, Angeline went back to their room to get herself a wine cooler. "I heard some girls in the hallway talking about a party on frat row," she reported when she returned. "You guys want to go?"

Jade's eyebrows went up. "A frat party? Our first night here?"

Veronica thrust her drink in the air. "HELL YEAH, BITCHES!"

Angeline giggled.

We'd learn soon enough that that's what Angeline did. She sipped on her wine cooler and giggled, a lot.

Veronica boomed and said *bitches* a lot. I kinda loved it.

Jade was clearly our leader.

After another drink for each of us (and a new wine cooler for Angeline), we got ready to go. Jade went and found the girls who'd been talking about the party, and they included us in their group. We walked from campus to a street down on Cain's frat row.

The whole block was packed, and it wasn't just one party. There were a few of them going.

A part of me was like, *What am I doing? I should go back to the room and call Blaise. I should tell him I'm here.* But the other part of me was like, *This is college. I should embrace this, and hell yeah to me for not just eavesdropping on a party for once.*

I was a mixed bag this evening.

I should've brought a wine cooler of my own. Though Jade had us covered. She had the serious party/tomboy look going, including a backpack full of drinks, and she was pulling it off glamorously. No joke. She didn't care how she looked, but she still looked good—tight tank top, tight shorts, sneakers, and a backpack.

I followed along toward the back of the group, because five more girls had attached to us when they learned we were all from the same dorm. Was this normal? I had no clue. But it was the first weekend, so the normal social rules might not apply.

We went past the first party to a bigger party.

I eyed a few of the guys on the front lawn because they looked so much like Zeke, they could've been twins. I mean, the faces were different, but the douchebag, bully/joker, preppy partier vibe was the same. They were throwing beanbags at a piece of wood with holes in the middle of it, and they were doing pretty well. They kept yelling, "Hole in one!" Then they'd cheer with their fists in the air and salute each other, downing an entire red cup of beer. Or I assumed it was beer. They'd done this three times by the time we got to their sidewalk.

Then I caught the end of what a girl in front of me was saying, "...he, like, moved from New York to California or something? I don't know, but Columbia was supposed to have him on their team. Something happened, and we got him on ours. He's a big deal, I'm telling you."

"How do you know this?" another girl asked.

"My brother's a junior on the soccer team. He swears he's never seen a player like this in person. This guy should've already been in Europe playing for one of their clubs."

"Why isn't he?"

The original girl shrugged. "I don't know. My brother said something like his dad was the biggest douche ever not to let him go over there."

"What's his name?"

I knew. My stomach was tight, but also blooming in pride.

"Blaise something. He's fucking gorgeous too." She looked up at the party. "Keep an eye out. My brother said the soccer team likes to party with these guys. That's how I knew about the party in the first place."

Blaise could be here.

Blaise could be here!

I wasn't nervous.

No. That was ridiculous.

For real, it was seriously ridiculous.

But... I did have a bad case of déjà vu. Blaise was already the popular guy.

I was once again on the outskirts.

All I needed were some woods and to get caught spying on a girl going down on him, and I'd be back in my social loner hell.

The butterflies and knots were all in a flurry inside me. They were spring-boarding off my intestines.

No.

Blaise got serious this month.

Therapy. Soccer. He'd said that's all he would do, and he was honest. He was always bluntly honest.

He'd told me he loved me, and the therapy was for a reason. Because he loved me. Because he didn't want to be a risk for me.

He did that for me.

I did not need to be nervous or scared.

This was *not* high school.

He had changed. I had changed.

We were good. We would be good, and besides—

I'd been so busy giving myself a pep talk that I'd missed how we'd walked past the guys on the front lawn. We'd gone up the front stairs and were now inside the house, the music almost deafening, and Jade took her leadership point again.

The bigger group of girls was breaking up, but Jade rounded the four of us back together.

She tightened her hold on her backpack straps and leaned in. "Okay. Here's the deal. This is not my first rodeo. I'm sure it's not yours either, and my brother's warned me about these parties.

They can get rowdy and crazy, and we can't be dumb bitches. That's why I brought our drinks with us. This isn't always going to happen. I heard they usually charge, and you have to buy a cup, but whatever. We're in the door, so if someone starts being an asshole, just go ask for an empty cup. Say your friend is a moron, and her beer is going to spill, and you want to save the beer. They'll give it to you. So, can we figure out the rules, and yes, we should've had this meeting before we left, but we didn't."

"Rules?" Angeline looked ready to faint. "What do you mean rules?"

"Rules for us. Like, we never leave someone behind. We keep an eye on our buddy. Like that. What do you think?"

"I like those rules." Veronica bobbed her head. "Let's go."

"No." Jade caught her hand, wheeling her back. She glared at her. "I'm asking what the rules are."

Veronica frowned. "My personal rule is to find a guy, climb on him, and stay there all night. If he becomes my boyfriend, that's cool. If he's my tree stump for a night, I'm okay with that too."

Angeline started giggling. Again.

Jade gave her a dark look. "Seriously?"

"Yeah. I don't get roofied. I don't drink shit other guys give me, and I'm a black belt in karate. Guys here aren't scared of me yet. I gotta strike while the iron is hot, because they'll learn real fast. You know what I'm saying?" She held her hand out. "Give me one of the bottles, and I'm good for the night. I'll see all you bitches at home."

Jade glowered, but pulled out the bottles. Veronica took the whiskey. I was kinda envious, looking at Veronica in a whole new light. I think my appreciation morphed into a girl crush. She marched off, her head high and her shoulders rolled back. The confidence alone was inspiring.

Angeline continued giggling.

Jade met my gaze. "We're on babysitting duty, I think."

I opened my mouth. Should I say anything?

Then a pair of arms wrapped around me. I started to scream as I was lifted off my feet, but then I heard the voice boom (we had another boomer) and instantly relaxed.

"THERE'S MY GIRL! HELL YEAH! FALLEN CREST IN THE HOUSE!"

It was Zeke.

And the butterflies took steroids, along with the knots, because I knew who else I was about to see.

Zeke lowered me, and I turned.

He wrapped his arms around me again, and I got a good hug instead. "Man. Hey. I was with your fan club last night. Shit got weird. Did Blaise tell you?"

"I—" choked. I choked. *He doesn't know?*

Jade and Angeline watched me intently.

"Hi, Zeke." I tried not to look, but I couldn't help myself.

Zeke chuckled, throwing his arm around my shoulders. He turned to my friends. "Hey. I'm Zeke. Who are you hot things?"

Jade's mouth snapped shut and she beamed, raising her chin in a flirty way. "Hi. I'm Aspen's roommate, Jade."

"Jade. Hmmm. I likey." He looked at Angeline. "Who are you?"

Angeline flushed all over and gripped her wine cooler with both hands. She used both hands to take a drink from it too. Then when she was done, she giggled.

Jade shook her head. "That's Angeline. She's one of our floormates. Her roommate is around here too."

"Floormates." Zeke clasped me tighter. "That's right. You're doing the dorm thing. Have you checked out Blaise's apartment yet? It's almost right next to the soccer complex. Our boy's got it going this year."

"What are you—" Jade's eyes bounced from Zeke to me. "How do you know Aspen, and where are you staying?"

His grin turned proud. "We went to the same school, and I

just got clearance. I'm here, like, *here* here. I'm rushing. My pops was a legacy, so they just moved me right in already."

Angeline's eyes got wider as Zeke spoke. Then she looked at me. "So cool," she said, just before she drank the rest of her drink.

Jade had another ready to go before she could resort back to her default setting. Her laughter had been funny at first, then endearing. Now it was getting annoying.

Zeke grinned. "She's funny. She could be a drinking game. Everyone do a shot when the girl starts giggling."

That made Angeline snort into her wine cooler.

He turned to me. "So, we're outside. Your boy's in a mood, and I'm thinking it's because he needs to get laid. What do you say? Come put him out of his misery?"

I closed my eyes. "Zeke."

"Come on. I'm pushing your buttons. He told me the whole deal, but you're here. He's here. It's time, little Monson."

Jade and Angeline (now recovered from her snorting/giggling spell) were following all this with extra interest.

Zeke didn't wait for a response. He led the way.

We fell in line, but it took a while. Zeke kept stopping to bump fists with guys, talk to people, get hugs from girls. It was like Fallen Crest. He was already the big man here. During one of those pauses, Jade leaned close to me. "You have a boyfriend?" She cursed. "Usually that's the first thing girls ask each other. I'm kicking myself now. The first thing I asked was whiskey or rum?"

I laughed. "I love that you asked me that." I took a breath, because she was giving me a pointed look. "And the answer is complicated."

Her eyebrows shot up. "Seriously, I want to hear all about this."

Angeline pushed in from the other side. "I think Veronica is outside. I can hear her."

We stepped onto the porch, and Veronica yelled, "Bitches!"

A guy yelled back, "Shut her up, Korchack."

Zeke glanced over his shoulder and winked at me.

"Zeke, don't make a big deal—"

Too late.

He hollered over Veronica, "Found someone for you, Blaisey boy."

Then he stepped aside, and there was Blaise, standing in a group of guys, his arms over his chest as they talked. He'd been mid-conversation when Zeke spoke up. He turned and looked right at me. His eyes widened, he stopped talking, and a second later he was coming for me.

The hunger, the desperation, the yearning—I could see all of that on his face, and I told my butterflies and knots to take a hike.

The next second, Blaise had me in the air, and he was walking backwards, taking me far away from everyone else. I could hear Zeke laughing behind us.

"I'll watch your girls for you, little Monson."

Blaise's mouth was on mine, and I ceased thinking.

Home. Home. Home.

I was home. I wanted to go to his home. Blaise was my home.

I chanted that in my head and wound my arms around his neck. People tried to say things to him, pat him on the arm. I could feel them, but Blaise ignored everyone. His mouth was on mine and then his hands were on my ass, urging my legs up. I wrapped them around his waist, and he dug in his pockets.

There was a smattering of laughter on the front lawn, and Blaise lifted his free hand. The laughter stopped, but one guy yelled after us, "Have fun, soccer star."

"Who's that?" I heard a girl ask.

When we reached Blaise's Wagon, he groaned, lowering me to my feet. "Holy fuck." He pressed me against the door. "Can we just—can we go to my place? I need to be inside you *now,* and we can do the talk afterward?"

I was shocked he was asking. "Hell yes."

He peeled himself away from me and opened my door.

He helped me in, darted to his side, and we drove a few blocks to an apartment building. He had underground parking. *Nice.*

Then we were in the elevator, and Blaise had me pressed against the wall, his mouth on mine. I stopped paying attention to our surroundings.

He picked me up and a little while later, he dropped me on a bed and climbed on top of me.

Blaise whisked my jeans off, grabbed my underwear, and they vanished. Then he slid inside. We were like animals. Too long, way too fucking long. He went in hard and fast, and then slowed, panting in my ear. "Holy—I can't—"

He was trying for control.

Hell to the no, no, no.

I grabbed his ass and pulled him into me. "Harder."

I moved my hips, slamming back against him, and that's all the response he needed. Blaise took me, pumping furiously. I came, and then he flipped me over and pounded me from a different angle, his hand bringing me to another orgasm right before he came inside of me.

Birth control is my friend. Thank you, reproductive prevention plans.

Yes, that was my thought. I couldn't move. I could only pant, gulping for air, sprawled out, and then he fell next to me.

His hand swept down my back, cupping my ass, and he moaned. "I have seriously missed you."

All those nerves and fear? Stupid.

I turned my head, but the muscles in my back weren't strong enough. I could only see him from one of my eyes. "Therapy was good?"

He swallowed, nodding. "Real good. I got the green light. I'm still a dick, but I'm not going to hurt anyone."

"You feel better?"

His face softened. "Yeah. I feel better. I did the work for you, but it was for me too. I'm good. I really am." He bent over, giving me a tender kiss.

That was enough for me. I mustered my strength and climbed over him.

He rolled to his back, his hands finding my hips, and looked up at me.

His grin was fully satiated, but I worked him hard again and lowered my hips. Once he was inside, I leaned back.

"We're good, then?" I heaved the words out as I rolled my hips forward and back, riding him.

He growled low in his throat. "Yes. We are good. I'm good. Are you good?"

Oh yeah. I was good.

I picked up the pace, and his hand moved between my legs. I was really good after that.

We didn't have any more of a talk that night. We went from his bed to the shower. Then he made food for us, and we went to his kitchen counter. He introduced me to his balcony. He was on the highest floor, and we kept everything dark behind us so we could see the party lights from frat row. I knew exactly which house was Zeke's.

After that, I made some phone calls, because that was one thing my roommate and I had remembered to do—exchange numbers. Jade wanted to murder Angeline, and Veronica had moved to Zeke's lap. I envisioned drama already, but then an hour later, Jade reported that they were all in the dorm and safe. I was supposed to check in in the morning, and she demanded a roommate breakfast. She also wanted to meet the boyfriend, her last text a tease as Blaise carried me back to his bed. He laid me down, disappearing into the bathroom.

Jade: Complicated, my ass. That hottie is yours and yours alone from what everyone is saying. Girls are seriously jealous of you. HAVE FUN! Talk tomorrow. I want to meet him.

Then my phone beeped again.

Unknown number: This is Angeline!!! We had so much fun. Your friend Zeke is cute and he rejected Veronica. She's already cyberstalking him. See you tomorrow!! Your boyfriend is really cute.

Unknown number: Veronica here. Girl. You have explaining to do. Tomorrow. Breakfast. You bring the coffees. Also, that Zeke guy is an asshole. I have to have sex with him.

I laughed, showing Blaise the texts when he came back in, wearing nothing. Which was the *best* ever.

He grinned, then took the phone as he slid into bed beside me.

He sent them all a group text.

Aspen: This is the boyfriend. Stop texting my woman. I got her for the night. Phone is off.

And he tossed it aside and claimed me, pulling me over him.

That's when I remembered. "My brother's in town. He wants to do brunch."

Blaise groaned, his hand smoothing down my back. "I have a feeling college is going to be interesting."

I smiled.

I had a feeling college was going to be perfect.

EPILOGUE

BLAISE

"**D**ude! No!" Zeke doubled over just as I killed him for the last time.

He tore off his headset and threw it at me. Catching it, I laughed, pulling my own off and setting both on the floor. The headsets weren't cheap. I scowled. "Sore loser, asswipe."

"Shut up." He got up, stalking to my kitchen. I heard the fridge open and he called out, "Why don't you keep any beer? That's like against the sacraments or something."

I laughed, getting up and heading to grab some water. "Sacraments? We're in college, not a religion."

He grabbed a sports drink, shooting me another glare. "College is a religion for some of us."

"Maybe for you. And I don't drink during season. You know that."

His scowl lessened. "Whatever." His phone buzzed, and checking it, he sighed. "I gotta head back to the house."

I frowned. Zeke didn't usually sigh when it came to his fraternity. He loved that house, a bit too much in my opinion, but that was Zeke. If he loved something, he really loved it. "Something wrong?"

"You know that party the first weekend?"

I nodded. I wasn't a big party person, but I went to a few. I mostly went to spend time with Zeke, and because it was expected of me. I lived alone, enjoying to keep my own place free of distractions like when others were studying or partying. Now that I was back playing soccer, I needed to be razor sharp on my focus. Aspen. Zeke. Soccer. School. Those were my priorities, for the most part. There were other annoying distractions, like Cross, but that was neither here nor there right now. So far I hadn't run into them too much, though I knew they'd attended my games a few times. Cross sent a couple texts congratulating me.

That'd been a different surprise. I still didn't know if I liked it or not. So far, it was a 'stay tuned' sort of deal.

"There's a guy that was macking on someone he shouldn't have."

I knew who he was talking about. I saw him, saw the girl too.

He was eyeing me.

Yeah. We both knew the girl.

He asked, "Are you going to say anything?"

I let out a breath. Fuck. I'd kept clear from any drama since starting school. Getting involved with my brother's crew, not something I wanted to voluntarily step into. I lifted up a shoulder. "I haven't decided yet."

"Well, Harper's causing problems since."

I didn't normally see Zeke like this. He was mostly smiling, albeit sometimes his smiles were dirty and aimed at scoping out females, but he was mostly in a good mood since coming to college. I rather thought he enjoyed the break from school, or the pressure of our last school. He was already known on campus, but it wasn't the same deal as it'd been at Fallen Crest Academy. Zeke was able to be like any other fraternity brother. Partying. Enjoying life. Women. He'd also changed since his 'punishment' from his dad. He was more cautious with things, so hearing his concern now, my stomach dipped.

Anger was starting to rumble.

I wasn't just protective of my girl.

"What kind of problems?"

Zeke's jaw clenched. He shoved his phone in his pocket, reaching for his keys. "Throwing his weight around." He shook his head, eyeing me again. "I gotta tell you something and you're going to lose it when I do."

I frowned. "What?" Alarm slithered down my spine.

I really did not like that look from him. Zeke was never scared to tell me something, and he was hesitating now.

"You know Aspen's in my bio class."

Fuck. I was really not liking this now.

My teeth were starting to grind against each other. "Finish it. Just fucking tell me."

"Harper's in that class, and he was saying a few things about Aspen yesterday."

"You're just now telling me this shit?"

What. The. Fuck?

He grimaced. "I know. I know! But, shit. I had words with him. I thought it was done, except..." His phone buzzed from his pocket.

And buzzed again.

And again.

Again.

It kept buzzing.

Zeke didn't move to look at it. He wasn't moving to look at me either. He was frozen, staring out my window, his jaw clenching over and over again.

A dark feeling took root in me.

It was low, and it was spreading.

Alarm was spiking all through me.

"Let me see your phone."

Zeke didn't answer. He also didn't move to get his phone.

"Zeke." I showed him my teeth. They were clenched too. "Your fucking phone. Now."

His eyes closed, and he cursed under his breath, reaching for his phone. He handed it over, and I put his password in. Yeah. He didn't know I saw him put it in, but too bad.

I was pulling up the messages, seeing it was all coming from a group text.

Scrolling up, I was ignoring what the others were saying, looking for the origin, and then I got it.

The world went black. Murderous.

My vision was fraying at the edges and I was locked in, right in. I was staring at an image of one of Aspen's early modeling gigs.

HarpAss: fucking hot, bro! Your boy gets to plow this bitch whenever he wants to? Sign me up!

Deke: I want a turn.

Abe: Get in line!

Hankinson: Meow.

Doehing: I want that pussy.

I was gone. Done. Every fucking one of these guys was going to hurt, and not giving one shit about Zeke, I clicked the video call.

I held the phone up, letting them see my face. Zeke saw what I was doing and lunged for me. "No!"

I waved him off, then someone accepted my call.

Harper. I remembered his smarmy little face now.

"Hey, asshole."

His eyes got big, but he tried to cover. "Phone said Zeke was calling—"

My tone went low and I wanted him to see what I was going to do. I wanted all of them to see what I was going to do. "You're going to get your ass beat by me, and then you're going to jail."

I knew this video was getting picked up by the others in the chat. Half of them were probably in the same room, and they all got quiet on their end.

Harper started to scowl.

I kept on, "This picture was taken when she was twelve years old, you sick fuck. She's modeling pre-teen clothes. Your comments turned this into child pornography. You know the guy who raised me? The assdick who's got a lawsuit coming for him? Guess what? He knows guys in the FBI. Guess what numbers it would be really easy for me to send this entire fucking group chat to? And if you don't think my dad isn't motivated to cut some form of deal, in any way possible, you're too stupid to have a phone. Deleted texts can be undeleted if you get my fucking drift."

Harper wasn't scowling anymore. He was staring back, a pale green color coming to his ugly face.

No one was texting anymore.

"You're going to delete this group chat. You're going to delete those pictures of Aspen, and you're not going to say another fucking word about my woman. Got it?!"

He swallowed.

I wasn't done. "And for the rest of you coward weasel fucks who are not chiming in, but I know can hear me, you're going to thank Zeke when he comes back because if he hadn't let me take his phone, I wouldn't be giving this warning. I would've collected every fucking piece of evidence that your group chat would've continued with and I would've gone straight to the authorities. You fucking pussy dicks don't know me, but you don't fuck with me. You got it? I would've gone to anyone to get your house shut down, and if you think you could intimidate me, then try me. Just fucking try me."

I ended the call and threw the phone at Zeke.

He caught it against his chest, not doing anything else. He stared at me, so still because he knew me. He knew me.

I wasn't okay with just that call, those threats. Not by a long shot.

He swallowed, his gaze bleak and then it was gone. It went hard and he asked, "You want to go now?"

I drew in a sharp breath. "Hell yeah."

He nodded. "Just Harper. I'm not going to clear it with the house, but it can only be him. The guys will understand."

My own phone buzzed and I pulled it out, every cell in my body stood on end.

Aspen: My parents are here. You're still coming to dinner, right?

One.

Two.

Three.

I counted all the way to ten, breathing in through my nose and out my mouth.

I needed to calm the fuck down.

I texted back.

Me: Yes. Can I pick you up, drive you there?

Aspen: Yes! I'll be ready in twenty minutes.

Twenty minutes. That gave me fifteen minutes to clear my head of murderous thoughts.

"What's going on?"

I typed back to Aspen.

Me: See you in 20.

I lifted my head, putting my phone in my pocket. "I have to do dinner with Aspen and her parents, but tonight I'm coming over."

He nodded, his face dark, as if a shadow hung over him.

I asked, "Will you be okay going in alone?"

"Yeah. You have a rep already. Some of the brothers heard about you in New York. They know not to mess with you. I'll be fine." He waved his phone in the air. "I know this worked. Half those guys are terrified of getting any rape charges against the house. What you said, about her being twelve, fuck. I know a few probably pissed their pants then and there." He paused, his face clearing, but a question lurked in his gaze. "Was that true? She was really twelve?"

I shrugged. "Fuck if I know, but she was young. I do know that."

He grinned, his shoulder relaxing. "That was a good bluff then. Worked."

"You'll be okay?"

His head moved up and down. "I'll be good. Don't worry." He went to the door, pausing before he opened. "About the other thing with Harper?"

My gut tightened. That other thing had to do with Cross and his group.

"Let's wait it out. I have a feeling they'll find me about it."

"I think that too."

He opened the door, one last glance back. "I'll see you tonight."

"See you."

"So, Blaise." Aspen's mom smiled brightly at me. We'd been at the restaurant for an hour. Most of the conversation had been small talk. They asked Aspen how her classes were coming, about her roommates. They wanted to hear about her dorm, general things. I figured out that they hadn't talked to Aspen prior to when I picked her up. This was the first visit since Aspen had come to Cain.

The shift of conversation was coming now, coming towards me.

Some of her smile was forced, but some of it was genuine. They'd been reserved about me since we met at high school graduation.

I got it. I did.

Parents seem to know I'm a dick, but I'd been nothing but good to their daughter. That had gone a long way. I knew Aspen's brother spoke for me too. They shared their concern, stating they heard I had a reputation for being a prick and worried how I'd treat Aspen. Him telling them I was wrapped around Aspen's pinkie helped. A lot.

But seriously, I got it.

I wouldn't like me too.

She continued, "Since our project was finished, we've been spending more time getting to know people in Fallen Crest. I have to say that it's been just lovely meeting your mother. Marie and Stephen make a wonderful couple."

Aspen seemed to deflate whatever breath she'd been holding. She blinked, giving me a smile at the same time squeezing my hand tight under the table.

I chuckled under my breath, squeezed her hand back before shifting our hands and running my thumb over the inside of her palm. She jerked, but I kept her hand in place, enjoying this slight torment. Her breath was growing shallow because of it. She'd be squirming in a second.

"My mom mentioned the same thing to me. She's enjoyed getting to know Malinda Strattan as well."

"Oh, that's right. Malinda uses her husband's name. I used to know her as Decraw back in the day."

I nodded, knowing there was history there.

"And soccer?" This question came from Aspen's dad. "I'm hearing exciting things about the Cain soccer team this year. It's usually their football team getting the attention."

This wasn't the first time I'd heard that as well.

I nodded, still holding onto Aspen's hand under the table, but I stopped teasing her. "Yes, sir. The team is good. Our goalie is one of the best in the nation."

"And you? What position do you play?"

"I'm a center forward."

"What does that do?" From Aspen's mom.

"I'm mostly on offense. I help move the ball forward, acting as a striker too."

"Right. You're the guy by the goal?"

"Uh. Kinda." There was more to it than that.

"You score the goals, though." Her dad waved his hand in the air, sitting higher, almost proud.

I hid a smile. "I score goals."

He dipped his head down. "Good. You help bring the wins in. Cain is known to produce quite a few professional athletes, in all sports."

"That's the goal."

"To go professional?" From her mother.

"Uh." I rolled my shoulder back. "I'm not sure, to be honest. A lot of those guys overseas have been in clubs since they were fourteen, younger sometimes. I'm behind."

"You could play professional here?"

I turned to her dad. "I could, yes."

He frowned a little. "But you're not sure if you want that?"

"Right now I'm just in college, spending time with your daughter. That's all I'm focused on." That wasn't totally true. Soccer was huge in my life right now, but I hadn't decided if I wanted to go abroad or not. And because of that, I wasn't lying when I said Aspen was part of my focus. She was. And training as hard in soccer as I could until I did decide.

"Right. Well, whatever you decide, you'll have our full support."

"Thank you, sir." I looked at Aspen's mom. "Ma'am."

Her smile was much more genuine now. The pride too.

But then again, this was also normal. Star athletes got a lot more attention than others. Aspen's parents were like others. But I caught a little look Aspen's mom shot her. There was a trace of hesitation and that made me feel better. She was still worried about her daughter, but time would tell. I didn't pull out a smooth facade, how some parents wanted, if only to appease their own inner doubt. That wasn't me. I would hope that Aspen's parents would come to know that as well, but I wasn't worried.

I loved their girl. It would be fine.

As if sensing my thoughts, Aspen patted my hand under the table. "I think I'm full. I can't eat anymore."

I shot her a dark grin.

She grinned back.

Aspen's dad noted the shared look and seemed to sigh. "Yes. I'll signal for the check."

"THAT WENT WELL."

I'd been kissing down her throat. We were lying on my bed and, if I didn't want to forget my promise earlier and just sink inside Aspen.

I lifted my head. "You want to talk about your parents now?"

She laughed, her fingers going through my hair. "No, but I'm happy."

A good feeling uncurled in my chest. My dick was already throbbing, but there was a warmth entwining with the lust and pleasure I always felt when I touched her. "Good. That's my job."

She smiled, the look turning almost dreamy and she rolled her head on my pillow from side to side. "I love you." Her eyes darkened.

I wasn't moving. No way now. "I love you back."

Her hips pressed up and her lips parted. "Now fuck me."

"I can do that." And a moment later, I was sliding inside of her.

ASPEN WAS CURLED in my bed, sleeping sound when I hit up Zeke on the phone.

I typed to him as I dressed in the bathroom.

Me: Heading over now.

He buzzed back a second later.

Zeke: Now?!

Me: Now.

Zeke: Okay. He's sleeping.

Me: Did he drink tonight?

Zeke: No. He was too scared to drink. Most of the guys were.

A deep satisfaction bloomed in my chest. That made me feel damned good.

Me: Then we'll wake him up. Be ready.

It wasn't a long drive to get to Zeke's frat house. There was an alley in the back, and a piece of the fence was loose. Zeke showed it to me the first day I was there, said we could use it to sneak in and out. Some of the brothers knew about it, some didn't.

He was waiting for me as I slipped through, dressed all in black. He handed over a small flashlight and a gag. Without saying a word to each other, we headed inside the house.

LATER, as we woke Harper up, as his eyes opened and he saw me standing over him, as he started to jump up, his mouth opening to yell for help, I would think about what we did that night. But in that moment, I didn't.

I wouldn't think about it in the way that I would regret it. No. Never that.

I enjoyed as Zeke stuffed a gag in his mouth, and as I yanked him off the bed. There was a thudding sound, but no one came to his help. Not one brother. We weren't exactly quiet about it. We dragged Harper from his room, and since his room was on the first floor, he only needed to worry about a few steps on the back porch.

Zeke stood back when we got him where I wanted him.

I stood back.

Harper realized it. I wasn't like him, and I say that because I know his character. He would've jumped me with five other guys. He would've had them hold me down.

I wasn't like that.

I let him get to his feet. I let him clear his head.

I gave him a fighting chance.

It wasn't my fault the fucker couldn't fight.

It wasn't my fault that I *could* fight.

I told Zeke to head back to the house half way through it, and I texted him once I was done. Harper was breathing and awake when I left him, but he was bleeding. And he would hurt. He would hurt for a hell of a long time, but there was no permanent damage.

It was later when I thought back to that night and I realized I wasn't hitting him just for Aspen. I was doing it for myself. I was doing it for Zeke. But I was doing it for my brother because there would be a time in the future when they would find out what else Harper did.

I was also doing it to set a precedence. Don't fuck with me and who I loved. And knowing that, knowing my message was good and received, I went back to my apartment.

I washed up, then crawled in bed with Aspen. I pulled her into my arms.

Tomorrow would be another day, but we'd be all right. I'd make sure of it. We'd be all right no matter *what* came our way.

"Blaise?"

"Mmm?"

Aspen's voice was sleepy. "You okay?"

I pressed a kiss to the side of her mouth. "Never better. Go to sleep."

And she did. So did I.

SECOND EPILOGUE

ASPEN

YEARS LATER

"Are you ready for this?" Jade asked as she took the seat beside me.

I shook my head. "Not in the least."

It was Blaise's last game as a Seattle Falcon. When he'd finished college, he'd taken a spot on the team. We'd been in Seattle for the last two years. But tonight was his last game with the Falcons—and in the United States. He'd joined a new club in Europe. We'd be on a plane in a couple weeks, heading to Hungary. The offer had been too big, and Blaise knew his time to be able to go over and play in their ranks was diminishing. With the Falcons, he'd quickly become one of the best in the league, but I knew he wanted to try his luck overseas.

"But I'm excited too," I assured Jade.

"I bet."

I reached over, took her arm, and gave her a squeeze. "I'm glad you came."

Her eyes got big. "Of course!" She pulled me in for a hug.

My throat was already swelling up. With the little one in me, my emotions were all over the place. And just thinking about him or her—we'd decided to be surprised—made me reach down and place my palm over my stomach.

He/she was kicking, and I smiled.

Blaise had been ecstatic when I told him.

After college, we'd wanted to enjoy living together while he started his soccer career, and I joined a marine-mammal-rescue nonprofit. My main task was to go out every day and rescue ocean mammals. There was never a shortage, sadly. Wrestling seals and cutting netting from around their necks had been the most terrifying at first, but then became my favorite job to do.

It was not something I thought I would've ended up doing, but camping on the beach was what got me started. Not a seal, but a sea lion was caught in another large net. Blaise and I caught him to cut it off.

After that, I was *in* in.

There was no going back.

Blaise and I still did our camping thing, and I say *our* because I'd converted him long ago. He was now the packer and planner for our trips, though I think that was because he always wanted to make sure our sites were somewhere Zeke could join us.

Yes.

Zeke.

You read that right.

Zeke now joined our camping expeditions too—he and his girlfriend. And I'm not naming names because the 'girlfriend' changed every two months. Though, that was a step up from how he was in college. Zeke had gotten a big rep for having only one-night stands.

"Blaise's family is coming tonight, right?" Jade asked.

I nodded. "They got their own seats because it's a surprise for him. He can see me, and if he looks up and they're sitting with me..."

Jade nodded. "Got it." Her smile was so big. "And that's awesome. I'm happy they're here."

Another arm squeeze, another look, and we were hugging again.

I couldn't stop the tears this time. I sniffled, trying to wipe them away.

I still hated crying, but the hormones didn't. The hormones loved crying, especially publicly.

A roar started in the stadium, and just like that, the game was about to start.

The players came out, and we all stood.

Blaise was one of the last to walk onto the field, and as soon as he appeared, a giant roar sounded through the stadium. This was the last game for the Falcons' newest star.

I knew Blaise planned to come back.

He wanted to be in Europe for a few years, then return and retire after a few more years here. There was a bit more leeway when it came to players' ages in the United States. Plus, we had family here.

Like I knew he would, Blaise turned his head as he strode out to the field. His eyes found me, as I'd sat in the same spot for every one of his games.

Jade sucked in her breath. "You're on the jumbotron."

I ignored that, because Jade didn't know we were going to be on the jumbotron quite a bit. News had broken about the pregnancy last week, and the attention had been intense.

When I fell in love with Blaise, if I'd known the amount of attention he was going to get—and I'd get by his side—I'll be honest... I don't know how I would've handled it. But, day by day, game by game, I'd slowly started to get used to it.

I went from being the invisible girl to having a jumbotron on me on the reg. That said everything right there.

Blaise smiled, kissing his fingers and holding them in the air to me.

I returned the gesture, then noticed many in the crowd doing the same.

They loved their DeVroe.

And yes, my throat was swelling and here came the tears. Again.

I'll have no working tear ducts by the time I have this kid. I'll be like a desert inside.

Jade sighed. "God, he's hot."

I glanced at her.

Her cheeks reddened. "Not your man—though he's hot, too." Her eyes went to his teammate.

Ah-ha. The last time she came to visit, I now realized it hadn't been an accident that Theo joined us for dinner.

And the night after.

And the night after that.

Why hadn't I noticed it before? And why hadn't Blaise told me? I needed to be looped in on this stuff. Jade had been my roommate, then my friend, then my best friend, and now my sister.

My phone buzzed.

Nate: Your man is looking ready to kill someone tonight.

I smiled.

Me: You know it. Probably envisioning your head on his opponent tonight.

Nate: Ha! Your man loves me. We both know it.

He was right.

Nate had started visiting more often, and he and Blaise had become almost joined at the hip. Nate didn't care about the age difference in the beginning of their budding bromance. He joked that hanging with him kept my brother young, but I always thought he liked Blaise so much because Blaise enjoyed pissing off some of Nate's friends.

Nate: You'll be around before you fly out?

Me: Of course.

Nate: Good. Love you. I already texted Blaise good luck, and he gave me a middle finger emoji back.

Me: And then he followed it with a kissing emoji, right?

Nate: How'd you know? *Wink emoji.*

I laughed.

Me: No clue.

Nate: Game is starting. Stop texting me. I have to start my cheers.

That was another new tradition. My brother liked to watch Blaise's games in a bar, and he always announced who his brother-in-law was and sent video of the entire bar cheering Blaise on. Most of the videos ended with more than a few patrons mooning the camera as well. Both Nate and Blaise assured me it was their inside joke. I wasn't privy to it, and I didn't think I wanted to be.

Either way, I was happy.

My brother was happy.

Blaise was happy.

His family was happy.

I felt a kick in my stomach.

Our little guy/girl was happy too.

And that, right there, was everything I could've asked for in life.

Another deafening cheer, and the game started.

Blaise kicked in two goals and assisted on another one.

The Falcons won.

We went to Europe. Blaise played for six more years.

Our little Zeke was followed by Crosston and Sailor—Cross a

little boy, and Sailor a little girl. She was the apple of all her boys' eyes.

No one could blame them.

∽

"Babe."

I woke to Blaise pressing kisses down my spine, pushing the sheets away.

I stretched, enjoying his type of alarm. It beat wails, screams, beeping sounds, toy cars being rammed into the wall, or just shrieks.

Then giggles split the air. That was the other good alarm.

I heard the little feet stampeding on the floor, and we braced, knowing we had imminent arrival in three...

Two...

The door slammed open, and Sailor appeared.

Her blond hair stuck up in the air. She had red marks around her mouth, probably juice stains, and her father's eyes were irritated. She crossed her arms over her little chest and puffed up. "Why are you both still in bed?"

Blaise groaned. "Sail—"

"Why, Daddy?!" She clambered onto the bed, crawling to us and settling on his chest, staring down at him. He jerked his head up, mock-glaring right back.

I just waited.

This was almost a tradition now, during the off-season.

This time, Sail broke first. Her face melted, and she started giggling. "You're funny, Daddy."

He swept an arm up around her and rolled. She shrieked, and then the tickling started.

I slipped out of bed, making my escape. I was taking advantage. I could do with a long, hot shower by myself. Hearing another shriek/giggle, I glanced back. Blaise had Sailor in the air, pretending she was an airplane, and she was loving it.

I got into the shower, and I was loving *that*.

A few minutes later an arm slid around my stomach as the water pounded down. Blaise settled his hips up against mine.

"You thought you could just slip away like that?" he growled.

I laughed, noting how similar my giggle sounded to Sailor's, but then his hand slid between my legs and my head fell back to rest against his shoulder. "The kids?"

"With my mom and Stephen."

Well, then....

I was going to take advantage of this too.

So we did.

If you enjoyed Rich Prick, please leave a review!
They truly help so much.

Blaise and Aspen's story is done,
but you can read more of them in Always Crew and Nate's book!

www.tijansbooks.com

LETTER TO THE READER

I'm going to be honest. I'm having a hard time writing this letter.

I tried writing it last week, and even the week before. Both times, nothing. And also, full disclosure that this letter is not going to be edited. This is coming real and raw from me, so that means it's not going to be smooth, perfect, and all correct-like.

Gah.

This is my absolute last thing that I have to do before finishing this book. After this, I'll get it formatted and then sent to my agent and then it's out of my hands. I always struggle at this juncture because it's no longer my book. It's yours. And all the love, tears, waking hours, lack of sleep, etc, all that stuff is now put in a book form for people to either love, hate, critique, praise, or ignore.

But wow. Whoa. This book.

This book!! I loved this book on another level like I loved Ryan's Bed. But different, you know?

That probably makes no sense, but onto the reason I'm even doing this letter in the first place.

I wanted to explain why Blaise didn't officially confront his mom about why she didn't tell Stephen about Blaise. I wanted to do that scene. I was planning on doing that scene. I tried to hint at her reason, her even saying a partial reason for it; but the truth is that my gut kept saying no.

I'm a writer that listens to my gut when it comes to books. Every time I don't, I always think back to how I should've so I've learned my lessons. And with this book, it kept telling me wait, wait, wait. Then I got to Blaise's counselor scene and it came out why he kept putting it off. I also kept thinking about the reality is that there are major issues in families that are never talked about. That's real life.

I trusted my gut.

Blaise was just not ready to open himself to that conversation. Not yet.

All that said, I loved writing Blaise and Aspen.

I *really* loved writing Blaise, but I can't promise if I'll write more Blaise and Aspen-centric novels in the future.

And even though this book is a standalone, I introduced one of the mean guys that'll be in Always Crew. Blaise and Aspen are in Always Crew as well. But again, who knows what will happen in the future.

I hope hope hope you enjoyed Rich Prick.

I hope you go on to enjoy the rest of the Crew Series, Nate's book, and so many more of my books that I've got coming.

Thank you all so very much!

-Tijan

ACKNOWLEDGMENTS

I've been wanting to write Aspen's book for a long time, and I always felt that I needed to write her book before I could write Nate's so expect her brother's book soon.

Now, about Blaise.

Blaise was a total surprise to me. He first shows up in Crew Princess. At the beginning of Rich Prick, I had no idea what layers he had in him. And as I went on, I grew more and more intrigued until now when he might be one of my favorites to write.

I truly loved writing Blaise and Aspen's story, and I hope you did as well.

Thank you to Jessica, Paige, Chris, Rochelle, Crystal, Eileen, Kim, Amy, and Susan! Thank you to Kimberly, Debra Anastasia, Helena Hunting, and Ilsa Madden-Mills. You guys all rock for constantly just putting up with me.

And last, thank you to the readers!!

ALSO BY TIJAN

Fallen Crest Series

Crew Series

The Boy I Grew Up With (standalone)

Other series:

Broken and Screwed Series (YA/NA)

Jaded Series (YA/NA suspense)

Davy Harwood Series (paranormal)

Carter Reed Series (mafia)

Mafia Standalones:

Cole

Bennett Mafia

Sports Romance Standalones:

Enemies

Teardrop Shot

Hate To Love You

Young Adult Standalones:

Ryan's Bed

A Whole New Crowd

Brady Remington Landed Me in Jail

College Standalones:

Antistepbrother

Kian

Contemporary Romances:

Bad Boy Brody

Home Tears

Fighter

Rockstar Romance Standalone:

Sustain

Paranormal Standalone:

Evil

More books to come:

Always Crew

Cut's Ryan

Nate

And more!

CPSIA information can be obtained
at www.ICGtesting.com
Printed in the USA
BVHW030922180620
581801BV00001B/72